# BUDDWING

## A NOVEL BY

## Evan Hunter

SIMON AND SCHUSTER · NEW YORK · 1964

FIRST PRINTING

LIBRARY OF CONGRESS CATALOG CARD NUMBER: 64–14426
MANUFACTURED IN THE UNITED STATES OF AMERICA
BY AMERICAN BOOK—STRATFORD PRESS, NEW YORK, N.Y.

*To Anita—with love*

*For when you're alone*
*When you're alone like he was alone*
*You're either or neither*
*I tell you again it dont apply*
*Death or life or life or death*
*Death is life and life is death*
*I gotta use words when I talk to you*
*But if you understand or you dont*
*That's nothing to me and nothing to you*
*We all gotta do what we gotta do*

—T. S. ELIOT

# 1

HE AWOKE.

He could not have been asleep for more than a few hours, and yet he felt curiously refreshed, coming instantly awake without passing through that fuzzy borderland he usually associated with rising. He knew exactly where he was. He seemed only mildly surprised to discover he was wearing his street clothes, but then he supposed one did not sleep in pajamas on a wooden bench in Central Park. He sat up and rubbed a hand over his face, not to wash away any weariness—more, he suspected, as a gesture of habit. Then he glanced across the path and beyond the iron railing to where the ground sloped to a small lake. The lake ended in a narrow finger capped by a huge outcropping of primeval rock, the man-made concrete of Fifth Avenue beyond and in the distance, and behind that a pale blue sky.

Who am I? he wondered.

The words flashed across his mind in brilliant, almost searing intensity for only a second, and then were extinguished by their own absurdity. He grinned at the foolishness of the thought,

9

grinned too because it was a beautiful day. The air was mild and warm; a balmy breeze reminiscent of somewhere in the tropics played at the back of his neck. He wondered what time it was. He looked at his wrist, surprised to see he had no watch, and then again wondered Who am I? This time the question did not seem as absurd. This time the question forced the grin from his mouth.

Well, I'm

He sat waiting. He did not panic. He sat calmly on the park bench. This is New York City, he told himself. This is Central Park. That's Fifth Avenue up there, I can see the tops of the buildings, who am I? Patiently he waited, the knowledge on the tip of his tongue. Of *course* he knew who he was; he was

He waited.

He felt suddenly uneasy, but he knew he would not panic. This was a temporary lapse of some kind, like forgetting the name of someone at a party, a simple block, momentary and transitory. He would not even allow his brow to furrow. He sat calmly and patiently, circling his own memory warily, like an animal preparing to spring on an elusive prey, cautiously, treading silently: I'm

But the name would not come.

Well, that's really ridiculous, he thought offhandedly, casually, I'm

Who?

The uneasiness was spreading. He glanced about him surreptitiously, as though this stupid *lapse*, this inconsiderate and grotesque inconvenience, were somehow something that everyone could see. But there was no one to see. He was quite alone on the bench and in the park. It must have been really very early in the morning; he could not even hear any sounds of traffic from Fifth Avenue. The uneasiness had started somewhere at the back of his skull, not in his mind, but physically at the base of his skull, the medulla oblongata. The medulla oblongata: Biology I at high school—*which* high school? It had then moved across his face; he could feel it tightening the flesh over his cheekbones and then spreading to his upper lip, the lips pulling taut, lodging in his throat when his cautious circling trap did not work, and then leaping instantly into his heart, fluttering wildly there. He would not panic. He told himself he would not panic. But the uneasiness was something very close to panic now, galloping in his heart. He suddenly clenched his hands.

Look, he told himself, you know who you are.

Well, then (cautiously . . . he almost dreaded thinking the words again, as if, presented again with them, he knew he would again have no answer, the words reluctantly refused to come . . . cautiously, very cautiously, no, it was no good playing tricks, it was no good creeping up like this) well, then, *who* am I?

I *know* who I am, he thought, I'm sitting here on a park bench, this is Central Park, that's Fifth Avenue over there, I'm in New York City, my name is

Oh.

Oh, hell, he thought.

What's the matter with me this morning? What am I doing here, anyway? I should be

The panic suddenly leaped against the walls of his heart. With a certainty sharp and clear and fierce, he knew he should be somewhere else, and he had not the slightest inkling of where that somewhere else was. And then, knowing he should be elsewhere, fearing his heart would burst through his rib cage and explode the flesh on his chest, lie beating in fear on the path before the bench, he suddenly wanted to know what he looked like. He brought his hands up instantly. They were trembling. He looked about him again to see if anyone had noticed the trembling. But he was still alone, quite alone, and his aloneness added a new dimension to his panic, as though he were trapped somehow in a horrible unending dream where he would interminably shout the question WHO AM I? and there would be no one to hear and no one to answer.

He explored his face with the fingers of both hands widespread. He seemed to have the right number of eyes, and a nose, somewhat long, and a thin upper lip, and high cheekbones—he supposed they were high; they seemed to end just below his eyes. The skin on his cheeks seemed taut, pulled tight, and he had a beard stubble.

He took his hands away from his face and studied them intently, as though wondering whether they were faithful recorders of his features, and it was then that he noticed the heavy gold ring on the third finger of his right hand. The ring had a black stone, and the stone was cracked, but there were no initials, no crest, nothing on the cracked black stone, no clue in the shining black-though-marred surface of the stone or the encircling gold to tell him what the ring was supposed to commemorate or mean other than decoration. He tried to take the ring off his finger, but it would not budge past his knuckle. Still sitting on the bench— the panic had fled before his curiosity now, an idle sort of curiosity—he put his finger into his mouth, wetting it past the knuckle, and then forced the ring off. He looked into the gold circle. In delicate script lettering the legend *From G.V.* was engraved.

G.V.

Who is G.V.? he wondered, and then became amused by the possibilities of what was happening to him. He did not know who he was, and he did not know who G.V. was, and he suddenly thought it funny that he did not know who anyone in this whole wide world was. Who is President Johnson? he asked himself, and was reassured by the very logic of his question; if he knew that Johnson was the President, then he knew who Johnson was. He found himself running through a list of names in his mind, as though arranging the geographical points on a map: Chairman Khrushchev, Pablo Casals, Sarah Vaughan, Fidel Castro, Tennessee Williams, Roger Maris, Marilyn Monroe, Ernest Hemingway; they're dead, he thought, they're both dead. And then he wondered if he himself were dead.

Well, if I'm dead, he reasoned, I feel pretty good, so what the hell? If I'm dead, then being dead is like waking up in Central Park on a nice spring day, so being dead can't be so bad. And then, as if the idea had been in his mind all along, as if he had only been playing some sort of hideous game with himself, he reached into his pocket for his wallet. He knew infallibly that he kept his wallet in the left-hand pocket of his trousers, the same way he knew that Lyndon Johnson was President of the United States, the same way he knew that this was Central Park. He reached into his pocket, and knew with the same infallibility that his wallet would not be there, but felt deeper into the pocket nonetheless, and then nodded in brief disappointment. As a matter of course, he checked his other trouser pockets, but there was no wallet. He had either lost it or had it stolen from him, which might after all explain what he was doing in Central Park on a Saturday morning when

Saturday.

He knew it was Saturday.

He sat quite still on the bench, looking off into the distance that was Fifth Avenue, lulled by the knowledge he knew he possessed, a knowledge of place and now of time; this was Saturday. He could not have told himself how he knew it was Saturday, but he knew it for certain, and then he wondered why on earth he felt there was someplace he was supposed to be on this Saturday morning. But the panic was gone completely now. He simply sat calmly and stared into space. The search that had started with the ring on his finger and then led to his trouser pockets, looking for his wallet, inevitably led to a curious probing of the pockets of his jacket. He was wearing a dark blue suit, he noticed, and blue socks and black shoes. His shirt was white, and a pair of gold cuff links showed where his jacket ended. He was wearing a gray tie with a tiny gold tie tack. He was hatless —that did not surprise him; he knew he never wore a hat. He found a package of L&M cigarettes in the breast pocket of his jacket, and he lighted one now—he was carrying matches, no lighter—and then he replaced the cigarettes in his pocket and continued searching through the other pockets. He found a slim gold pen and pencil set in his inside jacket pocket, and a small black address book behind them, and behind that a timetable for the Harlem Division of the New York Central. He glanced only briefly at the train schedule—it meant nothing to him—and then he opened the small black book, expecting it to be crammed with names and addresses, disappointed when he learned it was not. The pages were blank except for the first page, and written onto that page in a hand he did not recognize was: MO 6-2367. On impulse, he took the pen from his pocket, turned the barrel to bring the point into writing position, and directly beneath the MO 6-2367, wrote the identical legend, which he supposed was a telephone number, MO 6-2367. The hand he had not recognized was his own; the script was identical. He replaced the book, the train schedule, and the pen in his right inside pocket, and then searched the left inside pocket and found nothing. The left waist pocket of the jacket was empty as well. In the right waist pocket, he found two torn movie stubs. He had no idea whether they were old stubs or whether he had been to a movie last night, but a cold cunning recorded the fact that there were two of them. Whenever he had been to the movie, he had not gone alone. He stuck two fingers into the watch pocket of his trousers, expecting to find nothing, and was surprised to find two small gelatin capsules with white powder in them. He did not know what the capsules contained, or why he was carrying them. He put them back in the watch pocket.

He sat quietly for several moments more, thinking very calmly, and reasoning that the first thing he should do was call the number in the black book, if it was a number. What else could it be but a telephone number? He reasoned that the book was obviously new, and that the number must be an important one if he had jotted it down as the first and only item in the book. He knew it was not his own phone number because no one ever jotted down his own phone number. Unless he had recently moved, and had a new phone, and wasn't familiar with the number as yet, in which case he might possibly have written it down as a reminder. The possibility seemed extremely remote to him, but he nonetheless did not discard it. He moved it to a place at the back of his mind somewhere, a place where he was beginning to store a bank of knowledge about this person who was himself and whom he did not know. The knowledge was scanty at best, but at least he knew he was wearing a gold ring on his right hand and none on his left, which seemed to indicate he was not married. He also knew that G.V. had given him the ring, and he further knew that he was wearing gold cuff links and a gold tie tack and a fairly decent-looking suit. He opened the jacket now and looked at the label sewn into it. De Pinna's. An expensive suit. Whatever he was, he was not a pauper. The knowledge that he could afford gold cuff links and a gold tie tack and a suit from De Pinna's was reassuring, unless all these, like the gold ring, were gifts from G.V., whoever he or she was, in which case

He closed his mind against a dizzy spiraling that seemed endless and dangerous. The first thing he should do was call that number. He reached into his pocket for the black book again, and turned to the first page where the two numbers were written one under the other, the first already there when he had initially opened the book, the other that he had written to check the handwriting. MO 6-2367. Well, the first thing he would do was call the number, and yet something told him that there was no urgency about calling it, that once he called it, he would know nothing more about himself than he now knew.

Besides, he had no money.

He also had no watch, a fact that combined with the loss of his wallet and the absence of even any small change to lead him to believe he had been a robbery victim. And yet, his cuff links and tie tack had not been stolen. Would a thief have taken his wallet, his watch, and all his small change, without bothering to take his jewelry? Or had there been a thief and a robbery at all? Was it not equally possible that he had walked out of someplace, an apartment, a hotel room, someplace, anyplace, and simply left his wallet, and his watch, and his money behind? Perhaps he had never owned a watch to begin with. No, he hardly knew anyone in the world who did not own a wristwatch. Again, he was amused. Because not only did he hardly know anyone in the world who did not own a watch, he also hardly knew anyone in the world, period. Or, to be more exact, he *absolutely* did not know anyone in the world, never mind the hardly. He did not know a single living soul, unless perhaps he knew President Johnson and all the others whose names had flashed through his mind. Why not? Perhaps he called the President every night and said, "L.B., would you like to go bowling?" Perhaps he was a delegate to the United Nations. Perhaps, for Christ's sake, perhaps he was Adlai Stevenson himself. Why couldn't he be? He hadn't even seen his own face yet.

He suddenly touched the top of his head because the idea that he was Adlai Stevenson, that he was *really* Adlai Stevenson who had somehow through some curious quirk wandered into Central Park and been mugged and left on a bench, seemed very real and quite possible to him, and he knew that Adlai Stevenson was bald, so he touched the top of his head to see whether he was bald and really Adlai Stevenson.

He felt hair.

It was cut rather close to his head, not in a crew cut, but close nonetheless. Well, he was not Adlai Stevenson, which he supposed was something of a relief. This did not exclude the possibility that he was someone who *knew* Stevenson, and who *knew* Johnson, in fact someone very important who wandered in very high political circles—why couldn't he be? His suit had come from De Pinna's, and he was wearing gold cuff links and a gold tie tack, and he had obviously wandered out of the Sherry-Netherland where an important Democratic political function had been taking place, accidentally leaving his watch and wallet behind in the men's washroom where he had been standing side by side with Dean Rusk.

He rose from the bench.

The first thing he had to do, he now realized, was not what he originally surmised. The telephone number in the black book, if indeed it was a telephone number, still did not seem particularly urgent, nor did it now seem even terribly important. The most important thing he had to do was find a mirror someplace and take a good hard look at himself. He might surprise himself and discover he was Cary Grant. If there were some people around (where the hell had everybody in the city vanished to?) he would know right away if he was Cary Grant, because someone would most certainly stop him for an autograph, or perhaps someone would swoon—but unfortunately, there were no people around. Anyway, a dead swoon would not necessarily indicate that he was Cary Grant. It might only indicate that he was Burt Lancaster, or Frank Sinatra, or, as some swooning circles went, perhaps even Van Cliburn. He looked at his fingers. They were long and thin. Perhaps he *was* a piano player, or maybe a bongo drummer; the possibilities were limitless and, to tell the truth, a little frightening. Suppose, for example, suppose he found a mirror someplace, and he faced that mirror, and suppose he really *was* Cary Grant, but suppose he failed to recognize Cary Grant when he looked at him, then what? Suppose he simply saw some guy looking back at him, and he hadn't the faintest notion who the hell that guy was, Tony Curtis, or Dr. Schweitzer—please God, don't let me be Dr. Schweitzer.

He began walking.

The day was mild and clear, except for a haze that seemed to hang very high in the towers of the hotel buildings and apartment houses lining Fifth Avenue. He came out of the park and crossed immediately past the equestrian statue and to the fountain outside the Plaza. He looked around for a clock someplace, searching the tops of the buildings (Wasn't there a goddamn thing that flashed the time and the temperature every three or four seconds? Where the hell had that disappeared to?) but he could not find a clock. He knew it was very early in the morning, sensed that he had awakened only moments after the sun had cleared the horizon. The usual carriages were not waiting across from the Plaza; it was too early for that. Nor was there even a doorman on duty as yet outside the hotel. He pushed his way through the revolving doors and was walking toward the Palm Court when he glanced to his right and saw a man walking parallel with him.

The man startled him.

When he turned, the man turned. He realized all at once that he was looking at the doors of the men's room—he saw the sign GENTLEMEN—and that the twin doors were each broken into eight mirrored panels and that the man who was looking back at him was himself. The mirrored doors were divided by painted strips of wood, and he had to bend to see his own face because one of the horizontal strips crossed the mirror at just that point. His eyes met with the eyes of the crouching man in the mirror, and they both looked at each other unknowingly, two perfect strangers, neither knowing who the other was. He stepped closer to the mirror. The man was about thirty-five years old. His suit, though rumpled from a night's sleep, was obviously expensively tailored and fit him impeccably. His tie was knotted with a Windsor knot. He was wearing a shirt with a tab collar. His hair was a brownish black.

He looked into the other man's eyes, the eyes of the man who was himself, whom he did not know. The eyes were blue, flecked with white chips, the brows over the eyes somewhat bushy. The nose of the man, the stranger in the mirror, cleaved his face harshly, a little too large for the face really. The cheekbones *were* high; he had not been mistaken about that. The upper lip was not really as thin as he had imagined; he had a good mouth, this man in the mirror. He was, all in all, a good-looking man; he liked this man he saw in the mirror, but he did not have the faintest notion who he was.

Well, he thought, you're not Cary Grant.

He was fascinated by the mirror image. At the back of his mind, the store of knowledge added another kernel, added an image that he knew was his, an image he could now carry as an external shell inside of which he could operate, an image he had not possessed before. He had been only a bodiless mind moving through boundless space before this, but now the space had closed in and taken shape, had created a shell for itself, and the shell was this image staring back at him from the mirrored wall of the Plaza, an image he instantly liked, an image that fascinated him. He raised one eyebrow, a trick he had learned when he was sixteen; another kernel of knowledge was added minutely to the growing mound at the back of his mind. He was delighted by this person he saw, this face with its blue eyes and its uncombed but well-groomed hair, this broad-shouldered, narrow-waisted, obviously intelligent and good-looking gentleman who looked back at him from the mirror in appreciation of the stranger grinning at him with such undisguised joy. He backed away from the mirror, and realized all at once that he was hungry.

The hunger seemed to attack him with immediate violence, so that he knew it had probably been there from the moment he had awakened, but had been shunted aside in view of more pressing matters, like wondering exactly who the hell he was, for example. It was the hunger that lent sudden urgency to the telephone number—if it *was* a telephone number—he had found in the black book. He did not have any money, and in order to eat you had to have money. Perhaps the person at the other end of that number had some money to give him or lend him. Perhaps that person would know him and love him and feed him. He walked immediately to one of the house phones. He lifted it from the cradle and then opened the black book to the number again and waited until a hotel operator said, "Your call, please."

"Operator, would you get me MO 6-2367, please?"

"Are you a guest of the hotel, sir?"

"Yes," he lied.

"Your room number, please."

"407," he said.

"One moment, please."

He waited, half suspecting the operator was going through an elaborate register listing all the guests in all the rooms, and discovering either that Room 407 was vacant at the moment, or occupied by a spinster in her eighties. Instead, and to his immense relief, he heard a clicking sound that told him she was dialing, and then he heard a phone humming somewhere in the city, insistently calling a person who, for him, had no face and no name.

The phone rang once, twice, three times.

He waited.

It rang again, and again, and he was ready to hang up when a woman's voice miraculously said, "Hello?"

"Hello," he said, surprised.

"What time is it?" the woman said. Her voice was breathless, edged with sleep.

"I don't know," he answered. "Did I wake you?"

He heard a muffled sound, and then the woman, who had obviously just looked at the clock beside her bed, said, "For God's sake, it's six o'clock in the morning. Who *is* this?"

"Is this MO 6-2367?"

"Yes, this is Monument 6-2367. Who's this?"

"Who's this?" he asked.

"What is this, some kind of joke? Is that you, Sam?"

"Well, who's this?" he said.

"This is Gloria. What do you mean, who's this? Are you calling me, or am I calling you?"

"I'm calling you, Gloria," he said. Gloria, he thought. G.V. "How are you?"

"How am I? I'm half asleep, that's how I am. What is this? Is that you, Sam?"

Sam, he thought. "Yes," he said, "this is me. Sam."

"I thought so," Gloria said. "What do you want?"

"I want to see you."

"Why?"

"I want to talk to you."

"Why?"

"I . . . have to talk to you." He hesitated a moment, and then said, "I'm lost."

"Where are . . . what do you mean, you're lost? Lost, did you say?"

"Yes."

"Oh, Sam," the woman said, and there was so much despair in her voice that for a moment he thought she would begin to cry.

"Gloria?"

She did not answer.

20

"Gloria?" he said again.

"I'm here."

"Are you all right?"

"I'm fine. Why do you always call me when you're drunk? Will you please explain that to me?"

"I'm not drunk, Gloria."

"Then what the hell do you mean, you're lost? How can you be lost? Where are you?"

"I'm at the Plaza."

"What plaza?"

"The Plaza Hotel. On Fifty-ninth Street."

"Then how are you lost if you're at the Plaza?"

"Where are you, Gloria?"

"Home. What? I'm *home*, where do you think I am? You just *called* me, didn't you? I'm home in bed asleep. *Trying* to sleep. Oh, Sam, you drive me nuts. What is it you want?"

"I want to see you."

"When?"

"Now."

"No."

"Why not?"

"Because you'll want to . . . no. Forget it."

"Gloria, I *have* to see you."

"Why?"

"Because . . ." He hesitated. "Because I don't know who I am, and I'm hungry."

"You *never* knew who the hell you were," Gloria said, "and you've *always* been hungry. What's this supposed to be, news or something?"

"I really don't know who I am," he said.

"Yeah."

"Gloria?"

"Yeah."

"Let me come there."

"Why? So you can jump into bed with me?"

"No. I want you to tell me who I am."

21

"Oh, Sam, cut it out. It's too early in the morning for this kind of crap. You're who you are, who do you *think* you are? You're a pain in the ass, is what you are. Now hang up, and let me go back to sleep."

"No!" he said sharply. "Gloria, wait a minute."

He heard the woman sigh on the other end of the line. "I'm waiting a minute," she said. "But only a minute."

"I woke up in Central Park this morning," he said.

"So?"

"I don't know who I am."

"Sam, I don't understand you at all," she said. "*Not* at *all*."

"I'll explain when I get there."

"You won't explain nothing when you get here because you're not coming here."

"Your number is in my book," he said.

"What?"

"In my book."

"Yeah, and *your* number is in my book, sweetheart, and I know just what you want, and I'm not about ready to give it to you. If you think you're going to come up here and just . . ."

"No, I want to talk to you."

"Yeah, the big talker," she said, but he could sense she was weakening.

"I mean it. Let me come."

"I'm still asleep, I'm half asleep."

"We can have some coffee. We can talk."

"I'm going to put on my clothes, you know. You're not going to walk in here and find me in bed, if that's what you're thinking."

"That's not what I was thinking."

"Well . . ."

"Please, Gloria."

"Well . . . all right."

"I'll be right over," he said.

"All right," she said, and hung up.

The first thing he thought as he replaced the receiver was that he now had a name, Sam, not a very good name, but a name nevertheless, Sam, and then the second thought snapped into his mind fiercely. He had not found out where she lived. He picked up the receiver again, and immediately asked for the number again, and again told the operator he was a guest of the hotel, Room 407, and then waited while the phone rang at Gloria's apartment again.

"Hello?" she said.

"Gloria?"

"What now?"

"I forgot the address," he said.

"You what?"

"I for—"

"You for*got* the *add*ress?" She paused for an instant and then shrewdly said, "You *are* drunk, aren't you?"

"No, it's just that I can't remember anything. I already told you that."

"332 West Ninety-eighth," she said. "You forgot the address. Boy, that takes the cake!"

"I'll be up there in a few minutes."

"If you're at the Plaza, you won't be up here in no few minutes," Gloria said. "What are you doing at the Plaza, anyway? Having tea?"

"Yes," he said. He smiled. "Yes, I'm having tea with Adlai Stevenson."

"With *who?*"

"Stevenson."

"Well, don't bring him with you," she said. "My hair's in curlers."

"I'm sure you look lovely in curlers," he answered.

"And don't start any of *that* crap," she said.

"I won't start anything, Gloria," he promised. "332 West Ninety-eighth, right?"

"Yeah, yeah. Forgot the address. Maybe you'd better write it down, huh?" she said sarcastically. "So you won't forget it again, huh? Since you seem to be forgetting things lately?"

"That's a good idea," he said.

He took the black book from his pocket, and under the telephone number he wrote the address: 332 West 98th St. Then he closed the book and said, "Thank you, Gloria."

"Be careful," she said gently. "Don't fall under any goddamn subway train."

"I won't," he said. "Thank you," he said, and hung up.

He came down the wide front steps of the hotel, and he smiled and took a deep breath of air and thought, I have a name, I have a woman, and looked across to where the fountain splashed water idly and gently, and thought of other fountains, the one in Rome by Bernini, on the Piazza Navona, with the men covering their faces against the monstrosity of the church front opposite, designed by his rival, Borromini. I have been to Rome, he thought. Where else have I been? She seemed to feel I should have known the address, seemed to think it was incredible I should have forgotten it, 332 West 98th Street. Have I been there, too?

He sighed and glanced across the street to the canopy of the Sherry-Netherland, and saw for the first time the big standing sidewalk clock. How had he missed it earlier when he had wanted to know what time it was? Time seemed unimportant now that he had a name. He heard a sound overhead, and he glanced up at the sky and saw an airplane sharply metallic against the morning blue, and thought, Time, and then grinned and walked past the fountain, and hesitated on the corner for a moment, wondering which subway system he should take to 98th Street.

Sam, he thought. My name is Sam. Am I indeed the Sam she thought she was talking to, her own Wandering Sam who calls her when he's drunk, who's supposed to know her address the way he knows his own name, Sam? Well, maybe not, and probably not, but in another sense I *am* her Sam in that it was she who gave me the name. Her number is, after all, in my little black book, so who should know her own darling boy if not Gloria? Until she tells me otherwise, why, I *am* Sam, I have a name, and I have a woman who is expecting me at 332 West 98th Street.

Sam, he thought. Which, together with fifteen cents, will get me into the subway and on my way. My name is

The beer truck rolled past at that instant, coming east on 58th Street, and taking the corner onto Fifth Avenue, with the name of the beer splashed across the side of the truck, BUDWEISER, and the advertising slogan "Where there's life, there's Bud," and he added the Budweiser to the Sam, and he completed the thought and the name, Sam Budweiser, and then rejected it, clipping it short after the Bud; and hearing the drone of the airplane again, high overhead, and looking up and immediately associating airplane with wing, and then again merging the separate parts of the beer and the airplane, he made a compound called Buddwing, Sam Buddwing, which he rather liked. Sam Buddwing. I am Sam Buddwing, the hell with you.

He had a name.

# 2

THE CITY was beginning to come awake.
It was Saturday morning, and she was a little slow rising, a little
tardy in shaking the sleep from her bones. Here and there, as
Buddwing walked along Central Park South, a window shade went
up slowly and reluctantly. This was Saturday morning, and there
was no place to go, no hurry to get anywhere. This was Saturday, and the city came up out of sleep a little too early, through
force of habit perhaps, and then heaved an enormous shrug that
you could feel clear down to her bowels. Up and down the wide
street, steam hissed up from manhole covers. A lone cruising taxicab slowed as the driver spotted Buddwing, but it was too early;
the city was still restlessly stirring in a warm bed smelling of
Friday night's musk and Friday night's liquor and Friday night's
copulation. The cab picked up speed and passed him by; it was
too early.

He could hear the sound of birds in the park, a sound you
rarely heard in this city. He could hear them chirping in a hundred different voices, could hear their calls echoing among the

trees beginning to bud in the first sweet rush of spring, and then re-echoing across the balmy air, touching the bright yellow forsythia blooms ranged like golden asterisks against the park's stone walls, trilling across the red and pink cornelian cherry shrubs, dissipating on the air, seeming to vanish, and then suddenly replenished and replaced by another bird voice, another sharp trilling chirp, the chirps multiplied and magnified until it seemed a thousand birds, a million birds, were calling to the city, urging her to rise, willing her to rise.

In this enormous city, which had a name but was nonetheless anonymous, in this sprawling New York stirring now to test her early morning muscle, he walked anonymously, a man with a name who was anonymous to himself. And in his anonymity (Christ, how sweet the birds sounded) he felt a sudden joy that was somehow contained within a brittle shell of sympathy for every other anonymous son of a bitch who lived here. He knew this city was his. Whatever else he knew about himself, and he knew precious little, he knew that he had been born in this city, that he belonged in this city, that he felt this city's pulse as his own pulse, that she held an irrevocable and lifelong claim to his love and his hate, and that she would never let him go as long as he could breathe.

He could not count the number of times he had walked along Central Park South in his life. He tried now to remember other times on this wide street, tried to remember if there had been bird sounds then, tried to remember if he could see the haze slowly burning away over the roof of the Coliseum in the distance, could remember none of it, and yet knew with certainty he had walked this street in winter and summer, spring and fall, that it was as much a part of him as his liver or his heart. The city called to him that Saturday morning. He had found a new face by confronting himself in a mirror at the Plaza, he had stolen a first name from an unknown woman on a telephone, and then requisitioned a surname from a beer and an airplane: Sam Buddwing. And now Sam Buddwing—clean, new, somehow filled with joy and sadness—walked into a city he loved and hated, clean and new, and heard her calling to him.

Deep in her gut, he could feel the rumble of infrequent subway trains growling along subterranean tracks, clattering into nearly deserted station stops. He could visualize, he could *hear*, a drunk mumbling in his sleep on the platform, a young couple whispering to each other behind one of the pillars, her lipstick smeared, his hair tousled. He could roam this city in his mind, he could turn over every corner of her, inspect her armpits and her crotch, kiss her navel and her throat, plunge his hands deep into the hot spongy interior of her, and come out stinking of honey and blood, loving her, hating her. He could hear the tugs hooting their cry on the Hudson, thousands of miles crosstown, could feel the haze rising from the river, hanging in a veil beneath the George Washington Bridge, rising, rising; you could see the Palisades across the river. How many times had he shrieked on that roller coaster? How many times had he seen the posters for the amusement park, the young girl in her swimsuit standing beside the swimming pool, and known this was the real beginning of summer? How many times had he climbed those mysterious steps, the steps of Aztecs or Mayans or Apaches, leading up to Washington Heights? How many girls had he kissed in Poe Park near the band shell in the summer when Bobby Sherwood was playing "Elks' Parade" and the lights of Fordham Road danced in the distance? How many skirts had he raised by the banks of the Bronx River where the willows hung suspended over the water and lights reflected eerily in blackness? Oh, he knew this city; he loved this city, and he hated her.

He could remember

He could remember—and he delicately nourished the memory, delicately nurtured it for fear it would vanish completely, leaving him lost again—bicycles, bicycles along a silent summer path; the path wound alongside the river. He could remember her plaid skirt flapping as she pedaled the bicycle, dark hair blowing back and free from her face, a boy's bicycle, her brother's, and the flash of thigh and her laugh high and melodious on the still hot air under the viaduct arching overhead, the sudden trees, they parked the bicycles in deep shade. They took them off the path and lay them flat, crushing the new young grass. He explored her mouth, her black hair hung in a curtain over his face, he touched the warm inner softness of her thighs, he could remember.

Who?

A boy, so young.

A girl.

He did not know her name.

He remembered a vague Sam Buddwing, a boy wearing bicycle clips; the bike was black with white trim, he could remember that, but the boy he remembered was unclear and indistinctly formed. He could not see his face, only a thin angular body, and a head held somewhat the way the man in the mirror at the Plaza had held his head, but nothing more than that, and then even that was gone.

The empty city surrounded him.

He could hear the clatter of his own shoes on the pavement. The street was deserted now. He had a sudden desire to step off the curb and into the middle of the street, and run up the white line to Sixth Avenue. The desire paused. The city seemed more silent than ever. Even the birds were hushed. He wondered how he had expected to get into the subway when he had no money, and then an audacious idea came into his head, and he knew instantly that he would try it, and quickened his step to the kiosk. He was grinning broadly now, outraged by the audacity of his plan, knowing he would never have conceived it, never hoped to execute it, if he knew who he really was, if he had a real identity and a real name. But he was Sam Buddwing, and he didn't know a goddamn soul, and so he hurried down the steps, his eyes searching the ground as he walked.

He would need a piece of cardboard, or a slip of paper, no, cardboard would be better. He could see the change booth up ahead. There was only one man in it at this hour of the morning, and he was probably half asleep. Yes, it would work; he felt certain it would work. He found what he was looking for swept against one of the walls, a piece of white cardboard that had undoubtedly served as the inside backing for a candy bar. He picked it up and looked at it. It seemed wide enough, but perhaps it was a trifle too long. Carefully, he folded three-quarters of an inch from one end, and then cautiously tore the cardboard along the fold. Lifting his head confidently, he walked toward the change booth and then past it. He ignored the turnstiles and walked directly to the gate alongside them. He turned only casually toward the change booth, raised his hand palm outward with the white piece of cardboard cupped in his palm like a transportation pass of some kind, holding it for the change-booth attendant to see. The attendant looked through his bars, gave a brief nod, and went back to whatever he was doing. Buddwing opened the gate and walked on through. He kept walking without looking back, going down the steps to the Uptown platform.

When he reached the platform, he burst out laughing.

He knew the neighborhood Gloria lived in, because it was close to Broadway, and he used to work in a grocery store on Broadway when he was a boy going to high school. What was the name of the man who'd owned the store? It didn't matter. An Italian name. He had hated the man; the man had worn eyeglasses. He could remember that he had taken the job because he had needed the money for something. It had been a summer job, and he had been about sixteen. What had he needed the money for? Something.

The day he reported to work, the boss (Palumbo or Palumbi or something with a P, something Italian) had explained to him that his job would be primarily the delivery of groceries, but that occasionally he would help out behind the counter. He also told Buddwing that he could eat his lunch in the basement under the store, where all the soda pop was kept, but that he would have to pay him for any soda he drank.

Buddwing thought this was fair until the first day he went

down to the basement to have his lunch, and found there a veritable treasure trove of soda pop. Coca-Cola, Pepsi-Cola, Seven-Up, Canada Dry Ginger Ale and Orange Soda, Hoffman Cream Soda and Sarsaparilla were stacked in cases that almost reached from floor to ceiling, bottle upon bottle. He correctly figured that if he paid the boss five cents a day, six days a week, for the bottle of pop he had with his lunch each day, the grand and munificent total would come to thirty cents a week. He mused that if he were the owner of a fancy grocery store, he would certainly allow his lowly delivery boy to drink a meager bottle of soda pop once a day every day of the week without charging him for it. The boss, it seemed to him, was being a cheap bastard. Besides, he was earning only twenty-two dollars a week, and the boss could certainly afford to let him have a free bottle of pop each day, or at least a bottle of pop at wholesale, which Buddwing was sure was not five cents a bottle. Nevertheless, even though the boss's cheapness rankled, he went down to the basement for lunch every day for the first two weeks, and every day he opened a bottle of Coke and drank it with the sandwiches he brought from home, and then went upstairs and gave the boss a nickel.

Then, one morning while he was putting a carton of eggs into the refrigerator, he dropped the carton and broke eight of the eggs, and the boss told him he would deduct the price of those eggs from Buddwing's salary. That very afternoon, Buddwing went down to the basement to have his lunch as usual. But instead of opening a bottle of Coke, he opened a quart of Hoffman's Cream Soda and drank the whole quart, and then he opened a quart of Canada Dry Ginger Ale and drank half of that and spilled the rest down the open drain. When he went back after lunch, he paid his boss a nickel for the Coke he had not had. For the rest of the time he worked there, he stole the boss blind. He did not smoke at the time, but he stole cartons of cigarettes and took them home with him, and he opened canned fruits in the basement and had those with his lunch, and he sometimes would open six or seven quarts of soda, each a different flavor, and have

a few sips from each bottle, and every day he would go back upstairs and pay the boss a nickel for a bottle of Coke.

He could remember all this, but he could not remember what
the cheap bastard's name was, or what he had done with the stolen
cigarettes, though he had a feeling he had given them to a very
close friend of his who smoked, and whose name he also could
not remember. There was something else he could not or would
not remember about that lousy job on Broadway and 91st Street
—yes, that was where it had been—something else that troubled
him about that job besides the cheap bastard who could not speak
English, something else in one of the apartments he delivered to,
something. Or maybe a combination of somethings, maybe that.
He only knew that he remembered the job with a curious feeling of dread, and that the dread could not have come from the
memory of his petty thefts.

He wondered now why he had needed money that summer,
and he wondered too why even such a scanty memory of the job
seemed to fill him with such dread, and then he stopped wondering. There was simply too much to wonder about, too little he
knew. He hesitated in the lobby of Gloria's building. For a moment, he did not wish to go into the building, did not wish to find
Gloria, did not wish to find himself. Coming up Central Park
South, listening to the birds, sensing the city around him and
inside him, he had felt an anonymity that he instantly equated
with freedom. The freedom had caused him to pull his outrageous
trick on the change-booth attendant, and to sit in secret glee all
the way uptown to 96th Street. But now . . . now memory of
that grocery store job so long ago had triggered a reluctance in
him to know anything more about himself. He suddenly felt that
knowing himself would simply mean losing this freedom he had
newly found. Knowing himself would bring a responsiblity that
would not allow him to hold up a blank piece of cardboard as a
Transit Authority pass. Knowing himself would be frightening,
and he did not want to be frightened.

He found himself walking through the lobby and to the mailboxes. He was not at all sure that he would go upstairs once he

found out what apartment Gloria was in—he had not asked her on the phone, was that significant?—but there was a burning curiosity inside him that threatened to override both the earlier freedom he had experienced and the shudder of dread that had accompanied his recollection of the grocery store job. As he ran his index finger over the names in the mailboxes, he remembered Gloria's voice on the telephone, edged with sleep, somewhat breathless, a sensuous voice, and the things she had hinted at, the things she thought he wanted from her. He did not know whether he really wanted these things from her or not, or even whether he had ever had these things from her, and if he had had them whether they were good or bad. But he was curious, and he was also oddly excited by the idea of going into the apartment of a woman with whom he had perhaps been intimate, and not recognizing her but nonetheless knowing that he had perhaps been intimate with her; the idea was very exciting. He could feel a stirring in his groin that had nothing whatever to do with intellectual curiosity. His finger traveled along the nameplates a little quicker, almost passed one of the names by, and then retraced itself and stopped.

GLORIA OSBORNE

He searched the remainder of the row. There were no other Glorias, and no other names with the initial G before them. This, then, was Gloria. Gloria Osborne. Not the G.V. who was inside his ring, not the G.V. from whom the ring had come, whoever he or she was, but Gloria Osborne, whose hair was in curlers and who spoke with a sleep-fuzzed breathless voice, who promised by denial the things that would happen when he entered that apartment, Gloria Osborne.

As he walked out of the small alcove containing the mailboxes and toward the elevator, he found himself becoming more and more excited by what he was now certain awaited him upstairs. He pressed the elevator button and waited while the name Gloria Osborne echoed sensuously in his mind. Apartment 7A, the mailbox had said, Apartment 7A, and Gloria Osborne waiting to tell him who he was, to do with him the things they had doubtless done a thousand times before, Gloria Osborne. He got into the elevator and pressed the button for the seventh floor.

When the elevator stopped, he walked into the corridor and again hesitated. The excitement that had come with his thoughts of Gloria's voice, of Gloria's denying promises, suddenly died when he realized she probably would not know him at all. He would knock on her door, and she would open it and look at his face and not know him, and perhaps slam the door, and perhaps call the police; it was after all only six-thirty in the morning! His passion died limply. He stood in the corridor, lonely and drained and discouraged. She would not know him, she would not tell him who he was, she would not offer him her bed and her body and her warmth. He stood with his head bent, undecided, and then he thought, Why shouldn't she know me? I'm Sam. He pulled back his shoulders and began looking for Apartment 7A. He found it at the end of the hall. He hesitated a moment more before knocking, and then he raised his fist and rapped his knuckles sharply against the door.

"Who is it?" the woman said from inside the apartment.

"It's me," he answered. "Sam."

"Just a second," she said.

He waited. His heart had begun beating frantically inside his chest. She won't know me, he thought. Oh Jesus, she won't know me. It was not important now that he find out who he was; this did not seem important at all. It was only important that *she* should know who he was, that she should open the door and say, "Sam, oh Sam baby, where you been, honey? Come in," that she should open her arms and pull him close to her breasts and smother him with warmth and perfume, that she should *know* him. He waited while she fussed inside the apartment—what was she doing in there?—waited interminably, and then knocked again on the door, and she yelled, "Yes, yes, I'm coming," and still he waited; what was taking her so damn—the door opened.

Gloria Osborne was a big blond woman wearing curlers in her hair, and a quilted robe around her shoulders. She opened the door wide and peered into the hallway, and her face expressed the same shock that must have been on his the moment the door opened, because Gloria Osborne was perhaps fifty-three years old with pale blue eyes and a wide nose and a mouth that had vanished the moment she had removed her lipstick. He stood staring at her in disappointment and in anger, feeling she had tricked him with her breathless, sleep-edged voice, recognizing that what he had first accepted as breathlessness was really the sound of advancing middle age, hating her for having tricked him, and then seeing that she was staring at him in surprise and waiting for him to speak. Neither said a word. He thought of turning and running for the elevator, and then a horrifying idea rushed into his mind. My mother, he thought. This woman standing here with the machinery of hell in her hair, this woman with watery blue eyes and no mouth, is my goddamn mother!

"Miss . . . Miss Osborne?" he asked.

"Yes?" The voice was cautious, suspicious.

"*Gloria* Osborne?"

"Yes?"

"I . . ." He sighed heavily. "I'm Sam," he said.

"Yeah?"

He nodded. "Yes."

"You're not any Sam *I* know," she said.

"I just spoke to you on the phone a little while ago," he answered.

"Yeah," she said. She was still watching him suspiciously, as though trying to figure out what his game was.

"Your number was in my book."

"Yeah," she said.

He could see that she didn't believe him, so he instantly reached into his jacket pocket and took out the little black book and opened it to the first page and showed the page to her.

"Twice," she said, and she smiled.

"What?"

"It's in your book twice."

"Oh. Yes, I . . . I wrote it twice."

35

"Because you forget things, isn't that right?" The smile was still on her face, a curious smile he could not read. He was suddenly aware of the heavy scent clinging to her and realized that Gloria Osborne, his breathy-voiced telephone inamorata, had doused herself with perfume upon arising, but had not bothered to put on any lipstick. The implications of such an oversight were frightening.

"Well," Gloria said, "why don't you come in?"

"I don't think I should," he answered. "You see, I thought you might know me, but apparently you don't, so I'll just apologize for waking you up, and—"

"Don't be silly," Gloria said. "You're here, so come on in. I'll make you a cup of coffee."

"Well . . ."

"Come on."

"But . . . I'm not Sam," he said.

"Who *are* you?" she asked.

"I don't know."

"Then how do you know you're not Sam?"

"Am I?"

"How do I know?"

"I mean, do *you* know me?"

"I've never seen you before in my life."

"Then I can't be Sam, can I?"

"You can be whoever you like, baby. Napoleon, if you like. Only make up your mind. We're going to wake up the whole damn building." She paused, watching him. "Yes or no? In or out?"

He shrugged. "I guess I can use a cup of coffee," he said.

Gloria smiled, and said, "Then come on in."

He followed her into the apartment. The quilted robe was blue, and it spread over a very wide backside which she managed to jiggle ponderously as she walked, rather like a truck horse pulling a brewery wagon. He noticed that she was wearing tiny blue satin slippers with blue pom-pom puffs at each toe. There was a small mirror on the wall just inside the entrance, and she paused to glance at herself, and then turned her head daintily over one shoulder, and said, "Come on," in a trippingly light voice, slightly teasing, invitational. He would have left her in that moment, were it not for the fact that her number was, after all, in his little black book. He found, as he followed her into the small apartment, that a curious tug of war was going on in his mind, the antagonists in which stood at either end of a memory rope, one trying to pull him deeper into forgetfulness, the other trying to pull him up into complete recognition. He sensed that if he succumbed to either one or the other, he would be completely lost. The key to survival, he reasoned, was to maintain a balance between these two forces tugging at either end of his unconscious. So whereas he wanted to run from this blowzy broad in her blue quilted robe with her blue pom-pom slippers, his instincts told him to stay and hear her out. How had her number come to be in his book in his handwriting in his jacket pocket? He had to know, and yet he did not want to know, and the rope tightened in his mind from the strain at its opposite ends.

He followed her into a small living room furnished in a three-piece suite, one chair done in maroon, a second in gold, and the couch in a deep blue, all with heavily carved mahogany legs, all with antimacassars on the arms and the backs. A framed print of gondolas in Venice was on the wall over the couch, and a framed print of a Spanish lady with a mantilla over her head, strumming a guitar and singing, was on the wall over the maroon chair, which he now sat in. Gloria sat opposite him on the couch, tucking her legs up under her and pulling the flaps of the quilted robe down over her knees. She smiled maternally, and said, "The coffee's up. It should be ready in a few minutes."

"Thank you," he said.

"What's your name?" she asked. She asked it so casually, so offhandedly, that it seemed not at all like a trap. It seemed for a moment as though he were simply some stranger who had come to the door, whom she had accepted, and whose name she now wanted to know. The conversation on the telephone seemed never to have taken place.

"I don't know my name," he said.

"Then why'd you say you were Sam?"

"*You* said I was Sam."

"I never said no such thing."

"Well, what I mean is you *thought* I was Sam. On the phone."

"Who gave you my number?"

"I don't know."

"But it's right there in your book, isn't it?"

"Yes. It seems to be."

"Seems, hell. It *is*. Twice."

"That's right."

"Well, who gave it to you?"

"I told you. I don't know."

"Where are you from?"

"I don't know."

"How old are you?"

"I don't know."

"Where do you live?"

"I don't know."

"What's your Social Security number?"

"119 . . ." He stopped.

"Yeah, go ahead."

"I can't remember the rest."

"You married?"

"I don't think so. I'm not sure."

"Are you afraid of me or something?" Gloria asked suddenly.

"No. Why should I be afraid of you?"

"I mean, what's all this smoke screen for? What did Sam tell you, anyway?"

"What?" he said.

"Come on, mister, let's cut the crap, huh? You met my husband in some goddamn bar last night, and he gave you my number and told you to call me. Isn't that what happened? So here you are, so cut the crap and relax."

"Is . . . is Sam your husband?"

38

"Yeah," she said, "some husband." She paused. "We're separated. Didn't he tell you that?"

"No, I . . . I don't remember meeting him."

"Then how'd you get my number?"

"I don't know."

"Somebody must have given it to you, right?"

"I suppose so."

"Were you out drinking last night?"

"I don't remember where I was last night. I woke up this morning in Central Park, and that's all I know."

She stared at him curiously for a moment, her head tilted to one side, and then she said, "I think I hear the coffee," and rose massively and walked into the kitchen. From the kitchen, she called, "How do you take this, mister?"

He heard her words, and he sat quite still in the ugly maroon chair, and for the first time since he had awakened this morning he felt despair. He sat looking at his clenched hands, his head bent. She came into the doorway between the kitchen and the living room, the coffeepot in one hand, and she said, "Hey. How do you take it?"

He began weeping suddenly. He had not expected to cry, and when he felt the tears rolling down his cheeks, he turned his face away so that she could not see him. But he could not hide the heaving of his chest and shoulders, and she stood in the doorway dumbfounded, staring at him in confusion and sympathy. The tears came steadily, forced from his eyes by the great racking sobs that shook his body. She went into the kitchen briefly to return the pot to the stove, and then she came through the doorway again and walked to the big maroon chair where he sat. She perched on it beside him, and then wrapped both her arms around him and pulled his head onto the vast cushion of her breast, soft beneath the quilted robe, and said, "Hey, hey, baby, what's the matter? Hey, come on, now, what's the matter? Come on, now, baby, don't do this, please, this ain't right, now come on, baby."

He sobbed against the comfort of the breast beneath the quilted

39

robe, and he searched for his voice, and when he found it he said, between sobs, "I don't know how I take it."

"Huh?" she said, puzzled.

"My coffee," he answered. "I don't know how I take it."

"Huh?" she said.

"My coffee," he said again, and suddenly she began laughing. The laugh broke from her mouth in a raucous bellow. Her breasts shook, and her belly shook, and his head on her breasts shook, and as each convulsive wave of laughter rocked her body, its seismic echo vibrated through him so that he seemed to be laughing himself by osmosis, and then *was* laughing himself in actuality. Together they laughed while she hugged him fiercely and protectively to her breast, his laughter coming between the sobs, as though he were uncertain whether to laugh or continue crying, her laughter a warm canopy of sound that fell gently on his ears, that reverberated beneath his cheek where it lay pressed to her giant mother breast.

"Oh, my God!" she said. "You don't know how you take your coffee!"

"Yeah," he said, grinning, laughing, crying.

"Oh, my holy sweet mother of God!"

"Yeah," he said.

"Oh, God," she said, hugging him, kissing the top of his head, showering laughter and kisses on his face, crying herself now from the force of her own explosive laughter. "Yeah," he said, and she said, "God," and he said, "Yeah" again, and then they laughed more quietly for several moments, and then the laughter faded away, and then they were silent. He kept his head cradled on her breast. She stroked his face with her massive left hand. He felt warm and protected against her breast. He wanted to move the quilted robe aside and rest the flesh of his cheek against the flesh of her bosom, but he thought she would misunderstand. And then suddenly he knew that she would not; suddenly he loved this enormous aging Gloria with her hair in curlers and her quilted robe and silly pom-pom slippers and her great warm soft breast holding his head so gently cradled, and her rough left hand softly and caressingly stroking his face. He moved her robe aside, exposing her breasts.

"Yes," she said, "rest, baby, rest," and she pulled his head into her soft and yielding flesh, and he closed his eyes and smelled the heavy perfume of her rising from the cleft of her bosom. "What are we going to do about you, baby?" she asked, her voice a whisper now. "You poor dear baby who don't know who you are, what the hell are we going to do about you?"

"Don't know," he murmured.

"You got no idea?" she asked.

"No."

"Tch," she said, clucking her tongue, the single sound echoing the despair he had heard in her voice on the telephone when she had thought he was Sam, her husband, calling her because he was drunk again. "You don't know who you are at all, huh?"

"I don't even know how I take my coffee," he said.

"Yeah," she said, and burst out laughing again.

"Yeah," he said, chuckling against her breast.

"You take it black, maybe? Were you in the service?"

"I don't know."

"Because a lot of guys who were in the army or navy, they take it black. Sam was never in nothing, that 4-F bastard, but he takes his black."

"Then I'll take mine black," he said.

"You want me to go get it now?" she asked.

"Stay," he said, in sudden panic.

"Okay, okay," she said, and she patted his head gently, and he snuggled deeper into her bosom, closing his eyes again, strangely at peace. The peace did not last very long. The rope of memory that lay slack and limp at the bottom of his mind was suddenly snapped taut again, suddenly pulled tight from opposite ends. If the rope had not regained its tensile life, he knew he could have rested in the haven of her bosom forever, not caring who he was or where he was or why he was. He could have inhaled her cheap perfume and her honest sweat, allowed her smells and her warmth

to lull him to sleep, wrapping forgetfulness about him like a warm
blanket, curled on the pillow of her bosom. But he recognized
all at once, as if it were a new thought of which he had not until
now been aware, that he did not know who he was, and that if he
stayed here in this woman's arms, on this woman's warm breast,
he might never find out. So he pulled his head away from her with
a start, his cheek suddenly cold. He stared up into her face, as
though surprised to find these warm and protective breasts belonged to a person, and he looked up into her sympathetic blue
eyes and plaintively said, "You don't know me?"

She stared at him as if she would begin weeping, as if she
wanted nothing more than to tell him she knew him. But she
shook her head sadly, and said, "No, baby, I'm sorry. I don't know
you."

He sighed deeply, and then he got to his feet, moving out of
the chair. "I think I'd better go," he said.

"Where?"

"I'm not sure. But I don't think it's any good staying here."

"Have some coffee," she said. "It's all ready to pour."

"No. Thank you. Gloria . . . thank you very much. You're a
very nice person."

"Yeah," she said in embarrassment.

"You are, Gloria. Thank you. But I have to go. I just have
to go."

"Have you got any money?" she asked, her eyes suddenly narrowing shrewdly.

"Sure," he said.

She moved off the arm of the chair, and she said, "Wait. Don't
you leave, you hear me?" She went into the other room—the bedroom, he supposed—and came back carrying her handbag. She
opened it and held out a five-dollar bill to him. "Here," she said.
"Take it."

"I couldn't."

She did not say another word. She reached over and stuffed it
into the breast pocket of his jacket, behind his cigarettes. He

42

looked at her steadily for several moments, and then he said, "Why, Gloria?"

"You're lost and hungry, ain't you?" she said, shrugging. "Ain't that what you told me on the phone?"

He smiled and nodded. "Yes," he said, "I'm lost and hungry."

"Then go find yourself," she said.

# 3

HE began expecting some sort of shock the moment he left her apartment and walked down to the street. He did not know in what manner or form the shock would arrive when it did, but he felt an almost preternatural certainty that it would come—and soon. The shock expectancy did not frighten him. As a matter of fact, he felt rather gay and light-headed as he walked again to Broadway, and then turned right and began heading downtown.

He did not know to what he should attribute his sudden sense of exhilaration. He had known extreme peace and comfort, and a vast sense of security, lying on Gloria's bosom, had been reluctant to leave and begin his search anew. But now that he was once more embarked on his quest—and he had not the slightest idea where he was going, or where he should begin looking—he felt that odd sense of freedom again, as though he had shaken off encumbering shackles. It was only with the greatest effort that he could contain himself from running down Broadway. And yet, not five minutes before, he had not wanted to leave the security of Gloria's apartment.

He thought about Gloria now as he walked down the almost deserted street. It was perhaps seven o'clock in the morning and most of the stores along Broadway were still closed. He spotted an all-night cafeteria and decided he ought to have breakfast, but he no longer felt very hungry; this exhilaration inside him seemed to be all-consuming, obliterating all other feeling. He passed the cafeteria by. The thing about Gloria, he supposed, was that she was really a very repulsive woman, with her fat behind and her silly little pom-pom slippers, and yet he had not found her repulsive. He suddenly wondered if she had expected him to go to bed with her. The idea somehow pleased him because he was still partially in love with this fat slob of a woman who had no mouth but who had offered him warmth and comfort when he seemed to need it most. And yet he knew without doubt that if the matter had come up at all, he would have been obliged to refuse, and this puzzled him.

He felt strange about the money she had given him, too. He knew that five dollars was a lot of money to some people, and he suspected that Gloria was one of them. At the same time, he had a feeling that he was used to handling much larger sums of money, that he counted money in terms of thousands, and that five dollars was absolute chicken feed to his normal self. But he felt rich. He had taken the bill from his breast pocket and moved it to one of his trouser pockets, and he felt richer than he ever had in his life. He remembered with a wry grin that his life had really begun in Central Park little more than an hour ago, and that he had awakened penniless and nameless. So naturally five dollars would seem like a lot of money to him. But the thing about this particular five dollars, which he could feel in his pocket brushing the ends of his long fingers, was that it not only seemed like a *lot* of money, it seemed like *all* the money there was in the world. He felt enormously rich, overwhelmingly rich, all because he was carrying Gloria's five-dollar bill in his pocket.

That was the curious thing about Gloria, he realized. She caused him, in his present anonymous state, to accept—indeed to be delighted by—things he knew meant nothing in his ordinary life. My ordinary life, he thought. What is my ordinary life?

45

Maybe my ordinary life *does* include women like Gloria who offer me their fat and fleshy bosoms like gifts to a pauper. Maybe my ordinary life is constructed around an economy that does consider five crumby dollars a fortune. What the hell is my ordinary life, and how is this new life that began this morning in Central Park any less ordinary, any more extraordinary?

His exhilarating mood was being threatened, he felt.

He began whistling, not recognizing the tune at first, and then realizing he was whistling the main theme of a very well-known symphony, but he did not know which one. He began running through the names of composers in his mind: Tchaikovsky, Berlioz, Saint-Saëns, Shostakovich, Brahms, Beethoven, and Bach, Prokofiev, Copland, Bernstein. He supposed he had coupled Bernstein and Copland only because he could remember a record with Copland's *El Salón México* on one side and Bernstein's *Fancy Free* on the other, a curious combination for an A and R man to hit upon, but there it was nonetheless. Then he remembered that the record had a red label, and knew instantly it was a Columbia record, and then wondered how in hell he knew what an A and R man was, and then wondered if perhaps he wasn't in some way involved with the music business. He did not think he was, but he seemed to have been humming a symphony and he seemed to be familiar with a composer or two, and he also knew what an A and R man was, but then he supposed everyone did. He saw a man coming down the street, an old man with a grizzled beard, his hands in his pockets, staring at the sidewalk as he walked, and he went up to the man and said, "Excuse me, sir."

The man looked up at him suspiciously.

"Do you know what an A and R man is?" he asked.

"What?" the man said.

"Do you know what an A and R man is?"

"Well, now, just a minute," the man said. "A and R, huh?"

"Yes, sir."

"Aerials and Radios?" the man asked.

"No."

"Just a second, now, just a second." The man furrowed his

brow, thinking strenuously. "Aeronautics and . . . uh . . . Rockets? Rocketry? Is that it?"

"No."

"I'll get it, just a minute," the man said. "What's this for, anyway?"

"What do you mean?"

"Is this some television show or something?" the man asked.

"No, I just wanted to know," Buddwing said.

"Oh. Well, just a second, now. A and R, huh? Just a second. Automotive and . . . just a second . . . Research? That sounds right, don't it?"

"No," Buddwing said.

"Oh." The man looked disappointed. "Well, then, I'm sorry, fella. I can't help you."

"Thanks, anyway," Buddwing said.

"Don't mention it," the man answered, and he continued walking up Broadway, his head bent, his hands in his pockets.

Buddwing looked after the man for a moment and then thought, Well, *he* doesn't know what an A and R man is, so perhaps I *am* connected with the music business at that; or perhaps, considering the skill with which I handled the old gentleman, perhaps I am a professional survey taker. His joyous mood returned at once, powerfully, making him almost giddy. The staggering number of possibilities of things he could be—the doctors, lawyers, Indian chiefs; the butchers, bakers, candlestick makers; the princes, paupers, panderers and pimps; the artists, writers, actors, agents; the truck drivers, muckrakers, groundhogs, hemstitchers; chicken pluckers, aviators, pearl divers, bandleaders; bass fiddlers, ballplayers, lobster salesmen, thieves; anything, *everything*—the possibilities, rather than overwhelming him and leaving him weak, instead brought on a feeling of immense power. God, what a choice! he thought. I can be anything I want to be! I can start right this minute as a professional survey taker, Sam Buddwing Research, Inc., and go down Broadway asking everyone I meet if he knows what an A and R man is! I can stand on the corner and teach a class or preach a sermon! I can buy a chisel and become a sculptor or a burglar! I can find a scrap of paper and write a play or a pamphlet! I can be a lover or a hater, a creator or a destroyer, an artist or a critic! I can be whatever I want to be and whoever I want to be! I am new, I am clean, I am born, my God I am hungry!

He quickened his pace, searching avidly for a cafeteria now, wondering if he should turn back and go to the one he had seen earlier. He walked two more blocks downtown, and then decided to cut crosstown to Amsterdam Avenue, and then instead continued walking on Broadway, and found at last another cafeteria, which he walked into quickly, pulling a ticket from the machine, and lifting a tray from the pile of brown plastic trays, and then going down the line of food, eying each separate piece of food with a delight almost unbearable. He took a glass of orange juice and a grapefruit, he took two pieces of Danish pastry and a hard roll, he took three pats of butter, he took a cup of coffee and a glass of milk, and then he went to the rear of the line again and took a glass of tomato juice. He carried all these to a table at the back of the sparsely populated cafeteria and was about to sit when a voice behind him said, "That's my chair."

He turned.

He was looking at a very short man of about fifty years of age, who had a twitch on the left side of his face. The twitch made the man look very evil. It twisted his face at regularly spaced intervals, the mouth curling upward, the eye blinking, as if the man were some sort of infernal machine that had been short-circuited. The man was wearing a sports jacket over a sports shirt, a gray fedora on his head. He was holding a cup of coffee in his right hand.

"Go ahead, sit down," the man said.

"But you said it was your chair."

"There's four chairs at the table," the man said. "I should deny you a lousy chair? Go ahead, take the lousy chair."

"Well, thank you," Buddwing said, and he pulled out the chair and sat. The man stood by the table, twitching and looking at Buddwing's tray.

48

"You're expecting someone?" he said.

"What?" Buddwing asked, looking up. "Oh. No. No, I'm not."

"I thought perhaps you were expecting a breakfast club," the little man said, twitching. He pulled out a chair, put his cup of coffee on the table opposite Buddwing, and then said, "Since you ain't expecting nobody, I presume you won't mind if I join you?"

"There are four chairs at the table," Buddwing said, smiling. "I should deny you a lousy chair?"

"That's very kind of you," the little man said, twitching. "My cast bread is coming back upon the waters." He sat and watched Buddwing as he drank his orange juice, and picked up the glass of tomato juice. "You eat a hearty breakfast, don't you?" he said, twitching.

"Well, not usually. But I'm very hungry this morning."

"Listen, don't be so defensive," the man said. "You like to eat, so eat. Be healthy." He sipped at his coffee, and watched the tomato juice disappear from Buddwing's glass. Buddwing moved the grapefruit into place, and picked up his spoon.

"That's a lot of citrus," the man said. "You're expecting maybe scurvy?"

"No, I just feel hungry."

"Don't get so upset," the man said. "If you're hungry, eat. Who's telling you not to eat? Watch it, you almost got me in the eye with that one."

"What?"

"The grapefruit. You're squirting it all over the table."

"Oh, I'm sorry."

"That's all right, who's complaining? You want to squirt a little grapefruit in my eye, go ahead. My name is Isadore Schwartz, what's yours?"

"I don't . . ." he started, and then stopped. "Sam Buddwing," he said.

"Pleased to know you. You eat here all the time?"

"No," Buddwing said. "This is the first time I've ever been here."

"The food here is very good," Schwartz said. "As a matter of fact, I would go so far as to say the food here is gourmet food, and at very reasonable prices. I didn't think you ate here often because, to tell the truth, this is the first time I ever seen you in here."

"Yes, it *is* my first time," Buddwing said.

"That's what I said. You should come more often. The food here is of an excellent quality, believe me. I eat here all the time. Breakfast, lunch, dinner. That's because the food is so wonderful here." Schwartz paused. "It's also because I happen to own the place."

"Oh, is that right?" Buddwing said.

"Sure, I've been here for twenty-five years, right on this same corner. You didn't happen to see the name outside?"

"No, I didn't."

"Sure, right across the front. Izzy's Cafeteria. That's me, Isadore Schwartz. I got good food here, ain't that grapefruit good?"

"Yes, very good."

"Wait till you taste the Danish. You ever been to Miami Beach?"

"I . . . I don't know," Buddwing said.

"What do you mean, you don't know?"

"I forget."

"How could you forget a place like Miami Beach?"

"I don't know. I just can't remember if I've ever been there or not."

"That's like misplacing New York City!"

"I haven't misplaced Miami Beach, I simply don't remember if I've ever been there or not."

"Are you Jewish? If you're Jewish, you've *been* there."

"I don't know."

"What?"

"I said I don't know if I'm Jewish or not."

"Well, what are you then, an Arab?"

"I don't know," Buddwing said, and then moved aside his finished grapefruit and picked up one of the Danish pastries.

"What did you say your name was?"

"Buddwing. Sam Buddwing."

"All the Sams I know, they're Jewish," Schwartz said.

"How about Sam Adams?" Buddwing answered.

"He probably changed his name," Schwartz said.

"So did I."

"Ah-ha!" Schwartz said. "What did it used to be?"

"I don't remember."

"Why? You ashamed of being Jewish?"

"No. It's just that . . ."

"You should be ashamed of yourself, a nice Jewish boy like you."

"Well, okay, have it your own way," Buddwing said.

"How do you like that Danish?"

"It's delicious."

"Sure. The reason I brought up Miami Beach is because my Danish, the Danish you get right here in this cafeteria, is better even than what Wolfie's gives you in Miami Beach. You know Wolfie's? On Collins Avenue?"

"I don't think so."

"Well, whether you know it or not, this is better Danish. Take my word for it. Aren't you going to drink your milk?"

"Sure. I want to drink my coffee first."

"How can you drink it black like that?"

"I used to drink it this way in the service," Buddwing said, smiling.

"What branch were you in?"

"I don't remember."

Schwartz pursed his lips and looked at Buddwing seriously. "How can you not know what branch you were in?"

"I don't know."

"If you were 4-F, don't be ashamed of it."

"I don't think I was."

"What's the matter with you, anyway?" Schwartz asked suddenly. He stared at Buddwing, his face seriously concerned.

"Nothing. I just can't remember anything, that's all."

"Why don't you go see a doctor?"

"I might do that," Buddwing said. He finished his first piece of Danish, and then picked up the hard roll and spread the three pats of butter on it.

"You like butter, don't you?" Schwartz said. "Go ahead, eat. It's Grade-A creamery butter, straight from the cows."

"It's very good butter," Buddwing said, biting into the roll.

"When's the last time you ate?"

"I don't remember."

"Don't you remember anything at all?"

"Well, hardly anything."

"You remember my name?"

"Sure."

"What's my name?" Schwartz said, twitching, testing him.

"Isadore Schwartz."

"That's very good," Schwartz said. "See? Your memory ain't so bad, after all."

"Oh, I can remember everything that happened since I woke up this morning," Buddwing said.

"You think you'll remember where this cafeteria is?"

"I think so," Buddwing said.

"Good."

"Why?"

"Because I'd like you to come back. I like to see a man who knows good food. Where's your ticket?"

"What ticket?"

"The one you have to give the cashier on the way—"

"Oh. There it is. On the tray."

Schwartz picked up the ticket. "Forget it," he said.

"What do you mean?"

"I mean, forget it. This is on me, Isadore Schwartz. I like to see a man eating. Drink your milk."

"I can pay for my breakfast," Buddwing said.

"Don't I *see* you can pay for your breakfast? Do you look like a bum? Don't you think I got eyes? The only thing that's wrong with you is you can't remember anything, that's all."

"Well, I appreciate the gesture, Mr. Schwartz, but—"

"What gesture? This ain't a gesture, it's a reality, a fact. I, Isadore Schwartz, am paying for your breakfast, Sam whatever the hell you changed your name to."

"Buddwing."

"That's right, Buddwing. Where'd you pick a cockamamie name like that?"

"From a beer truck."

"It sounds like from a beer truck, believe me," Schwartz said. "You ain't gonna drink your milk?"

"I was just coming to it."

"Take a bite of the cheese Danish," Schwartz said. Buddwing picked up the Danish and bit into it. "How's that?"

"Delicious."

"I know it is. Drink your milk. That's Grade-A homogenized, from the same creamery the butter comes from. Here you don't get pyok water when you order milk. It's *some* milk, ain't it?"

"It's delicious," Buddwing said.

"You ought to go see a doctor, you know that?" Schwartz said. "You shouldn't put off ailments, no matter how small they seem. I'm telling you. My brother Dave, he had an ingrown toenail, he didn't see a doctor, it was murder, believe me. Go see a doctor."

"Well, maybe I will."

"Though I must admit you eat like a healthy young horse. How old are you, anyway?"

"I don't know."

"Don't it bother you, not remembering anything?"

"Well . . . yes and no."

Schwartz nodded gravely, and then twitched. "You better go see a doctor, Sam. Otherwise, twenty years from now, you'll wake up in some small town in Minnesota, you'll be married with four kids, and you'll suddenly remember you ain't Sam Buddwing at all, you're really Max Lipschitz and you got a wife and a grown daughter up in the Bronx. That could get very complicated."

"I guess it could."

"Go see a doctor. They're all lousy finks, I know, but maybe you'll be lucky. Maybe you'll find one who can help you."

"Well, I thought I'd scout around a little on my own," Buddwing said.

"Well, listen, it's up to you. It's your life, I'm only telling you what I would do. I'm talking to you like a father or a brother, the way I talked to Dave when he had the ingrown toenail." Schwartz shrugged, and then twitched. "*He* wouldn't listen to me, either."

Buddwing drained his glass of milk and said, "Well, maybe I *will* go to a doctor." He paused. "Listen, I wish you'd let me pay for my own—"

"Wouldn't hear of it. Go on, you're my guest. Can't I have guests here? I'm here breakfast, lunch, dinner, I can't have a guest to talk to every now and then? This is like my home. Consider yourself a guest in my home."

"Well . . . thank you," Buddwing said.

"My pleasure." Schwartz rose. "Come back again, we'll talk some more." He put his hand on Buddwing's shoulder gently, and added, "And don't be ashamed you're Jewish. It's nothing to be ashamed of. Some of the finest Christians, they're Jews, believe me."

He nodded, twitched, and then walked away from the table. Buddwing could see him at the cashier's booth, giving the cashier the ticket, and then pointing out Buddwing, identifying him so that the cashier would let him pass through when he left. He waved at Buddwing and then went behind the steam table and through a door which presumably led to the kitchen. Buddwing suddenly wondered whether or not Schwartz was married and then, for no apparent reason, thought how nice it would be if he was not married and could meet Gloria. He basked in the idea of Gloria and Schwartz together, visualized them as husband and wife, and then suddenly frowned because he could not imagine them in bed together. The frown deepened. Rather than being unable to imagine them making love, he found that he could now imagine them all too vividly, that he could see Schwartz taking

Gloria into his arms, his hands touching her breasts and her thighs, climbing onto the huge mother hulk of her, entering her. He could hear Gloria moaning as though in pain, and he wanted to shout to Schwartz to stop it, don't you know you're hurting her, and he was suddenly filled with an enormous hatred for the imagined image of Schwartz the lover. I could have had her if I had wanted her, he told the image of Schwartz. Leave her alone, you're hurting her, you bastard, can't you hear her whimpering?

He picked up his paper napkin with a harsh decisive motion and wiped it across his mouth. As he walked away from the table, he was filled with a vague fury. And yet he felt he should love this man. Schwartz had fed him, hadn't he? Schwartz was willing to pay for his meal, wasn't he? But the image of Schwartz grinding against his beloved Gloria, Buddwing's own Gloria whose breast he had known—this image persisted until he reached the cashier's booth. The cashier looked up at him, smiled, and said, "Mr. Schwartz has taken care of it."

"How much was it?" Buddwing asked.

"A dollar thirty-five," the cashier said.

Buddwing took the five-dollar bill from his pocket and put it on the cashier's rubber-nippled pad. "Take it out of this," he said.

"But Mr. Schwartz . . ."

"Yes, I know. I'm afraid I can't accept his kindness."

"But . . ."

"Please," Buddwing said, and he gave the five-dollar bill a gentle nudge with his forefinger.

"Well," the cashier said dubiously, "all right." She took the bill and pushed some buttons on her machine, and his change came clattering down the chute, a dime, a nickel, two quarters. She opened the cash drawer and handed him three dollar bills. He pocketed the entire amount, smiled at her again, and then walked out into the street. He had three dollars and sixty-five cents; he was still rich. He began walking.

The feeling of dread started almost immediately, and he did not know what caused it until he realized he was on 92nd Street and Broadway, and that the grocery store he had worked in when he

was sixteen was on the next corner. He wanted to turn back, run
to Schwartz's cafeteria, tell the cashier it was all right for
Schwartz to pick up the tab, and then seek out Schwartz and talk
to him some more, tell him he did not mind about him and Gloria,
after all Gloria was a woman more Schwartz's age, he understood,
it was all right. But his legs kept moving him toward 91st Street,
and the feeling of dread mounted. All he had to do, he knew, was
walk into the grocery store and ask the owner who he was, I
worked for you when I was sixteen, don't you remember? I
dropped a carton of eggs. You made me pay for them. Remember
me? And the owner would look at him over the rims of his glasses,
and he would nod vaguely, and then smile dimly, and then say,
Why, sure, I remember you. You're

I don't want to know, he thought. I don't want to know, you
hear me? I don't want to know!

He walked toward 91st Street.

He knew he would go into the grocery store and ask his
questions.

# 4

IT SEEMED not to have changed at all.
It was on the same corner, the windows stacked high with canned goods, the two grocery wagons on the sidewalk, the bicycle with its basket parked in the rack. The doors to the basement were open wide, and a seventeen-year-old boy in a white grocer's apron was on the sidewalk, sweeping. Buddwing supposed it was eight o'clock or a little after, and then remembered that his long-ago working day had begun at eight and ended at six. He walked into the store.

There were no customers. He supposed it was too early in the morning for that. He looked toward the rear of the store and immediately saw the refrigerator, and remembered again the time he had dropped the eggs, and then a voice on his right said, "Yes, sir, can I help you?"

He did not want to turn for a moment. He kept staring at the glass-fronted refrigerator case and remembering the broken eggs, and then he sighed, and turned, and walked toward the counter. The man behind the counter was perhaps Buddwing's age, with black hair and deep brown eyes. Buddwing knew at once he was not the owner of the store, and this strengthened his desire to get out of here. If the owner wasn't around, well then, the hell with it. He had tried, hadn't he?

"I'd like to talk to the owner," he heard himself saying.

"I'm the owner," the man behind the counter said.

Buddwing looked him over carefully. "I used to work here," he said. "Oh, I don't know, maybe twenty years ago."

"Yes?" the man said, waiting.

"The owner wore eyeglasses. He was an older man."

"Mr. Di Palermo, yes," the man said.

"Yes. Yes, that was his name." Buddwing paused. "Where is he?"

"He's dead," the man behind the counter said. "He's been dead, oh, five, six years."

His first reaction was one of soaring joy; the old man was dead, good! And then he felt immediate guilt, as though he were somehow responsible for Di Palermo's death, having wished it so often and so fervently in the past. He was sure both his joy and his guilt were showing on his face. He cleared his throat.

"And you own the store now?" he asked.

"Yes. I bought it from his widow."

"I see."

"Yes." The owner hesitated. "Was there anything I could do for you?"

"I don't think so. I wanted to see Mr. Di Palermo, but I guess that's impossible now."

"Yes, that would be impossible," the owner agreed.

"You wouldn't have his records or anything, would you?"

"His what?"

"Records. You know, maybe his Social Security records or something. You wouldn't have them filed anywhere, would you? The names of people who worked for him? Anything like that?"

"Do you mean from twenty years ago?"

"Well, yes," Buddwing said.

"No, I wouldn't have any of his records," the owner said mildly.

"I see. Well, then . . ." Buddwing shrugged. "I guess that's that." He smiled and looked around. "The place hasn't changed much." He paused. "How much do you pay your delivery boy?"

"What?" the owner said.

"Your del—"

"Well, I . . . I really don't think that's any of your concern."

"I guess not. Well, thank you," Buddwing said cheerfully, and he waved at the man and walked outside. The seventeen-year-old kid was still sweeping the sidewalk. Buddwing watched him for several moments, remembering himself in the same white apron, sweeping the same damn sidewalk, and then he walked over to the boy.

"Hi," he said.

The boy looked up, startled. "Hi," he said cautiously.

"Are you the delivery boy?"

"Why?" the boy asked.

"I used to deliver groceries here," Buddwing said, smiling. "When I was your age, more or less."

"Yeah?" the boy said.

"Yes." Buddwing kept smiling. "I used to get twenty-two dollars a week." He paused. "How much do you get?"

The boy kept studying him suspiciously. "I pay my taxes," he said at last. "Both Federal *and* state."

"No, no," Buddwing said, "listen, I'm sure you pay your taxes. Why wouldn't you pay your taxes?"

"Well, a lot of kids with odd jobs, they figure nobody's going to know the difference," the boy said.

"You think I'm an internal revenue agent, is that it?" Buddwing asked, amused.

"I don't know what you are."

"Neither do I," Buddwing said cheerfully. "How much *do* you get a week?"

"Anyway, it's deducted. I mean, the boss deducts it even before I get my check."

"Certainly," Buddwing said. "That would seem to be the proper procedure."

"It is," the boy said firmly.

"So how much do you get?"

"Before taxes, you mean?"

"Yes, before taxes."

"Why do you want to know?"

"Because I think the man I used to work for was cheating me. There used to be a different owner here. I think twenty-two dollars a week was very little for the job. Don't you?"

"Well, the dollar isn't worth as much today, you know."

"That's true. I still think twenty-two dollars was pretty cheap. For the amount of work involved."

"I get fifty," the boy said. "That's before taxes."

"That's very good," Buddwing said. "Fifty."

"Which makes it about right, doesn't it? The dollar's worth about half now, isn't it? I mean, you must be forty or so, so if you worked here when you were my age . . ." The boy did some mental arithmetic. "Hell, that was even before the *war!*" he said, astonished.

"Yes, it was," Buddwing answered. Forty, he thought. He says I must be about forty. The man in the mirror had not looked that old. "Well, thanks a lot," he said. "I appreciate your telling me."

"I got to admit," the boy said.

"Yes?"

"Twenty-two bucks *does* sound a bit cheap."

"Yes, that's what I thought. Well . . ." He shrugged. "So long."

He walked away from the boy and the store, filled with a righteous anger that was very satisfying. He seemed content to learn that he had indeed been cheated those many years ago, and he wondered why he had never come back to the store before this to discover the exact extent of Di Palermo's thievery. He felt vindicated now for his own petty thefts, the drinking of all that soda pop, the stealing of the cigarettes. He had simply been taking, in merchandise, what he should have been receiving in cash. And he was glad Di Palermo was dead. Glad because the old man had been a rotten thieving crook, and also glad because now Di Palermo could not tell him who

He stopped in the middle of the sidewalk.

Well, I really *must* find out who I am, he thought.

He tried to tell himself that the relief he now felt was simply caused by the absence of Di Palermo, admitting that he had always been somewhat frightened of the old man. The relief had nothing to do with the fact that Di Palermo, now dead and gone, could not possibly identify him. And anyway, he reasoned, even if he were alive, would he really know who I am? He knew a skinny sixteen-year-old kid who came to work bleary-eyed each morning, who shoved that broom around the sidewalk until it was time to begin deliveries, Apartment 4A, 2117 Riverside Drive, a shudder went up his spine.

I don't know that apartment, he thought.

I'm glad you're dead, he thought.

I'm glad I broke your lousy

The boy on roller skates came down the sidewalk at a furious rate of speed. Buddwing heard the familiar grating sound of worn wheels against pavement, and looked up just as the boy approached him. He tried to sidestep, but the boy swerved at about the same moment, so that the two came together in a curiously clumsy embrace, each trying to support the other, losing the battle and clattering to the sidewalk in a scramble of arms and legs and flying skates. There was a brief silence, and then Buddwing sat up and looked at the boy. "You okay?" he asked.

"Yeah," the boy said. He was about nine years old, a blond kid with blue eyes. He was wearing short pants and a striped T shirt. One skate had come loose from his foot, dangling there from the strap. He did not examine himself for cuts or bruises—his knees were scabby and scraped and black-and-blue from previous accidents—but instead immediately looked at the dangling skate, and said, "Oh, hell, it opened again."

"Your skate?" Buddwing asked.

"Yeah." The boy got to his feet and, on the one skate still operative, skated over to the curb. He promptly sat again, removed the dangling skate from his right foot, and reached into his pocket for a skate key. Buddwing walked over to the curb and sat beside the boy.

"You know how to fix it?" he asked.

"Sure," the boy said. "Only thing is the nut is stuck."

"You want some help?"

"I can do it myself," the boy said. He shoved both parts of the skate back to the proper size, and then fitted the skate key to the nut on the underside. "The thing keeps opening," he said. "That's pretty dangerous, you know. You could hurt yourself if you're going very fast and your skate opens."

"How fast do you go?" Buddwing asked.

"Oh, I guess about twenty m.p.h.," the boy answered. "You see what I mean? The nut is stuck, that's why I can't tighten it. I think it's rusty or something."

"Do you want me to try it?" Buddwing said.

"Well, you can if you want to, but it's rusty, all right. Here." He handed Buddwing the skate and the skate key. "You live in this neighborhood?" he asked.

"No," Buddwing said.

"I didn't think I saw you around." He watched as Buddwing struggled with the nut on the bottom of the skate. "It's rusty, ain't it?" he said.

"It sure is."

"Yeah, I told you. Where *do* you live?"

"Oh, another part of the city," Buddwing said.

"Pretty nice there?"

"Yeah, it's okay," Buddwing said.

"You got a playground there?"

"Yes."

"We got one here, too," the boy said. "You busy or anything?"

"What do you mean?"

"Pete is sick, he's my best friend. I thought maybe if you weren't doing anything, we could take a walk over to the playground. It's only a few blocks." The boy shrugged.

"Sure, I'd like to," Buddwing said.

"I mean, with that lousy rusty nut, I can't skate any more, anyway. That ever happen to your skates?"

"It used to," Buddwing answered.

"Yeah? How'd you fix it?"

"Well, I mean it used to happen when I *had* skates."

"Did you lose them or something?"

"No. I just outgrew them."

"Oh." The boy nodded. "You ought to get a new pair." He took the skate from his left foot, and said, "I just want to put these in the hallway," rose immediately, and ran into a building two doors up. Buddwing waited on the sidewalk. In a few moments, the boy returned. "Okay," he said, and began walking. Buddwing fell in beside him.

"What's your name?" the boy asked.

"Sam Buddwing."

"I'm Eric Michael Knowles," the boy said.

"Glad to know you, Eric."

"Have *you* got a middle name?"

"No," Buddwing said.

"Well, that's all right," Eric said. "Pete's middle name is Farley. The thing about him, though, is he always gets sick on weekends. That makes it rough, you know. He's got a lot of toys. Sonar Sub Hunt, and Stratego, that's a game, and a skeet shoot, and even a set of H-O tanks."

"Of H-O what?"

"Tanks."

"You're welcome," Buddwing said, and Eric laughed immediately.

"You want to hear a dirty joke?" he asked.

"Sure," Buddwing said.

"A boy fell in the mud," Eric said. Buddwing laughed, and Eric watched him curiously for a second, and then laughed with him. "That's really a very old one," he said. "Do you get it?"

"Sure," Buddwing said.

"What is it?"

"Well, a boy fell in the mud."

"Yeah, but what's so funny about that?"

"Well, you asked me if I wanted to hear a dirty joke."

"Yeah, I know." Eric paused. "What's a dirty joke?"

"Well . . ." Buddwing hesitated. "I don't know," he said at last.

"Then why is it funny?"

"Well, I guess a boy falling in the mud is pretty funny." Buddwing said.

"Yeah, and pretty dirty, too." He shrugged. He looked at Buddwing shrewdly and then said, "It's a good thing the army's got those things that can go through the mud, ain't it?"

"What things?" Buddwing asked.

"You know. Those big metal things with treads on them."

"Tanks?"

"You're welcome," Eric said at once, and then burst out laughing. "You're welcome," he repeated, almost under his breath, as though savoring the joke a second time, and storing it in his memory. "The playground is up there, near the Drive," he said.

"Yes, I know."

"I thought you didn't live around here."

"I don't. But I know where the playground is."

"It's a pretty corny playground," Eric said. "You want to walk by the river instead?"

"Okay."

"I'm not allowed to walk by the river because you have to cross the parkway, and also a kid drowned there last summer."

"Well, I'm allowed to," Buddwing said.

"Then I guess it's okay, huh?"

"I guess so."

"I always wanted to throw stones in the river. Do they arrest you if you throw stones in the river?"

"I don't see why they should."

"Let's do it, then."

"Okay."

They walked in silence to Riverside Drive and then into the park and past the playground and over to the path bordering the

Henry Hudson Parkway. An iron railing separated the path from the grassy slope that led to the road below. They climbed the railing and then waited for a break in the traffic and ran across the parkway to the grass on the river's edge. Buddwing could see the cliffs of New Jersey on the opposite shore, and uptown the double-decked span of the Washington Bridge. A squadron of destroyers was moored mid-river. He could hear the loud-speaker on one of the destroyers calling the men to their work stations. There was no mist now. The destroyers bobbed lazily in sharp gray silhouette. The sky above the Jersey shore was clear and blue.

"What kind of boats are those?" Eric asked.

"Destroyers."

"Wow," Eric said, and then made a hissing sound. "I'll bet I can hit one with a stone."

"Go ahead. Try."

Eric searched in the grass, found a stone, and then pulled back his arm and hurled with all his strength. The stone fell into the water some ten yards away. "A little short," he said. He paused thoughtfully. "Do you ever wish you were really strong?" he asked. "I mean, really, really strong? The strongest man in the world?"

"Yes, I do sometimes," Buddwing said.

"I'll bet Superman could hit one of those boats with a stone."

"I'll bet he could."

"If *he* threw a stone," Eric said, "it would have so much force, it would probably put a hole in the boat, don't you think?"

"I guess it would."

"Well, sure, he can jump over buildings and everything." Eric paused. "How does he do that, anyway? Jump over the buildings?"

"He gives a mighty leap."

"I don't know, it just seems funny to me that he can jump over buildings. And fly around in the air. I mean, even if he's very strong, how does that make it he can fly in the air and go jumping over buildings? I don't get that at all. Do you get that?"

"I guess he flexes his muscles or something."

"Yeah, but he ain't got wings, hasn't. So I don't see how he can fly." Eric shook his head. "What would you do if you were the strongest man in the world?"

"I'd do what Superman does. I'd use my strength for good."

"Yeah, me too," Eric said dubiously. He hesitated. "Though, maybe sometimes, I'd also, well, do a couple of bad things." He hesitated again. "Would you?"

"Maybe, but not very often."

"Oh, *no*, not very often. Just once in a while. What did you say your name was?"

"Sam."

"But no middle name."

"No."

"Do you think Superman is real?" Eric asked.

"I don't know. What do you think?"

"Well, I guess I'd think he was real if he didn't fly in the air and go jumping over buildings. I don't know, that makes him seem not real to me. Doesn't it make you feel that way?"

"I guess so. I don't really see how he can fly or jump over buildings," Buddwing said.

"Sure, that's impossible."

They walked in silence for a while. The day was warm, the air was balmy, the sky was blue. Upriver, he could hear the sudden sharp blast of a tugboat's horn.

"Do you know what I want to be someday?" Eric asked.

"No, what?"

"A garbage man."

"Oh? Why?"

"Because they get to collect all kinds of things. You know how much stuff people throw out? Boy, you'd be surprised! Also, I like the smell of garbage."

"Do you really?"

"Yeah. I like the smell of gasoline best, but garbage I like next. It's got a good smell. Not like gasoline, but different. Those

66

garbage men wear uniforms like army guys, too, did you ever notice that?"

"Yes, that's right. They do."

"Sure. How much do garbage men make?"

"A pretty good salary," Buddwing said.

"A hundred dollars?" Eric asked.

"A week, do you mean?"

"No, not a week," Eric said. "A hundred a *week?* Oh, no. I meant, well, I don't know, how much do you *think* they make?"

"I guess about a hundred a week, or maybe a little more." Buddwing paused. "Plus all they can eat."

"What do you mean? All they can . . ." and then Eric burst into delighted laughter. "Garbage, you mean?" He laughed again. "Who would want to eat garbage?" he said, and shoved out at Buddwing playfully, and laughed again.

Out on the river, the destroyers began piping the men to quarters for muster. The high shrill bosun's whistle cut the air, traveled to the shore.

"I can whistle almost like that," Buddwing said.

"So can I," Eric answered.

"I mean, without a whistle."

"So can I," Eric said.

"I mean loud."

"What do you mean?"

Buddwing drew his lips inward, folding them in over his teeth, placing his tongue behind them. He forced air into the cleft, and an ear-shattering, piercing whistle came from his mouth.

"Wow!" Eric said. "How do you do *that?*"

"I'm not sure."

"Teach me how to do it," Eric said.

He spent the next fifteen minutes trying to teach Eric the new whistle. At the end of that time, Eric had succeeded only in producing a gravelly mixture of forced breath and saliva. Exhausted, they lay back on the grass at the river's edge and watched the water traffic. Occasionally, one or the other of them spoke, but for the most part they were silent. Eric fidgeted a lot, moving his hands or his feet, or working his mouth, but he seemed content to sit by the river watching the tugs and the smaller craft, and an excursion boat that moved smoothly past, and a tanker that appeared from nowhere, huge and black, with strange foreign markings on its hull. A dazzling parade of clouds marched solemnly over the brow of the Jersey shore, steadily and slowly pushed across the sky by gentle winds, clean and white, gleaming with captured sunlight. The breeze was balmy. It caressed Buddwing's cheek, gently riffled his hair. He almost dozed.

He drew himself back to the edge of consciousness. Fear suddenly crowded into his mind, and with it the same premonition of shock he had felt when leaving Gloria's apartment. He sat up abruptly. Eric was sitting beside him, his arms clasped about his knees, looking out over the water. He turned.

"I thought you were sleeping," Eric said.

"Almost," Buddwing answered. He wiped his hand over his face. The fear would not leave him. "Are you ever frightened?" he asked.

"Sure," Eric said.

"What frightens you?"

"Dracula," Eric said. "I saw him on television. Boy, he's a real scary guy."

"I meant, do real things frighten you?"

"Well, *he's* real, isn't he?"

"No, he's made up," Buddwing said.

Eric shook his head. "No, he's real," he insisted. "I *saw* him. He's a real person. I mean it. It wasn't a cartoon or anything, Sam. He was *real*."

"But that was an actor," Buddwing said. "Bela Lugosi."

"No, it was Dracula. That was his name. Dracula. He was a vampire."

"Yes, I know who you mean."

"Then you saw him, too?"

"Yes."

"Well?"

"Well, what?"

68

"Well, was he real or wasn't he? You *saw* him, didn't you?"

"Yes, I saw him."

"Well?"

"He was real," Buddwing admitted.

"Sure," Eric said. He paused. "Are you scared now?" he asked.

"A little."

"What of? Dracula?"

"No. Not Dracula."

"I get scared just talking about him," Eric said. He shuddered.

"Well, what *are* you scared of, if not him?"

"I don't know."

"There's no ghosts, you know," Eric said. "Mommy told me that."

"I know there aren't."

"There aren't, *are* there?" he asked doubtfully.

"No. No ghosts."

"Or monsters either?"

"No. No monsters either."

"Then what are you scared of?" Eric asked.

"Nothing," Buddwing said, and he smiled. "There's nothing to be afraid of." He rose and extended his hand to Eric. "Come on," he said. "It's time to go."

"Why?"

"Well, we can't sit here all day."

"Why not?"

"There are things to do," Buddwing said.

"We *are* doing things," Eric replied.

"I know. I meant . . ."

"Don't you like it here?" Eric asked.

"Yes. Yes, I do," Buddwing said, and there was an oddly wistful note in his voice.

"Then stay."

"No, I . . ." He looked at Eric's face, the wide-open blue eyes, the plaintive mouth, and very gently he said, "You see, I lost something, Eric. And I have to find it."

"What did you lose?"

"Myself," he said.

Eric studied him for a moment, the blue eyes solemn, not sure whether this was another joke or not. And then he broke into cautious laughter and began walking up toward the highway with Buddwing. "How can you lose yourself?" he asked. "That's impossible."

"I don't know how," Buddwing said, smiling, "but I seem to have managed it."

"Well, who are *you*, then?" Eric asked. "If you lost yourself, then who are *you*, huh?"

"Well, that's what I have to find out, you see."

They paused at the highway's edge, waiting for a lull in the traffic. They crossed then, and again climbed the iron railing and walked up the steep grassy bank to the path. As they climbed the white steps near the Soldiers' and Sailors' Monument, Eric asked, "What do you get if you find it?"

"What do you mean?"

"Yourself, I mean. If you find yourself, what will you get? Is there a reward?"

"Oh, certainly," Buddwing said.

"How much?"

"Three cents and a collar button."

Eric laughed.

"And also a used peach pit," Buddwing added.

"What can you do with a used peach pit?" Eric asked, still laughing.

"You can make a peach-pit ring out of it," Buddwing said. "Don't you know how to make a peach-pit ring?"

They were coming up 90th Street now, walking toward West End Avenue. The sun slanted through the canyon ahead of them, dazzling in its brilliance. They walked in deep shade, but the sun was ahead of them, a bright dagger-shaped wedge of light, capping the buildings.

"No, I don't," Eric said. "Will you show me how to make one?"

"Too early," Buddwing said. "Peaches aren't in season yet."

"When are they in season?"

"During the summer."

"Will you show me how to make one in the summer? If I don't go to camp?"

"If you don't go to camp," Buddwing promised, "I will show you how to make a peach-pit ring in the summer."

"You think we'll still be friends this summer?" Eric asked.

"I hope so."

"I do, too. You're a nice kid," Eric said.

He looked at Eric, and for a moment his eyes filled with tears. He blinked them back. "Thank you, Eric," he said. "You're a nice kid, too."

They had reached Broadway. They stopped on the corner where they had met.

"Well, I'll see you," Eric said.

"You bet."

"You won't forget my name, now, will you? Eric Michael Knowles."

"I won't."

"Or the peach-pit ring?"

"No, I won't forget."

"Okay, Sam," Eric said, grinning. Then he winked and said, "I'll see you, huh?" and went into his building.

The shock was waiting at the next corner.

# 5

HE WAS shocked only because he thought he had forgotten her, and then doubly shocked because even when he remembered her, he could not really remember who she was. She came out of a building on 89th Street and walked quickly to the curb, obviously looking for a taxicab. She was a girl of seventeen, with long black hair that was pulled to the back of her head in a ponytail. He could not see her eyes from this distance, but he knew they were a dark brown, and he recognized instantly the long-legged lope that took her to the curb. She was wearing black stretch tights under a black skirt. She wore a black sweater, too, and her pulled-back hair bobbed like some strange proud crest of feathers as she moved hurriedly to the curb, so that she resembled a rather tall and scrawny, black-legged, black-crested, black-breasted bird. He saw her raise her arm to hail a cruising cab, saw the taxi move toward the curb, saw her hand dart out to open the door of the car, and began running toward her instantly.

"Doris!" he shouted. "Doris!"

The girl did not turn; the girl gave no sign that she had heard him at all, even though he was shouting at the top of his voice. The taxi door slammed just as he approached the corner. He crossed the street against a light, and the taxi emitted a brief cloud of exhaust fumes and pulled away from the curb. He stood on the corner and frantically shouted, "Doris! Doris!" but the taxi was moving away, and he stood in undecided panic for just an instant, and then brought his lips back over his teeth and, using the whistle he had tried to teach Eric, hailed the next taxi that came by. He scrambled onto the back seat and said, "Would you follow that taxi up ahead, please?" and the cabbie turned to look at him with a curiously sour expression, as though he expected to find a private eye in a trench coat and was disappointed to find only a rather ordinary-looking man in a blue suit. He nodded perfunctorily and set the cab in motion. Buddwing leaned forward, watching the rear of the girl's cab, wishing his own driver would go a little faster, and then finally saying, "Don't lose it, huh?"

"Mister," the cabbie said with infinite patience, "I am going as fast as the law allows. You want to pay the fine if I get a speeding ticket?"

"Yes," Buddwing said at once, knowing the possibility of the cabbie's getting a ticket was extremely remote, and also knowing that his verbal agreement could hardly be held binding should the matter ever come to a legal test. "Yes, I'll pay the fine. Now, hurry up, will you?"

"You'll all pay the fine," the cabbie said wisely, "until it comes time to pay the fine. Then nobody wants to pay the fine."

"I don't want to lose that cab. It's very important to me."

"It's very important to me that I don't get in trouble with the police in this rotten city," the cabbie said. "Besides, the driver up there ain't allowed to go any faster than *I'm* allowed to go. So sit back and relax, like the sign says, and leave the driving to us, okay?"

"All right, but don't lose it," Buddwing said, still leaning forward.

"I get it, I get it already," the cabbie said. "You don't want me to lose that cab, right?"

"That's right."

"I get it. Relax."

Buddwing could not relax. His mind was swarming with a hundred thoughts, who was that girl in the cab ahead, he had called her Doris, who was Doris, how did he know her, how much would it cost to follow her through the city of New York with a meter ticking away, was it forty-five cents already, how much money did he have left, Doris, who was she, who?

"Look at that stupid bastard, did you see that?" the cabbie said suddenly. He leaned his head toward the window, and shouted, "Make up your mind, you jerk!" and then turned the wheel sharply and almost collided with a moving van that had come up on the right of the taxi. "They shouldn't be allowed to drive," he muttered. "They take the car out on Saturdays and Sundays, and louse up the entire city, as if it needs lousing up. Man, you got to be out of your mind to drive a taxicab, I'm telling you. Where's that broad going, anyway?"

"What broad?"

"The one in the cab up ahead. It's got to be a broad, don't it?" The cabbie shrugged. "Otherwise, what are you getting in such a sweat for? I had a blond broad in here the other day, she gets in the cab stoned drunk at two o'clock in the afternoon, she wants me to take her to Oyster Bay. You know where Oyster Bay is? That's a ritzy section in Long Island, all society people. She's wearing this black cocktail dress, two o'clock in the afternoon, she smells like the Schenley distillery, she wants me to take her home to Oyster Bay. I say to her where in Oyster Bay, lady, she says, 'On the water.' I say *where* on the water, lady, she says, 'Do you want me to take your number?' Right away, they want to take your number. Somebody wrote someplace once that the way to scare all the cabbies in New York City is to tell them you're gonna take their number. So take my number, I tell her. If you want to take my number just 'cause I'm asking you where in Oyster Bay you want to go, which is an out-of-town call

74

anyway, and which you got to pay special out-of-town rates for, then go ahead and take my number. But if you want to be more sensible about it, lady, why, just sit back and relax like the sign says, and give me your address in Oyster Bay, and then we can all have a nice drive because the traffic shouldn't be too bad this time of the afternoon. Well, she don't take my number. Instead, she sits back and relaxes all over the place, though she still don't give me her address, how the hell am I supposed to know she lives on a big estate with tennis courts and a swimming pool, and the place don't have an address? No numbers, you know what I mean? Just a mailbox on a road near the water, like she said. But the way she relaxes is she sits way back and relaxes, I mean, man, she *relaxes*. Then she begins singing very dirty songs like 'Minnie the Mermaid,' in this low drunken dirty voice while I keep watching her in the mirror, looking up her dress, I swear to God I almost crashed the cab four times. Man, what an afternoon that was. In this business, I'm telling you, you got to be out of your mind. The payoff is she gets to this swanky estate, on the water, just like she told me, and she goes inside to get some money to pay me, and she comes out, and on a twenty-eight-dollar ride, she gives me a quarter tip. I say to her, lady, I say, you sure you can afford this with them tennis courts and that swimming pool in there, you sure this ain't going to break you? So she gives me a real sweet sexy-looking smile, with this blond hair hanging down over one eye, and she says, 'Mister, you never had a ride like that in your life,' and then she goes marching up the front walk, and just before she goes in the door she turns to me and gives me a bump and a grind like as if she's in a burley joint in Union City. A quarter. Was it worth it, I'm asking you? Man, this business."

"They're turning," Buddwing said.

"I see they're turning, relax."

"Where are we?"

"We're on Sixty-seventh Street and Central Park West. Will you try to relax, mister?"

"Where are they going?"

"How do I know where they're going? Is she an out-of-towner? It looks to me like we went all the way from Broadway to Central Park West and now we're heading toward Broadway again. That's sure the long way around the mulberry bush. Relax, will you?"

"You're letting that truck get between us!" Buddwing shouted.

"You want me to fight with a truck?"

"I want you to follow that cab!"

"I *am* following it!"

"You're going to lose it if they make that light on the corner!"

"I don't control the traffic lights in this city, mister. You got a complaint, go tell it to Commissioner Barnes, maybe you can help him louse up the works a little more."

With a heartsick sigh, Buddwing saw that Doris's taxicab had indeed gone through the green light on the corner, and that the light had now changed to red. The truck stopped, blocking the entire street ahead of Buddwing's taxi, so that he had to crane his head out the window to try for a glimpse of the other cab, which seemed to be proceeding west on 67th Street.

"Now you'll lose it," he said. "I *told* you not to lose it."

"I still got my eye on it," the driver said. "It's stopping in the middle of the next block."

"Well, hurry up, will you please?"

"The light's still red."

"It's changing. There! Go ahead!"

"Shall I drive right through the truck? Or under it? Which?"

"Give him the horn."

"He's moving."

"Can you still see them?"

"The girl's getting out."

"Then hurry!"

"Hurry, hurry, nobody's got time to relax in this rotten city." The cabbie shook his head and waited for the truck to make its turn onto Columbus Avenue. He stepped on the gas then and drove recklessly up 67th Street. Doris's cab was just pulling away from the curb. Buddwing leaned forward and saw only her

black-stockinged legs mounting the front steps of a brownstone.
He reached for the money in his pocket. The fare was seventy-
five cents. He gave the cabbie a dollar bill, and quickly stepped
onto the curb.

"Doris!" he called.

The door of the brownstone closed behind the girl.

"Doris!" he called again, and then quickly ran up the front
steps of the building and tried the front door. It was locked. He
debated ringing the superintendent's bell, then wondered what
he would say to the man when he came to the door, and decided
against it. Sighing, he came down the steps again and stood on
the sidewalk next to the garbage cans waiting for pickup.

The city was wide awake; he had not noticed that. He had
spent too much time with Eric by the river, and then had become involved in following Doris, so that the city had quietly
and secretly come awake all around him. He paused on the sunwashed sidewalk now, and tried to get his bearings, amazed that
the city was alive, feeling its breath again with a fierce nostalgic
intensity.

The block between Amsterdam and Broadway was a short one
and consisted of crumbling brown tenements surrounded by the
new construction that had come on the heels of Lincoln Center.
The parking lot on the corner of Broadway was called the Phil-
harmonic, and the huge structure behind it was called Lincoln
Square Motor Inn. Up the street, running at a ninety-degree
angle to the tenements, was an apartment building complex named
Lincoln Towers. In the midst of all this culturally inspired splendor, the tenements crouched like cockroaches under a shiny new
kitchen sink, waiting to be stepped on by urban renewal. But,
Buddwing noticed, the people on the street went about their
business as though nothing at all was happening around them,
nothing was threatening their way of life.

A woman in a bathrobe, a scarf on her head, was walking a
poodle on a leash. The superintendent next door was out sweeping his sidewalk. A young girl in a tight short skirt came out of
one of the buildings carrying two empty milk bottles and head-

77

ing for Broadway. There were traffic sounds now, the groan of buses, the fainter purring sound of automobiles, the creaking clatter of a horse-drawn wagon that lumbered past the corner. There was a lazy somnolence to the horse and wagon, and to the day itself. The city was awake and alive, but this was Saturday morning, and there was no rush as yet. The city had rolled out of a warm bed, opened a window wide to a balmy spring breeze that gently lifted curtains, savored the mild air, and then consumed a leisurely lazy breakfast. And now she came forth to greet the day, awake but unhurried, still dressed casually; this was Saturday, tonight would be Saturday night and she would emerge sleek and pleasure-bound, but for now she could sweep her sidewalks and walk her dogs and go to the corner store for the morning milk, and idly watch a horse-drawn wagon, the horse's brown back gilded with sunlight, make its way in a lazy clatter up the avenue.

A stickball game was being formed halfway up the block, but there was no rush to get it going. There was instead an examination of the broom handles that would serve as bats; this one had a crack near its fatter end, it simply wouldn't do. And then there was a bouncing of balls against the asphalt; the pink Spalding bounced highest but nonetheless had to be tested, the balls held in separate hands and dropped simultaneously, a white one and a pink one, the choice being made. There was a slow and easy choosing of sides—odds, evens, one, two, three, shoot. The boys stood around in a patient circle while the wheat was separated from the chaff, a skinny kid with eyeglasses being the last chosen, accepting his misfit role with tolerant reluctance. There was a painstakingly slow chalking of the bases on the street, the chalk ran out, another color had to be used, third base was a bright yellow against the black, home plate was a lurid green. There were a great many practice pitches and a great many practice throws, and then another examination of the stickball bats, and a final rejection of a red broom handle. Another worn-out broom was brought, beaten against the fire hydrant to loosen the wire, and then the wire holding the straw bristles to the handle was

78

carefully unwound, the bristles finally shaken loose. The new bat was tested, and seemed to prove itself adequate, and the game was ready to begin. But there was still no rush. This was Saturday; even stickball could be calm and easy.

He supposed he would have to wait for Doris to come out since he did not know where she had gone exactly, and since he could hardly go ringing strange doorbells and asking for her. He looked across the street to a candy store, and decided he would have a cup of coffee there, sitting near the open door so that he could watch the front of the brownstone in case she emerged. He crossed the street—the opening pitches of the stickball game were being tossed not fifty feet from him—and saw first the electric clock in the candy store window. The time was 9:10 A.M. Then he saw the newspaper stand outside the store, and he thought it would be nice to buy a newspaper. He stopped beside the stand and was reaching for the *New York Times* when his eye was pulled back sharply by the bold shrieking black print on the front page of the nearest tabloid. He knew immediately that *this* was the shock he had been expecting ever since he had left Gloria's apartment. Not Doris who had appeared suddenly and splendidly in big-bird, black-legged surprise, but *this*, this that stared up at him from the newsstand, shouting, screaming, *this*.

He almost rushed away from the newsstand. He thought, hastily, That isn't me. And then he reached out for the newspaper, his hand trembling, and he carried it with him into the candy store and placed it on the counter before him, not looking at the headline again, and he said to the man behind the counter, "A cup of coffee, please, light with one sugar," and did not even realize he had automatically remembered how he took his coffee. He almost forgot all about Doris in the next few moments. He had taken the stool at the end of the counter so that he could see through the open door to the street outside and the brownstone across the way. But he did not even glance through the door now. He simply kept staring at the black headline on the front page, finally reading it, and then reading it over and over again, seeing the small type that told him the story was on p. 3, but not wanting to open the paper because he was afraid there might be a picture there, and he would recognize the picture as himself, and then he would know for certain, then the headline would be clear, the ominous black type would assume even more frightening dimension, growing until it obliterated the city and the world and the universe.

The man behind the counter put the cup of coffee down on the counter before him and said, "You taking that paper, mister?"

"Yes," Buddwing said.

"Then I'll add it to the check."

"Yes, do that," Buddwing said, and the counterman turned away as though he had won a major triumph.

The headline on the front page, shrieking, told Buddwing that a mental patient had escaped last night from a Long Island hospital. The headline did not spell out the words "Long Island," it simply abbreviated them, using the letters "L.I.," and Buddwing thought it was somehow odd, although he knew it was perfectly acceptable, that the newspaper should be shrieking about the escape of a madman, and yet should use a commonplace abbreviation like L.I. He thought suddenly of the woman who had gone to Oyster Bay and then given the cabbie a twenty-five-cent tip. He wondered what the woman had looked like beneath the open naked cavern of her black cocktail dress, and then he turned to page three.

There was no picture on page three. He wondered why there was no picture. Didn't madmen have their pictures taken? Didn't mental hospitals, like jails, mug and print anyone who came through their doors? The story told him that a man named Edward Voegler had escaped from Central Islip State Hospital on Long Island last night, shortly after the evening meal. Voegler— and he remembered with panic the initials in the ring on his right hand, G.V.—had apparently gone out of the dining room and then had walked into the director's empty office and stolen a shirt, a tie, and a suit of clothes from the director's closet. The story did not say what color the suit was, but in his certainty that he was this man Voegler, Buddwing knew the suit was blue.

Voegler, the story said, was thirty-eight years old, about six feet tall, and extremely dangerous, a paranoid schizophrenic with a severe persecution complex and delusions of grandeur. The story then went into a quasi-medical explanation of schizophrenia and paranoia and explained what a man with a persecution complex and delusions of grandeur might be expected to do, ending with the number that should be called if anyone happened to run across Voegler.

Buddwing read the story three times.

The legend inside his ring had read "From G.V." and he again wondered who G.V. was, but this time his wonder was edged with terror. He surmised that G.V. was the wife or mother of this man Voegler, who he knew without doubt he himself was. Edward Voegler. He repeated the name in his mind. It did not have a familiar feel, and yet who else could he be? Had not the newspaper story mentioned Voegler's seemingly normal behavior interspersed with exceedingly unusual speeches and deeds? Had not his own behavior been odd and somewhat . . . well, crazy, yes . . . stopping a stranger on the street and asking him what an A and R man was, spending an hour or more with a young boy by the river, chasing a strange girl (She is not a strange girl, goddamn you! She is Doris! I *know* her!) in a taxicab and waiting now for her to emerge from the building across the street?

He looked quickly through the open door and across the street. The face of the brownstone was still sealed tight. He turned back to the newspaper and read the story a fourth time. Of course, he thought. What else was my attitude toward Di Palermo than a paranoiac symptom? Severe persecution complex, of course— why the hell else would twenty-two dollars be so important to me? Twenty-two lousy measly dollars—I who spend thousands a year! There! he thought. Delusions of grandeur! And what about the way I treated Mr. Schwartz, who offered to pay for my breakfast? What kind of behavior was that? Who the hell would behave that way except an escaped lunatic named Edward Voegler, who is me, who goddamnit is me, me, me!

Is he? he thought.

Is Edward Voegler really me, and am I really him? And if I am, what the hell do I do now? Should I call that number, let them take me back to that horrible place, *what* horrible place, how do I know of its horror if I'm not indeed Edward Voegler, the escaped lunatic, what had the headline called him, a schizo, yes, schizo escapes l.i. asylum. There was a poetry in the words. L.I. Asylum. He thought back to a headline he had seen in the *Daily News*, oh, long ago—why was it he could remember all the stupid trivial paraphernalia of his life, the inconsequential trimmings, and not any of the really important things, like whether or not he happened to be Edward Voegler, escaped lunatic, or madman, or schizo, or whatever he was? The headline had appeared when the men down at Canaveral had sent up a rocket containing white mice. The rocket was supposed to send radio signals back to earth before the eventual return of the mice, but those brilliant spacemen had gloriously fouled up the experiment, and the rocket was not sending back any radio messages, and it looked as though those red-eyed litle rodents would go spinning through space eternally. The headline on the *Daily News* that day— What made him think he didn't like that newspaper? That headline had cheered up his entire day!—had read simply:

MISSILE MUM,
MICE MISSING

God, that was a great headline! The man who wrote that headline should have been given a medal and a ticker-tape parade down Fifth Avenue in an open car with Mayor Wagner taking off his hat and holding it up to the crowd like a panhandler!

I *must* be crazy, he thought. I'm sitting here with a cold cup of coffee, light with a little sugar—I take it black, isn't that what Gloria said? Sam takes it black—remembering a headline I saw years ago, when the headline on the newspaper right in front of me is telling me I'm a nut who stole some director's nice blue suit (and undoubtedly his gold cuff links and tie tack) and ran off with a case of paranoid schizophrenia and a severe persecution complex with delusions of grandeur. Where the hell is Doris? Isn't she ever coming out?

She suddenly seemed like his only salvation. Doris in the building across the street, with her long bird legs and her flowing black crest, old Doris would know all the answers. He would wait for her to come out, and then he would simply say, "Hi, Doris, remember me? It's nutty old Ed Voegler; we used to know each other before I got committed. Remember? I used to tell you about all the hatchet murders I was planning. Come on, you remember, don't you?"

And Doris would look at him and say, "Why, you silly boy, you. You're not Ed Voegler at all, whoever *he* is. You're Myron Goldfarb, who used to take me cycling in the Bronx, don't *you* remember?"

Oh, yes, he thought, oh yes, I remember those sun-stained days, yes, yes, I remember, but hasn't Edward Voegler got a memory, too, and isn't his as confused and as terrified as my own, this paranoid schizophrenic who took his evening meal and then ran for freedom? Didn't *I* run for freedom this morning, up Central Park South with the birds singing their sweet and piercing song in my ears? Didn't *I* run for freedom?

"There's more of them guys on the outside than on the inside," the voice beside him said.

He wheeled on his stool. The boy standing next to him was no more than sixteen years old. He was wearing a black leather jacket with silver studs in the collar. His sideburns were long, and his eyes were wide and blue in a guileless open face seeking conversation.

"Are you talking to me?" Buddwing asked.

"Yeah, sure," the boy said.

"What did you say?"

"I said there's plenty of them nuts walking the streets."

Buddwing smiled. "Yes," he said, "I'll bet there are."

"How'd he get out?" the boy asked.

"He just left."

"Don't they have fences around them places?"

"I guess they do."

"So what kind of fences do they have where some nut can just march out like that?" The boy shook his head.

"Maybe he cut a hole in the fence. Or dug under it," Buddwing said, and then wondered if that was what Voegler had done, what *he* had done.

Two other boys seemed to materialize out of nowhere. They were sporting sideburns, too. One of them was wearing a gray sweat shirt with a black line drawing of Beethoven stamped onto the front. The other was wearing a blue sports shirt over which was an open red vest. They took up positions slightly behind the boy in the black leather jacket, and joined the conversation easily and naturally.

"I wonder if he really only escaped last night," the one with the Beethoven sweat shirt said.

"What do you mean?" the one with the red vest asked.

"Well," Beethoven explained with patient logic, "that's only what they're *telling* us. Suppose he *really* escaped last week, or maybe even last month? Maybe they've been looking for this creep all that time, and they couldn't find him 'cause he's hiding out in the bushes someplace, you know, so they figure that *now* maybe they better warn the people, you dig?"

"That sounds crazy," Red Vest said, but Buddwing did indeed dig what Beethoven was saying because it suddenly opened a new line of thought for him, and the thought was overwhelming. Suppose, he thought, suppose I am *not* Edward Voegler but simply a very nice ordinary man, a garbage man perhaps, who doesn't happen to remember who he is? But more than that, suppose I haven't really known who I am for a week, maybe, or even maybe a month, just as Beethoven said? Suppose I have been waking up every morning for the past month without having the slightest idea who I am?

"You may be right," he said to Beethoven, looking at the face above the sweater for the first time. The boy had long brown hair and gray eyes, and really a remarkably handsome face, with

a short pug nose and full lips, like one of the carved angels on
the roof of Il Duomo in Milan; Italy again, hot, the roller in the
typewriter had melted because the typewriter had been near the
window with the sun beating in on it and the temperature had
been a hundred and two in the shade, the roof of the cathedral
with its gingerbread icing, the way her hair had been framed by
a sky of molten brass, brass against brass, her hair, Milan.

"Sure," Beethoven said. "You think they're gonna tell *us* anything? And get theirselves in hot water? It's only 'cause they can't
find that kook is why they're telling us about it now."

"Well, maybe so," Red Vest said. "What do you think?"

He addressed this to Leather Jacket, who was obviously the
leader of the trio. L.J., the boss, shrugged as if such speculation
were beneath his lofty consideration. "Who cares?" he said. Red
Vest, who looked somewhat like an Indian, with a swarthy com-
plexion and black crew-cut hair with incongruously long sideburns, shrugged too. Whatever was all right with L.J. was all
right with him, it seemed, and besides, who cared?

"Did they finally get that stickball game going?" L.J. asked
Beethoven.

"Yes, they did," Buddwing answered.

"Takes them an hour to get a game started," L.J. said, accepting Buddwing into the conversation casually and easily. "You
ever see a bunch of guys take so long to get something going?"

"No," Buddwing said. "It's Saturday, though, so I guess there's
no rush." He picked up his cup and sipped at the coffee, pulling a
face.

"What's the matter?" L.J. asked. "Your coffee get cold?"

"Yeah," Buddwing said.

"Hey, Artie," L.J. said to the counterman, "why don't you
give this guy a cup of hot coffee?"

"I *gave* him a cup of hot coffee."

"Yeah, well, it's ice-cold now."

"That's all right," Buddwing said.

"Come on, break your heart, Artie. Give the guy a fresh cup.
And bring us all some while you're at it."

"None for me," Red Vest said.

"You think coffee grows on trees?" Artie said.

"As a matter of fact, it does," Buddwing answered, and the boys all laughed.

"Where you think it grows?" Beethoven said, laughing. "In the dirt, like potatoes?"

"The comedians," Artie said. "Here's your coffee."

Buddwing noticed that he put down three cups, and wondered if he was expected to pay for the fresh cup L.J. had demanded. L.J. picked up his own cup of coffee and then started to walk toward one of the booths in the back of the place. He stopped, turned toward Buddwing expectantly, and said, "Whyn't you sit back here with us?"

Buddwing was about to refuse. But the open innocence was still on L.J.'s face, as though he were asking for contact somehow, as though it were very important to him that Buddwing join them.

"All right," Buddwing said. "But I have to keep an eye on that building across the street."

"Oh, yeah?" L.J. said. "How come?"

"I'm waiting for a girl to come out."

Red Vest made a clucking sound with his tongue, and Beethoven picked up his coffee cup and shouted at the counterman, "Hey, Artie, you think girls grow on trees, too?"

"He thinks girls grow in Macy's," L.J. said, and everyone, including Buddwing, laughed.

"Wise guys," Artie said, but he was smiling.

They made themselves comfortable in the booth, L.J. and Buddwing on one side, Red Vest and Beethoven on the other. L.J. picked up his coffee cup, sipped at it, and then turned to Buddwing and said, "We're always putting him on. Artie. He's a nice guy. The guy up the block, he always chases us when we hack around. Not Artie."

"He does seem like a nice guy," Buddwing offered, though he really held no opinion of Artie whatever, and was in fact still wondering whether he was expected to pay for the second cup of coffee.

"You connected with the television studio?" L.J. asked.

"What do you mean?" Buddwing said.

"ABC. Over near the park."

"Oh. No. No, I didn't even know there was a studio around here."

"Yeah, there's always a bunch of actors going in and out of there. You're not connected with it, huh?"

"No."

"I thought maybe you were connected with it. You look like an actor or something."

"I do?"

"Yeah. Don't he look like an actor?"

"Yeah," Beethoven said, smiling angelically, "he looks like Boris Karloff."

"More like Peter Lorre," Red Vest said.

"Wise guys. You see? They can't take nothing serious," L.J. said.

"We're very serious," Beethoven said.

"Oh yes, very serious," Red Vest said.

"You really waiting for a girl?" L.J. asked.

"Yes, I am."

"What's her name?"

"Doris."

L.J. thought for a moment, his brow wrinkling. "Doris," he said, "Doris." He turned to the other boys. "You know any Doris on this block?"

"There's a Dotty," Beethoven said.

"No. This is Doris," Buddwing said.

"What's she look like?" L.J. asked.

"Black hair, brown eyes, very long legs."

"How old is she?"

"Seventeen," Buddwing answered without hesitation.

"That's kind of robbing the cradle, ain't it?" Red Vest said.

"What do you mean?" L.J. protested. "Maybe he likes them

young." He looked at Buddwing seriously, and said, "How old are you, anyway?"

"Thirty-five," Buddwing said.

"That's not so old," L.J. said.

"That's pretty old," Red Vest said. He grinned at Buddwing and added, "I'll bet you can remember the chariot races."

"I can remember the building of the pyramids," Buddwing said.

"Dotty has blond hair," Beethoven said idly, and then shrugged and picked up his coffee cup.

"No, this is Doris."

"But there ain't no Doris on this block."

"I think you made her up," Red Vest said.

Buddwing smiled. "No, she's real, all right."

"Naw, you made her up," Red Vest said, and he winked at the other boys. For a moment, Buddwing felt a twinge of anticipation. He was sitting in a booth with three boys who looked like all the pictures of juvenile delinquents he had ever seen. They had accepted him into their circle unquestioningly, had joked with him, had demanded a fresh cup of coffee for him when his first cup had grown cold. But now he grew suspicious of them. Why were they being so friendly? Was their easy banter leading to an argument, leading to an excuse for them to jump him? Cautiously, he lifted his cup, avoiding their eyes, and cautiously he sipped at his coffee.

"Does she put out?" Beethoven asked idly.

Buddwing dared to raise his eyes. He looked into Beethoven's face, and could read nothing on it. Carefully, he said, "Well, I don't know."

"Oh, yeah, he don't know," Beethoven said, and laughed gently. The laugh seemed to dissipate whatever anxiety Buddwing had been feeling. He looked into Beethoven's gray eyes and at his soft face, and he listened to the boy's warm chuckle, a chuckle that conveyed such a sense of cheerfully shared conspiracy that Buddwing knew instantly his suspicion had been illfounded, and instantly he relaxed.

"No, really," he said, smiling. "I don't know whether she does or not."

"Yeah, he don't know," L.J. said. "Just look at him."

"*Everybody* puts out," Red Vest said. "That's a fact."

"This guy thinks the whole city is a whorehouse," L.J. said.

"It is," Red Vest answered.

"Then what does that make your mother and your sister?" Beethoven asked with sweet simplicity.

Sipping at his coffee, Buddwing thought, I have had this conversation before.

"My mother puts out, that's for sure," Red Vest said, "and my sister's only eight."

"That's very mature," L.J. said, laughing. "What's holding her back?"

They all laughed, and Red Vest said, "Yeah, you guys. Boy." He turned to Buddwing. "You ever see a bunch of hornier guys in your life?"

"Who, *us?*" L.J. said in astonishment. He nudged Buddwing gently and said, "*This* is the guy who's horny. Look at him. Sitting here and waiting for a chick, when it's only nine o'clock in the morning."

"Well, it's really nothing like that," Buddwing said. "She's really a very nice girl."

"Who said she ain't nice?"

"She's probably sweet as can be."

"Mmm. Sweet."

"With that black hair and those brown eyes."

"Yeah, and the long legs."

"I dig long-legged chicks," Red Vest said.

"You dig anything that walks with a skirt on it."

This identical conversation, Buddwing thought.

"You know what I dream sometimes?" Red Vest said confidentially. He lowered his voice and leaned across the table. "I dream of all these beautiful long-legged chicks walking around naked, but there's no body from the waist up, you know what I mean? Just this pussy on legs, that's all. I dream it all the time."

"You're nuts, that's why you have such dreams," L.J. said, and Buddwing thought again of Edward Voegler, of Central Islip State Hospital, of the newspaper's shrieking headline.

"Mmmm," Red Vest said, "*eat* them all up. Mmmm," and he licked his lips.

"You know who's the sexiest girl on this block?" Beethoven asked idly.

"Who?" Buddwing said.

"Yeah, look at him, he wants to know," Red Vest said. "I thought you were waiting for Doris."

"I am."

"So what do you want to know about some other chick for, huh?"

"Yeah, wait'll we tell Doris," Beethoven said. He grinned at Buddwing, enjoying the banter immensely.

"What, is he *married* to her?" L.J. asked. "Boy, you guys, you never . . ."

"It's plain to see he's bugged over the girl," Red Vest said, shrugging.

"*Are* you bugged over her?" L.J. asked Buddwing.

"Well, I like her a lot," he answered.

"Then I don't think you ought to tell him about this other chick," L.J. said to Beethoven.

"Okay, I won't," Beethoven said.

"No, go ahead, tell me," Buddwing said.

"Naw, I don't think I should."

"I think Doris would get very angry if we went telling him about some other sexy chick, that's what I think," L.J. said.

"That's what I think, too," Beethoven said.

"Me, too," Red Vest said.

"Me, too," Buddwing said, and they all laughed.

"Louise," Beethoven said suddenly. "Louise Ambrosini, that's who the sexiest girl on this block is."

"Louise Ambrosini!" Red Vest said, shocked.

"Yeah, that's who."

"She's an old lady!"

"She's a young mother. And don't yell. There's people here who know her, you realize that?" Beethoven lowered his voice. "You know what she does?"

"What does she do?"

"Oh, boy, wouldn't you like to know what she does."

"Yeah?" Red Vest said, leaning forward. "You mean it?"

Beethoven nodded his head and smiled in a superior manner.

"I don't believe it," Red Vest said. "She's got a baby in a carriage!"

"She's also got a husband in the navy," Beethoven said, "that's what *else* she's got. In the *navy*. In *Florida*. That's what."

"What are you saying?"

"Me? Nothing," Beethoven said innocently.

"You mean . . ."

"He means Old Louise is available," Buddwing said.

"If *he* knows what I'm saying," Beethoven said, "how come *you* guys don't know what I'm saying?"

"It must be a meeting of the minds," L.J. said.

"Yeah, it must be a meeting of the world's great thinkers," Red Vest said.

Beethoven laughed and said, "You hear that? We're the world's great thinkers."

"Sure, I knew that all along," Buddwing said.

"Let's go see how that stickball game is doing," Red Vest said.

"Sports fans," L.J. said, his voice deepening in imitation of a radio announcer, "here we are on Sixty-seventh Street, between Amsterdam and Broadway, about to witness the opening game of the spring classic."

"He wants to be an announcer, this guy," Red Vest said.

"Really?" Buddwing asked.

"Well, I thought of it," L.J. said modestly.

"He's very good at it," Beethoven said, looking at L.J. in a friendly, encouraging manner, and then turning to Buddwing and trying to convince him. "Really. He's got it down pat. And he knows all the rules, too, and the batting averages, things like that. He's very good at it, really."

"I'll bet he is," Buddwing said.

"Well, my voice ain't so hot."

"You got a very good voice," Beethoven said. "Don't you think he has?"

"Very good," Buddwing said. "It's a good deep voice."

"Not too deep, though," Red Vest said. "It's just right for a radio announcer."

"Yeah, if it's too deep, you can't hear them so good," Beethoven said. "His voice is just right. You should hear him sometime. He really does a good job."

"You should see *this* guy draw," L.J. said.

"What do you mean?" Buddwing asked.

"Well, I'm not so good," Beethoven said.

"He's great, he really is. I can't even draw a straight line, but you should see some of the pictures he does. Hey, why don't you run upstairs and get some of your pictures?"

"Naw, come on," Beethoven said.

"He's got a picture, it's all in color," Red Vest said, "of the rooftops on this block. You ever been up on a roof?"

"Yes," Buddwing said. "Yes, I've been on a roof."

"Well, he's got it all down, you know, the television antennas, and the way the tar gets, and the bricks, and even there's a pigeon coop on one of the roofs. He's got an eye, boy! When you gonna do our pictures, huh?"

"I'll do them," Beethoven said.

"He's always promising he's gonna draw our pictures," L.J. said, "and he never does."

"He took this girl to the park, though, and he drew *her* picture, didn't you, hah? Ah-hah?"

"She posed for him," L.J. said, grinning.

"You should see *that* picture," Red Vest said. "Hey, come on, go upstairs and get them, okay?"

I have heard this talk before, Buddwing thought, I have been in this candy-store booth with these same boys, and we talked of sex and dreams, we talked of ambition and desire, we shared together, we felt what is in this booth now, a pride and a joy and a warmth, I know these boys.

"Come on, let's go watch that game," L.J. said.

"I have to keep my eye on the building," Buddwing said.

"You can watch it from the street, it ain't going no place."

"I guess not."

"Boy, this Doris must be *some* chick," Beethoven said.

They moved out of the booth and toward the door of the candy store. Artie looked up from his newspaper and said, "Forty-five cents for the coffee, and five for the paper, if you don't mind."

He's not charging me for the extra cup, Buddwing thought, and immediately said, "I've got it."

"No, no, let me take it," L.J. said.

"No, that's all right."

"Come on, there's *three* of us, for Christ's sake. That ain't fair. Hey, come on, really."

"No, don't worry about it," Buddwing answered, and he put fifty cents on the counter, the two quarters he had got as part of his change in Schwartz's cafeteria. He still had the dime and the nickel in his trouser pocket, and he wondered abruptly how many bills he had left. He had spent a dollar for the taxicab, and now an additional fifty cents—should he tip Artie?—how much did that leave him? Were those *three* bills in his pocket, or only two? How long would his money last, and how long would it be before they dragged him, Edward Voegler, back to Central Islip and started giving him shock treatment, or put him in a tub full of steaming water covered with a rubber sheet . . . why, that was Olivia de Havilland in *The Snake Pit!* he thought suddenly, and wondered all at once whether he had ever really been inside a mental hospital, whether he was really Edward Voegler, the escaped paranoid schizophrenic.

Well, Doris will tell me, he reasoned, if she ever comes out of that damn building. She's been in there for more than a half hour now; isn't she ever coming out? The hell with her, he thought suddenly. I have my own friends, I have my own life to lead—and then he recognized how absurd this reasoning was. The three boys he had met were hardly his friends—why had he thought they were his friends? Simply because they had shared some time with him, simply because he had felt a momentary spark of sympathy from them, the idle angelic smile of Beethoven, the reminiscent gutter talk of Red Vest, the playful nudges of L.J.? They were not his friends; they were simply some guys he had stopped to talk to on a mild spring day. And yet he still felt very close to them as he walked out into the spring sunshine and heard the sudden sound of stickball bat against rubber ball, and then the clattering noise of the broom handle being dropped on asphalt.

He blinked his eyes against the sun. The bat was rolling, he heard the sound of it, it seemed to be the only sound on the street. The sun was bright in his eyes, memory sharp and swift and sudden, blinding in its intensity, rooting him to the sidewalk in a brilliant splash of canyon-filtered sunshine, it is too still in this house.

The sunshine is coming through a small window in the entry hall. It crosses the air with flecks of dancing dust motes, the apartment is very still. He can hear a clock ticking someplace in the living room, and another sound below that, a swishing sound, he cannot place it, he does not know what the sound is. They are the only sounds in the apartment, this house is too still. He does not move from the doorway because the stillness has reached out for him, is surrounding him now, it is too still, too unreal, he has walked into something that threatens to suffocate him. The dust motes seem to move more quickly, to whirl and to advance upon him with the stillness, he knows something is wrong, he cannot move.

The carpet is deep and green and he turns his eyes to it now, really listening, but pretending he is only studying the carpet in this silent house, where are the noises? He can see separate strands of wool in the carpet, he can see a stain, his ears are reaching for sound, but there is none, they are always mistaking her for Italian, *Ma lei è italiana, sicuramente?*, and she answers always with a strange pleased mysterious smile, *No, non sono italiana,* but tells them nothing more, it is too quiet in this apartment. He wants to scream.

The dust motes tirelessly climb the shaft of sunlight.

"Hey, are you coming?" L.J. called.

Buddwing blinked his eyes. He was breathing hard, and his hands were clenched at his sides. He blinked again and looked toward the voice, the calling voice, and saw someone in a black leather jacket whom he recognized only dimly. Did he know this person? Had he ever really known this person, had he . . . yes, of course, L.J., of course, the boys, of course, yes, he knew them, surely he knew them, surely they were very important. He was taking a step toward his friend in the black leather jacket when the door in the brownstone across the street opened, and his heart quickened, and he turned as she came down the steps.

# 6

SHE HAD already reached the sidewalk by the time he crossed the street, moving swiftly on her long black legs, turning east immediately and striding toward Broadway with her head bent and her ponytail crest flying.

"Doris!" he shouted, but she did not turn, and he yelled, "Doris!" again and then began running after her. Behind him, he could hear L.J. calling to him, but his voice sounded very far away and indistinct. Doris was wearing black pumps with tiny French heels, and she scuttled over the sidewalk in giant flying steps; God, she was a fast walker. "Hey, wait up!" he called. She did not turn. Running, he caught up to her and fell into step beside her.

"Hi," he said.

She turned toward him, startled, and the first thing he noticed was that her eyes were not brown, they were green. She looked at him with that peculiarly suspicious shocked incredible outraged look most New Yorkers wear when they are accosted by total strangers, and then performed the magic trick of tilting her nose snobbishly, raising her eyebrows aloofly, and twisting her mouth disgustedly, all at the same time. She quickened her already breathtaking pace, her little behind pumping vigorously as her long legs chewed up concrete, and left him behind her on the pavement.

"Hey, Doris!" he yelled, and ran to catch up with her again, falling into step beside her once more. "Slow down, will you?"

"I am *not* Doris," she said. She had a bright perky little voice heavily garnished with the tones and rhythms of New York, familiar to him, pleasant to his ears.

"Sure you are," he said.

"Will you please get away from me?" she said, but she turned to take a look at him, and then again lifted her nose, and raised her eyebrows, and twisted her mouth, and would have begun walking faster but he suspected she was getting out of breath.

"I've been waiting for you for a half hour," he said. "What took you so long in there?"

"That," she said, "is none of your business." She looked at him sideways, and again lifted her nose, to give the impression she was looking down at him, although he was at least five or six inches taller than she. Still, she was a pretty tall girl, five-six or five-seven, he imagined. Her nose was slightly longer than he remembered it, but very nicely shaped, with a slightly precocious *Saturday Evening Post* tilt to it. Her lower lip protruded a bit, in either a purposeful or natural pout, he wasn't sure which. She kept walking speedily, and he walked beside her, listening to the noise of her shoes on the sidewalk. Every now and again, she stole a glance at him as if ascertaining that he was still there. Finally, she stopped dead in the middle of the sidewalk, put her hands on her hips, which were very narrow and practically non-existent, a boy's hips almost, and said, "Would you like me to call a cop?"

"Well, no," he said. "As a matter of fact, I wouldn't. What do we need a cop for?"

"*You* don't need a cop, but I think *I* do," she said.

97

"Well, Doris, if you feel you need—"

"And my name is *not* Doris."

"Then what is it?"

"My name is . . . that's none of your business," she said.

"Well, it *is* my business because I've been waiting for you."

"Nobody asked you to wait for me," she said.

"Didn't you hear me calling you on Eighty-ninth Street?"

"On where?"

"Eighty-ninth Street. And Broadway. Where you got the cab."

"You followed me here? All the way from . . ."

"Well, I yelled after you, but I guess you didn't hear me."

"No, I didn't hear you."

"Well, I sure yelled loud enough."

"What did you yell?"

"I yelled 'Doris!' "

"I am *not* Doris," she said.

"Then what *is* your name?"

"My name is Janet, and goodbye," she said, and turned away from him and began walking at her furious clip again, her head bent, her black ponytail angrily bouncing along behind her, trying to keep the wiggle out of her behind, but failing miserably. He began running again, but saw that she had stopped on Columbus Avenue to wait for the light, so he took his time catching up with her and then said, "What were you doing in that brownstone, Janet?"

"I was visiting my brother. Is that all right with you?"

"That's fine with me. What was *he* doing there?"

"For Pete's sake, he's a writer, he *lives* there," Janet said. "Listen, I wish you'd stop talking to me. And following me. Really, I wish you would. I'll call a cop, I really will."

"Why?"

"Because you're bothering me, can't you see that?"

"How am I bothering you?"

"By talking to me and . . . and *following* me, for Pete's sake."

"Well, you look like someone I know," Buddwing said.

"Who? Oh, never mind, don't tell me. Doris." She made an open-fingered gesture with her right hand, bringing the hand close to her face, her eyes opening wide, and then she rolled her eyes as if she would go out of her mind if she heard the name Doris one more time.

"Yeah," he said, "Doris."

"Doris, Doris, all *right*."

"May I walk with you?" he asked.

"No."

"Why not?"

"Because I don't want you to."

"Even if I don't talk to you?"

"Look," she said angrily, "it's a free country, and I can't stop you from walking wherever you want to." The light changed, and she crossed the avenue. He walked beside her, but he did not speak to her. She still glanced at him occasionally, but made no other acknowledgment of his presence. They walked in silence all the way to Central Park West, past the Tavern-on-the-Green and then onto the 66th Street footpath.

"Where are you going?" he asked.

"I told you not to talk to me. Listen, you'd better not get funny," she said. "This is Central Park, you know."

"So?"

"So you get funny in Central Park, and boy! I'm telling you."

"I slept here last night," Buddwing said.

"Where? You mean here? In the park?"

"Yes."

"You look it," Janet said sourly. "You need a shave." She glanced at him briefly, and turned away. "If there's one thing I can't stand, it's a man who needs a shave." She glanced at him again and said, "My brother always needs a shave, too. His whole damn apartment needs a shave, if you ask me. Boy, what a rattrap. And I mean rattrap, believe me. I mean, he's got brazen rats in that apartment who come right out and sit on their hind legs and *stare* at you, for Pete's sake, actually *stare* you down. And I mean *rats*, not mice."

"Missile mum, mice missing," Buddwing said.

"What did you say?"

"Nothing."

"I thought you said something."

"No, I was just mumbling."

"Oh."

They were deep in the park now, deep in the midst of park noises: the joyous sound of shrieking children chasing each other in circles, climbing on the rocks, shooting imaginary guns; the imperious sound of Swedish governesses pushing polished baby buggies, shouting to sibling wards in Greta Garbo tones, tall and statuesque and blond like Nevada show girls; the impatient sound of taxicabs winding on the transverse road, the gunning of engines, the honking of horns; the sweet sound of gentle laughter, of lovers lying on the grass, a boy stretched back with his arm behind his head, one knee bent, a young redheaded girl leaning over him with her long hair falling loose, their shared laughter, the gentle touch of their hands; the distant sound of a baseball game somewhere, the excited voices of young boys in competition; the steady beating rhythm of a skip rope slapping against the path, and little girls' voices in unison chanting, "Double-ee-Dutch, double-ee-Dutch"; the chattering sound of bulging women with knee-length silk stockings, sitting with widespread legs on sunwashed green benches; the sounds of an oasis.

"Well, we seem to be walking together after all," Janet said, and she smiled such a radiantly lovely smile, shy and rare, dimpling the corners of her mouth, that he fell in love with her in that instant, and then immediately suspected he had been in love with her all along.

"Yes, I suppose we are," Buddwing said.

"You're not a degenerate or anything, are you?"

"No, no."

"God, I can't stand those spooks who rub up against you in the subway."

"Neither can I."

"They rub up against *you*, too?" she asked, astonished.

"No, no, I meant I can't stand the ones who rub up against *you*. You, Janet."

"Oh, thank you," she said, and gave a curious giggle. "Are you picking me up?" she asked.

"Would you like to be picked up?"

"Well, no, not particularly. But I don't mind talking to you. You seem all right."

"Thank you."

"It's a lovely day, isn't it?"

"It's a beautiful day," he said, and added, "You're a beautiful girl, Janet."

"I'm not really," she said. "My nose is too long, and my legs are too skinny. That's why I'm wearing these black tights. They make your legs look better, did you know that?"

"No, I didn't know that."

"Well, they do. Thank you for saying so, anyway."

"Saying what, Janet?"

"Well, what you said."

"I'm sorry, what . . ."

"About my being . . ." She turned away from him shyly. Her voice dropped. "Beautiful," she said.

"Where are you going now?" he asked.

"Oh, to my analyst," she said. "He's on Park and Sixty-fifth. I don't have to be there until ten-thirty."

"Well, that gives us a little time."

"Yes," she said. She turned to look at him, and he saw how very green her eyes were, reflecting the freshness of the spring grass all around them, glowing with sunshine. "Hey, you know, I really shouldn't be doing this," she said. "Talking to you like this. How do I know who you are?"

"Who do you think I am?"

"Oh, boy, you sound just like my analyst! He always wants to know what *I* think about something. I ask him something simple, like where he went to medical school, and he says, 'Where do you

*think* I went to medical school?' " Janet shrugged. "He went to
Cornell, in case you're interested." She pulled a wry face and
added, "I'm sure that's very fascinating to you, the fact that my
analyst went to Cornell."

"I *am* fascinated," Buddwing said.

"Ho-ho, I'll just bet you are. How old are you, anyway?"

"How old do you think I am?"

"There you go again, you'd better watch it. Hey! *You're*
not an analyst, are you?"

"No, I think I'm a patient, as a matter of fact."

"Well, welcome to the club. What's your doctor's name?"

Buddwing smiled and said, "Voegler, Dr. Edward Voegler."

"Thank God we don't have the same analyst," Janet said.

"Voegler's the resident psychiatrist at Central Islip State
Hospital," Buddwing said.

"Really? I know Central Islip."

"How do you know it?"

"Oh, one of my instructors made a joke about it, in a Psych
course. I'm really *raw*-ther well oriented psychologically, as you
can see. Anyway, they first performed frontal lobotomies at
Central Islip, and apparently they did a great many of them there
because everyone in the profession began calling it Central Icepick. You know, they do a lobotomy with a long—"

"Yes," Buddwing said.

"I wonder if your Dr. Voegler performs lobotomies."

"I wonder."

"Why don't you ask him?"

"I will, the next time I see him."

"How often do you go?" Janet asked.

"How often do *you* go?"

"Four times a week."

"Me, too," Buddwing said.

"Been going long?"

"Oh, on and off."

"How long?"

"How long have *you* been going?"

"Two years," Janet said.

"Me, too," Buddwing answered.

"Well," Janet said. "Anyway, how old *are* you? You still haven't told me."

"Guess."

"That's the same thing as asking me how old I *think* you are. You know all the tricks, don't you?"

"A few," he said.

"Mmmm, I'll bet," Janet answered, and she gave a low sexy chuckle that startled him. "I think you're twenty-eight. Right?"

"Wrong."

"Twenty-six?"

"No."

"If you say you're younger than that, you're a liar."

"I'm much older than that," Buddwing said.

"How much older?"

"I'm about thirty-five."

"What do you mean 'about'? When were you born?"

"This morning," he said automatically.

"Ask a stupid question," Janet said, and nodded her head. "Thirty-five, huh? Well, well. I'm with an Older Man."

"How old are *you?*" he asked.

"Nineteen. Well, I'll be nineteen next month."

"When is that?"

"The twelfth."

"Of what?"

"May." She looked at him curiously. "Next month. May. This is April."

"Yes, it feels like April."

"It's a beautiful day."

"Yes."

"I was fishing," Janet said, "but you didn't say it again."

He took her hand and stopped walking, and she stopped beside him, and he looked into her face and said, "You *are* beautiful, Janet. You are the most beautiful girl in the world."

She tilted her head to one side and gave a small embarrassed shrug, lifting one eyebrow at the same time—she seemed capable of the most extraordinary simultaneous body movements—and then said, in a very soft voice, "Yeah?"

"Yeah," he answered.

"You're holding my hand."

"I know."

"Aren't you ashamed of yourself, an old thirty-five-year-old lecher?"

"No."

"Mmm," she said. She looked into his face and then shook her head and drew her hand back gently and said, "Listen, you'd better go easy."

"Why?"

"Why? For Pete's sake, I don't even know your name!"

"Sam Buddwing," he said.

"Or whether you're married or not."

"I'm not."

"Or engaged or anything."

"I'm not engaged."

"Or . . . who you *are*. I mean . . ." She shrugged again. "Well, let's just go easy, huh? I mean, let's take it easy, okay? Because, listen, I'll tell you the truth, you're a pretty attractive guy, you know?" She took a deep breath. "I mean, considering everything."

"Like what?"

"Like you're old enough to be my father, for Pete's sake!"

"Okay," he said.

"Yeah, okay, what does okay mean? I'm not in the habit of . . . well, I don't dig this Electra bit, you know? Well, at least I didn't used to. Or I suppose I *used* to, when I was a kid—you know *all* girls go through that—but I've *resolved* it, and listen, you're attractive as hell, I don't even know what I'm *talking* about!"

"That's good."

"Who's Doris?" she asked.

"I don't know."

"No, huh? You followed me all the way from Eighty-ninth Street because you thought I was her, and now you don't know who she is."

"I thought *you* could tell me who she was."

"Doris Kantor is the only Doris I know. She's in my History of the English Language course."

"Where?"

"Hunter College." Janet paused. "I'm a sophomore." She paused again. "Is Doris Kantor your Doris?"

"No. You're my Doris."

"If I'm going to be *any*thing, I'd better be your *Janet*," she said, and she turned to stare at him steadily.

"All right," he said.

"All right what?"

"You know."

"Say it."

"You're my *Janet*."

"Mmm," she said, and her eyes held his steadily, and again there was that same sexy understatement on her face, deep and somehow hungry. "We'd better go easy," she said again. She looked at her watch. "And we'd better hurry. I don't want to be late. Does yours charge you when you're late? Or when you miss a session?"

"Oh, yes," Buddwing said.

"Mine does, too. That seems awfully unprofessional to me. Will you wait for me? I'll only be fifty minutes—well, you know that. Will you?"

"Yes."

"Okay. Listen . . ." She shook her head. "No, never mind."

"What is it?"

"Nothing. Only . . . listen, you better not hurt me."

"What?"

"I don't want to get hurt by you." She paused. "I'm . . . I'm a very vulnerable person. If you're a son of a bitch or anything, well, let's just shake hands now, okay?"

"I'm not a son of a bitch," he said.

"Because I'm . . . I'm not just a quick college-girl roll in the hay, if that's what you think I am."

"I don't know *what* you are, Janet, or *who* you are. I only know that I love you."

She stared at him silently.

"You shouldn't have said that," she said.

"Why not?"

"Because you don't mean it. And . . . I told you . . . I'm . . . I'm a very vulnerable person and I . . . I find you terribly attractive . . . and those are magic words. You . . . you have to be very careful with magic."

"I'll be very careful. I love you, Janet."

"Ahh," she said.

"I do."

"Ahhh." She closed her eyes and smiled, and then she opened her eyes suddenly and said, "Come. Please. I'll be late." She took his hand, and they walked swiftly across the park, and then onto Fifth Avenue, and across Madison, and over to Park. They stood holding hands on the corner of Park and 65th. "Wait for me," she said. "Will you wait for me?"

"You know I will."

"Listen, don't love me yet," she said. "Please wait."

"Why?"

"I'm afraid of things that come too fast."

"Don't be."

She squeezed his hand and nibbled at her pouting lower lip, and then reached up suddenly and kissed him on the cheek.

"I *really* want to kiss you," she said, "but that'll do."

"All right."

"For now."

"Yes."

"You won't go away?"

"No."

"You'll wait right here?"

"Yes."

"I must be crazy," she said, and she turned and ran under the awning and into the building.

# 7

HE STOOD watching the lobby, the light streaming through a courtyard window, as she walked across it. She stopped at the elevator, unaware that he was watching her. She pushed the button, and then turned idly to look out at the street again. She saw him in startled pleasure, grinned, lifted her hand, wiggled the fingers on it, brought the hand to her lips, and threw a kiss. His heart soared. He watched as she got into the elevator, and then he did a small pirouette, and gave a short twisting jerk of his head and began walking down Park Avenue. He smiled at everyone he passed. He felt that the sky would open at any moment and shower golden coins on him, they would fall tinkling at his feet, he would wade through them and not bother to pick them up, they would clink and glitter as he walked airily through them, Jesus, she was beautiful.

Janet, Janet, Janet, her name sang in his head, plummeted to his heart like a stone dropped in a well of sweet water, echoed, echoed, Janet, Janet, Janet. Her eyes were green and deep and young and surprised and alert and questioning and new with discovery. Her hair was black and shining like a crow's wing and a cold night and a polished seashore pebble. Janet, oh Janet —her face, delicately shaped, palely turned, the honest thrust of her nose, and the curved indentation surprised by her upper lip, the cheekbones daringly molded, the tendril of black hair escaping to lie against the jaw, the entire face in motion, eyes and nose and mouth jubilant and fresh and alive—I love you. You have tiny perfectly formed breasts; I watched your breasts beneath the black armor of your sweater. When you lifted your arm, when you put your hand beside your face with the fingers widespread in exasperation, your breasts rose and flattened for an instant, and then filled your sweater again when you lowered your arm, small and young and infinitely sweet, I love your breasts. I love your eyes, I love your hair, I love your long legs in their black tights and the promise of spring juices in you, the low chuckle in your throat, the lust that fills your green eyes, unaware. Oh my Janet, your mouth is sweet and wet and bruised by love, your lower lip is swollen with pollen. You walk with a headlong rush, there is an electric energy in you, a rhythm that gushes from your mouth in a broken Bronx college-girl jargon, that tilts your narrow hips, that drives the blossoming female bulge of you, full and achingly free beneath the black skirt. I want to touch you, I want to hold your slender naked body in my arms and touch you. I know what you are like, I know what you will be, my love my Janet.

I need a shave, he thought.

She didn't like the fact that I needed a shave; she said it rather petulantly, as though how dared I even attempt to pick her up when I needed a shave? But of course I wasn't trying to pick her up; she simply reminded me of Doris. How had I ever mistaken her for Doris in the first place? Doris has brown eyes. Had. And Doris was seventeen, I can remember, certainly I can remember. So how could she possibly have been Doris, when Doris is probably as old as I am now? Doris is probably fat and sluggish and stupid—who *cares* about Doris? Anyway, Doris was fourteen, not seventeen.

Wait, he thought.

He seemed terribly confused all at once. His pace slackened, and for a moment he did not know where he was. He looked around him to get his bearings. Yes, this was Park Avenue; that was the old New York Central Building far down at its end, blocking the avenue, and rising above it like a majestic finger, the new Pan American Building. Yes, this was Park Avenue. How the hell could Doris have been fourteen? And who cares?

*I* do, he thought fiercely. I care. I *did* care. I cared very deeply, and that matters to me. It is important to me that I know I cared about someone and something, that . . . that

No, wait, he thought, please. It isn't all gone, it really isn't, it hasn't all been for nothing. God why did she have to

Wait.

Please.

Wait.

I

can remember.

If you will only grant me, please, a little

time.

Please.

I desperately need a little time, only to organize my thoughts, only to prepare myself, you see, that's all, simply to prepare myself for a life I

Grant me this, please.

"I *know* who Doris is," he said aloud, fiercely. A man walking past turned to look at him, and then hurried by, glancing back once and not again. Buddwing shook his head to clear it.

She was fourteen when I met her.

That is how she can be both fourteen and seventeen. That is logical and clear, and not at all mysterious.

He moved away from the side of the building.

She was fourteen when I met her, he repeated to himself; I can remember exactly what she was wearing. She had a plaid coat, the dominant color of which was a very pale shade of lavender, and she was wearing saddle shoes that were very dirty. She looked very dirty all over, as a matter of fact, though she certainly was not; it was simply that her black hair was very wiry and always looked uncombed and also this was a time when girls were wearing very sloppy sweaters. So the effect was one of total slovenliness, though she wasn't really dirty. She was a very clean girl. She told me that later, the time, well, that was later, the time she called me a sailor. You see, I *do* remember, there is nothing here I have forgotten. I have almost total recall, I can remember it all, even the buttons on the very pale lavender coat, which were rather large cloth-covered buttons, the cloth echoing the strongest color in the plaid, which was a thin square of deeper purple.

And we were going out to Coney Island; it was toward the end of the season. That's why she was wearing the plaid coat in the morning, but she took it off later in the day, and then was wearing it again at night when we made the long ride back in strange Brooklyn subway cars until finally we transferred to the White Plains Road line, and by that time she was asleep. I wasn't supposed to be with her—that is, she wasn't my girl, she wasn't even my date. The entire thing was rather confused, because we were still kids, you see. I was only fifteen, a year older than Doris, and dating was something still a little beyond our reach. This was a gang sort of thing, with my cousin Mandy

Yes, Mandy. Why yes, Mandy.

Isn't it odd that I can remember Mandy when I haven't seen her . . . why, it must be . . . it must be fifteen years, twenty years? But I can remember her very clearly now with her hatchet face and her thick body and her piano legs. And of course it was Mandy, who was always running around in her stupid cheerleader sweater and leading everyone as though she were standing in a stadium somepla

I played football.

No.

But I remember something about a stadium.

I *must* have played.

But . . . it was Mandy who organized the trip to Coney Island, and I spent most of the day watching Doris, and that was the beginning of it. She didn't seem very much interested in me. I bought her two hot dogs, but she kept walking alongside the thin fellow with the very long hair and the duck's-ass haircut, I hated that creep. He was older. He was seventeen. I think my cousin Mandy had her eye on him. But so did Doris, and I spent thirty cents for hot dogs, a lot of good that did. She fell asleep on the way home. I asked if I could walk her to her house, but she'd already made plans with that thin lanky creep.

I *must* have played football.

Because I remember a plaid coat and a stadium.

If it wasn't Doris in the plaid coat, then who was it?

Look, I'm doing very well, I really am. I remember this all very well, oh, a few odds and ends left out, I don't . . . I don't know what she called me; that seems to be the difficult part, remembering just who I was at that time, just who this boy who fell in love with Doris was or . . . or . . . I can't remember the house I lived in or what my mother and father looked like, but I do remember her, I do remember all the heady moments of that first long love, the bicycles on the path that day . . . well, that, yes, that first time.

We learned each other, I suppose. We learned the mysteries through each other, the mysteries of touch. I never drew her picture the way Beethoven did with his girl, I never used that as an excuse, but we spent days in the woods together, long days when we would take the bicycles at nine o'clock in the morning, carrying picnic lunches, and spend the morning and most of the afternoon in the woods near Tibbett's Brook. And we learned, we explored, we touched, we felt. She was my girl, you see, but more than that, she was everything female, the pulsing softness of her would sometimes leave me stunned with wonder. I can remember the first time I touched her breast, the breast of a girl, *any* girl—

I can remember that so clearly, the pure silent shock of it. I can remember the first time she opened her blouse and showed herself to me, I can remember staring at her, and then touching her in new wonder, seeing what my hands had known for months, her eyes averted shyly, I can remember. I can remember her with enormous tenderness, I can remember almost all of the love I felt for her, the odd bright quickening of my heart whenever she came into view with that silly plaid coat and that slightly embarrassed look on her face as though her own emotions were overwhelming and somehow shameful.

It is odd how much I loved her, and yet how suddenly that love grew cold and died. There was a break so sharp and so clean that it was almost a knife thrust, a piece of clinical surgery, delicately removing the heart and holding it pulsing in the hand before dropping it in a surgical container. She was everything in the world to me, and then she was nothing. I told her on the trolley car coming back from Mount Vernon where we had gone to the Loew's there to see a movie—I think it was *Strike Up the Band* with Judy Garland and Mickey Rooney. I think it was that, though it may have been something else; my mind was really concentrating on how I would tell her. I had discussed it that summer with L.J. and Beethoven, we had gone someplace for the summer, I don't think Red Vest was along; no, he didn't come into the crowd until later. But I had discussed it with the boys in the quiet dark, lying in our separate beds in the small wallpapered room. I can remember the woman who made salads, yes, we were busboys, that's right, her name was Gladys, she was a big woman who had a son in college, she lived on Fordham Road. I can remember she got into L.J.'s bed one night, but I don't think he did anything with her, and yet I can't for the life of me understand why she got into his bed, had he said he was cold? I could never understand it. But I had discussed Doris with them, it seems there was another girl involved, or perhaps that was only the excuse I seized upon, perhaps it was finished with Doris long before the boys and I left for the mountains, yes, of course, it was in the

Borscht Belt someplace, Goldschmidt's Hacienda? No, that was only what we called it, well.

I told her on the trolley car. It was September; the boys and I had just come back from Goldschmidt's. She was wearing my silver scholarship pin on the lapel of that same plaid coat, or perhaps it was a different coat, I only remember fastening my eyes to the silver high school scholarship pin. The pin made it easier to tell her. L.J. had said the best way was clean and sharp, so I kept staring at the silver pin, and I said, "There's something I have to tell you, Doris," but she already knew. I saw the sudden lowering of her brown eyes, and then I saw the way her hands were fluttering in her lap, and I knew she already knew, I hadn't even kissed her in the movies, the things we used to do in the movies. "I want to break off," I said, clean and sharp, just the way L.J. said I should do it, clean and sharp, I could feel that gleaming surgical knife sliding in between her ribs. She nodded.

"All right," she said. She did not raise her eyes.

Clean and sharp.

Nothing is clean and sharp. I saw her again when I was home on leave from the navy, oh, it must have been two years later. Her father was a trumpet teacher, when I got to her house that day he had a kid in the living room, and the kid was running up and down his chromatic scales. I wore dress blues, and the flattop hat which I never got a chance to wear except in New York, and I had three rubbers in the elastic band behind the crest of the hat. I took her to a movie, and then parked my father's car on a hill overlooking Ely Avenue.

I had known this girl, I had known her very well. And she stopped my hands, and said, "No. I've heard all about you sailors." I took her home. I guess that was her revenge, I guess she was entitled to a small revenge after the entrance of a surgical knife on a trolley car on a bright September day. But the thing that bothered me—the *real* revenge, the revenge she hadn't even intended—was not that she was denying everything we'd known together, the time we got caught in the rain and the lightning crashed in the trees around us, and we couldn't stay dry, we were soaked to the skin waiting for the storm to pass, wanting to touch each other again, and then finally running out of the woods, and we stopped at a gas station to hide from that fearful rain, she was sixteen then, this was the spring before we broke off, and her blouse was stuck to her, the attendant watching her, I wanted to hit him, to kill him. Not the things we *did*, not her denial of these, not her pretending we were strangers when we were really all either of us had known up to a certain point in our lives, but . . . but denying *me*. Not the things. *Me*. Pretending I was only a sailor, only another sailor, she had heard all about us *sailors*. I was *me* underneath those dress blues, she had held *me* in her hands, she *knew* me, I was not a goddamn sailor, I was

I was

Tears were streaming down his face. He tried to see through the tears because he knew he had to find a barbershop, had to get a shave before he met Janet again. He wiped his eyes with the backs of his hands, and he thought, Well, that was long ago, that was even before Beethoven died, what the hell, why bring it up now? What's it got to do with anything? She didn't know who I was that night in the parked car, she thought I was some goddamn sailor, and now it's twenty years later, however much later, and now I don't know who I am, so what the hell difference does it make?

He saw a clock in a restaurant window. The time was 10:50. What time had Janet's hour begun? 10:30, isn't that what she'd said? That meant she would be out at 11:20; he had a half hour to get a shave. If he could find a barbershop.

He walked to Lexington Avenue and then made a right turn, heading downtown. He saw the barbershop in the middle of the next block, and was approaching it when his vision blurred.

# 8

HE thought at first his eyes were still tearing, but when he rubbed at them he found they were dry. It was then that he really thought he was Edward Voegler, the escaped madman. He blinked his eyes shut, and then opened them again suddenly, as though anxious to prove the blurring was only a momentary thing. But as he looked down Lexington Avenue, he could see only a curious optical chaos, and he thought, I'm in the middle of some kind of paranoid fit; something dreadful is about to happen to me. He did not know what this fearful thing would be. Perhaps he would fall to the sidewalk frothing at the mouth like an epileptic, perhaps he would rush down the street, berserk, and break store windows or strangle women and children. He knew only that something was wrong with his vision, and that this curious lopsided askewness made it seem as though *everything* were wrong, outside his body and deep inside it as well. He kept looking through his own eyes as though he were someone trapped in a room with rain beating against the windows. But no, his vision wasn't actually *blurred*, no, not that way, not the way rain will dissolve a window, not the way watercolors will run into each other. Instead, it was as though there were a single sharp image, and then a ghost of that image, overlapping it, so that there were two images, side by side and partially covering each other, the ghostly image on the right dissolving somewhat, as if its edges were melting. At the same time, there seemed to be a curiously odd flicker somewhere off to his side, a pulsing flicker of light that he could not focus because it was somehow behind the field of his vision, far behind his right temple, but he could see it nonetheless, a flicker, flicker, flicker of light, colorless, on, off, on, off. A throbbing pain was beginning in his left temple, and he had the strangest feeling that the left-hand side of his face was going numb, and that his left hand was getting thick and clumsy, the way a hand feels when it has fallen asleep. He was frightened because he did not know what was going to happen next, and he suspected it would be something terrible. But at the same time, he knew this thing that was happening to him had happened to him often before, that he had learned to live with it, and that it would not really be so horrible after all. He found that he could walk quite well despite the strange double-exposed landscape ahead of him, that he could reach for the handle on the barbershop door and touch it with a great degree of accuracy, and open the door, and walk into the barbershop, all without falling. The flickering light was stronger now, like a candle guttering in a sharp wind, just beyond his field of vision, behind his right temple. The barber smiled at him, and there were two faces superimposed, one of the faces melting away at the edges, the barber's nose smearing into his mustache, the other image sharp and clear beneath the superimposed and slightly askew one.

"How much do you charge for a shave?" he heard himself asking the barber.

"Seventy-five cents," the barber said.

"All right," he answered, and he was about to sit in the chair when an inspiration came to him.

The pills, he thought.

The gelatin capsules in my watch pocket. That's what they're for. They're to clear the vision, they're to take away this stupid throbbing pain, they're to put out the flickering light.

He stopped before the chair, and the barber looked at him curiously, the sharp left image and the dissolving right image both smiling up at him expectantly.

"Yes?" the barber said.

"Could I have a glass of water?" Buddwing asked, and then felt a sharp pang of warning. You don't know what those gelatin capsules contain, he reasoned calmly. If you are Edward Voegler and you stole this suit from the director's office, those capsules could contain *anything*, Nembutal or Pentothol or even *arsenic!* Well, now, let's be reasonable, he thought. Nobody's going to put arsenic in gelatin capsules, now, are they? And besides, if this *is* the director's suit, and I must say it fits me pretty damn well for another man's suit, but if it *is* his suit, the odds are pretty good that the director of Central Icepick would be carrying *medication* in his watch pocket and not poison. Yes, but the medication could be a sedative—isn't that what they use in institutions today? Well, don't *you* know? If you're Edward Voegler, don't you know what they use in the nuthouse? What do they use on *you*, Mr. Voegler? On me, they use a straitjacket, and leg irons, and a club; that's what they use on me, all right, smart ass? They throw me in a little Oriental cell with bedbugs in the mattress and cockroaches crawling over the walls, and lice nesting in my hair, okay? They beat me regularly, and they give me mildewed bread and polluted water, and there is a sadistic God . . . *guard* . . . who tells me I am as sane as he is, but those are the breaks, Mac. That's what they do to me, okay?

"Here you are," the barber said, holding out the glass of water.

"Thank you," Buddwing answered. He reached into the watch pocket, caught one of the capsules between his index finger and his third finger, put it into his mouth without looking at it, said "Cheers" to the barber, and washed the capsule down with a swallow of water.

"I have a terrible migraine headache," he explained, and instantly felt this was the truth. He sat in the chair, and the barber put his striped cloth around Buddwing, and then eased the chair back. Buddwing put his feet up on the chair rest, and felt the barber's hands working lather into his face. He was suddenly overcome by a delicious feeling of luxury—the warm soap, the barber's gently kneading hands. He closed his eyes. He could see the flicker even in the darkness, a steady beating on-and-off light that took on a yellow color when his eyes were closed. But with his eyes closed, he was no longer troubled by the superimposed image, and he felt himself relaxing completely. Besides, he instinctively knew this was nothing but a migraine, and that he was probably subject to such attacks and carried the capsules in his watch pocket for just that reason. Instinct. That was the key. If he simply followed his inst

Key, he thought.

Why, I don't have any keys.

He recognized this with some surprise, and he tried to remember his awakening in Central Park early this morning—it seemed like eons ago—and going through his small store of worldly possessions. He catalogued them in his mind now, just as he had found them when he awakened, and wondered if he had noticed then that he had no keys. I awoke with a gold pen and pencil set, a black book with the number MO 6–2367 in it, a New York Central timetable, a package of cigarettes and a book of matches, two torn movie stubs, and two gelatin capsules. That's all I had. No wallet, no watch, no loose change. And no keys.

But he had not noticed the fact that he was carrying no keys until just a few seconds ago, and this seemed ominous to him now. *Everybody* carries keys, he thought. Wait a minute, not everybody. A man in prison does not carry keys. A man in a mental hosp

The throbbing at his left temple increased sharply.

He became terribly frightened of the capsule he had swallowed so casually. What mysterious powder was inside that gelatin, and now inside his body, working its way into his bloodstream? If he awoke without keys, *and* without a wallet, *and* without a watch, *and* without money of any kind, was it not entirely possible and in fact likely that he had come directly from an institution where patients do not normally carry any of these things? But wait, what was he doing with a pen and pencil? *Please excuse the crayon I used to write this, but I am not allowed to have anything sharp.* Well, the pen and pencil were in the suit, and if the suit was not his, then *they* were not his, and neither were the train schedule or the black book or the movie stubs or anything. I have no keys, and I have no possessions: a man without keys is a man without anything. No house, no car, no safe-deposit box, no ski rack, no responsibilities.

Nothing.

I have nothing, and I am nothing.

He felt the barber's razor scraping against his jaw. Slit my throat, he thought, why the hell don't you? I have nothing, I am nothing; I'm as good as dead, anyway.

The flicker behind his right temple had faded somewhat. He was sure now that the capsule he had taken contained a sedative, and that he would fall asleep in the barber's chair, and lose Janet forever. He wondered what time it was.

The clock.

It is ticking in the living room. She does not want to buy the clock; she says it is too expensive. The flea market in London, Portobello, the street band that marches through playing "Midnight in Moscow," is that only last summer? And she does not want to buy the clock, too expensive, we mustn't let a flea market fool us. Now the clock hangs on the living room wall, and the sound of it fills the apartment, with the other swishing sound running beneath it in counterpoint, I will drown.

He counts seconds.

He is frozen and cannot move. They should not have bought that clock, they should never have gone to Milan, because in Milan, too hot, in Milan is where they look at each other in suffocating heat, and see, and wonder where it all has gone. And to buy the clock in London, against her wishes, this is only an echo of Milan where recognition is swift and cruel and searing. The clock ticks so loudly in the silent apartment. He cannot move, it is too late, the clock is throwing minutes into the room, the clock is ticking off hours, the clock is ticking off a lifetime, and it is too late, and he will not move, too late.

He knows where. He knows instinctively.

Dan is on the telephone, no there is something wrong, the sequence is wrong, there is something he will not allow himself to see. Dan is talking in his coldly soothing voice. The telephone is trembling in his hand, but Dan keeps talking calmly and interminably, infuriatingly, as the telephone trembles. Arrangements, people, let me help, what do you *want*, Dan? can't you leave me alone? can't you hear that goddamn ticking clock? don't you know what it is saying? can't you stop? can't you stop? can't you please for God's sake stop?

"There we go," the barber said. Buddwing opened his eyes. The barber was taking off the apron, raising the chair. He looked at himself in the mirror.

"She gave me a haircut," he said.

"What?" the barber answered.

"Well, long ago."

"Who?"

"I don't know," Buddwing said. He smiled weakly. "How much is that?"

"Seventy-five. Like I told you."

Buddwing reached into his pocket and took out a dollar bill. He handed it to the barber and glanced at the clock. It was 11:15. "Keep the change," he said recklessly, and then walked out.

His head was still throbbing as he turned the corner onto Park Avenue. Janet was standing under the canopy, looking up the avenue impatiently when he came up behind her. He put his hands up quickly, circling her face and covering her eyes. She gave a startled little shriek, and then relaxed against his hands and said, "Let me see. Who can it be? Your hands are very gentle, you must be very nice, whoever you are. Let me see."

"Well?" he said.

"Mmm, I like your hands on my face. I'm never going to guess."

"You have to guess."

"Give me a clue," she said, moving back and a little closer to him. "Are you very handsome?"

"Yes, terribly."

He could feel her body against his, feel every slightest move she made.

"Are you very tall?"

"Very tall."

"And very young?"

"No, I'm very old."

She pulled his hands from her eyes with her own, and whirled into his arms. "You're young," she said seriously. She kissed him swiftly on the mouth and said, "We're going to get arrested." She moved away from him, taking his hand. They began strolling up the avenue. "Where would you like to go? It's only eleven-thirty, and we have the whole day."

"There's a slight problem," he said.

"There are no problems," she answered.

"Yes, there are." He reached into his pocket and took out the remaining dollar and the dime and the nickel. He held them on his palm and said, "This is all the money I have."

"There are still no problems," she said. She grinned and added, "I should have realized you were a gigolo. Do you want to walk a little?"

"No," he said.

"What do you want to do?"

"I want to make love to you."

"Oh?"

"Yes."

"I told my analyst about you," she said, ignoring his statement.

"What did he say?"

"Nothing. He just sat there. At least, I *think* he was sitting there. I can't see him because he's always behind me. For all I know, he knits or cleans his nails or goes to the window and sails paper airplanes."

"What did you expect him to say?"

"I expected him to say nothing, which is what he always says. Do you mean what did I *want* him to say?"

"Yes."

"I wanted him to say, 'Why, Sam Buddwing sounds like a wonderful person, God bless you, my child.' But I don't need him to tell me that." She squeezed his hand. "I live on Eighty-ninth Street, you know."

"No, I didn't know that."

"Yes. Where I got into the cab. Eighty-ninth and Broadway." She paused. "I tried to get an apartment on the East Side, near the school, but I couldn't." She paused again. "I live alone. A lot of the kids have roommates, but I don't. My parents live in the Bronx, on Kingsbridge Road. Do you know where that is?"

"Yes. I used to live in the Bronx."

"Oh, really? Where?"

"Well, it was a long time ago."

"Yes, but where?"

"I . . . I don't remember."

"That's a fine example of mental block, isn't it?"

"I suppose so."

"If your parents are anything like mine, I'm not surprised. I sometimes wish I could just block them out of existence. Boy, did they raise a stink when I moved. But my brother had left the year before, you know, so I insisted on equal rights. Women are entitled to equal rights, don't you think?"

"Absolutely."

"Sure. Did you want to come home with me?"

"If that's where you want to go."

"I don't know where I want to go, Sam, or what I want to do," she said seriously.

"Then let me decide."

"I don't like other people making decisions for me."

"Then let's walk."

"I don't want to walk."

"Well . . . what *do* you want, Janet?"

"Oh, I don't know," she said petulantly. "Let's walk."

They walked in silence for several blocks.

"My brother's a writer, did I tell you that?" she asked at last.

"Yes."

"The Pied Piper."

"What do you mean?"

"With his rats."

Again, she was silent. Buddwing, walking beside her, suddenly knew how he could find out who he was. The idea was so simple that he wondered why he had not thought of it before this. He would simply go to De Pinna's, where the obviously hand-tailored suit he was wearing had come from, and ask them who had ordered the suit. He was sure they would have a record of some sort, and perhaps the tailor might even recognize him. There was, of course, the danger that they would tell him the suit had been made for the director of Central Islip, but even that would not be so bad because then he would at least know for sure he was Edward Voegler.

"Mike hasn't decided which school he wants to belong to yet," Janet said. She saw the puzzled look on Buddwing's face, and said, "My brother. The schools of writing."

"Are there different schools?" he asked.

"Oh, yes, dozens," she said knowingly.

"Why doesn't he try combining them all?"

"No, no, Mike has to find his own *chemin*. That's what he calls it. He keeps pecking away at his typewriter and telling me, 'Jan, I've got to find my own *chemin*.' And I'm the one seeing an analyst." She shrugged. "He'll never make it, you know. I can tell."

"How can you tell?"

"Just by looking at him. I go into that apartment, and he's living there like a pig, you know, an absolute pig. His underwear is all over the floor, and there are dirty dishes in the sink, and cigarette butts everywhere you look, and he sits at that typewriter like some kind of beat mystic or something, and he barely looks up when I come in."

"Why do you go?"

"Well, I love him, you know," Janet said simply. She shook her head. "But he isn't going to make it, and I know he's not, and I wish I had the courage to tell him. I have this horrible vision of one day going there, ten years from now, and knocking on the door. The whole area will have been reclaimed by Lincoln Center, except for the building Mike lives in. I'll go into his apartment, and the rats will have taken over. Mike'll be sitting at that crumby table he uses for a desk, in a typing position, but all his bones will have been picked clean by the rats." She shuddered and clutched his arm and said, "Oh, that's *horrible*, isn't it?"

"Yes."

"Maybe I *wish* he'd get eaten by the rats, I don't know. Otherwise, why did I think of it?" She shook her head again. "Listen," she said.

"I'm listening."

"You won't, will you?"

"Won't what? Get eaten by rats?"

"No, I'm serious. I mean hurt me. You won't, will you?"

"No. I won't."

"Because I'm a pretty mixed-up girl, you know, and I don't need anything like that right now. I've got enough troubles, with my brother and everything. I mean, this may be the romance of the century and all that, but I'll tell you the truth, I'd rather pass it by if it's going to make me unhappy. I'm unhappy enough as it is."

"I won't make you unhappy, Janet."

"I just have the feeling I shouldn't start up with you, that's all."

"What do you want me to say, Janet?" The throbbing pain in his left temple, which he had thought was easing, now seemed stronger.

"I think I want you to say goodbye."

"All right, then."

He made a motion as though to move away from her, but she caught at his arm and drew him back sharply. "No!" she said. "I want you to tell me everything'll be all right."

"I love you," he said.

"That's not what I want to hear."

"Janet, I don't know what you—"

"It's not just going to bed with me, is it?"

"Janet, I told you I love you!"

"I *know* you love me. But . . . can't you say the rest?"

"What rest? What is it you want to hear?"

"That it's not just going to bed."

"It isn't," he said wearily.

"Then tell me."

"It isn't just going to bed."

"Tell me you'll take care of me."

"I'll take care of you, Janet."

"Will you protect me, and love me?"

"I'll protect you, yes, and—"

"And keep me warm?"

"Yes, Janet, I'll keep you—"

"And make me happy. Will you make me happy, Sam?"

"I'll make you happy. I'll love you. I'll always love you."

"All those things? Will you do all those things?"

"I will, I will."

"Say it."

"I will love you and . . . and protect you and . . ."

"Keep me warm . . ."

"Yes, and keep you warm, yes, and make you happy, I will do all those things, Janet, I promise."

She looked at him with sadness in her eyes, and then she gave a brief discouraged nod and said, "You'll screw me, Sam, that's what you'll do. That's *all* you'll do." She sighed heavily. "Will it upset you if I pay for a cab?" she asked.

His headache was gone by the time they reached her apartment. That was all right, but everything else was all wrong. She had been inordinately silent in the cab on the way crosstown and uptown, staring through the window on her side while the pulse in his temple pounded and throbbed. She had not touched him, had not even held his hand, had simply sat far over on her side of the taxi staring through the window. He had felt the headache recede and then emerge more strongly again, recede further, emerge, recede and then fade and then vanish completely, to be replaced by an anger that gathered force as her silence continued. He had promised not to hurt her, but now he wanted only to hurt her. He had promised to protect her, but now he wanted to destroy her. Her silence infuriated him. As the cab wound through the park and then emerged on Central Park West and continued west to Broadway, coming closer and closer to her apartment, he found himself building furious fantasy after fantasy, of beating her, of forcing her to her knees, of striking her repeatedly across the face. Her silence excluded him, and angered him; her silence shut him out of a world he was desperately trying to re-enter. When the cab stopped in front of her building, she paid the driver without a word, raising a disdainful eyebrow, he thought, and then stepped out of the cab and went directly into the building without waiting for him and without looking behind her to see if he was following. The hell with you, he thought, and he almost turned and began walking in the opposite direction, but something pulled him to her, the knowledge that she was a thin thread connecting him with the life of this city, perhaps the *only* thread. He did not want that thread to break. He followed her into the building.

Her apartment was on the third floor. She unlocked the door and waited for him to enter the kitchen, and then locked the door behind him and slipped the chain on it. She turned toward him and smiled briefly, a very curious grudging smile, and then put her arms around him and kissed him. She kissed him with surprising ferocity, moving her lips and grinding her teeth against his, and thrusting her hips forward. He could feel the hard bulging mound of her beneath the straight black skirt, pushing against him fiercely, and then she ripped her mouth from his and looked directly into his face with an anger in her eyes, a fury he had not seen there before, and she said, "Go on in. I'll be with you in a minute."

She indicated the other room with a toss of her head, and then turned and went into what he assumed was the bathroom. He suspected she was going to put on a diaphragm and the knowledge distressed him because this was not at all what he had expected of her, not the experienced insertion of rubber and cream, not this cold-blooded intensity that seemed to be on her face, that seemed to govern the movement of her body, frightening him. He walked into the other room. The bed was still unmade, the sheets rumpled from the night before. The room seemed to be a combination bedroom-living room, with bookshelves on one wall, and a record player, and a stack of 45 rpm's on the floor beside the player. A framed photograph of a boy in an open-throated white shirt was resting on a shelf beside the bed. He did not know why, but he assumed it was her brother. He sat on the edge of the bed and took off his shoes, and then lay back against her single pillow, which was stained with lipstick.

He hoped she would not come to him naked. He thought that if she came to him naked, he would leave the room immediately. He could hear water running in the bathroom, and then silence. She is taking off her clothes, he thought, and was suddenly saddened by what seemed to be an exaggerated theatricality, the setting of a stage, the costuming of performers; it had not been this way with Doris long ago. He closed his eyes and waited. He heard the bathroom door opening, and then whispering shut behind her, she closed it so gently, and then heard the padding of her bare feet across the kitchen linoleum. She stopped beside the bed. He opened his eyes.

She had loosened the pony tail, and her hair fell softly about her face now, intensifying the green of her eyes and the paleness of her cheeks. She had taken off the black skirt and the tights and the French-heeled pumps, but she was still wearing her sweater and he knew from the soft yielding look of its front that she had first removed her bra and then put the sweater on again. Below the sweater, she had put on white cotton panties, flat over her stomach, cut high against her full thighs. Her narrow hips were tilted forward in a phony model's stance that magnified the thrust of her crotch, made it seem pulsing with an eager forward inner rush of its own. He reached out his hand, palm upward, and seized her between the legs.

"You're still dressed," she whispered.

She fell onto the bed beside him, his hand still clutched relentlessly between her legs. She undressed him swiftly, contorting her body the way she had contorted her face earlier, performing innumerable physical tasks simultaneously, her hands busily working as she loosened and unfastened and stroked and unbuttoned and teased, her lips covering his mouth and then sliding over his throat when she unbuttoned his shirt, her thighs rotating against his restless hand between them, her back arching, and then twisting, rolling onto her side, unloosening his belt, and thrusting her hand deep, rooting blindly, grasping him harshly and fiercely and possessively, pulling him rigidly free, and giving a faint rushing moan, her legs moving again in a rocking piston motion, one leg jutting straight suddenly to hook his trousers with the heel of her foot, the other leg still bent, the knee coming up against his chest, polished white, and then throwing his shirt wide and bending over almost double to kiss his belly and his groin, her mouth opening over him in a sidelong wet and sliding motion, and kicking his trousers free, and lifting her own sweater to reveal the small perfect breasts and puckered schoolgirl nipples, Doris, he thought, Doris. She rolled her body onto his and slid her hands flat beneath the elastic of her panties, pushing them downward swiftly over her flat stomach and deep navel, freeing her crotch from his hand, moving rapidly out of the panties, knee bending, and then rolling onto him again. She hesitated over him for a moment, spread-legged, teasing him, poised, and then descended in a kind of harsh and vicious glee, covering him, pulling him into her. "Oh, love," she said. "Oh, love."

He came at once, and in the moment of his coming he hated her vehemently and he almost wept at his own anger. She continued to grind against him mercilessly, repeating the words "Oh, love," lovelessly. He did not help her. He was sure she was unsatisfied when finally she stopped; he didn't give a damn.

The room went still.

He lay exhausted and spent and angry on the twisted sheet.

He looked at her silently. Her eyes were closed, she was still breathing harshly, her hands clung to her own breasts, holding them tight.

In a little while, he rose and began dressing. She did not say anything. She watched him quietly, lying on the bed in angular tense softness, the white curve of her hip in negative silhouette against the dark wall behind her, her head propped on one hand, her elbow bent. When he was fully clothed, he walked to the kitchen door. He took the chain from its slot, and unlocked the door.

He looked back at her briefly where she lay on the bed still and silent with her head on her hand and her elbow bent, gazing at him with anger and fear in her green eyes.

"Goodbye," he said, clean and sharp.

"I knew," she answered, and he went into the hall and closed the door.

# 9

HE went down the steps quickly, propelled by an anger bordering on revulsion, wanting to get away from the girl as quickly as possible, frightened because he had nowhere to go, furious because he had lost himself again on the tangled sheets of her bed. He did not know what he had expected from this girl, but he knew it was not a coldly mechanical lay in a room with her brother's picture near the bed. He had felt something fiercely alien emanating from this girl, and it had been contagious so that whatever they did together had become a war—what the hell had they been trying to prove? He recognized all at once that at least part of his anger now was founded in disappointment. He had not expected a practiced woman; he had wanted a young girl shining with truth, rare and awestruck beneath his hands, succumbing to his supplications, the way Doris had been long ago. This girl, this Janet in the clothes and in the body of his Doris, had promised innocence and delivered experience. But more than that, she had brought to him something he did not deserve. She had come to him with a hatred . . . no, not a hatred, a seeking, yes, a seeking as blind as his own, knowing he would not satisfy her needs, and blaming him for it beforehand. Each grinding movement of her body had become a whiplash, each uttered "Oh, love!" had become an urgent plea, denied in advance each time it was spoken. It could have been otherwise, and this was why he hated her now. And yet, with a calm reasoning that was yet more infuriating, he knew it could never have been otherwise and that he had been a fool to even hope for anything but what had happened.

Hating her, he walked up Broadway angrily, not knowing where he was going, and not caring, striking three matches before he finally lighted his cigarette, and then discarding the cigarette at once as he went into the subway kiosk on 96th Street. He saw no one. He was in a cold and isolated shell of anger and self-pity, and everyone who passed him was an obstruction, something to be overcome, something to push aside, something that stood between him and where he wanted to be.

He did not know what he hoped to find in Central Park, or even whether he could again locate the bench upon which he had awakened earlier that day. He knew only that he thought of that bench as his birthplace, and that his encounter with Janet had shaken something deep inside him, so that now not only his identity was in doubt, but his very existence as well. He wanted to see that bench again. He wanted to reassure himself that he had indeed awakened there this morning, that there was indeed a measure of reality to his life.

To his surprise, he found the bench without any difficulty, but it seemed a little more weatherbeaten than he had remembered it, scarred by time, decrepit. An old man and an old woman were sitting on the bench in bright sunshine. She was reading a newspaper, and he was sitting with his eyes closed, his head tilted back, his gnarled hands resting on the head of his cane. Buddwing looked at the bench and at the old couple, feeling oddly dispossessed, wanting to go to them, wanting to say, "I beg your pardon, but this is *my* bench, this is where I was born, don't you see?" He walked past the bench rapidly. The depression was still

with him, but now it threatened a vaster gloom. It seemed to him
as he passed the bench that he was about to lose even the things
that were comparatively fresh and new, that six o'clock this morning was about to recede into an irredeemable past as obscure as
the deeper past from which he had come. He sensed that Gloria
and Schwartz, were he to see them again, would now be as old
as the man and woman who sat on his bench in brilliant sunshine;
Eric would be a teen-ager; L.J. and the others would have advanced to middle age; even Janet, whom he had left not twenty
minutes ago, would now be a fat neurotic matron. He could not
imagine having moved so far and so fast in the space of six hours,
and yet he knew that the present was being threatened by the
recent past as well as a past that was unfathomable.

It was high noon in New York. Fifth Avenue was alive with
tourists and shoppers. Everything had changed; this was not the
landscape he had known earlier this morning. Harsh out-of-state
accents jangled on his ears and his nerves, people jostled him, the
sounds of traffic boomed interminably, the sun hung suspended
in the sky directly overhead, a giant unblinking eye. He shoved
past a group of excited children coming out of F.A.O.'s, and then
quickened his pace, anxious to get anywhere out of this crowd.
Snatches of conversation touched his ears, fading into his auditory
range as he walked, fading out again as the talkers passed beyond
him and out of his life, throngs of strangers he had known briefly
and not at all well.

He walked with his head level as the stream of people moved
against him, parting before him, the out-of-town women with
their spring hats, the New York girls with their perky rapid walk
and their darting shopping eyes, the strolling Park Avenue gentlemen with their homburgs and their gloves, the dancers heading
for 57th Street, with bowling-ball backsides and muscular calves
and a curious identifying duck waddle, the old ladies and the
young actresses in mink, the homosexuals strolling with discreet
fingertip touches, the idle traffic cop watching the snarl of automobiles and buses and taxicabs, the delivery boys carrying cardboard cartons of coffee, the geographically incongruous whore,

the young Boy Scout staring up at the buildings, all of whom he knew briefly in the few seconds it took for their faces and their voices to come toward him, and abreast of him, and then disappear behind him.

You either own this city or you don't, he thought. There were days, golden days in a bottomless past, when he had walked this magnificent street and felt as though the city were his, he was the sole property owner and this crowd of people rushing past was only leasing the sidewalks from him, the buildings, the very air. On those days, he had wanted to embrace the entire Parisian hulk of St. Patrick's Cathedral, wanted to kiss Cartier's glittering windows, run his hand over the sleek thighs of the Tishman Building. You possess this city completely or you don't possess it at all, he thought. You either know who you are, or you don't. And when you don't, they all rush past you like a great ant army intent on their own ant business, and you catch the vibrations of their antennae, but the signals mean nothing. He suddenly realized that De Pinna's was across the street—had he been heading there all along? The end of doubt, the end of anonymity, was across the street. He would inquire about his hand-tailored suit, and learn his name, and come out again knowing who he was, owning the city.

The light turned from red to green, the DONT WALK changed to WALK. He started across the street. When he was a boy, there were only lights without written directions, and even then the lights were ignored, and you ran across the street whenever there was a break in the traffic. He could remember walking up 120th Street to First Avenue, and then racing across the wide cobblestones and gaining the opposite curb. The coal station with its big green wooden doors would be on his left, and trolley cars would be running along the avenue, the sound of their gongs sharp and strident, sparks flying from the overhead cable. He could remember especially the dead cold winter days of Harlem and all the anticipatory joy that came with the first brisk warning flutter of autumn. He could still recall the sudden appearance each fall of jellied apples and charlotte russes. He could remember Halloween, the chalked sticks and the stockings full of flour, chasing schoolgirls down the narrow gray canyon of a city street. 120th Street between First and Second Avenue, *that* was the scene of his infancy and his childhood, not Central Park. He could remember this all, his knickers falling down over his knees to his ankles, and all of it was somehow intertwined with the image of the tall man with white hair and thick eyeglasses who was his grandfather. There was always steam coming from the pressing machine in the back room, Uncle Freddie grinning at him—"Hey there, how are you?"—and pulling down the padded top of the machine, and then depressing the stick lever, the steam hissing up from beneath the pads and hiding Uncle Freddie in a thick white cloud. He could remember election night in New York when he was a boy, the enormous bonfires in the street, the older boys running into the gutter to feed wood to the flames, the stickers for Alf Landon, which his father had got from the Republican Club and which he and Eric had stuck to parked automobiles all up and down First Avenue. He had worn the maroon plaid mackinaw his grandfather had made for him, and a fleece-lined aviator's helmet with goggles. Eric, of course, had been the first kid on the block to wear the aviator's helmet and goggles, and then every kid in the world had them. They were very good for election night when the bonfires threw smoke and sparks into the air.

Quiet, how quiet it was on a winter's afternoon, walking from the school to the tailorshop near 117th Street—his mother worked in those days, she had a job somewhere in a mailing room, his Aunt Martha would give him lunch—feeling the cold on his cheeks, his cheeks a flaming red, the aviator's helmet strapped under his chin, and the celluloid goggles pulled down over his eyes, one hand in the pocket of his maroon mackinaw, the other gloved and holding his strapped books, the cobblestones on First Avenue shining and gray. The tailorshop always seemed to beckon intimately. Grandpa would put the light on in the window early in the afternoon, and as the gray of Harlem's winter turned to dusk, the storefront would glow with warmth. There was a little bell over the door of the shop, and Buddwing would reach up to grab the handle, and the bell would tinkle, and Grandpa would look up from behind the counter, and Grandma would turn from the sewing machine, which was near the front window, and Grandpa would always say, without ever changing a syllable, "Come in, you must be frozen. Annie, make him some nice hot chocolate." And then he would follow Grandma behind the counter, Grandpa would ruffle his hair as he went past and into the back room where Uncle Freddie would be running the pressing machine—"Hey there, how are you?"—and he would stand with Grandma near the hot plate while she made him his chocolate. There was a telephone on a shelf over the long cutting table opposite the pressing machine. Grandpa always had orders for Salvation Army uniforms, and the white S's and A's he would later sew onto the collars were always scattered on the cutting table. There was so much warmth in that shop. He would stand near the hot plate while the steam of the pressing machine filled the air, and then he would take his chocolate and go behind the counter with Grandpa and tell him what had happened in school that day. Grandpa would always listen very intently, his head cocked to one side. His hair was white even then. Buddwing supposed his hair had been white for as long as he had known him. And Grandpa would cluck his tongue, or say this or that about one or another of the teachers, or nod his head in approval, or ask Buddwing to repeat all the exciting details of a new project, all the while taking care of customers who came into the shop, and gently warning Buddwing not to spill chocolate on any of the clothes.

He knew suddenly why he had taken the job in Di Palermo's grocery store the summer he was sixteen.

He had taken the job because he owed his mother twenty-five dollars.

Well, that, he thought.

Well, I remember the shop. And I knew who I was *then*, by God; I knew it every morning and every afternoon, winter and summer, too, the summer I showed Eric how to make a ring from a peach pit, rubbing it on the sidewalk until it was thin and flat, and then scooping out the center with a knife until it fit his finger. Grandpa taught me how to do that; he learned it in the old country. He was a very nice guy, was fifty dollars enough?

Well.

He walked into the men's department of the store and thought, Well, I was only a kid, I was only sixteen, it was enough, and immediately saw the suits and coats and jackets and trousers hanging in orderly rows on the racks and remembered his grandfather's rack, with the long hooked pole, and his grandfather stretching up to take down a garment for a customer. He felt intuitively that he was very close to gaining an important piece of knowledge about himself, and he looked around immediately for someone to help him. There were several salesmen on the floor, and one customer, an old gentleman in a tattersall topcoat who kept poking his cane at the sports jackets hanging on one of the racks, as though testing their durability. Buddwing walked to the nearest salesman, a young man in his late twenties who was sporting a brand-new mustache, which he kept twisting in an attempt to train it up and away from his lip. The salesman dropped his hand and said, "Yes, sir, can I help you?"

Buddwing hesitated. He felt again the same queasy uncertainty he had known in the lobby of Gloria's building, the same dread he had experienced before entering Di Palermo's grocery store. He wanted desperately to know who he was, but something equally desperate pulled him back from the imminent knowledge; something warned him to tread with care lest he destroy himself.

"Yes, sir?" the salesman said.

Buddwing wet his lips. "This . . . suit," he said.

"Yes, sir?"

"Was it hand-tailored?"

The salesman looked at him curiously for a moment, and then said, "May I see the label, please, sir?"

Buddwing unbuttoned his jacket. The salesman studied the label for what seemed like an inordinately long time. You are going to tell me in a minute, Buddwing thought. You are going to say, Yes, sir, this is one of our hand-tailored suits, and then you are going to consult your records and tell me the suit was made for that director at Central Islip. You are going to tell me I am Edward Voegler. Then I will know. Then it will be over.

"No, sir," the salesman said. "This is one of our ready-to-wear garments, made for us expressly in England last year. It was part of our line last fall."

"Last fall, I see," Buddwing said.

"Yes, sir."

"Thank you."

"Not at all, sir. Was there anything I could show you, something in a—"

"No," Buddwing said. "Thank you." He turned and walked out of the men's department. He felt nothing at all. Nothing. Neither disappointment nor glee, happiness nor gloom.

Nothing but an overwhelming need to urinate.

He walked toward 49th Street rapidly, and then turned right off Fifth, going past the skating rink, and crossing the street, and continuing on past the RCA showrooms with idiot high school kids making faces on the see-yourself television, and then to the Rockefeller Center Garage where he made an abrupt left as though he had done this many, many times before. He went into the westbound waiting room, and past the newsstand—the afternoon dailies had picked up the story of the escaped madman and headlined it—and then past the cashiers' booths, and the telephones, and the elevator leading to the ladies' room upstairs, and the pay lockers, and then took the steps down to the men's room. A man was washing his hands at the sink as Buddwing entered the room, and another man was at one of the urinals. Buddwing unzipped his fly and was reaching into his pants when the man standing beside him at the urinals turned and said, "This is a stickup, mister."

The first thing that popped into his mind was the joke about the midget in the men's room. Then, reacting instantly to the danger, he swung out at the man only to discover that the man had swung first and indeed had struck him on the point of the jaw. He found himself staggering back from the urinal and almost colliding with the sink, and then he remembered the other man who had been washing his hands, because this other man suddenly struck him on the back of the neck with what seemed like a sledge hammer. Okay, he thought, you want to get rough, huh? and the first man slugged him in the face again, and he almost went unconscious.

To him, there was something hilariously comic about the fact that his fly was open while these two assassins continued to batter him back and forth between them. He tried to strike out at each in turn, but whenever he did, it seemed the one behind him got in a blow at just the precise moment he himself decided to strike, so that none of his fierce attacks ever got further than the planning stage. He thought it was funny that General Sarnoff up there in the RCA Building had not the faintest notion that someone was getting his brains beaten out in the men's room of the Rockefeller Center Garage, and he thought it especially funny that these two guys were exerting so much energy to knock him unconscious when he wasn't even carrying a wallet, didn't in fact have more than the single dollar that was all that remained from Gloria's foundation grant. He also thought it would be comical when the police found him dead and bleeding on the floor of the men's room with his fly open but without any other clue to his identity. While all these screamingly funny thoughts bounced through his head, his assassins continued to bounce him off the tiled walls of the room and the metal wall of one of the booths and the porcelain wall of one of the urinals, and he was amazed by his own resiliency, and amazed too that he was not out cold by this time. He was vaguely aware that his nose was bleeding, and he thought, All right, already, cut it out, but the two men showed no indication of cutting out anything but his heart perhaps, seemed determined in fact to slug him into oblivion if it took all day, which it seemed to be taking. He was about to throw in the towel, about to tell the referee there was one man too many in this ring, the fight was fixed, when all at once he heard a voice saying, "Hey, whut the hell're you guys doin'?"

A fist caught him on the side of his head, forcing him to turn toward the doorway, and he saw a short squat man in a sailor's uniform entering the room with his fists clenched. The image of the sailor blurred in that instant because another fist hit him on the other side of his head, and he fell backward and into the nearest urinal. He got up quickly, his trouser leg wet with a pine-smelling antiseptic, just in time to see the squat sailor hit one of the men on the bridge of the nose. Now we're talking, he thought, and he sailed back into the fray to collide with the fist of the man who had been standing near the sink, and found himself falling right back into the urinal again. He got up with the seat of his trousers wet this time, and smelling even more of the aromatic antiseptic, and he was about to lend the sailor a helping hand when he saw that the sailor was in no need of a helping hand. The two men were lying unconscious on the tiled floor of the room, and the sailor was clutching at Buddwing's jacket sleeve and whispering urgently, "Man, le's get the hell out of here 'fore the shore patrol arrives."

He followed the sailor up the steps, trying to cup his hand under his bleeding nose so that he would not stain the steps, reaching for a handkerchief in his back pocket, finding none, and then accepting the sailor's handkerchief gratefully as they came past the pay lockers and into the waiting room. They walked directly into the street, the sailor setting the pace, Buddwing following. When they reached Sixth Avenue, the sailor stopped for breath.

"How's that nose?" he asked.

"Fine," Buddwing said, dabbing at it. He looked at the sailor now and saw him clearly for the first time. He was a boy of about twenty, with a square face and jaw, a spate of freckles across the bridge of his nose. His eyes were blue, and he spoke with a thick Southern accent. He had a huge barrel chest and short legs. He wore his hat on the back of his head, and his hair was straight and blond. The rating on his sleeve told Buddwing that he was a second-class signalman.

"Anything I cain't stand," the sailor said, "it's a unfair fight. Whut was they after?"

"My money, I guess," Buddwing said. He pulled the handkerchief away from his nose and looked at it. The bleeding seemed to have stopped.

"Man, in this town you cain't even take a leak 'thout somebuddy jumpin' on you. You're right lucky I happened along when I done."

"I know," Buddwing said. "Thank you." He dabbed at his nose with the handkerchief again, and then handed it back to the sailor.

"Might's well keep it," the sailor said. "I stole it from the clothesline, anyways. Your fly's open."

"What?"

"I said your fly's open," the sailor said again, and then immediately added, "Mah name's Jesse Salem, whut's yours?"

Buddwing first zipped up his fly, and then took Jesse's extended hand. He had a firm grip, and huge hands with large knuckles, the hands of an habitual street fighter.

"I'm Sam Buddwing."

"Pleased t'know you," Jesse said. "You know wheah we can find a head that ain't got no holdup artists in it? I *still* got to go, man."

"Me, too," Buddwing said, smiling. "Up this way." They turned left on Sixth Avenue and began walking downtown.

"What ship you off?" Buddwing asked.

"The *Meredith*," Jesse said. "Tha's a tin can."

"I know."

"How come?"

"Man's name. Got to be a tin can."

"You an ole navy man?"

"Yes," Buddwing said immediately, and without doubt.

"What kinda ship was you on?"

"Same as you. A tin can. The *Fancher*."

"I think we ran into her when we was up in Japan," Jesse said.

"That's just where I *left* her," Buddwing answered, grinning.

"No kiddin'? In Japan? When was that?"

"After the war." He paused. "World War II. I left her in
Sasebo and came back on a transport for discharge."

"Where'd you put in? San Diego?"

"No, Treasure Island. Off San Francisco."

"Yeah, nice town, San Francisco. Where's this head, man? I
got to go something fierce."

He took Jesse into the men's room of the Automat between
45th and 46th. When they came upstairs again, he asked, "Have
you had lunch yet?"

"No, but I ain't partial to the idea of puttin' nickels in slots.
Tries my patience."

"There's a hot-dog joint down the street," Buddwing said. "Let
me buy you lunch."

"You don't hafta," Jesse said.

"I want to."

"Well, okay, so long as you understan' you ain't beholden."

"I understand that," Buddwing said.

"Well, good, then."

They continued walking downtown again. The day was still
mild and clear. Buddwing walked with a long quick stride, and
Jesse struggled to keep up with him on his shorter legs.

"How'd you like Japan?" Buddwing asked.

"Loved it," Jesse said.

"What towns did you hit?"

"Well, Sasebo, same as you. And Nagasaki, and Yokohama, and
Tokyo."

"Ever get up north?"

"Ain't Tokyo up north?"

"I meant up near Russia. Hakodate, up around there."

"No. Where's that? On Hokkaido?"

"Yes."

"No, we never got up that way. We sure had some good times
in Japan, though."

"We sure did," Buddwing said.

They found the hot-dog joint on the corner of 44th and Sixth,
and they stood at the sidewalk counter and each had a hot dog

with sauerkraut and mustard, and a cup of coffee. The total came to seventy cents.

Buddwing took the last dollar bill from his pocket. He put it on the counter, and the counterman rang up the sale and then returned a quarter and a nickel to him. Buddwing looked at the unequally divided thirty cents and wondered whether the counterman expected him to tip a nickel, a quarter, or nothing. He would have wanted to leave a ten-cent tip, but the division of the change now made that impossible. He did not want to seem cheap by leaving a five-cent tip on a seventy-cent order, or cheaper by leaving nothing at all. At the same time, this money was all that divided him from complete bankruptcy, and he did not feel he could extravagantly leave a quarter. He was about to ask the counterman to break the quarter for him, when Jesse nudged him in the ribs and said, "Take a look at that, mate."

Buddwing turned and followed Jesse's stare. The thing he was being asked to take a look at was a black Volkswagen that had managed to stall itself directly in the middle of the side street approaching the Sixth Avenue corner. As small as the car was, it had effectively blocked traffic on either side of it, and a medley of angry truck and automobile horns was honking all the way up to Broadway. A Chinese girl sat in patient inscrutability at the wheel of the car, trying the starter at judicious intervals while the horns frantically honked behind her, failing to change the situation an iota. A younger Chinese girl sat beside the one at the wheel, and she craned her head over her shoulder periodically to look behind her at the honking vehicles. As Buddwing watched, the younger girl stuck out her tongue at the honkers and then turned back to her companion and said something to her that caused her to laugh and then glanced up and saw Buddwing watching her from the sidewalk, and impulsively stuck her tongue out at him, too. Buddwing smiled.

"She's giving you the old come-on," Jesse said. "Why don't we go see if we can't just help those sweet little things?"

He moved away from the counter swiftly, walked directly to

the driver's side of the car and, leaning on the door, bent down to the open window and said, "Can I be of some assistance, ma'am?"

The Chinese girl, with her foot on the clutch and her hand on the ignition key, turned to look at Jesse in brief scorn, and then said, "Get lost, sailor."

"I think maybe you've gone and flooded her," Jesse said, grinning. He turned to Buddwing, who had come from the curb to stand in the middle of the street, and said, "Don't you think she's got her flooded, Sam?"

"I think she has," Buddwing said, and he bent down to look into the car, but Jesse was blocking the window and all he could see was the younger girl's face, and her solemn brown eyes studying him.

"I'm a machinist's mate," Jesse said, lying conversationally. "I can help you get it started, if you want me to."

The driver studied him again, speculatively, and then said again, "Get lost."

"Let him try, Sally," the younger girl said. She kept looking at Buddwing as she said this, her face unsmiling, the slanted brown eyes watching him as she delivered the words to Sally. Sally turned to her and said something in Chinese, and the younger girl answered in Chinese and then gestured with one slender hand thrown back over her shoulder toward the trucks and cars that were creating a powerful din behind them. Sally shrugged and said, "Okay, okay," and then turned to Jesse and smiled, and said, "All right, mate, go ahead."

Jesse opened the car door, grinning, and Sally slid over on the seat toward the other girl, making room for him. He gestured with a palm-upward hand at the vehicles lined up behind the Volkswagen and shouted, "Keep your shirt on!" and then slid onto the seat. Buddwing stood in the gutter, watching the three cramped onto the tiny front seat of the car. Jesse studied the instrument panel with the scrutiny of a physician doing a yearly checkup, and then ducked his head below the wheel (Buddwing became suddenly aware that Sally was wearing a dress cut in Oriental style, slit very high on each side) and studied the brake pedal and the accelerator and the clutch and even the knob that turned on the heater, taking what seemed like an inordinately long time with his head bent and with Sally beside him, her leg and thigh showing in the slit of her skirt. Then he raised his head and said, "Yep," mysteriously, and tried the ignition key. The car did not start.

"I'll have to look under the hood," Jesse said, and he opened the car door and stepped into the street again. A crowd had begun to gather now, curious passersby stopping to peer at the small car with the two Chinese girls, and at the sailor who again shushed the honking trucks and cars with an angry wave of his arm. Most of the pedestrians crowded the sidewalk, but some were bold enough to come into the street, forming a loose circle around the car, watching Jesse as he went to the front of the car, hearing Sally as she leaned out the window and said, "No, the engine is in the back." The beat patrolman stopped on the corner and watched the crowd and listened to the honking horns and some choice bits of truck-driver Anglo-Saxon, but did nothing to relieve either the congestion or the mixture of gaiety and anger that seemed to converge on the corner. The gaiety was undeniable, a holiday mood seeming to settle on the crowd of people who swarmed about the small car as Jesse inspected the engine. The spectators all wore those oddly self-conscious smiles that seem to say, "Aren't these people crazy? Isn't this crazy?" but are at the same time slightly embarrassed because the wearers of the smiles are enjoying the insanity and are indeed a part of it. The anger was undeniable as well, a fury in the sound of the horns echoing up and down the street, truck drivers who had delivery schedules to meet, cab drivers who wanted to drop off their fares and pick up new ones, gentlemen in Cadillacs and Continentals who were in a hurry to get crosstown to Sutton Place, all of them leaning on their horns in a frenzied cacophony as Jesse studied the compact engine and then came to the front of the car again.

The crowd, the traffic, the gaiety, even the anger reminded Buddwing suddenly of Japan, where the slightest unexpected incident would draw a throng of Japanese, all laughing behind their white face masks, but laughing with the anger of a defeated people who were now suffering foreigners on their soil. He looked again at the Oriental girl who sat on the far side of the car, and he was surprised to see that she was still studying him curiously, as if she were not really a part of this shameful spectacle, and as if she suspected Buddwing was not a part of it, either. Jesse climbed back into the car, and Sally slid over on the seat again, her leg and thigh winking, and once again he tried the ignition, and the car started.

"There you are," he said, and at the same moment a cheer went up from the crowd in the street and on the sidewalk, and as though stilled by a sudden and mysterious command, all the horns behind the Volkswagen went silent.

"Where are you girls all going?" Jesse said, sitting behind the wheel and showing no indication of moving.

"Downtown," Sally said. "Home."

"To Chinatown?" Buddwing asked, bending down to look into the car.

"Yes," Sally answered.

"Why, that's just where we were going," Jesse said. "Ain't it, Sam?"

"Yes, sir," Buddwing answered, and he smiled at the other girl to let her know this was not where they had really been going, but that if it was all right with her, they would make it their destination now. The girl understood the smile completely, it seemed, because she turned to her friend—Buddwing assumed Sally was her friend; she could just as easily have been her sister or her cousin or her aunt—and said, "Why don't we give them a lift, Sally? They *did* start the car for us."

"All right," Sally said quickly. "But please get in before they start blowing their horns again."

The trigger-happy motorists behind the car, as if submitting to Sally's prophecy, began leaning on their horns in renewed fury. Jesse, ignoring them, got out of the car and said, "Whyn't you two get in the back, and Sally and me'll sit up front? That okay with you, Sally?"

"All right, all right," Sally said, sliding over onto the driver's seat again, and Jesse said, "I'll drive if you want me to," and she said, "All right, all right," and slid back onto the seat the younger girl had vacated. The younger girl was now climbing into the back seat from her side of the car, and Buddwing was trying to get into the back seat from his side, with both front seats bent forward at the same time, and with neither being able to squeeze past the bottleneck. In the meantime, the truck drivers were beginning to lose their patience, and the door of one of the truck cabs opened and a very burly man wearing a cap with a pencil stuck in it and a plaid shirt began lumbering toward the Volkswagen. As he approached the car, Buddwing allowed the young Chinese girl to get into the back seat first, and then collapsed on the seat beside her with an awkward backward-falling motion. Jesse got into the car and, smiling, said, "Well, now we all settled, huh?"

"What the hell are you doing up here?" the truck driver bawled. "Celebrating Chinese New Year's?"

"Go blow it out," Sally said in English, and added something probably appropriate in Chinese. Jesse stepped on the gas, crashed the red light on the corner, waved at the startled cop, and turned left on Sixth Avenue.

"You're going the wrong way," Sally said.

"I know. This's a one-way street."

"Well, do you know where Chinatown is?" she asked.

"Sure," Jesse replied. "Right near the Golden Gate Bridge."

"You got the wrong city, mate," Sally said, and then she turned toward the back seat and giggled, and Buddwing saw the flash of a gold tooth at the side of her mouth and knew with certainty he was in Yokohama. They had stolen a trolley car there . . . well, not stolen it, simply commandeered it, shoving the conductor to one side, and taking his place at the electric throttle while the passengers around them laughed behind their face masks, hating. There was something about this ride in the Volkswagen that reminded him of that wild trolley-car ride, Jesse turning left again on the next corner, and then hitting Seventh Avenue, and then

147

weaving in and out of the traffic plunging downtown to the heart
of the garment district, delivery boys shoving their wheeled dress
carts, even on a Saturday, Puerto Rican seamstresses hurrying
back from their lunch hour, even on a Saturday, models walking
in tight short skirts, crowds pushing their way through Macy's
doors, the imposing monolithic hulk of Pennsylvania Station, and
then the relative silence of the dead streets between 31st and
14th, windows reflecting the afternoon sunlight, the long Japanese afternoons, the smell of fish and of flowers, the silent
shuffle of sandals on cobblestoned streets.

They had come up out of Sasebo by train, he and Jesse, and
they had been drunk even before they boarded, loading up on
Japanese beer in the USO and then reeling to the train station.
They had sung all the way to Yokohama, *Pardon me, boy, is this
the Yokohama choo-choo? Track ee-chee-nee, we've got to be
back by three*, making up the lyrics as they went along, offering
seats to surprised Japanese ladies, staggering and giggling, and
searching for words in a language as alien as the landscape, *We
can afford, to board, the Yokohama choo choo. Got yen to spare,
we'll have an oh-hai-oh there!* The roadbed was lined with bud-
ding cherry trees, the blossoms opening pink and white and red
against the rolling green terraced hills beyond as the train, a
Toonerville tinkertown train, chugged and rattled along the
track, throwing coal cinders back through the open windows of
the car, dirtying their summer whites. The Buddha sat in immense splendor miles from the track, but it seemed close enough
to touch, dominating the hillside and the entire landscape, a huge
stone idol, unseeing, seeing all, as the train clattered past and
they sang the song that linked them with a world they knew.

In Yokohama they drank more Japanese beer in a Japanese
dance hall and danced with thirty-year-old hostesses who were
wearing Western clothes, the kind of simple cotton frocks twelve-
year-olds were wearing in the States. And then they commandeered the trolley car, and ran like hell from the shore patrol,
two marine bastards in a jeep who sat with their white helmets
and white leggings and white clubs, one of them yelling, "Hey,

you sailors! Come back here, you hear?" while he and Jesse ducked into a bombed-out alley, eluding them. And then they met the girls, one o'clock in the afternoon, Yokohama in skeletal ruins, rubble piled in the streets, met them on the roof of the servicemen's club where Jesse posed for his picture with one of them, the older one with the gold tooth. They walked downstairs again later, there were cherry blossoms even in the rubble, and stopped to watch the Japanese street artist who was drawing a picture of an Army sergeant while little girls with straight hair and sniffly noses stood around and watched and grinned, and the girl he had met on the roof of the servicemen's club covertly slipped her hand through his arm.

"Whereabouts you going, exactly?" Jesse asked.

"We're going home," Sally said. "I told you."

"And where's that, exactly?"

"Exactly?" Sally said, and giggled. "He wants to know exactly, Tina."

"Well, now, sure I do," Jesse said.

"It's *exactly* on Mott Street," Sally said, giggling. "Do you know where that is, exactly?"

"Well, not exactly," Jesse admitted.

"Do you girls live together?" Buddwing asked. "Tina? Is that your name?"

"Yes, that's my name," Tina said. She had a very small voice, faintly touched with an Oriental flavor, a slight musical quality. "What's *your* name?"

"Sam."

"Why'd you want to know if we live together?" Sally asked, turning to face Buddwing.

"I'm just curious."

"Are you sisters?" Jesse asked.

"No, we're not sisters," Sally said, smiling, and then turned again to Buddwing and again asked, "Why'd you want to know if we live together?"

"Because he was hoping maybe you'd invite us in for some tea," Jesse said.

"Chinee tea velly good tea," Tina said in a mock Chinese sing-song.

"Velly velly good," Sally said, picking up the phony accent. "Hot and holly."

"I mean, after all, we did get this jalopy started for you, and looka me driving you all the way downtown. That deserves a cup of tea, don't you think?"

"At the very least," Sally said, and she giggled.

"What you like with your tea?" Tina asked. "We got fortune cookie, almond cookie, vanilla, chocolate, strawberry ice cream, orange sherbet, kumquat."

"I'd just like a nice cup of tea and maybe some soft music and a place to put up my feet," Jesse said. "Man, I been on the go since four o'clock yesterday."

"You like we play nice music on samisen?" Tina asked.

"I like you play nice music on record player."

"Well, we see," Sally said. "You make turn here, please, this Canal Street."

They came into the maze of Chinatown and cruised the streets looking for a parking spot. This was not the nighttime Chinatown of red and green neon, of tourists trying to decide which restaurant to enter, of brilliantly lighted souvenir shops with paper dragons and cardboard swords, of teen-agers in search of firecrackers. This was a neighborhood, and it happened to be Chinese, the way that side street in Yokohama had happened to be Japanese, with people living here and going about the daily routines of their lives. The neon signs did not shout their intentions at one-thirty in the afternoon. Huge muted Chinese calligraphs stood white and pale against the sides of tenement houses. The souvenir shops seemed gathering the strength of their motley wares for the Saturday evening onslaught, Chinese women dusting porcelain Chinese warriors in window fronts, a Chinese man hanging a colored paper lantern, pulling it taut and testing the light bulb, a feeble glow in an afternoon window. Boys and girls stopped to talk to each other on the street, in English, and old men lingered about newsstands, reading the front pages of Chinese-language newspapers. Women moved in and out of the markets, the food in the windows rare and exotic to Buddwing's eyes, the water chestnuts and green onions, the ginger syrup and kumquats, the octopus and lychee nuts. As he stepped out of the parked car into the spring afternoon, he found himself looking into the open kitchen door of a restaurant, and seeing the hanging pigs on their great hooked chains rotating slowly over a smoke oven. The pungent smell of roasting pork touched his nostrils, evoking a stronger memory, the cleavers in a neat row hanging above the chopping block, the sea bass marinated and ready to roast, the rows of frogs' legs tied in neat pairs for hanging in the L-shaped oven, these, these; he took Tina's hand as she stepped out of the small car.

"Well, do we get the tea?" Jesse asked.

Sally put one hand on her hip and extended her leg, bending it slightly, the pale white length of her thigh showing in the deep slit. Tina was wearing a blue skirt and a white blouse, with a tiny gold pendant watch around her throat, and she looked much less Chinese than Sally in her green silk, high-necked, thigh-slitted dress. Sally was thoughtfully considering Jesse's last question now, her pale brow faintly wrinkled, her teeth gnawing on the inside of her mouth. Whatever decision was being formed in her inscrutable mind apparently had little or nothing to do with Buddwing or Tina. Buddwing immediately suspected that Sally, who seemed to be close to thirty-five if not over the hill and gone already, had her own apartment here in Chinatown and was now debating whether or not to share humble abode and hot and holly tea with two strange white devils, one of whom was sailing man. The decision, in any case, contrary to the one made in the car where Tina had advised and Sally had accepted, was one that Sally would undoubtedly reach independently, with neither counsel nor debate from Tina. So they all stood on the sidewalk in dumb anticipation while Sally wrinkled her brow and jutted her hip and extended her bent leg and nibbled at the inside of her mouth, and the neighborhood Chinese women came and went with their marketing baskets.

"Well, what the hell," Sally said at last, "let's have some tea."

It was going to be a monumental drunk, one that Buddwing would remember for years to come. It was going to be one of those roaring, boistering, sex-filled, whiskey-filled afternoons where nothing mattered but the wild soaring joy of letting go, and even that was not a conscious thing.

The apartment was not as Oriental as he had thought it would be, not as Oriental as the small wooden hut on the Yokohama side street had been in May of 1946. A Chinese man was sitting on an upended milk box in front of the tenement doorway as they climbed the front steps, following Sally. He looked up in brief disapproval and then went back to watching the street. There had been smoke coming from the shack in Yokohama. It had been in a row of shacks on a street behind what must have been a major thoroughfare before the bombings. A small path led to the door of the shack. They had followed the older woman with the gold tooth, and the younger girl shuffling along behind her, up the path to the door of the shack and then had entered. There was the smell of woodsmoke. A small hibachi burned in the center of the room. Sally opened the door to her apartment, and they followed her into the kitchen where beaded Oriental curtains hung at the far end, separating it from the living room. A calendar was on the kitchen wall, a Chinese girl decorating its face. There were a range and a sink and a refrigerator and an enamel-topped kitchen table. Sally walked directly to the beaded curtains and held them aside for Jesse and Buddwing. They walked into the other room, and Tina and Sally followed them. The décor here was faintly Oriental, twice removed, Sally's honorable ancestors being honored more in the breach than in the physical actuality. There was a couch bought from one of the modern foam-rubber places on Park Avenue South, and a very low slatted table before it, and on the other side of that a pile of brightly colored cushions. Another calendar—Japanese, not Chinese—hung on the living room wall, and an abacus was on the top of a modern chest of drawers on the opposite wall. There was, too, an open game of mah-jongg and—on the wall above the chest of drawers—two delicate Chinese prints of birds. Aside from these touches—the calendars, the abacus, the game, the prints— the apartment could have been any one of a hundred apartments in the neighborhood where he had been born and raised. No, there was one other thing, and it was this that brought back with peculiar pungency the Yokohama shack: the faint aroma of burning incense.

"Do you really want tea?" Sally asked.

"Well, like what did you have in mind?" Jesse said.

"I thought maybe a drink, but . . ." Sally shrugged. "You think it's too early for the fleet, Tina?"

"It's too early for *me*, that's for sure," Tina said.

"Tina just sniffs the cork," Sally explained, "and right away she's back in the Tang dynasty."

"What's that?" Jesse asked.

"The Tang dynasty? Before the Ming," Sally explained.

"The Ming dynasty," Buddwing said, trying to be funny, "is the dynasty run by the Emperor Ming in Flash Gordon."

"Who's the Emperor Ming?" Tina asked.

"A very tall, bald-headed man in a robe, with a pencil-line drooping mustache. Ming. Haven't you ever read Flash Gordon?"

"No," Tina said.

"How old are you?"

"Twenty."

"I read Flash Gordon," Sally said, "and I resented the heavy being Chinese."

"He wasn't really Chinese," Buddwing said.

"Well, he sure as hell *looked* Chinese. As a matter of fact, I had an *uncle* who looked just like Ming."

"Did I hear somebody mention a drink a little while back?" Jesse asked.

"I thought you were the big tea man," Sally said, smiling.

"I am the big B-Man," Jesse said. "B for bourbon."

Sally went into the kitchen, and Jesse knocked over the pile of colored pillows and settled himself on one of them. Buddwing and Tina sat on the couch. The incense was very strong in his nostrils now. It seemed to be emanating from somewhere behind the couch, but he could not locate the burner. Its aroma filled the room. He looked at the girl sitting beside him, the Japanese girl with her painted face and her incongruous garb. In the other room, the woman with the gold tooth was bustling about. The sun slanted through the shack's one window, touching the glowing coals of the hibachi in the center of the room. Jesse was making himself comfortable on the floor. There was the sound of sandaled feet outside, the babble of Japanese calling to each other, the cries of a fruit peddler wending his way through the neighborhood. There was always a smell of fish and smoke, always; it hung over every Japanese city like something you could touch, a curious smell that was October even when it was May. It came through the open window now, and mingled with the fainter aroma of the incense. A potato was baking on the hibachi. The woman came back from the other room and smiled, the gold tooth flashing in her mouth, and that was the beginning of it.

Sally and Jesse both drank bourbon with a little water, please, while Buddwing and Tina drank Scotch neat on the rocks, and it was along about the third drink that Buddwing realized they were roaring down the pike toward a monumental drunk. The drunk started in the apartment off that side street with bourbon and Scotch, and with music on the record player, and with Sally suddenly getting up and beginning to do a dance alone as if there were nobody else in the room. Tina kept giggling all the while Sally danced, and Buddwing slipped his hand up under her skirt, and she squeezed it between her thighs and then he had another drink while Jesse applauded for Sally, and then they all had another drink—Tina was on his lap now—and that was when Jesse took Sally in his arms and kissed her.

Buddwing was a little surprised when Jesse began kissing Sally because he knew that Jesse was madly in love with a Mexican girl who lived on the outskirts of San Antonio, and who had taught Jesse how to hypnotize people. Jesse was a devout believer in black magic, something everybody on the ship joked about, but nobody made fun of the way he could hypnotize people. They would all crowd into the sonar shack, which was maybe six feet by six feet, and Jesse would fix those blue eyes of his onto the middle of somebody's forehead, and then just begin moving his forefinger back and forth. "Now, you jes keep a-watchin' my finger," his voice would say. "Now your eyes are gettin' heavy, your lids is gettin' heavy," his voice would say. "You cain't hardly keep 'em open," his voice would say, and before you knew it, just like in the movies, the guy he was hypnotizing would shut his eyes and do whatever Jesse told him to do. He had Andy Grange jumping around on the deck and barking like a dog one time, and another time he hypnotized Mr. Carver at Mr. Carver's own request, but then when he had him in a trance he was too chicken to give him any orders, Mr. Carver being the senior communications officer aboard, and not a man to go messing around with.

Jesse loved that Mexican girl with all his heart, and he never stopped talking about her to whoever would listen, which was practically everybody on the ship. His descriptions of her became more intimate each time, so that eventually the tiny sonar shack was crammed with listeners who hung breathlessly on his every word. He started by describing the texture of her coffee-colored skin, and her coal-black hair and eyes, and then he went on to describe each part of her anatomy in painful detail, lacing his descriptions with wild tales of the voodoo stunts she had performed. He told them of the time she had bitten into the neck of a live chicken and smeared her naked breasts with blood and then kissed him with the blood still hot on her lips. He told them of the time she had summoned her dead sister from the grave, and of the time he had laid her in the back room of a funeral parlor. He told them of just about everything they had ever done together or planned to do together, sex and black magic mixed, chili sauce and incense, tortillas and smut. He left nothing to the

limited imaginations of his shipmates, so that before long the
fiery-eyed incantating wench in San Antonio became the girl
who was waiting back home for every man on the ship.

And now here he was kissing Sally as if he had forgotten all
about his Mexican girl back home, but Sally wasn't having any
of it, not right now she wasn't. Sally, of the entire four, seemed
to sense most clearly that a majestic drunk was being formed
and started, and she had no desire to spoil it by hopping into bed
with Jesse—not right now, at any rate. Sally had the good sense
to know that sex was going to be a part of this free-swinging
drunk, but that it had to be a controlled and time-biding sex that
permeated the entire afternoon, and not something that would
threaten or otherwise mar the shining surface of the high they
were all building. Sally was a shrewd and experienced girl, and
Buddwing knew immediately that they could not have been in
surer hands than hers—hell, he had known that about her the
moment they had met on the roof of the servicemen's club. But
even then—even knowing that Sally with her gold-toothed grin
was the more experienced of the pair, was the one who would lead
the fun and set the pace—he had been drawn to the quietly smiling, secretly amused Tina, mainly because she reminded him of
a life he had left back home, a life he desperately missed.

The majestically building drunk was all a part of missing the
life back home, of obliterating it, of blurring its edges so that it
would not seem like the reality any more. Japan was certainly
not the reality. The stupid sailor suit he wore was not the reality.
The destroyer sitting in the harbor with its ensign flying on the
fantail and its "Request permission to come aboard, sir" was not
the reality, but it was all the life there was, and he suffered it
with a dull patience because he knew that someday it would be
over, someday he would go back home again and see L.J. and
Beethoven and Red Vest and all the others. No, he would never
see Beethoven again because Beethoven had been caught in the underwater barbed wire when the marines invaded Tarawa, and he
had been machine-gunned to death by the Japanese as he struggled
to free himself. A letter from L.J. had told him what had hap-

pened to Beethoven on Tarawa, and he had wept silently in the dim radar-illuminated stillness of C.I.C. aboard the *Fancher*. There were friends aboard the *Fancher*, yes, but none of them could compare to the boys he had left at home. And so this drunk, all the drunks, all the stumbling, falling-down, staggering, whorehouse-hopping drunks from Norfolk to Pensacola to Guantánamo Bay to Colón (he had received L.J.'s letter in Panama; he had wept in the radar shack while a balmy tropical breeze sifted through the open bulkhead door) to San Diego to Pearl to Sasebo, and now in Yokohama, all these drunks were only an effort to re-create something real and meaningful in his life, only a meager and foolish attempt at substitution. The something real and meaningful had existed in those Harlem streets when his closest friend was a boy named Eric Michael Knowles whom he had taught to make a peach-pit ring, had existed in that cloistered tailorshop with the tall white-haired man who was his grandfather. He had found reality again in the Bronx after he had moved, found it in a tightly secure structure the nucleus of which was L.J., Beethoven, Red Vest, and himself. And then, somehow, the entire structure had weakened—had fifty dollars been enough?—and had collapsed in the confusion of World War II and the United States Navy. Now, with Tina, he tried to recapture something he had known a long time ago, perhaps the innocence of Doris, the shining innocence of those cycling afternoons, perhaps the serenity of a calm and uncluttered existence that held no responsibilities and no pressures. Now, with a whore he had picked up on the roof of the Yokohama Servicemen's Club, he drank himself into a lulling stupor. This was not the reality, and he knew with grim certainty that the reality he had known would no longer be there when at last he returned to it. The whiskey was a hedge against recognition—the whiskey and the gently inquiring touches along the inside of Tina's thigh, the secret promise in her eyes, lust and liquor fumed inside him, drowning all else; this was going to be the longest afternoon in his life. He knew he would be subtly changed before it ended; he knew that once he was discharged from the navy, he would return to a different landscape where he would pad as softly as a stranger—and he knew who would be waiting.

They came roaring out of Sally's apartment at close to two o'clock, heading for the roof of her building. Jesse wanted to carry the girls up the steps, but Sally—in her good-sensed, cautious, sex-conscious, drunk-conscious way, wanting to preserve this marvelous high, wanting the high to go on and on and never end until they were joyously exhausted and naked—took Jesse's hand in her left hand and then grabbed Buddwing's hand in her right, and the three ran laughing up the staircase together, leaving Tina behind on the landing below. They stopped just outside the door to the roof, and Jesse yelled, "Hey, where's Tina?" and then dropped Sally's hand and ran back down to scoop Tina off her feet, struggling and giggling, and then climbed and staggered back with her in his arms to where Sally and Buddwing stood just outside the fire door.

"He's a kook," Sally said, and then kissed Buddwing firmly and teasingly on the mouth and laughed again, and kissed Jesse as he put Tina on her feet before them, and it was then that Buddwing realized the four of them would end up in the same bed together. Laughing, they pushed open the door and lurched out onto the tarred roof where the city suddenly opened beneath them like a cracked piñata, spilling its bridges and spires, its ribbons of asphalt and water. The view was overwhelming; it almost sobered them on the spot. But Jesse had thoughtfully remembered to bring a bottle of bourbon from the apartment, and he lifted the front of his jumper now to reveal it where it was tucked into the waistband of his trousers. He pulled the cork and tilted the bottle to his lips, and then passed the bottle to Buddwing. Sally urged him to drink—"Go ahead, sweetie, take a swig"—even though he needed no urging, touching him expertly and casually, never forgetting that sex was a part of this marvelous experience they were sharing, sex was the ultimate goal, but prolonging the sex in an ever-conscious, hand-touching, thigh-flashing, high-giggling way which Tina shyly approved with a faint, excited, drunken smile.

"Hey, looka these birds here!" Jesse shouted, and he ran across to the other side of the roof where a meshed pigeon coop rested against a parapet. "Hey, birdie, birdie," he said, "hey, sweet birdie, birdie," poking his finger through the mesh while Tina giggled and Sally fell against him laughing.

"Get away from those birds!" a man on the roof opposite yelled, and Jesse burst out laughing.

"Why? They your birds?" he shouted back.

"They my friend's birds," the man answered. He was Chinese and his voice was high and angry, and he waved his fist up at them as he spoke.

"Screw you *and* your friend's birds," Sally said, and she suddenly threw open the door to the coop and yelled, "Shooooooosh! Everybody out! Everybody out!"

Laughing, Jesse plunged his hands into the coop and yelled, "Just for that, ever'body out!" and the pigeons flapped frantically into the air while the Chinese man on the roof below waved his fist and yelled, "I get the police! You see!"

"You get the *bird*, man, tha's what you get!" Jesse shouted, and they all burst out laughing.

Sally's hands were in constant motion; she touched, she persuaded, she never let any of them forget what was in store if only they could preserve this miraculous high. Tina's blouse was unbuttoned—Buddwing had unbuttoned it in the apartment—and she fumblingly tried to rebutton it as they stood laughing on the roof in the glare of the afternoon sun, listening to the angry Chinese man, and then gave up the task and said, "The hell with it." Sally said, "Attagirl," encouragingly, and tilted the bottle to her lips, managing to lean against Buddwing at the same time with a strong full-fleshed thigh pressure against his crotch.

His lust was turning to a dull ache inside him, and running beneath the constant ache was an insistent warning. He was very much a part of this drunken spree that he was sure would turn into a drunken orgy, but at the same time the little warning trill kept sounding over and over again, and it told him they must not get into trouble with the police because he had no identification, and because he was Edward Voegler, an escaped maniac. He wanted to get off the roof, wanted to go back to Sally's apartment before the Chinese man made good his threat to call the cops. He was possessed by the wildest sort of fantasy, wherein Sally stood spread-legged in the center of her living room with the beaded curtains behind her, and he seized the hem of her dress in his hands, and then ripped it upward along the line of the slit, kept ripping it up past her hips and her waist and her breasts until she was standing in only her slim Chinese undergarments. At the same time, drawn to Sally because she made it impossible to forget her, he was intrigued by the drunken, smiling, seeming virginity of Tina, and further excited by the notion of the four of them together in the same bed. The entire feeling, he realized, was somehow wrapped up with L.J. and Beethoven and Red Vest, whom he had not seen since the war began. And then, with drunken clarity, he realized that he was as much excited by the idea of getting into the same bed with Jesse as he was of getting into that bed with the girls. The notion startled him and almost tore the drunk to shreds. He had awakened this morning knowing nothing at all about himself, and it suddenly occurred to him that perhaps he was a fag.

With recognition of the word, with full-bodied acknowledgment of the word and of the image it instantly brought to mind, that of a painted, marcelled, mincing homosexual faggoty fruity queer, the drunk came dangerously close to evaporating entirely. To preserve the drunk, he took the bottle from Sally's hand and swigged mightily from it, and then to preserve his masculinity, to reassure himself that what he wanted to do was climb onto Sally while Tina somehow climbed onto him, he handed the bottle to Jesse and put his arms around both girls, clear around Sally so that he could touch one small rounded breast under the silk Chinese dress, and only partially around Tina so that he could pat her behind in the tight blue wool American skirt, and he said, "Come on, Sally, let's go back to the apartment."

"What do you want to do there, huh, baby?" Sally asked, pushing his hand away from her breast, and then circling out of his arms like a dancer, and looping her arm through Jesse's.

"I want to tear that slit of yours clear up to your throat," Buddwing said drunkenly.

Tina giggled and said, "He wants to tear off a piece, Sally, that's what he wants to do."

"Yeah, you tear my dress, you bastard, and you'll pay for it." Sally said, and then they went down to the apartment.

They tore off her dress, of course.

The three of them, Jesse and Tina and Buddwing, tore her dress to shreds while Sally stood giggling and coaxing and tormenting in the center of the living room. And then they wrapped her naked in the beaded drapes they had pulled from the ceiling, and dragged her into the bedroom where they all fell laughing onto the bed. As the edges of the fine high drunk were turned back by their increasing animal awareness, as their naked bodies emerged and gleamed triumphant through the alcohol maze and the clouded stupor, as the smell of sex enveloped them with its strong and fiercely clinging perfume, as their arms and legs and mouths and hips took on a driving power of their own, almost sentient, moving with a predetermined will as deep as a race memory, until what they were doing finally replaced the alcohol and made them as high and as heady as their earlier drunk had made them—through it all, Buddwing felt himself intricately involved and yet curiously apart. There was something enormously threatening about what was happening. He and Jesse never once touched in the ensuing tangle of bodies and mouths, but he was consciously aware of his friend, though only as an embodiment of L.J. and Beethoven and Red Vest, and not as himself, not as Jesse Salem who had a Mexican girl back in San Antonio. The fear of homosexuality dissipated in the stronger glare of their wildly heterosexual performance, and yet he felt threatened in an oddly obscure way, as though all this frantic activity were a screen for something deeper inside him which he was about to lose. It was this knowledge of impending loss that was threatening, he realized, and not what they were actually doing. He felt as if this conglomerate act, this immodest, immoral, and probably unlawful act, were the culmination of a phase of his life, a clearly defined section of his life that had been building steadily and irrevocably toward this confused climax. And therein lay the threat, a threat to the very fabric of his existence, a threat to the core of whatever knowledge he possessed of himself and of the world thus far. He knew that nothing would ever be the same once he left this apartment, once he disentangled himself from Jesse and the two girls. There was enormous security in this bed in this room because whatever they did they were doing together, blameless, anonymous, in their miniature gang structure. The unknown lay beyond this room, down those steps, somewhere outside. He clung to his companions, he held Tina fast to him, he crushed his lips to Sally's mouth, he felt Jesse's reassuring nearness. He did not want to lose them. He held them close because he was holding life itself. But his mind could not escape the knowledge that this would end soon, perhaps too soon, and there was sadness in the certainty that from now on, and possibly forever, he would have to walk alone.

He left Jesse and the girls at four in the afternoon.

They said goodbye to each other without any real sense of loss. If they avoided each other's eyes, it was not because they felt any real guilt for what they had done, but only because their excesses seemed somehow pointless.

He knew exactly where he wanted to go.

# 10

THE PARK outside New York University was a miniature of the larger park in which he had awakened this morning, and he entered it now with a pleased feeling of correctness. His life, he felt, was somehow starting anew, and there was something unexplainably fitting about this repetition, as though the fresh beginning were not really totally unexpected, but rather an extension of what was already there. He found a bench in the sun, and he sat on it with the rather complacent air of a man who knows exactly what is going to happen next and is prepared for it.

Grace was going to happen next.

He spread his arms along the back of the bench and faced the college. The Washington Arch and Fifth Avenue were behind him and to his left. He could feel the strong afternoon rays touching his head and shoulders, and he wished he could turn his face to them, but he knew that Grace would come down the front steps of the school soon, and he wanted to see her when she did. In his mind, he acted out a little pantomime, Grace appearing suddenly with her books on her arm, wearing sweater and skirt and going to a bench at the other end of the park; he rising and going to sit beside her. He smiled in anticipation, and listened to the sounds of life around him.

Somewhere behind him, two men were playing chess; they were old men, judging from the sounds of their voices. *"J'adoube,"* one of them said, and the other answered, "You're always *adoube*-ing. Keep your goddamn hands off the pieces!" A folk singer with a guitar—he sounded colored but Buddwing wasn't sure—began singing "Greensleeves" in a gently keening voice, and overhead an airplane droned a noisy counterpoint. Students with Saturday classes sat on the benches chatting, filling the air with a pleasant buzz. He could feel the city behind him and around him, pulsing with life. He sat in sun-stained brilliance, the nucleus of a city teeming with millions, and for a moment he was completely alone and private, sitting in sun-enclosed secrecy as the city went its busy way, unaware. In secret silence, he could feel a sense of true identity slowly and tentatively seeping into muscle and bone, with the same penetrating force as the sun that touched his shoulders, spreading, warming, lulling.

His grandfather had died in the dead of winter; he had often thought of the old man as being lowered into a cruelly cold and stubborn, unreceptive earth.

As he sat in the sun, two overlapping memories seemed to enter his mind in swift succession, each rushing in its haste for recognition, one more frightening than the other, and yet neither as frightening as he knew they should be. The first concerned the death of his grandfather and the second

He frowned because the second memory seemed to concern the death of his grandfather as well, and yet he knew it was impossible for his grandfather to have died twice. His grandfather had died once and forever on January twelfth; the date was firmly fixed in his memory because it had been two days after his sixteenth birthday. The wake had been held in Harlem on a bleak and dreary day, the sky a uniform unbroken metallic gray across the tops of the Second Avenue tenements. The funeral parlor was on the ground floor of one of those tenements.

Well, that day, he thought. There was something wrong about that day.

The thing that was wrong about that day was the fact that his grandfather was dead and lying in a coffin—that was what was wrong; that was all that was wrong. But that in itself was not frightening—why had he thought it was frightening? He could, in fact, visualize the old man with his white hair against the white satin of the coffin, his eyes closed, his waxen hands clasped gently over the prayer beads on his chest. He could remember the funeral parlor in vivid detail, the banks of flowers heaped around the coffin and on the floor, the permeating perfume, the rows of folding wooden chairs. Grandma sat on one of the chairs in a black dress with a dazed expression on her face, accepting the condolences of the mourners. His grandfather did not look at all like himself; there was something strange and different about his face. But there was nothing frightening about this memory of the funeral parlor; there was instead a gentle tender whispering aura about the scene as he pictured it in his mind.

Yet the day had been frightening.

He shuddered with the memory even now, but at the same time he felt his fear did not concern anything that had happened on the day of the wake, but instead something that had happened much later on, when it was warm, yes, the summer, yes, Di Palermo's grocery store, Apartment 4A, 2117 Riverside Drive, no!

His mind clamped shut.

He retreated gracelessly, backing away from the second memory because there was horror implicit in it. Deliberately, he sought the comparative safety of the first memory, even though he knew the two were linked and that one owed its existence to the other. And then, like a faintly rattling warning wind, came the chilling knowledge that memory upon memory upon memory were inextricably linked, horror upon horror were waiting to emerge from the shadowed corners of his mind to force a confrontation, and the knowledge routed him completely.

Where's Grace? he wondered, and he looked again toward the steps of the school, not seeing her, but focusing his attention steadily on the steps anyway, knowing she would arrive soon. The delaying tactic did not work. His mind drifted back again to that day of his grandfather's wake in Harlem, but now the memory seemed less frightening than before, so that he concluded it was an absolutely safe memory; it was only the *other* memories he had to watch out for. He sought the memory of the wake almost eagerly now, nudging it into his mind, while all the time the warning continued to rattle, the warning that told him once he opened the floodgates there would be no stopping the rush of memory—he would be trapped in a thundering cascade; he would drown.

He had walked from the funeral home with his cousin Mandy. She was three months older than he, and she was not wearing her stupid cheerleader's sweater for a change, but was wearing instead a simple black dress. They walked the streets of Harlem with a total ease, because they had both been born into its poverty and its filth, and even though they were now clean-washed residents of the Bronx, the residue stuck to their bones like part of their flesh. The flowershop was on Third Avenue and 116th Street, across the way from the Cosmo Theater, which his mother had often taken him to when he was a boy. They went into the shop to price a floral wreath for their dead grandfather because they both felt they were old enough now to express their own sympathy, even though Mandy had told him in utmost secrecy that she had never been overly fond of the old man, a confession Buddwing accepted with a feeling of resentful anger.

He had never made a large purchase in his life before, and he knew that he would have to borrow money from his mother in order to meet his half of the obligation. There were a great many floral wreaths in the shop. The woman who waited on them wore a green apron with pins stuck all along the straps, and she was very patient in helping them to decide. They eliminated wreath after wreath, until finally there were only two wreaths to choose from. One of them cost seventy-five dollars. The other cost fifty.

"I think we should take the fifty-dollar one," Mandy said.

Buddwing shook his head. "No. Let's take the seventy-five-dollar one."

"It's too expensive," Mandy said.

"It's for Grandpa," Buddwing answered.

"It's still too expensive."

The woman with the green apron said, "The fifty-dollar wreath is very nice."

"Yes, but this is for our grandfather, you see," Buddwing said.

"Yes, I understand," the woman said. "But the fifty-dollar wreath is very nice."

"I think we should take the more expensive one," he said to Mandy.

"That would cost us thirty-seven-fifty apiece," Mandy said. "That's really too much money."

"I think the fifty-dollar wreath would make a nice remembrance," the woman in the green apron said.

"It's, you see, he's our grandfather," Buddwing said lamely, and the shop went still.

"Would there be a ribbon on the fifty-dollar one?" Mandy asked.

"Yes, of course."

"Could it say 'In Loving Memory'?"

"Yes, if you like."

"That would be nice," Mandy said, turning to Buddwing. "I think that would be nice, don't you?"

"The same kind of ribbon that's on the other one?" Buddwing asked.

"Yes, the same ribbon," the woman said. "It's really a very nice wreath, you know."

"It's just that fifty dollars seems so . . . cheap," Buddwing said.

"Oh, no," the woman said, looking offended. "Fifty dollars is a nice price to spend for a wreath. Oh, no, it's not cheap at all."

"He used to make all my clothes, you see," he said, and the woman looked at him blankly. "My grandfather."

"Come on, we have to decide," Mandy said.

"It'll look very lovely with the ribbon on it," the woman said.

"The red ribbon? Is that what you'll use?" Buddwing asked.

"Yes, if you like."

"I think the red is good, don't you, Mandy?"

"Yes. Yes, I think it'll look nice with the red."

"And would you deliver it to the funeral parlor?" Buddwing asked.

"Yes, we certainly will," the woman replied.

"Fifty dollars, you know, it seems . . ."

"We'll take the fifty-dollar one," Mandy said. "With the red ribbon saying 'In Loving Memory.' " She paused and looked at Buddwing. "Okay?" she asked.

"Well, okay," Buddwing said.

"Sure, it's good enough," Mandy said.

They told the woman in the green apron they would be back in a few minutes with the money, and that meanwhile she should attach the red ribbon to the fifty-dollar wreath. Then they walked out of the flowershop and back to the funeral parlor. His mother wanted to give him the twenty-five dollars as a gift, but Buddwing insisted that it be a loan, and he told her he would take a job that summer to earn the money to pay her back. When the wreath arrived later that afternoon, all the relatives clucked their tongues and wagged their heads in appreciation, and said, "Ahh, look, the kids bought him flowers." Buddwing felt oddly guilty.

He continued to wonder about that day long after they had buried his grandfather in the hard winter earth, long after spring had come and summer was near. In idle moments, he would reconstruct the conversation in that flowershop, and the words that resounded most clearly in his mind were the ones Mandy had delivered just before they had left: "Sure, it's good enough."

Good enough for *what?* he wondered. Good enough for the old man who inconsiderately died when I loved him so much? Good enough for the old man who welcomed me to his shop every afternoon, "Come in, you must be frozen. Annie, make him some nice hot chocolate"? Good enough for *what,* Mandy? Oh

God, why hadn't he argued more vehemently, why hadn't he convinced her that fifty dollars *wasn't* enough, that the extra twenty-five dollars was only a way of saying, "Grandpa, I *really* loved you, not fifty dollars' worth, not even seventy-five dollars' worth, but the world, Grandpa, I loved you the world"? Why hadn't he convinced her?

The job he took that summer was a constant reminder of his grandfather, even before

No, he thought.

No, there's no sense going over all this; there really isn't. I took the job, I paid her back the lousy twenty-five dollars!

He tried to make his mind go blank, the way Jesse had taught him to do aboard the *Fancher* during the war, a prerequisite for self-hypnotism. Before you could learn to hypnotize others, Jesse had said, you had to learn how to hypnotize yourself. He thought of snow, of whiteness, emptiness, open space, nothing, and then wondered what was keeping Grace, and then forced Grace out of his mind; the trick was to make the mind entirely blank, to push out any thought, even a random thought, to sit in unblinking blankness, to think of nothing but peace, nothing but emptiness, nothing, nothing at all.

Into the white blank nothingness of his serene mind, into the clear empty space surrounded by air transparent and pure, into this carefully controlled empty blankness came the single image of a boy pushing a grocery cart, and he obliterated this image at once, forcing it out and away, leaving the clean open space again and the blankness which nothing could invade the apartment building in red brick facing the water and the service elevator with the colored operator who always offered him cigarettes he suspected they were marijuana he told him his father was a cop and he wasn't allowed to smoke ha his father wasn't even a cop, he closed his mind down again. If whiteness didn't work, you went to black; you closed the mind in tight like the diaphragm of a camera, tighter and tighter, the shutter closing and blotting out everything in contracting blackness, the straight-edged circle in the center coming down smaller and smaller, showing less and less light, until there was only a pinpoint, and then you forgot the allusion of a camera's shutter entirely, a camera was a thought, you obliterated the camera image, and with it the pinpoint of light in the center of your mind, you closed down to total darkness, you swam, not swam, you floated, not floated, you *allowed* the blackness, dark and darker.

Nothing.

He looked like Grandpa.

No, he did not look at all like Grandpa; he was an old Jewish man, and he sat with his shawl wrapped around him, and his yarmulka on the back of his head, and his hands shook, and he coughed all the time, I did not want to go near him at first, I was afraid I would catch his disease, whatever it was.

Into the blackness now, he knew it would not work, into the blackness, you taught me a trick that doesn't work, you son of a bitch, into the blackness came memory, pushing back the blackness, seeping into the center of the dark plane, and shoving the blackness back like a parting curtain, pushing its edges out of the mind until only the memory was there, vague and badly defined, the first time he delivered groceries to Apartment 4A, 2117 Riverside Drive, and the colored girl opened the door, and the old man with the shawl and the yarmulka was sitting by the window in sunshine.

Into the memory, a side theme of the memory, came the image of his grandfather lying in his coffin, and he knew now why his grandfather did not look the same. They had taken off his glasses. He had never seen his grandfather without glasses before, and this man in the coffin looked particularly vulnerable, as though expecting a blow in the face, I told her fifty dollars wasn't enough. And then the second memory, the memory of the apartment, expanded and grew, brighter now, its edges more clearly defined with a sharpness that was painful, and he knew that terror lurked just beyond the pain, and he tried again to shut out the memory, but it would not go. It came instead in flashing vignettes, seconds long, the first time he had explained to the old man about the

Zwieback in the order the day before, the time the old man asked
him to stay a while and talk to him, the time the old man

A shudder ran up Buddwing's spine.

There had been a gentleness about that old Jewish man, a blue-
veined, translucent gentleness as he sat in the sun and chatted with
Buddwing each time he delivered an order. The shawl he wore
on his shoulders was made of silk, blue and white, with white
tassels, and he wore the black yarmulka perched precariously, almost rakishly, on the back of his skull. They never talked for more
than ten minutes at a time, sitting by the window overlooking the
Hudson River, the sunlight streaming in past the lace curtains,
the colored girl humming around the house as she did her work,
and the old man's voice gently asking questions, wanting to know
all about the job, wanting to know what Buddwing's future plans
were, wanting to know all about Buddwing's friends, all about
Buddwing's dreams. He told the old man that his closest friends
were L.J. and Beethoven and Red Vest, and he explained how
Beethoven was an excellent artist and hoped to go to Pratt Institute after he got out of high school. He told the old man about
Doris, and how he had given her his silver scholarship pin—"You
gave her a medal?" the old man asked. "You're serious with this
girl?"—and sitting there in the warm sunshine with the old man
was somehow reminiscent of coming to the tailorshop and going
into the back room where Uncle Freddie had the pressing machine
going, and Grandma was making hot chocolate, and then coming
out to join Grandpa at the counter, leaning on the counter and
sipping his chocolate and telling Grandpa everything that had
happened. Ten minutes at a time, perhaps once or twice a week,
until Buddwing began to look forward to his visits, and then the
end of the summer grew near.

The woman who answered the door that day was not the
colored girl. He had never seen this woman before in his life, but
she was wearing black, and the apartment behind her was ominously still, and then he saw the other people, strangers, and he
froze on the sill of the apartment.

His eyes opened wide. The strange woman standing in the doorway looked at him curiously.

He saw the coffin.

He saw the old man in the coffin.

He must have asked, "Is he dead?" because the woman was saying, "Yes. Yes, he is dead." He dropped the package of groceries and turned and ran and almost collided with the wall. The colored elevator operator asked him why he was crying, and he said, "My grandfather is dead," and then went down to where the grocery cart was waiting. He did not deliver any of the other orders in the cart. He went back to the store and told Di Palermo he was feeling sick, and then he took the subway home and thought all the while that if he had only insisted, if he had only convinced Mandy to spend seventy-five dollars instead of fifty, if only they hadn't given him such a lousy cheap crumby wreath, *Sure, it's good enough,* the old man would still be alive.

Now, sitting on a bench in Washington Square Park, tears came into his eyes again, and he tried to blink them away, looking across at the steps of the school again, and desperately willing Grace to appear.

Oh, Jesus, why did you have to die? he thought, and he rubbed his fists against his eyes, and blinked at the building, and knew suddenly that Grace would not come, there was no Grace. He rose from the bench. His feet were unsteady beneath him. He stumbled, regained his footing, and looked about him curiously, as if uncertain where he was. Who . . . who was I waiting for? he wondered. Grace? But there is no Grace, you see. There is no grace for a cheap son of a bitch who defiled his grandfather's memory, God, God, even the ribbon was shabby, "In Loving Memory," you piano-legged bitch, you *hated* the old man, you *said* so, there is no grace, you will find no grace in this secret park.

Where is she? he thought, and suddenly all reason seemed to leave him, the hope of finding Grace mingling with the despair of never finding her again until he wanted to shriek aloud, and then did shriek the single word, "Grace!" and knew he was insane.

He stopped in the middle of the footpath and stared at the

ground helplessly. He suddenly felt robbed of all volition, void of any sense of direction, powerless to move. He had come here to find a girl named Grace, G.V., the initials in his ring, and now those twin memories had caused him to realize she would not be here, had caused him to know with terrifying certainty he would not find her at N.Y.U., though this was where he had found her, why wasn't she here now? Why? he asked, and suddenly he did not want to know more, he did not want memory. Jesse, teach me, he thought, teach me to make my mind a blank, I do not want to know the rest, there is no Grace.

I know who I am, he thought.

"I'm Edward Voegler," he said aloud, and nodded.

Bellevue Hospital was on 26th Street and First Avenue.

They would put him in a padded cell and he would forget the whole damn world.

Quickly, he began walking out of the park. He had almost reached the sidewalk when the policeman stopped him.

The silence, which had surely been there all along, suddenly registered on his ears as a total absence of sound. The cop materialized soundlessly, stepping into his path with a nightstick stretched between two hands, held horizontally somewhere between his waist and his knees, as if he were ready to use it momentarily. The chess players were silent, the folksinger was silent, the chattering students were mute; he knew now they all must have looked up in surprise at his first outburst and then grown ominously still when he announced to the world at large that he was Edward Voegler. Again, a crosscurrent of thought entered his mind; he *was* Edward Voegler and this kind policeman would only help him to get to Bellevue immediately; but he was *not* Edward Voegler and this goddamn Keystone caricature was only going to complicate things.

"What seems to be the trouble, mister?" the cop asked, his hands still at the ready on the nightstick.

"No trouble at all," Buddwing answered curtly, and moved to walk around the cop, but the cop took a quick sideward gliding step into his path again, and the nightstick moved up just a trifle higher toward his waist. The cop was redheaded and freckled, with a sour expression on his face. Buddwing hated him instantly, partially as a conditioned response of all New Yorkers to cops, and partially as recognition of a very personal obstacle in his path. The cop knew he was hated as a symbol and suspected he was hated as a person because he happened to have halitosis, but he stood before Buddwing in placid immovability with an expression on his face that silently imparted menace to the nightstick. Behind him, the chess players had turned from their game and were giving the encounter their undivided attention. The folk singer, surrounded by a group of teen-age boys in dungarees and a scattering of girls with smoky Cleopatra eyes, had shoved his guitar onto his hip and was staring at the cop.

"Well, it looks to me like you're yelling all over the place," the cop said.

Buddwing backed down with a pacifying, cop-fearing grin on his face. He was carrying no identification, and whereas he would not have minded being taken to Bellevue, he did not particularly want to be taken to jail first. As a matter of fact, the more he thought about it, the more he began to realize he did not want to be taken to Bellevue either. So he grinned mealymouthed and said apologetically, "I'm sorry if I was noisy, officer. I guess I didn't realize I was being loud."

"Yeah, well, there's such a thing as disturbing the peace, you know," the cop said, unmoved, and all at once Buddwing knew this was going to be bad.

"I'm sorry, officer," he said.

"I could pull you in for disorderly conduct, you know that, don't you?" the cop asked.

"I didn't realize I was creating a disturbance," Buddwing said.

"Mmm," the cop said, studying him. The Negro folk singer had moved closer with his assorted collection of beatniks and music lovers, and the chess players had managed to gather around themselves a group of Saturday students who were asking what all the fuss was about. The cop, aware of the audience behind him, and seeming to feel his authority was being openly challenged if not severely threatened, stepped a little closer to Buddwing and said, "What are you doing here outside the school in the first place?"

"I was just sitting on a bench taking the sun," Buddwing said.

"Yeah, well, why'd you pick here to do it?"

"Isn't this a public park?" Buddwing asked.

"Never mind what it is, just answer what I told you."

"It seemed quiet and peaceful and sunny, so I decided to sit here, that's all," Buddwing said. "I didn't realize there was a law against that."

"There ain't," the cop said in a placid, line-of-duty, not-about-to-take-any-crap voice, and then added imperturbably, "How about showing me some identification, mister?"

There followed an ominous silence during which the cop surmised he had accidentally struck pay dirt and Buddwing instantly knew he was trapped. The crowd, which had moved in from the benches and the walks to form a loose curious circle around Buddwing and the cop, was part of the silence in a patient, tentative way, as though undecided which of the pair to choose as its champion. The cop was staring at Buddwing calmly and impersonally, and Buddwing stared back at him in fear and anger, and weighed the silence and the temper of the crowd, and knew that lynch parties sometimes started with just such a silence.

"I'm not a vagrant," he said.

"Who said you were?"

"I was simply sitting here in the sun."

"Doing what? Watching the college girls?"

"No, but . . ."

"Watching the young college girls?" the cop said, certain he had hooked onto something big now, maybe the Boston strangler in town for the weekend. His nostrils dilated with the smell of blood; his hands tightened on the nightstick. The absurdity of the situation almost caused Buddwing to smile, but he recognized that even a trace of humor now would be his undoing. Mention of college girls and all the sneakered tweedy virginal images they conjured had caused a noticeable stir in the crowd surrounding Buddwing and the cop. He heard the buzz that swept through the onlookers and he was tempted to tell them he had been to bed with a college girl only this morning, how about *that*, huh? Where was our fat minion of the law and protector of the people *then*, huh?

In his most dignified voice, he said, "I wasn't watching the college girls, officer, although I don't believe there's any law against that, either, is there?"

"No, none at all," the cop said calmly. "Let me see your identification."

"I told you I am not a vagrant."

"You seem to know all about vagrancy, don't you?"

Buddwing smiled at the policeman while inside his head the thought of flight took visual shape in the form of a blinking Broadway sign: RUN, *run*, RUN, *run*, RUN! He heard himself telling the officer they were making a mountain out of a molehill, weren't they, or some such stalling nonsense, while the sign kept blinking on and off in his head. Smiling, talking, stalling, he laid his careful heroic plan: he would kick the cop in the groin, grab the guitar from the Negro folk singer, and bat the cop over the head with it. He would then leap over the bench and run into the Village where he would lose himself. "After all, officer, there's really nothing so unusual about a respectable citizen sitting on a park bench taking a little sunshine, now, is there?"

"That's right, so let me see your identification," the cop said.

He was ready to lift his knee in a sharp crotch-splitting piston kick when one of the chess players, an old man with white hair and thin-fingered hands, said, "He was only sitting in the sun, officer."

"Nobody asked you," the cop said.

"I'm simply offering my observation."

"Nobody asked you for your observation," the cop said.

"I can back up his testimony," the other chess player said, a short bald man wearing a large, faded blue cardigan.

"This ain't a trial," the cop said, "and mind your own business."

"I thought this was a free country," one of the smoky-eyed girls said.

176

"Who asked you?" the cop asked.

"What are you going to do next?" the Negro folk singer said. "Stop us from singing here in this park?" thereby opening a few old wounds and causing the cop to turn to him with a sour, pained expression.

"Well, well, another county heard from," the cop said. "Why don't you all go home and mind your own business?"

The Negro did not wish to go home to mind his own business, because he had been one of those protesting folk singers many months back, and he considered civil rights his one and only proper business, and besides he did not like fuzz of any kind or shape. He also did not particularly like white men, although he was shacking up with a redheaded white girl on Delancey Street, but of course that was not a white man. The smoky-eyed girls and the dungaree-clad boys did not wish to go home to mind their own business because they had no business to mind except protecting the artist in a free society, and so they pressed closer to the Negro in support since he was an artist and colored to boot. One of them said, "Why don't you go play in traffic, officer?" and the rest chimed in with other clever taunts like "Come arrest my mother, she's a pusher," and "What's the matter? Graft a little slow today?" while the cop's sour, pained expression began to change to a patiently suffering martyred look. He had a sudden vision of a riot starting on his beat, which would not be his beat very much longer if a riot started on it, especially a riot led by a nigger. Staten Island took on very large and very real dimensions in his mind.

The colored folk singer, encouraged by his supporters, began playing and singing "Freedom," which sounded very Communistic to the cop, and which he needed like a hole in the head, a Communist nigger-led riot on his beat! The two aged chess players were maneuvering around the edges of the crowd as though trying to determine which was the most vulnerable spot on the board and then, apparently having discovered it, ran off in the opposite direction. Meanwhile, some of the Saturday students had managed to get hold of a huge piece of cardboard and were lettering a crude sign reading STOP POLICE BRUTALITY! A few Bowery winos who were *really* vagrants, and who had *really* come here to ogle the tweedy sneakered college girls, were beginning to sing "Peg o' My Heart," and some curious college instructors had come out of the school to stand on the front steps or drift toward the crowd, puffing their pipes and smiling, and thinking how nice it was to be young in New York in April.

The cop took off his hat and wiped the sweatband, which was an old New York fuzz trick of stalling, and which the Negro folk singer recognized at once. He began singing louder, trying to drown out the winos. The cop had never known the words to "Freedom," and he had forgotten the words to "Peg o' My Heart," so he put his hat back on his head and wondered how all this had started. He had the strangest feeling all at once that things like this *always* seemed to start on his beat, and he wondered if he should transfer to the Fire Department. While he was wondering this, a pickpocket began plying his trade on the edge of the crowd, and one of the winos goosed a pretty virginal college girl who had taken on half of Fordham's football team the season before but who now shrieked in outraged surprise nonetheless. The cop was too busy to notice these petty infringements of the law because in his mind he had already mushroomed this minor demonstration into a forced march on City Hall. "Freedom" segued into "Blowin' in the Wind," and "Peg o' My Heart" into "I'm Looking Over a Four-Leaf Clover." The Saturday students raised a second crudely lettered sign, BAN THE BOMB!, and tried to march in tempo to both songs simultaneously. The two aged chess players had run around the park enlisting an army of octogenarians from the other benches, and they descended on the crowd now like a frail wedge of pawns aimed straight at the king's heart.

The cop said, "Now, look, let's talk this over peaceably," but one of the smoky-eyed girls was beginning to take off her blouse in misguided protest while the winos sang "We Shall Overcome" and the Negro folk singer modulated into "Did Your Mother Come From Ireland?" The goosed college girl slapped the man

178

standing behind her, and apologized when she recognized him as her seventh-hour Anthropology instructor. *"J'adoube, j'adoube!"* one of the chess players was shouting, and the cop was shouting, "Now, calm down, everybody!" and the marching Saturday students were shouting *"Viva* Bertrand Russell!" and just then one of the winos, a secret wood-alcohol drinker, dropped dead in the middle of the crowd while the smoky-eyed girl twirled her brassière triumphantly in the air.

By that time, Buddwing was deep in Greenwich Village, six blocks away.

# 11

THE THING that amazed him, of course, was that they had all come to his rescue without even knowing who or what he was. He could have been Edward Voegler or he could have been Sam Buddwing or he could have been Adolph Hitler, for that matter, and none of them would have cared. Standing there arguing with the cop, he had possessed no more identity than he had awakened with this morning, and yet they had rallied to his cause and taken up his banner. So what the hell did it really matter? Whether he was anybody or nobody, who really gave a

"Just a second, young man," the voice on his left and slightly to his rear said, and he stopped dead in his tracks with a heart-lurching suddenness, and only then realized how frightening his brush with the law had been. He turned swiftly in reflex, expecting to find the chief of police or perhaps the district attorney and finding instead a man of about sixty who was puffing on a pipe and smiling.

"Yes?" Buddwing said.

"Mind if I talk to you?" the man asked.

"Yes, I do," Buddwing said. He was beginning to get tired of talking to strangers. He wanted to see a face he knew; he wanted to shake a familiar hand.

"Well, that's all right," the man said, and he fell into step beside Buddwing.

"Maybe you didn't understand me," Buddwing started. "I said—"

"Oh yes, I understood you."

"Well, if you don't mind—"

"I saw what happened back there," the man said.

"Are you a detective?"

"No, no," the man said, chuckling. "No, what ever gave you that idea?"

"Well, what do you want?"

"I thought the entire thing was very interesting," the man said. "I was sitting opposite you when you first came into the park. Did you happen to notice me?"

"No, I didn't."

"Mmm, well, yes, I was." The old man struck a match and held it to the pipe. "I was there when you jumped to your feet and shouted 'Grace,' and I was also there"—he puffed at the pipe, trying to rekindle it—"when you . . . *puff, puff* . . . when you . . . *puff, puff* . . . mmm, there it is."

"When I what?"

"When you said you were Edward Voegler," the old man said, and smiled.

He paused.

He kept smiling, silently.

Then he said, "*Are* you Edward Voegler?"

"Why?" Buddwing said.

"I'm curious."

"Everybody's all at once so damn curious about me, aren't they?"

"Madmen always attract curiosity," the man said calmly, puffing on his pipe.

"No, I'm not Edward Voegler," Buddwing said quickly.

"Then why did you say you were?"

"Is there a reward? Is that it?"

"No, not that I'm aware of. The newspapers didn't say anything about a reward."

"Then what do you want?"

"I want to talk to you."

"Why?"

"Because you said you were Edward Voegler, which is a rather dangerous thing to say in a public place if you aren't him." He paused. "I believe you are."

"Why should you believe that?"

"Because you wouldn't show that policeman your identification."

"I don't *have* any identification," Buddwing said.

"Precisely."

"But that doesn't mean I'm Edward Voegler."

"Then who are you?"

It always gets back to that, Buddwing thought wearily. It always gets back to the question for which there is only one answer.

"I don't know," he said.

"Ahhh."

"Anyway, what the hell is it to you?"

"Let us simply say I'm an interested citizen."

"Let us simply say goodbye," Buddwing answered.

"Ah-ah," the man said, hooking Buddwing's arm. "No."

"Look, mister," Buddwing said warningly, "don't fool around with me. I'm stretched pretty thin, and I'm just liable to—"

"No," the man said, shaking his head. "I'm going to help you."

"How?"

"How would you like to be helped?" the man asked.

"I'd like you to vanish," Buddwing said.

"That wouldn't help you."

"I didn't ask for you."

"I know. I appeared of my own volition."

"Well, disappear of your own volition."

"No," the man said, and he shook his head again.

Buddwing, watching him, thought, I suppose I'll have to hit him. The thought wearied him. He wanted only to be left alone. He wanted only to wander the city nameless and homeless. Why wouldn't they let him do that in peace?

"Mister," he said, "you're an old man. You're a frail old man. I don't want to have to break away from you by force, mister, but I'll do it, I swear to God, unless you take your hand off my arm. Now, will you please do that, mister, and forget you ever saw me? Or do I have to hit you? I don't want to hit you, mister, believe me, but I don't want to be bothered by you, either."

"I'm not bothering you," the man said, but he did not remove his hand from Buddwing's arm.

"Mister, I'm very tired . . ."

"Yes, I know that . . ."

"And I don't know who I am . . ."

"You're Edward Voegler . . ."

"And I don't want to have to argue with you, and I *especially* don't want to have to hit you. Now, please let go of my goddamn arm!"

"No," the man said. "I want to help you."

"Who the hell are you?" Buddwing asked.

"God," the man answered.

They stood on the Greenwich Village sidewalk at five o'clock with the sun hovering in the sky behind the women's house of detention. Around them and behind them and beyond them, in a realistic bas-relief, were the jewelry shops and leather shops, the faggot clothing stores, the bakeries and delicatessens and restaurants and art supply houses. The minuscule sounds of the city, compounded to a steady hum, filled the air with life, and the man puffed on his pipe and looked at Buddwing seriously and seriously told him he was God, and Buddwing wanted to believe him.

He wanted to believe him because he thought again, for the second time since he had awakened, that he was dead. If I'm dead, then she's alive, he reasoned. What was it she had once said, how had she described Hell? They had been driving through the

Holland Tunnel, and she said, "This is what Hell should be, you know. Just driving through a tunnel like this forever, without being allowed to change lanes, and with policemen standing on the ramparts waving you on, and with signs telling you to maintain a uniform speed, eternally." If I am dead, then she is alive, he thought, and all these people walking in the street are dead, so why can't this man be God, why the hell not? If he's God, then everything that's happened to me since I woke up this morning has only been a preliminary to this confrontation. My soul rose up out of that supine image on the bench, ectoplasmic and double-exposed, just like in the movies, and it's been wandering in search and now here is God, puffing his pipe and waiting expectantly for me to kneel and kiss his ring, and he will know who I am.

"How do I know you're God?" Buddwing asked, testing him hopefully.

"How do you know I'm not?" the man answered.

"Well, where are your credentials?"

"Where are yours?"

"You can't just walk up to someone and expect him to believe you're God."

"What do you want me to do?" the old man said, and smiled. "Perform a miracle?"

"Yes," Buddwing said.

"I don't do miracles after five o'clock," the old man said.

"What time is it now?"

The man looked at his watch. "Ten after five."

"Just a little after closing time," Buddwing said. "Stretch a company rule. Make that automobile over there fly up over the rooftops."

"God never stretches company rules," the man said.

"Superman could send that car up over the rooftops," Buddwing said tauntingly.

"I am not Superman, I am God," the man answered.

"You don't look like God."

"How do you know what God looks like?"

"He's a kindly man with eyeglasses and white hair."

184

"That's my father," the old man said seriously.

"I didn't know God had a father."

"Everybody has a father," the man said.

"Not me."

"Even you."

"Anyway," Buddwing said, "I don't believe in God."

"Do you believe in me?"

"Not if you're God."

"Well, I am God."

"Then I don't believe in you."

"But you're talking to me."

"Yes, that's true."

"Well, who or what are you talking to, if not God?"

"I'm talking to an old nut who followed me from N.Y.U."

"That is only a symptom of your condition."

"What condition?"

"Your insanity. It is a well-known fact that crazy people think everyone else is crazy."

"But *you* think *I'm* crazy," Buddwing said.

"Of course."

"Then *you* must be crazy."

"God can't be crazy," the man said.

"You know all the answers, don't you?"

"Most of them."

"All right," Buddwing said, "am I dead?"

"Of course not."

"Are *you* dead?"

"God is immortal," the man answered. "He never dies because he is all-powerful."

"Then why don't you do just a little miracle?"

"I don't choose to," the man said with dignity. "If you won't accept me on faith, then you shouldn't accept me at *all*."

"Okay, I don't," Buddwing said.

"But you'll be sorry," the man added.

"Why?"

"Because I'll yell at the top of my lungs that you're Edward Voegler, and they'll put you in a strait jacket and take you away."

"That would be very petty of you," Buddwing said. "If you're really God—"

"God *is* very petty," the old man said calmly.

"Yes, but not in such a petty way."

"In *any* way he wants to be."

"Why'd you let Beethoven die?" Buddwing asked suddenly.

"He was getting old," the man answered, "and besides I never liked his music."

"I wasn't talking about *that* Beethoven," Buddwing said. "There!" he added triumphantly. "You don't even know who the hell I mean!"

"I know *exactly* who you mean."

"Yeah, who do I mean?"

"You mean Beethoven." The man paused. "He died because it was his time."

"Who decided that?"

"I did."

"Then you're a murderer."

"God cannot be a murderer," the man said.

"And you killed all the others, too."

"What others?"

"All of them, all of them! Don't play dumb with me, you phony bastard."

"God cannot be a phony bastard," the old man said.

"No, and you can't be God, because you don't even know who the hell Beethoven is or was. You don't even remember that you killed him on Tarawa! You don't remember anything, you phony bastard!"

"I remember everything," the man said.

"Yeah? Well, who am I? Do you happen to remember that?"

"Yes. You are Edward Voegler."

"Wrong!" Buddwing said. "Ha!"

"God cannot be wrong."

"God can be wrong and petty and a phony bastard besides,"

186

Buddwing said. "I reject you! I reject you because you're a murderer and a thief! You stole my identity this morning, and you stole Beethoven's when you killed him on Tarawa."

"On the contrary," the old man said, "I did not steal his identity."

"No, huh?"

"I gave him one," the old man said.

"How do you figure—"

"Because you will always remember that he was killed on Tarawa. That is his identity. I have made him immortal in your memory."

"And what have you done for *me* lately?"

"You asked me who you were, didn't you?"

"Yes, and—"

"And I told you. You are Edward Voegler."

"Convince me."

"I do not perform miracles after five o'clock."

"The hell with your miracles, just convince me! I'll be whoever you want me to be, if you'll only convince me!"

"You must convince yourself," the old man said.

"How?"

"You must have faith."

"In what?"

"In me."

"Why you? You're crazier than I am!"

"There," the old man said softly. "You *do* know, don't you?"

"I know nothing."

"You know you're crazy. And you also know you are Edward Voegler."

"I never heard of him."

"You are a paranoid schizophrenic," the old man intoned hypnotically. "You belong in Central Islip State Hospital where you stole a director's suit last night after dinner. You must go back there."

"I don't want to go back. Not there, and not anywhere!" Buddwing shouted. "No!"

The old man leaned closer to him. Buddwing saw his eyes for the first time. They were clear and blue and staring at him brightly, reflecting the late afternoon sun. They were the eyes of a lunatic.

The old man's hand was on his sleeve again, the fingers tightening in the blue cloth like a claw. The old man's breath was foul, and words tumbled from his mouth in a litany as he leaned closer to Buddwing, his eyes burning intensely. For a moment, Buddwing saw them as a pair, the insane old man who thought he was God, and the paranoid schizophrenic named Edward Voegler, both involved in a lunatic dialogue that had no connection with reality. And then, standing side by side with insanity, his eyes locked with the eyes of insanity, his sleeve gripped in the clutch of insanity, he knew all at once that this man was not his brother, and it was then he decided finally and with complete conviction that he was not Edward Voegler.

The old man was still talking. His speech was pleading and threatening, cajoling and abusive. He conjured images of Heaven and Hell, of sin and redemption, while Buddwing half listened, overwhelmed by an enormous sense of relief: he was *not* Edward Voegler, he was *not* insane. And then, because he had lived with the notion since 9:10 this morning when he had first seen the headline outside the candy store on 67th Street, because the notion had grown within him and become an image to fall back upon when all other hope of identity failed him, he stared blankly at the truth and willed it to be untrue. He wanted to be anyone, if only Edward Voegler, a poor confused madman who had stolen a director's suit and fled. He wanted to be anyone, no, he wanted to be *someone*.

"Listen to God," the old man was saying. "Listen to the voice of God, for He will lead you into green pastures and—"

"Listen to me," Buddwing said.

"Listen to God."

"No! You listen to *me*. I'm *some*body, do you understand that?"

"You are Edward Voegler, and I—"

"No, I'm *me*, and you're a crazy son of a bitch who thought you saw yourself in me. Well, I'm not Edward Voegler, I'm not insane. I'm me, you understand? And I'm tired of people looking at me and seeing only themselves! From now on, you look at me and you see *me*, or you see nothing at all! Nothing! Now, get the hell away from me, before I tell that cop on the corner you're God. Go on, get out of here!"

"If you tell him I'm God, I'll tell him you're Edward Voegler," the old man said slyly.

"Good. Maybe he'll believe us both and lock us both up. How would you like that?"

"You are messing around with the Almighty, you little bastard," the old man said suddenly.

"God shouldn't curse," Buddwing said, smiling.

The old man stared at him with insane malice in his eyes, the pipe, dead again, clenched tightly in his fist. Without warning, he turned toward the policeman on the corner and shouted, "Help! This man is Edward Voegler, the escaped maniac!"

For a shocked ten seconds, Buddwing could not believe the old man had really carried out his threat. Then he saw the cop turn slowly toward them, and he heard the old man shouting again, "Help! Help! Escaped maniac! Help!" and for the first time since he had awakened he knew real panic.

Blindly, he ran.

He ran toward the sun, west, fixing it in his mind as a goal, and wanting to reach it before it descended into the river. Behind him, he could hear the old man and the cop shouting after him in unison, but he ran for the sun, thinking if he could only reach the sun before it went out, everything would be all right. Their shouts diminished behind him, or perhaps were overwhelmed by the noise of his own ragged breathing. As he ran, he thought how curious it was that if you sat on a park bench in New York and minded your own damn business, a cop would come over to you and ask to see your identification; but if you raced along the city streets, running like a thief for the sun because you wanted to catch it before it fell, why, no one gave you more than a sideward glance. He smiled as he ran. He could feel his feet thumping against the pavement with good sole-rocking thwacks, could feel each pumping stride jarring his calves and thighs. He sucked in breath after breath; he could feel the hot air in his throat and lungs, could feel his body responding to the pavement and the exertion of his flight. You never run, he thought. You grow up, and you never run any more.

The cop and the old man were lost somewhere behind him now; they were no longer a threat. But he kept running anyway, wanting to reach the river and catch the sun. He ran through a city that had suddenly become one-dimensional, as though viewed from a seat at the extreme side of a motion-picture theater. The people, the buildings, the trucks parked outside the meat market between Ninth and Tenth, the overhead span of the Henry Hudson Parkway flashed past his eyes in flat unreality; only the river and the sun were real, and these only as half-understood goals. You son of a bitch, you gave him identity, did you? he thought. By killing him. You made him immortal, did you? I'll always remember him as the one who was killed on Tarawa, is that it? And how will I remember the others, you son of a bitch? Have you made them immortal, too? He had to get to the river before the sun went out.

It was not what he had expected. The river's edge was crowded with buildings and ships. He had wanted a dock he could sit upon; he had wanted to look up at the living sun and find its reflected stain on the water. Where are all the free spaces? he wondered. You've cluttered up the whole damn world with your dockside shacks and your cargo ships. Where can I sit to rest? He kept running, turning abruptly upriver, his eyes searching the waterfront, his legs weary now, his heart pumping furiously, his lungs aching. He did not know how long or how far he ran searching for a break in the unyielding barrier that kept him from the river, running against the southbound traffic that roared on the highway overhead. It had not been this way long ago, when he had idly watched a squadron of destroyers midstream, and a friend of his had tried to hit the nearest ship with a stone.

When he saw the activity up ahead, he knew he had come uptown at least as far as the forties, and he knew if he ran a step farther he would collapse and die without ever seeing the sun. He did not want more confusion and noise. He almost turned and began running downriver again, but something drew him toward the huge black-and-white hull of the ocean liner poised against the sky; something drew him toward the sound of disembarking passengers, the honking of taxicab horns, the shouts of porters and customs officials. As though this were the sun itself, he moved toward the throng of people fluttering about the dock, and then he stopped running.

He stood with his arms hanging and his shoulders loose, sucking in great gulps of air. There was sound everywhere around him, voices in English and in Italian, a poodle barking from the open window of a parked black Cadillac, squealing children, the gunning roar of engines. He saw a woman coming through the dock gate, and a man ran to embrace her, and he suddenly felt more alone than he ever had in his life. The passengers were all pouring into the street now, all being embraced and kissed and greeted, and he stood on the edges of the throng, breathing raggedly and watching the exchange of love, and all at once he began weeping.

He wept bitterly. He was still struggling for breath, and each swallow he took ended in a convulsive sob that almost choked him. He stood unseen and unheard on the edge of the boisterous crowd, weeping. A ship's porter shouted, *"Presto! Le valige della signora!"* and a cab driver yelled, "Anybody for Idlewild? Idlewild here, who's going to Idlewild?" A baby suddenly began crying in its mother's arms, and a man testily snarled, "I thought *you* arranged for transportation." A fat woman in a mink stole erupted with a cheery "Yoo-hoo! Arthur! Yoo-hoo! Here we are!" Here we are, he thought, and the tears streamed down his cheeks.

He wept for himself, he supposed, and he wept for all the dead people in the world who would never again know the warmth of human arms around them, never again feel the brush of welcoming lips against their cheeks, never again hear a fat woman in a mink stole yelling "Yoo-hoo! Here we are!" He came very close to recognizing the truth about himself in that moment. As he sucked air into his lungs and into his body—perfume, oxygen, carbon monoxide, fumes of Diesel, body odors, river smell, a trace of whiskey—and heard the sounds of life around him, standing on the edges of life, the rim of the sun, he suddenly wished to re-enter it and hold it close, and this was when the masquerade almost collapsed. His name almost materialized in his head and on his tongue; he almost knew exactly who he was and how he had happened to awaken in the park this morning. In another moment perhaps, in another five seconds, the knowledge would have rushed free and clear, erupting from where it was hidden. He would have known.

A look of frozen expectation must have covered his face. He stopped breathing abruptly, as though afraid this truth balanced precariously on the edge of his consciousness could be toppled into the abyss by the smallest breath. He hung poised, waiting, dreading the knowledge, but ready to welcome it the way these returning passengers were being welcomed everywhere around him, longing to be a part of them again, desperately wishing for re-entry; it would come, it would come at any moment, he knew, he *knew*; he waited with his teeth clenched and the tears running down his face.

He saw Grace.

For a moment, he thought, No, I am not really seeing her, I am only afraid of the truth. But then his heart leaped in recognition, and he began moving toward her quickly. She is not Grace, he thought, don't you remember, *won't* you remember? He was moving toward her rapidly as she stepped through the crowd and around it, walking with a group of people who were laughing and pounding a young man on the back as he struggled toward a taxi with his luggage. Buddwing almost cried out to her. Wait, he told himself. Listen. You'd better face this. You'd better face it now. He hesitated.

They had put the boy into the taxi, and two girls and another boy climbed into it beside him. The cab pulled away, leaving Grace and five other people on the dock. He noticed that she stood slightly apart from the group, as though not really a member of it. Another cab pulled up. Buddwing expected all of them to get into it, expected Grace to drive away leaving him only with this insistent, clamoring, edge-of-mind knowledge that threatened to crack his skull wide open, that and thirty lousy cents, not enough to follow.

The cab moved away. Grace was still on the dock, standing alongside a young man in a tweed jacket. The young man took her arm. Together, they began walking east.

Who else can she be? he thought, and he began following them.

Behind him, he heard a little girl say, "Daddy, that man is crying."

# 12

Shⴄ LOOKED much the same, yes, per-
haps a bit thinner, her blond hair a little shorter, but she was
Grace, yes, and he felt an enormous sense of peace settle over
him as he began following her and the young man. They seemed
in no particular hurry to get wherever they were going, which
was why, he supposed, they had not taken a taxicab with the
rest of their group. They strolled idly, enjoying the mild spring
evening, chatting, laughing occasionally, their laughter drifting
back to him where he followed some fifty feet behind them.

The presence of the young man did not disturb him, although
he felt somehow it should. As he watched them strolling, there
seemed to be the same rightness he had felt when sitting in
Washington Square Park, a correctness about the situation which,
rather than excluding the young man whose arm she held, made
him an integral part of it. Watching Grace and the young man,
he had the peculiar feeling that he was watching himself, that
she was chatting with him, Buddwing, that she was turning her
head every now and then to laugh at something *he* had said, that

she was not really with the young man at all. He smiled. He felt
his position to be both superior and advantageous. He could, in
effect, walk side by side with Grace in the presence of the young
man, and at the same time he could follow behind and observe her
from a distance.

Her hair bothered him a little because Grace had always worn
her hair very long, flowing past her shoulders and down her
back, and this girl wore it clipped short like a rolled gold helmet,
evenly cropped at the nape of her neck. She was thinner, too, a
lot thinner than he had first thought, moving with casual an-
gularity in her sweater and skirt and high-heeled pumps. But
he supposed she was Grace, after all, because her walk seemed
somehow familiar and well-remembered, as did the way she held
her head, the way she placed her hand gently on the young man's
arm to emphasize a point.

He followed them down 44th Street, and then the young man
stopped on the steps of a building between . . . Eighth and
Ninth, he supposed it was, and he and Grace chatted there while
two Puerto Rican kids impatiently waited for them to get off
the steps so they could resume their game of stoopball. Buddwing
understood now why they had not taken a cab along with the
rest. The young man obviously lived here, fairly close to the
docks, and Grace probably had felt like walking, maybe she had
some shopping to do, or maybe she just enjoyed walking in the
spring air, yes, he remembered Grace liked to walk a lot. They
finally shook hands in farewell. The young man went into the
building and Grace continued walking east toward . . . yes, it
was Eighth Avenue, and then crossed the avenue, heading toward
Broadway.

The theater district was curiously still at this hour. It must
have been six or a little after, he supposed, and everyone seemed
to have gone indoors in preparation for the evening. The girl
was walking rapidly, but he sensed she still was in no hurry to
get anywhere, since she stopped every now and then to study the
photographs outside a theater, or to read a three-sheet as she was
doing now, her face turned in profile, forehead, nose, jaw, and

throat combining in a sweeping fluid line that denied its own thrust and achieved a look of serene order. She turned toward him briefly, as though sensing his intent gaze upon her, and he turned away quickly and lighted a cigarette under the marquee of a theater, but not before he had seen the deep brown flash of her eyes and felt an exultant rush of joy at this last confirming aspect of her features. He busied himself shaking out the match and putting the cigarettes back into his pocket until, from the corner of his eye, he saw her begin to walk again.

Her movements all seemed impulsive and unpremeditated. She walked almost completely past Mackey's and then suddenly arrested her step and turned toward the window as though the decision had been made abruptly and without prior thought. She studied the theater posters there, nibbling on her thumb, and then abruptly turned away again— in mid-glance, as it were—and began walking rapidly again, cutting across the street and into Shubert Alley. He followed her through the narrow passage, aware of the silence of the streets, aware of distant voices only as muted sections of an orchestra, the abrupt whine of a truck starting behind him at the *Times* delivery depot, the hollow echo of a newsboy shouting his headlines on Broadway, the pleasant hum of two dancers chatting outside the Shubert, and then they came into 45th Street, and she turned right toward Broadway, and he suddenly realized she knew he was following her.

What had earlier been a direct utilitarian walk now became a subtly seductive prance. She stepped out with a deliberate sway now; she brought each foot down firmly as if sensuously aware of the high-heeled shoes, as if certain each clicking jog would send a subsequent tantalizing ripple to her behind. Where her movements had been sudden and disjointed before, they became studied and deliberate now. She turned her head to look at signs and passersby, showing her profile, tilting her nose, her face assuming a studied look of indifference that sang to him loudly. She tossed her short hair, she smiled at a small boy carrying a shoe-shine box, she stopped at the window of a petshop on Broadway and rapped the glass, trying to catch the attention of the puppy inside, and then turned her face fully to Buddwing, with a sudden raising of her eyes, blinding, and turned away to lead the pursuit.

He knew he would have to approach her soon.

There was a muted excitement on Broadway as the city tentatively ventured outdoors in search of Saturday night. She was waiting for his approach, he knew that now, waiting with an impatience that was wearing thin, seemingly oh so interested in everything that was happening around her, the teen-agers lounging outside the Paramount, the Times Square fags boldly sniffing the air, anticipating the darkness that would soon enshroud them, a tenor saxophone starting in one of the bars, "How High the Moon" with a split reed, the Bronx women in their mink stoles and their escorts in Saturday night blue, entering restaurants and studying marquees, the shopgirl hurrying home with a small white cake box dangling from a string, the girl who stood on the sidewalk bent over a newsstand, delicately picking the New York *Post* from the stack of papers, her long black hair hanging over one eye, her sneakered feet in an unconscious ballet position. The city was poised, coiled as tight as a spring, and all of it was interesting to her, oh so goddamn interesting, she examined it minutely with her eyes, she sniffed each savory aroma, her ears caught each innuendo of sound, but he knew she was anticipating him, and he knew he would have to approach her fast or lose her. She stopped to wait for a light change on Broadway and 43rd, and he took a deep breath and walked up to her.

"Hello, Grace," he said.

She turned as though discovering him in surprise. "Hello, Seymour," she said.

"Is that my name?" he asked.

"Is Grace mine?"

"Yes."

"Then yours is Seymour."

They began walking together naturally, as though they had met by prearrangement and were now idly filling each other in on the day's activities.

197

"I don't think Seymour is the right name for me," he said.

"I don't think Grace is right for me, either," she answered.

"It's the perfect name for you."

"No, I'm not at all graceful. And I'm much too short. A girl named Grace should be at least five-seven."

"You're about five-four," he said.

"Yes, I am."

"You're tall."

"How long have you been following me?" she asked.

"When did you discover I was following you?"

"I asked first."

"I saw you on the dock."

"I saw you when I stopped to look at the sign outside the St. James." She paused. "What's your name?"

"What's yours?"

"Grace," she said, and smiled.

"Okay, mine is Seymour."

"I'm not really Grace. Why do you call me that?"

"Because that's your name."

"No."

"Then what is it?"

"I'm not sure I'll tell you."

"Okay. Would you like a cup of coffee or something?"

"Sure."

"Well, I don't have any money," he said.

"Then why'd you ask me if I wanted coffee?"

"I thought you might like some," he said. He paused thoughtfully, and then said, "You have a beauty spot near your left shoulder, haven't you?"

"No," she said. "I haven't."

"Yes, you have."

"You must be thinking of another Grace."

"No, I'm thinking of you." He held out his right hand. "You gave me this ring."

"I'm sorry, but I didn't." She looked at the ring. "I wouldn't have given you a ring with a cracked stone."

"What kind of ring would you have given me?"

"I wouldn't have given you any ring at all."

"Besides, the stone wasn't cracked when you gave it to me. I broke it yesterday."

"How?"

"I banged it against the wall."

"Why'd you do that?"

"Because you got me angry."

She stopped in the middle of the sidewalk and looked at him curiously, her brown eyes narrowing. "You really *do* think you know me, don't you?" she said.

"Yes, I really think so," he said.

She kept staring at him. "You know, you say it with such . . . certainty that . . . you make me feel I ought to know *you*."

"Well, I think you ought to," he answered.

"Yeah, huh? Why?"

"Well, I'm a very nice person to know."

"Mmmm," she said, and she smiled. "I thought I was pretty hip," she said, and she shook her head.

"What do you mean?"

"I'm falling for the oldest line in the world."

"What line?"

" 'Haven't we met before? You remind me of someone I know.' *That* one."

"Oh, that one."

"Yeah."

"But it's not a line," he said.

"I'm Grace, huh?" she said, nodding.

"Yeah."

"Mmm," she said. She kept nodding. "And you're Seymour."

"Well, no, I'm not Seymour."

"Then who are you?"

"I don't know. Who do you think I am?"

She shrugged. "You'd have to tell me a little about yourself before I could even guess. How old are you?"

"Thirty-nine. How old are you?"

"Twenty-eight."

"What were you doing at the dock?"

"Meeting a friend. Well, an acquaintance really. He's in the Peace Corps, and he just got back from Africa. He used to be a social worker, you see." She paused. "That's how I know him." She paused again. "I'm a social worker, too, you see."

"Oh, that's good," he said.

"Why?"

"Well, you're probably very good at interviewing."

"Yeah . . . well . . . mmm," she said, and shrugged. "You're married, aren't you?"

"What makes you say that?"

"I can tell." She paused. "I'm always getting involved with married men. I don't know what the hell it is." She shook her head. "Do you have any children?" She shook her head again. "Never mind, don't answer. You've probably got six of them." She paused, studying him. "What do you do for a living?"

"Is this the interview?"

She smiled. "Yeah, sure, this is the interview."

"I'm a pretty bad subject," he said. "What do you *think* I do for a living?"

"Let me see your hands." He held them out to her, and she looked at them briefly, and then dropped them, and was thoughtfully silent as they began walking again.

"Do you know what a tort is?" she asked.

"Sure."

"What is it?"

"It's a civil wrong or injury to a plaintiff."

"What's a misdemeanor?" she asked quickly.

"Any crime that isn't a felony," he answered.

"And what's a felony?"

"A crime punishable by death or imprisonment in a state prison."

"What's the maximum penalty for burglary?" she asked.

"I have no idea," Buddwing said.

"Okay, what's the name of the most popularly used reference book on evidence?"

"I don't know."

Grace nodded in disappointment and studied him again. She seemed to be preparing a further list of questions in her mind, and then suddenly she asked, "What's a catheter?"

"A hollow tube."

"What's it used for?"

"For draining off body fluids."

"Is morphine a depressant or an excitant?"

"A depressant."

"What about codeine?"

"An excitant."

"And scopalamine?"

"Is that a drug?" Buddwing asked.

"Yeah, well, skip it," Grace said. She thought for a moment, and then asked, "Who wrote *Gone With the Wind?*"

"Margaret Mitchell."

"Who published the book?"

"I don't know."

"What are the names of some New York publishers?"

"Doubleday, Random House, Macmillan . . ."

"What are pages?"

"Pages?"

"Yes."

"Do you mean *pages?* Like in a book?"

"Never mind," Grace said. "If the market is bearish, what does that mean?"

"Weak."

"What's it called when it's strong?"

"Bullish."

"What's the current quote on A.T. & T.?"

"I don't know."

"General Motors?"

"I don't know."

"I.B.M.?"

"I don't know. What's an A and R man?" Buddwing asked.

"What?"

"An A and R man."

"I don't know," Grace said. "What is it?"

"Ah-hah," Buddwing said, and they both laughed.

"All right, I give up," she said. "Is that what you are? An A and R man?"

"Nope."

"Then what are you?"

"I don't know," he said.

"What do you mean?"

"I don't know anything about myself."

"What?"

"I don't know who I am," he said, and shrugged almost cheerfully.

"Really?" she said, and stopped on the corner suddenly, looking at him with what he realized was professional interest, a social worker's curious, sympathetic, detached, probing look.

"You're serious, aren't you?" she said.

"Yes."

"About not knowing who you are, I mean."

"Yes, that's right."

"You're not kidding me? I mean, this isn't part of your line?"

"No. No."

"Mmmm." She kept studying him thoughtfully, nibbling at the inside of her mouth. "How long . . . when did this happen?" she asked.

"This morning. When I woke up."

"Mmm. You just don't know who you are, huh?"

"That's right."

"Mmmm."

He could feel the professional interest completely overwhelming whatever other interest had previously existed. He felt a bit put out by this new turn of events, as though he had suddenly become a client in her case load rather than a person. He did not want to be a client; he wanted to be himself. And he had thought

Grace, of all people, would certainly see him as himself, rather than as some damn stupid client in a case load. He knew immediately that he had to get her off this track, had to swing the conversation back to its main topic, which was, after all, a man and a woman on a street corner: Out *here*, Miss Jones, a man is a man and a woman is a woman.

"Look," he said, "let's not worry about—"

"Haven't you got any identification on you?" she asked.

"No. But I wish you wouldn't worry a—"

"And no money, you've already told me that."

"That's right. Listen, do you think we could—"

"Do you have anything at all that might—"

"I don't see what difference—"

"—help to identify—"

"Look, couldn't we just forget it?"

"But I want to help, you see."

"Yes, but . . ."

"I want to help," she said, very softly.

"Well . . ."

"*Are* you carrying anything that might—?"

"I have an address book with a telephone number in it," he said wearily.

"Have you tried calling the number?"

"Yes. She doesn't know me."

"Who would that be?"

"A woman named Gloria Osborne."

"Would you mind if *I* called her?"

"What good would that do? I went to see her. She doesn't know me."

"Did *you* recognize her?"

"No."

"Do you know where we are?"

"Sure. We're on Broadway."

"What city?"

"Oh, come on, Grace. New York."

"Why do you think my name is Grace?"

"You haven't told me it isn't, have you?"

"Yes, I have."

"Well, you haven't told me what it *is*. I mean, if it isn't Grace."

"Mmm," she said. "Do you live here in New York?"

"I think so."

"Would you happen to remember where?"

"No." Buddwing paused. "I have a New York Central time-table in my pocket, if that means anything."

"Oh? May I see it?"

Buddwing shrugged and handed her the schedule. "Oh my, there are a great many towns on the line," she said gently, professionally. "Is it possible you're *from* one of these towns?"

"No, I don't think so. I'm from New York, I think."

"Do any of these town names mean anything to you? Do you recognize them?"

"Recognize them?"

"Well, do any of them mean anything to you?"

"I know where they are, if that's what you mean. I know what towns they are."

"Bronxville?"

"Yes, I know where that is."

"Does it mean anything to you?"

"No."

"White Plains?"

"No."

"Valhalla?"

"No."

"Chappaqua?"

"No."

"Mount Kisco?"

"None of them mean anything to me."

"How about Katonah?"

"None of them."

"Croton Falls?"

"I told you . . ."

"Do you have any idea why this timetable would be in your jacket pocket?"

"No."

"Are you carrying anything else in your pockets?"

"Yes. A pen and pencil set, and two theater stubs."

"Legitimate?"

"What?"

"The legitimate theater?"

"No. Movie stubs. They're movie stubs."

"Would you remember which movie?"

"Something with Kim Novak."

"When did you see it?"

"Last night."

"Well, now we're getting somewhere, aren't we?" she said, and smiled such a goddamn solicitious social-worker smile that he wanted to punch her in the mouth.

"Are we?" he asked.

"Well, we know you went to a movie last night, and obviously someone was with you, since there are two stubs."

"I knew that when I woke up this morning," he said coldly.

"Where was that?"

"In Central Park."

"Did you know where you were at the time?"

"Yes."

"Were you surprised? Waking up in Central Park?"

"I don't remember *what* I was. I think I was confused. Because I didn't know who I was."

"What I meant was—"

"It's a little eerie waking up and not knowing who you are, you know," he said sarcastically.

"Yes, I know," she said sympathetically, and smiled. "What I was driving at was whether the neighborhood seemed strange to you."

"Central Park?"

"Yes, Central Park."

"How would Central Park be strange to anyone who lives in New York?"

"I meant the surrounding neighborhood."

"Fifth Avenue?"

"Yes, if that's where it was."

"Yes, that's where it was," Buddwing said.

"Did it seem strange to you?"

"No, of course not. How the hell could Fifth Avenue seem strange? That's a pretty stupid question, isn't it?"

"I'm sorry, but—"

"I mean, I've lived in New York all my life; how could Fifth Avenue seem strange? It's Fifth Avenue, what else could it be?"

"Of course," Grace said understandingly.

He was getting angrier every moment they talked. Her professional interest seemed to have moved beyond that now, seemed to have overgrown its own bounds and become a directing force. Doggedly, she persisted in shoving him toward a truth he did not wish to recognize. Stubbornly, he resisted. What's the matter with you? he thought. Why won't you just accept me? Do we have to go all over this? Don't you know how much this hurts?

"What's my last name?" she asked suddenly.

"How would I know?" he answered coldly.

"Well, you seem to think I'm Grace."

"I'm not sure any more," he said sharply, hoping to hurt her.

"But Grace what?"

"I haven't the faintest idea," he said.

"Could it be the same as *your* last name?"

"Yes, I suppose it could."

"Is it possible she's your wife?"

"It's possible," he said. "Anything's possible."

"Well, *is* she?"

"No."

"How do you know?"

"I don't know for sure."

"Then she *might* be, isn't that so?"

"Yes, she might be. But she isn't."

"How old is she? Would you remember that?"

"She's thirty-six," he said. "She looks younger."

"When did you see her last?"

"I don't know."

"Try to remember."

"I can't remember."

"Tell me what you do remember."

"I don't remember anything at all about her," he said, hoping that would be the end of it.

"Well, how about your parents, then?"

"My mother has no mouth," he said, and then frowned in puzzlement.

"What?"

"I mean she has very thin lips," he said quickly. "When she takes off her lipstick, her mouth vanishes."

"Is she alive? Your mother?"

"Yes. Wait, I don't know. I think so. Maybe."

"And your father?"

"He owns a cafeteria," he said immediately, and immediately felt confused. She was confusing him, the bitch.

"What's his name?"

"Isadore Schwartz." Confusion and anger. Why was she

"Well, there you are," she said, smiling. "If *his* name is Schwartz, then *your* name must be—"

"No. I changed it," he said tightly.

"To what?"

"Buddwing." Leave me alone, he thought.

"Well, in any case—"

"That's not my name, either," he said angrily.

"Then what *is* your name?"

"For Christ's sake, don't *you* know?" he shouted.

"No, I'm afraid I don't."

"Must we start with a goddamn argument?"

"Don't shout at me," she said.

"Why the hell must we—"

"I said don't shout. I'm trying to help you."

"Well, I don't need your goddamn help."

"I'm not sure you *know* what you need," she said.

"I sure as hell don't need *you*."

"I wish you wouldn't shout. People are looking at us."

"The hell with people," he said triumphantly: if she was at least aware of people as people, then perhaps she would begin to recognize *him* as a person, too. "Do we have to start with an argument, Grace?" he asked gently.

"Start?"

"Yes, *start*. Do we have to argue?"

Her face was now very serious, and her voice very low, and she said, "I'm not starting anything. Not with you, mister. You've got too many problems."

"So have you," he answered, and she looked at him in startled surprise, and he knew he had finally and magically pierced the social-worker armor to reveal the soft and throbbing vulnerable flesh beneath it. She kept staring at him. Something was happening in her eyes and on her face. Something terrible was happening, and he watched it and wished for a moment that it would not happen because he knew that once it did, they would be tied to each other forever.

"My problems are my business," she said softly.

"Yes. And mine are mine."

"Okay, so let's keep them separate and apart," she said.

"Okay, let's do that," he said, and turned from her abruptly and began walking away, feeling he was escaping, feeling an enormous wave of relief.

"Hey!" she yelled after him.

He stopped and turned to face her.

"What are you going to do now?"

"What difference does it make?"

"Well . . . you can't just go wandering around."

"Why can't I?"

"Because you need help."

"Every goddamn person on the face of this earth needs help," he said angrily.

"Won't you let me take you to a hospital?" she asked gently.

"I can find my own way to a hospital, thank you."

"Is that where you're going?"

"No."

"You should."

"Why? Are *they* going to tell me who I am? I'm eight million different people—how the hell are *they* going to know who I am?"

"Look, I . . ." She lowered her eyes. "I didn't mean to make you angry."

"I'm not angry."

"I'm sorry."

"Forget it."

"I suppose I . . . I suppose I *did* lead you on."

"I suppose you did."

"And I *was* flirting with you," she said.

"I know you were."

"But I can't get involved with you, that's all there is to it."

"Sure. Nobody wants to get involved with anybody. Why the hell should you be any different?"

"I'm not usually afraid of involvements," she said.

"Then what *are* you afraid of?"

"Look . . ." she said. She shook her head. "Look, I don't owe you a goddamn thing. You have no right to talk to me this way."

"I'll talk to you however the hell I damn please," he said.

"No, you won't," she answered, her eyes flaring, "and don't you ever forget it!" She seemed not to realize that she had, in that moment, given their tenuous relationship both continuity and longevity. He stared at her silently and said nothing.

"Well," she said, "why . . . why don't you go?"

"All right," he said, but he did not move.

"I can't go around feeling sorry for every damn stray dog who crosses my path."

"All right," he said.

"I've got enough troubles of my own."

"All right."

"I don't want to know you," she said. "This is *just* what I don't want, this . . . this goddamn intimacy. So . . . so just disappear, will you? I'm not about to get involved with you, no, sir."

"Okay, so long," he said, and again he turned.

"Wait a minute," she said.

"What do you want?"

"Have you got any money?"

"You know I haven't got any money."

"Have you . . . have you had dinner yet?"

"No."

They faced each other silently. She would not say more, and he sensed it. He kept watching her, waiting for her to speak, and knowing she would not. I know you too well, he thought. I know every goddamn corner of your mind.

"Do you want to have dinner with me?" he asked.

"You don't have any money," she said. Her voice had become very gentle, almost shy. She smiled shyly and looked up at him, waiting.

"That's right, I don't," he said.

"You mean you want *me* to pay for your dinner?"

"Well, I hadn't really thought of it that way. I just thought it'd be nice to have dinner together."

"That's kind of nervy, isn't it?" she asked. A coquettishness was creeping into her manner, replacing the shyness, or perhaps merely an extension of it.

"Is it?" he asked.

"Well, sure it is," she said. "Very nervy."

They were not talking about dinner at all. He suddenly remembered a long discussion he and Jesse had had aboard the *Fancher* one night, and then pushed it out of his mind and walked very close to where she was standing by the lamppost.

"I *am* hungry," he said.

"So am I."

"Where would you like to eat?"

"I didn't know it'd been settled."

"It's settled," he said.

She stared at him in silence for a long time, and then she said, "Yes, I suppose it is."

# 13

As they moved through their courtship
—and he thought of it as that, no matter how brief it was—
Buddwing felt himself becoming more and more involved in an
intense inner reality that seemed as clearly defined as whatever
was happening in the outer space through which he and the girl
moved, inexorably pulled toward a conclusion he knew would
no longer be valid when they reached it.

This curious dichotomy of logic puzzled him. He knew that
this girl whose hand he held was Grace, and that their lives
would become inextricably bound together, but he felt a curious futility about their early exploration of each other, as
though it would lead only to an inconclusive end. But how
could its conclusion be in doubt when everything they did together seemed to prepare naturally and easily for the next thing
they did, and then to prepare for what followed that, building
toward the only possible conclusion, the inescapable conclusion?
And yet, he had the feeling that the end—why did he even *consider* an end, why did he allow his mind to entertain thoughts of

an *end* when this was only the beginning?—would leave him exactly where he had been all along.

It seemed to him that there were definite echoes of Doris in this girl; she moved like her sometimes, and sometimes she even sounded like her; all right, what the hell, so she was something like Doris. But if a person followed that line of reasoning, he would have to conclude that every woman in his life was simply an echo of the woman who had preceded her. Grace was an echo of Doris, and Doris was an echo of his goddamn cousin Mandy with her piano legs, and Mandy was an echo of the first woman he had ever known, his mother. Well, okay, if a person wanted to get involved with all that Freudian jazz, well then, okay, Grace *was* an echo of his mother thrice removed, okay? A subtle refinement of the rather coarse and sometimes gross woman who had been his mother, okay? The same blond hair, and the same height more or less—he always thought of Grace as being tall, almost as tall as his mother had been—and the same directness and the same trigger-quick suspicious mind, and the same full breasts; okay, I'm falling in love with my own mother, okay? Well, now, just a minute, don't draw any hasty conclusions. So you kind of like this girl, fine, you've got a little lech for her, fine, she does look a little bit like your dear mother the queen, the same blond hair, but let's consider all the aspects of this, shall we? After all, if we are going to go searching through the involuted labyrinths of your mind, we must also inspect the possibility that not only does this sweet young social worker remind you of herself, who she most certainly is, this figure of beauty and Grace who she undoubtedly is and is not, and not only does she remind you of your dear late lamented mother with no mouth and blue pom-pom slippers and full and eagerly comforting breasts, and oh yes Mandy with her piano legs, your older cousin full of bursting vigor and sex, oh yes, all of these various and assorted women, but does she not remind you too of another sweet and angelic face, the cherub face on the roof of Il Duomo in Milan, the face that belonged to Beethoven who was machine-gunned to death in the underwater barbed wire off Tarawa? If we are to pursue these separate though tangential paths, where, then, will the conclusion lie? The conclusion will lie in endless repetition and inconclusion, that's where. The conclusion will lie in the knowledge that you are not yourself at all but merely a collection of neurotic responses to random stimuli.

He remembered again the conversation he and Jesse had had one night aboard the *Fancher* shortly after the hurricane that had overtaken them on the way to Japan. They were trying to explain a theory to one of their shipmates, a radar striker named Starkey, getting more and more excited by their idea. Starkey would not or could not grasp their meaning.

"Don't you see?" Jesse was saying. "I say 'Good morning' to you, right? But you don't hear me say 'Good morning,' you only hear what you *want* to hear, and what you hear is 'How are you?' So you answer, 'I'm fine, thanks, how're you?' but instead I hear you say, 'Nice day, isn't it?' and I answer, 'Beautiful day,' but you hear me say, 'Got the sniffles, can't kick otherwise.' Don't you get it? It's possible. We're telling you it's *possible*."

"No, it ain't," Starkey replied. "Because if we hear only what we want to hear, then by God we're *seeing* only what we *want* to see, too."

"Why not?" Jesse said. "Why isn't that possible, too? You trying to tell me we all see things the same way?"

"No, but if we're both looking at an apple, we know by God it's an apple and not an orange."

"How do you know we're both calling an apple the same thing?" Buddwing asked.

"What do you mean?"

"How do you know an apple isn't an orange to me?"

"Because an apple is an apple, that's why."

"But suppose I just heard you say, 'An orange is an orange'?"

"That *ain't* what I said."

"How do you know it's not what you said? How do you know you heard what *I* said?"

"I got ears, ain't I?"

"Yes, you've got a nose."

"I said *ears*."

"Yes, I heard you. You said nose."

"Don't you see what he's trying to do?" Jesse said to Starkey in exasperation.

"Yeah, he's trying to mix me up, that's what," Starkey said.

"He's trying to explain something, you goddamn fool."

"He's trying to explain that what I hear and what I see ain't what I hear and what I see. Does that by God make sense to you?"

"It makes a whole hell of a lot of sense," Jesse said.

"Yeah, well, I think you've both gone Asiatic," Starkey said, and he stretched himself out full length in his sack and turned his back to them.

They left the aft sleeping compartment and went out to stand on the fantail. The war was over, the *Fancher* was running with lights again, they stood in semidarkness near the stacked garbage cans and talked in excited whispers, involved in a highly philosophical discussion for which neither of them was adequately prepared. Looking back on that night now, he recognized just how specious their theory had been. They had, after all, communicated. Moreover, they had both used words that each had readily understood. If they had seriously accepted their own theory, they would have been forced to believe that Jesse was supplying all the dialogue in a conversational stream that was quite different from the one Buddwing pursued, the one in which *he* was the sole creator. And granting this, it would have been necessary to grant the inevitably following premise as well: that one of those separate though concurrent conversations had simply vanished into air, leaving neither trace nor memory of itself.

Something was eluding him now, too; something had vanished as surely as that second hypothetical conversation. He moved through his courtship with Grace in the midst of a clamoring mingled reality, a disjointed conglomeration of thoughts and images from within and without, pulsating with life, each as real in its shimmering presence as the other. The reality was this girl who went through the exploratory rite with him, but the reality was also Grace, and crosshatched through these two concurrent truths was another and terror-ridden truth, so that reality upon reality, truth upon truth crossed and recrossed, tumbled and swam. Surely these Saturday night people surrounding him, these pleasure-bound faces, these bodies in their twentieth-century finery, these sleek and shining automobiles, these curving neon tubes, these pavements, these streets, this city, surely these were as real as the girl on his arm. But a more youthful Grace was just as real, a Grace with brighter hair and a firmer body, a Grace in college-girl sweaters and skirts, this was real, too, this lived inside him, he could see her, he could touch her, he could reach out and touch her.

He moves out of the living room he approaches the door he can hear the swishing sound behind the door why should it frighten him he puts his hand on the doorknob it takes forever for his hand to open the door he sees the tile first there is something glittering on the tile.

The motion picture something stupid and shallow Kim Novak and three married men Dan sits beside him clever stupid insipid Dan they do not speak.

"Do you like Chinese food?" the girl asked.

"Well, I was in Chinatown this afternoon," Buddwing said.

Grace, where are you?

When he and Dan came out of the movie theater the streets are cluttered with the Friday night throng, they buy the little black address book in a novelty shop on Broadway, Dan gives him the number, you won't forget to call, will you? no I won't forget, you won't forget now, will you? no, I won't forget I won't forget I won't forget.

He would not forget, he would never forget.

He would forget immediately.

He would forget almost everything they did the moment they did it, so that their life together would become an unremembered series of incidents leading to a final lapse.

There was in this girl, in Grace, there had been from the very beginning, a contradiction of personality that bewildered and intrigued him. She seemed to be a curious mixture of innocence

and guile, of gaiety and brooding intensity, of high-minded purpose and of loose resolve. Perhaps he saw in her a mirror image
of the person he had become; perhaps this was why she seemed
so enormously attractive. His discharge from the navy had been
abrupt and somehow unsatisfactory, a four-day stay at Treasure
Island, and then a cattle-car cross-country trip and a whirl-
wind formal severance at Lido Beach. He could remember taking
a bus across the Whitestone Bridge, his eyes drinking in the
city in the distance, aware that a woman was holding onto a
strap just to his right, but unwilling to give her his seat because
then he would not have been able to see the skyline. He took a
taxi from Gun Hill Road, and all the while a single thought kept
echoing in his head, I'm going home, I'm going home, but he
had not as yet given "home" a binding definition—where was
"home?" Wasn't "home" the Whitestone Bridge, and the magnificent skyline in the distance? Wasn't "home" this familiar
stretch of Gun Hill Road? Wasn't it Evander Childs High School,
and Bronxwood Avenue, and the rutted, potholed streets? He
paid the cab driver and stood on the sidewalk with his seabag
and looked up at the frame house and thought again, I'm going
home, and the thought lingered in his mind as he walked up the
driveway and then into the house, and stayed in his mind as he
embraced his mother and his father, they both looked so much
older, I'm going home. He sat in his own living room and told
them of his adventures in Japan, and all the while he thought, I'm
going home, because somehow none of this was home.

Beethoven was dead; none of the boys even mentioned his
name. They went to see his mother once, but she wept when
they arrived, and they never went again. L.J. had met a girl in
Boston, and was seriously considering marrying her. Red Vest
said he was bored and was thinking of re-enlisting. They spent
the summer at Orchard Beach, reminiscing, but something was
wrong, this was not home, these were not the boys he had once
known. At the end of August, Red Vest went back into the army.
In September, L.J. went to Boston to propose to the girl he had
met there, and Buddwing enrolled at N.Y.U.

He first saw her in the small park outside the school in the middle of October. He was sitting on a bench with his back to the sun, watching the front steps of the building. Behind him, he could hear two men playing chess. Someone was strumming a guitar. She came down the steps and a student called, "Hi, Grace," as she passed, and she nodded and smiled briefly, and then went to sit on a bench at the other end of the park, facing Washington Square West. She opened a book in her lap and began reading. He must have watched her for perhaps ten minutes before he finally rose and walked to where she was sitting. He sat down beside her and immediately said, "Hello, Grace."

"Hello," she said, and then at once, "Do I know you?"

"No."

"Oh. Okay." She paused. "What do you want?"

"I want to talk to you."

"I'm studying."

"That can wait."

"That's what *you* think," she said, and went back to her book.

"What *is* that?" he asked.

"What is what?"

"The book."

"Greek Mythology," she said. "Hey . . . uh . . . you don't mind, do you, but I'm really trying to study."

"That's all right."

"Yeah, well . . . huh?"

"I said that's all right."

"Sure, but I can't study if you keep talking to me, you know what I mean?"

"How old are you?" he asked.

"Eighteen. How old are *you?*"

"Twenty-one."

"Okay, *now* may I study?" she asked.

"I've got a better idea."

"What?"

"Let's go for a walk."

"And what happens when I flunk Mythology?"

"I don't know. What happens?"

"I'll hate you forever, that's all."

"Well, I wouldn't want you to do that."

"When were you born?" she asked suddenly.

"January."

"January what?"

"The tenth."

"Mmm, that's Capricorn. Well, that explains it, I guess."

"What does it explain?"

"Well, never mind," she said mysteriously. "What's your favorite month?"

"March."

"March? *Nobody's* favorite month is March."

"Mine is," he said. "What's yours?"

"October." She shook her head. "March. I never heard anybody say that in my life."

"March is a good month," he said, feeling obliged to defend it. Grace shrugged. "October makes me very sad."

"Why should it?"

"Because everything dies in October," she said solemnly.

"If it makes you sad, why should it be your favorite month?"

"Because I'm a very sad person." She closed the book, and looked at him seriously. "I cry an awful lot. Do you?"

"No, not too often."

"But you do cry?"

"Yes. Sometimes."

"I didn't think men cried."

"Well . . ." he said, and shrugged.

"They used to, of course, when they wore armor. In those days." She paused. "I think it's very manly of you to admit that you cry sometimes." She paused again. "I cry all the time, *all* the time. I see a bird, I cry. I pick up a saltshaker, I cry." She shrugged. "My brother calls me The Weeper."

"Well, we'll just have to make you laugh, then," Buddwing said.

"That's very difficult to do."

"Why?"

"Because I have no sense of humor," she said.

"Oh, sure you do. Everybody has a sense of humor."

"No, I haven't. Really. Not the tiniest shred. Tell me a joke, you'll see. Not a dirty one, though."

"Not a dirty one, hmmm," Buddwing said. "Well, let's see." He thought for several moments and then said, "I don't know any clean jokes."

"Well, as long as it's not *too* dirty," Grace said.

"How about a limerick?"

"Okay."

"While Titian was mixing rose madder—"

"He spied a young lass on a ladder," Grace said. "I know that one."

"Well, don't you think it's funny?"

"Well, I think it's *clever*, yes, but it doesn't make me laugh."

"Mmm," Buddwing said.

"Yes. I really *am* The Weeper. My brother is right."

"You seem . . . very young," he said suddenly.

"What do you mean? Younger than eighteen, do you mean?"

"Yes," Buddwing said.

"That's because I'm a virgin," she told him.

"Well, I don't know if that has anything to—"

"Oh, yes, it's true. You look around you sometime. The virgins seem very young; that's because we're all so pure and innocent, you know, pish-posh," and she laughed.

"Well, there," he said. "You laughed."

"Oh sure, I *laugh*. It's just I haven't got a sense of humor."

"Oh. I see. Well, *would* you like to take a walk?"

"I don't know. Are you going to get serious or anything?"

"What do you mean?"

"Are you going to fall in love with me? You know."

"Well, I . . . well, I don't know."

"Because I can't fall in love with anyone just now, you see."

"Why not?"

"I don't want to."

"That's no answer."

"I want to finish college and then go on for my master's. Falling in love would just screw everything up, you see."

"Oh, sure, I can understand that," Buddwing said.

"But if you want to take a walk, that'd be all right, I guess."

She smiled briefly and rose from the bench and smoothed her skirt, and he looked at her appraisingly and said, "I think Grace is the perfect name for you, do you know that?"

"No, I'm not at all graceful," she answered. "And I'm much too short. A girl named Grace should be at least five-seven."

"You're about five-four," he said.

"Yes, I am."

"You're tall," he said, and they began walking.

"I really should be studying my mythology, you know."

"I'll help you with it, how about that?"

"Do you know mythology?"

"No. But I can use your book."

"Well, all right," she said, and she handed him the text.

"What'll the test cover?" he asked.

"The chapter on the constellations as related to. It's up front there someplace. This really is a stupid course, you know. I took it because somebody said it was a snap, but it seems to be more work than all the others put together. Are you a good student?"

"Well, I don't know yet."

"I'm terrible. I hate to study is what it is. I always say I'm going to make the dean's list, and then I never do. Because I don't study, that's what it is. Anybody can come along and ask me to go for a walk, and I'll say sure." She smiled. "Well, go ahead, ask me some questions."

"All right, what's the Pleiades?"

"The Seven Sisters."

"What are their names?"

"Alcyone, Merope, Celaeno, Taygeta, Maia, Electra, and Sterope."

"That's very good. What are they doing up there in the sky?"

"Well, Zeus changed them into doves first, to escape the attentions of Orion, and when that didn't work, he made them stars."

"Very good. Do you know the names of the Seven Dwarfs?"

"Yes, of course I do."

"Name them."

"Listen, we're supposed to be doing mythology," she said, laughing.

"They're sort of mythology."

"Yes, but not Greek."

"No, Disney. What's the difference? I'll bet you can't name them."

"Oh, sure I can. Dopey . . ."

"Everyone says Dopey first, have you ever noticed that?"

"Doc, Grumpy, Sleepy, Happy . . ."

"Yeah, go ahead."

"Sneezy, and Sleepy."

"You said Sleepy twice."

"Dopey, Doc, Grumpy, Happy, Sleepy, Sneezy, and . . ." She paused. She wrinkled her brow. "All right, who's the seventh one?" she asked.

"Orion," he said, and she laughed again. "See? You laugh all the time."

"Well, I guess I find you pretty funny," she said seriously. "Maybe I ought to go back and study, after all. In the library or someplace."

"Why?"

She shrugged. "Well, I have to graduate, you know, and then go on for my master's."

"Yes, I know that."

"So I don't want to get involved, that's all." She shrugged again.

"Walking through Greenwich Village on a nice fall day is hardly an involvement, now, is it?"

"I don't know, you look like you're just about ready."

"Ready for what?"

"And also you're Capricorn. To tell you the truth, you make me kind of itchy."

"Mmm. Well," he said abruptly.

"I didn't mean that the way it sounded. I mean, you don't make me *physically* itchy or anything."

"No, I just make you uncomfortable."

"That's right."

"Thanks."

"I didn't mean it that way, either."

"How *did* you mean it?"

"It's just I have to get my degree, you see—"

"Yes, and go on for your master's. I know."

"Yes, that's right."

"Okay," he said.

"You get upset pretty easily, don't you?"

"No, not usually," he answered.

"You sure *seem* upset. You should see your face."

"Well, a guy doesn't like to be told right off the bat that a girl's got to get her goddamn degree and then . . ."

"Go on for my master's."

"Yeah, go on for your master's."

"Mmm," she said.

"You know I'm a veteran, you know that, don't you?" he asked suddenly.

"No, I didn't."

"Well, I am."

"Well, that's very nice," she said. "Are you going to school on the G.I. Bill?"

"Yeah." He nodded angrily and said, "I just thought you might like to know."

"I'm glad you told me."

"I mean, I've been around the world, you know. I just got back from Japan a little while ago."

"How was it?"

"How was what?"

"Japan."

"Oh, fine. Fine." He nodded again and said, "So what I mean is, you know, just because a guy asks you to take a walk, it doesn't mean he's ready to marry you tomorrow. I mean, maybe you ought to understand that."

"Oh, I understand it."

"Sure. I know how important your degree is, and all that, and your master's, too, but don't go running for the hills every time a guy asks you to take a walk, is all I'm saying."

"Oh, well, sure, I understand that."

"Well, good."

"And I'm not running for the hills."

"Well, that's fine," he said.

"Did you want to take me out or something, is that it?" she asked.

"Well, I did have something like that in mind," he said angrily, "but I wouldn't think of upsetting the entire American system of higher education."

"When did you want to take me out?"

"I thought Saturday night."

"I don't see what you're so upset about," she said. "We just *met*, you know, on a park *bench*, you know. We're practically strangers."

"So?"

"So you don't have to get so upset, that's all. I told you honestly what my plans were. I'm going to get my degree, and then—"

"All right, all right, for Christ's sake," he said.

"Well, I happen to prefer honesty," she said.

"All right. What time shall I pick you up Saturday night?"

"I'm not even in the city on weekends," she said.

"What do you mean?"

"I'm only here during the week. I go home every Friday afternoon."

"Home?"

"Yes. To stay with my folks."

"So what?"

"It's a long drive."

"I'm willing to make it. What time shall I pick you up?"

"I didn't know it'd been settled."

"It's settled," he said.

She stared at him in silence for a long time, and then she said, "Yes, I suppose it is."

Her brother's name was Dan, and the German shepherd was called Duke. He hated them both on sight. Dan's hair and the dog's hair were the same color, a sort of malicious brindled brown. Dan's eyes were brown and suspicious; Duke's were exactly the same color, and positively paranoid. Dan spoke in a deep guttural voice that seemed to originate somewhere deep in his bowels. Duke was continually growling accompaniment to anything Dan said, like an echo in a rat-infested sewer.

Sometimes, at night, after he had left Grace and was trying to get some sleep, he would think of Dan and Duke and the two would get mixed up in his mind. Which was the dog and which was the man? Or were they both dog-men? He concocted an elaborate fantasy in which Dan and Duke became secret army weapons, trained to kill all ex-navy men on sight, especially if they happened to be dating Duke's . . . Dan's . . . sister. Neither was a man and neither was a dog; that was the beauty of the weapon. The victim never knew which of the two would give the kill signal, which would be the one who leaped for the jugular. In his fantasy, sometimes Dan would be stroking Duke's head and whispering, "That's a good boy, kill, yes, that's nice, sic 'im," and other times it would be Dan lying prone at Duke's feet while Duke gently scratched his neck and whispered the soothing words of death. He knew for sure that Duke was a son of a bitch; about Dan, he could only guess.

"How old are you?" Dan asked, the first time they met.

"Why do you want to know?" Buddwing said, and Duke growled. He looked at the dog. "What's the matter with *him?*" he asked. "Doesn't he like people?"

"There's nothing the matter with him."

"Then why is he growling?"

"That's not growling, it's talking," Dan said. "I asked you how old you were."

"And I asked why you want to know."

"Because you're dating my sister, okay? She's just a kid."

"She's eighteen."

"That's just a kid."

"I don't think so."

"No, huh? Well, she happens to be my sister."

"So what?" Buddwing said, and he watched both of them closely, waiting for one or the other to give the kill signal, waiting for one or the other to spring for his throat. "I'm not dating you and your talking police dog, I'm dating her."

"Yeah, and I think you're too old for her."

"I'm twenty-one," Buddwing said.

"I'll just bet you are," Dan answered, smirking. The dog, on cue, smirked at the same time.

"How old do you think I am?"

"Twenty-five, at least."

"Well, you happen to be wrong."

"When were you born?"

For an insane moment, Buddwing wanted to lie. With instant death grinning at him from the dog-men, he wanted to say he had been born in 1842 and was really a hundred and four years old. He had been taking secret youth tablets that kept him virile and leching for eighteen-year-old girls. Duke growled warningly, or perhaps it was Dan.

"I was born on January tenth, 1925, how's that?" he said. On impulse, he added, "I'm Capricorn."

"This is 1946," Dan said. "Which makes you twenty-one. *If* you're telling the truth."

"Why wouldn't I be telling the truth?"

"Look, buddy, you don't fool me. You've been around."

"So?"

"So my sister hasn't."

"You want to know something, buddy?" Buddwing said.

"What?"

"I'm going to *marry* your sister someday, how about that?"

"What?"

"Yeah," Buddwing said, nodding. "Talk it over with your goddamn dog."

The restaurant was on West 56th, small, and French, and not
too crowded. They sat at a table near the window and watched
the setting sun turn the windows across the street to brass. They
could not see the sky except in the reflecting glass opposite. The
sky was a broken complex of rectangles, gold and fiery red at
first, and then turning to lavender, each rectangle reflecting its
own jigsaw segment, a deeper shade of violet now, a thousand
windows echoing the subtle shift to purple, the red tones vanishing completely to leave a deeper blue, and then window after
window going blind as darkness came and the night was upon
them.

They did not yet know each other. They sat at the window
table and talked eagerly, anxious to exchange views and back-
grounds, pleased with each other's good looks, smacking their
lips over the wine, and telling each other how good the food was,
considering each posed question as though life or death depended
upon the response. They exchanged deep glances tentatively,
touched hands exploringly, laughed a little too loudly at each
other's witticisms, were a trifle too eager to create for each other
the image of a present person who was the sum total of a vivid
and exciting past, sharing incidents and embarrassments, recklessly
revealing all. Their window world seemed exclusive and self-
contained, but they consciously played to the other diners as
well, willing them to acknowledge their splendor, their total
absorption with each other, the fun they were having, terrified
that without appreciation their romantic exploration would wither
and die.

They ordered brandy after the meal. They rolled the snifters
in the palms of their hands, and stared deeply into each other's

eyes, creating a privacy that was instantly destroyed because they demanded acknowledgment of it from everyone in the restaurant. He recognized her performance, and he recognized his own as well, but for him there was something more, which he suspected she did not yet feel, and perhaps would never feel. She understood romance, yes, this was an inherent part of her, the sadness of October, but in her mind romance was still *Ivanhoe* and *Wuthering Heights*, the Pleiades and Edna St. Vincent Millay; romance was still an admiring audience who could look at a window-framed couple and appreciate their handsomeness and long for their communication. Romance was still the phony tinsel Hollywood crap, the Lux Radio Theater every Monday night, "This is Cecil B. DeMille, coming to you from Ho-o-o-llywood," kleig lights glaring, admiring eyes, "My, how beautiful her long blond hair is! How radiant she is!" He shared the romantic notion, and he played to the others in the restaurant because he knew that playing to the crowd was an essential part of romance, without which it could not exist. But he was more than just an actor going through a performance for a preview audience. The thing he felt inside him *had* to be shared because it was too exuberant to be contained.

He was falling in love.

And because he was falling in love, he wanted everyone in the place to stand on his chair and cheer wildly and throw kisses and applaud. He wanted everyone to know that this rare and foolish thing was happening to him, look at it happening to me, for Christ's sake, look at it *happening*, isn't it marvelous, don't you want to share it with me? Look! Look!

She did not want involvements. She had said so from the beginning.

"Where would you like to go now?" he asked.

"Let's take a ride in Central Park," she said. "In a horse and carriage. Let's look at the stars. Let's count the stars."

"And find the Seven Sisters."

"Safe from Orion."

Romance.

"I love you," he said.

"How much do you love me?" she whispered.

The windows were fogged with steam. The stars were gone, and a sharp wind had arisen; it looked as if it might rain. Grace was in his arms, partially leaning against him, looking directly into his face. The wind howled over the hood of the car in frenzy, as though wanting to tear it apart. In his mind, he could visualize the wind ripping the hood off and sailing it down the hillside where they were parked, two blocks from her house. It would descend over the roofs of the toy houses below, and then skim the Mount Kisco treetops to land solidly upon Dan and Duke where they were taking their nightly stroll. The army would give them both heroes' burials in Arlington Cemetery. DAN-DUKE, the tombstone would read, SON OF FANG. He watched the hood of the car, fully expecting it to blow off at any moment. He would not be at all surprised if it did; something happened to the damn car every time he borrowed it from his father. Flat tires, motor trouble, burned-out wires, the horn sticking—it was always something. "I don't understand," his father said each time. "I never have any trouble with it."

"Well, how much *do* you love me?" Grace asked.

"I'll bet that hood's going to blow right off," he said.

"Or *don't* you love me?"

"I love you, Grace."

"Well, how much?"

The question was childish and stupid, Roxane demanding eloquence from Christian. She was nineteen years old now, her breast was resting against his arm on the wheel, her legs were bent under her, the skirt pulled back over her thighs, she felt warm and ripe and bursting in the secret steamed cocoon of the car, and all she wanted to know was how much he loved her.

"I love you more than anything in the world," he whispered.

"Oh, well, what does *that* mean?" she said. "That could mean *any*thing."

"It means I love you," he said.

She stared at him silently. She kept staring at him, saying nothing, the child's look slipping away unexpectedly, an uncertain, puzzled, thoroughly adult expression moving onto her face.

"Why . . ." she started, and then hesitated. "Why do you love me?" she asked.

He did not answer for a moment, and then it was too late to answer.

"I mean," she said, "why *me?* Oh please, why *me?*"

The sound of her voice almost brought him to tears. He heard a vast sorrow in that voice, as though a thousand jacks and skip ropes, pigtails and braces, cotton slips and plastic blue barrettes were falling into the wind, sighing in a broken jumble. He heard in that voice the mystery of alien inanimate things, lipsticks and mascara, garter belts and bras, hooks and eyes, and diaphragms. He heard (I have heard the mermaids singing each to each) beyond, an echo of that childlike, forlorn, sighing sound carried on the wind high and clear and sharp, all the uncertainty of total commitments, all the sudden insecurity of complete and trusting exposure, the fragile splintering of a chrysalis, and he clutched her to him fiercely and joyously, and then was frightened lest her wings dissolve in powder. They were both trembling. He kissed her hair and her closed eyes, and he said, "Ahhh, ahhh," for in this steamy interior of a clopping horse-drawn carriage in Central Park, in this cloistered private brimming place, though she had said she did not want to become involved, she had suddenly and without warning fallen in love with him.

"I love you, Grace," he said. "Oh God, how I love you!"

She moved deeper into his arms, and smiled, and sighed, and said, childlike, against his chest, "I love you, too."

He lost his heart to her completely the summer she cut his hair on the desert sands beyond the valley of Sorek, after he had killed a young lion for her and caught three hundred foxes and slain a thousand men with the jawbone of an ass.

It was one of those haze-filtered days when the sun seemed to consume the entire sky, stretching from horizon to horizon in uniform unrelieved brightness, vague in intent, as though it could turn itself to rain or brilliant sunshine with equal ease. They had taken his father's car out beyond Jones Beach, having to stop only once when the radiator boiled over ("I don't understand," Grace said. "*I* never have any trouble with it.") and parking it finally on a strip of sand facing Gilgo. The ocean was calm that day, reflecting the opalescent sky in silvery tumidity. The beach was almost deserted. There was no breeze; the sand barely stirred. She wore a two-piece bathing suit, with the bra straps lowered, a curving line of white showing on the slopes of her breasts where her tan abruptly ended, the beauty spot near her left shoulder almost lost in the bronze of her skin. She was reading the Sunday *Times* through sunglasses, commenting on each world situation as the magazine section revealed it, reading a book review aloud to him, one hand resting on his head, the fingers toying with his hair. "You need a haircut," she said idly, and then read him passages of an article on Nantucket from the travel section, and then began leafing through the main section—"A man got bit by a shark. Do you think there are any here?"—pausing to examine the advertisements, "Do you like this dress?" sharing the newspaper with him as he lay beside her with his eyes closed against the searing glare of the milk-white sky. "I could cut it, you know," she said.

"Cut what?"

"Your hair."

"No, thank you," he said.

"Mmm, well. They're already showing the fall clothes, look at that. Do you like tweeds?"

"Yes."

"Why won't you let me cut your hair?"

"Because you're not a barber."

"You look terrible," she said. "Shaggy and hairy. Let me cut it. Please."

"Why?"

"It's sexy," she said, and she shrugged.

He turned his head to look at her, the sky bright and glaring behind her, squinting up at her. Her long blond hair was pulled to one side of her head, woven in a thick strand there, tossed carelessly over her shoulder. The sunglasses were perched on the end of her nose, the brown eyes peering expectantly over them, a thin confident smile on her mouth. She sat back on her own legs bent under her, rising from the chaos of the *New York Times* scattered on the blanket around her, blond and sun-limned and sitting bustily erect with her slender hands folded in her lap, patiently waiting.

"When'd you get so sexy, all of a sudden?" he asked.

"The beach always makes me sexy," she said.

"Mmm?"

"Yeah."

"Where would we get a scissors?"

"I have one in my sewing basket." She reached for the basket, and he caught her hand.

"You brought that along on purpose, didn't you?" he said.

"No, I was going to work on my hanging."

"Your *what?*"

"My hooked wall hanging. You *know* I'm making one, so stop looking so surprised. I've been hooking for a long time." He burst out laughing and she said, "What's so funny?"

"Don't you know what hooking is?"

"No, what is it?"

"It's something sexy," he said.

"Yeah?"

"Yeah."

"You always invent these things, don't you?" she said. "Just to make me feel very young and innocent."

"No, really. A hooker is a—"

"Yeah, yeah, sure," she said.

She took the scissors from her basket, and he sat before her unprotestingly while she cut a huge hole in the *New York Times* and then put it over his head like a barber's apron. She got on her knees behind him, and examined his head with her fingers widespread. "You really have big ears, did you know that?" she said. "They stick out all over your head."

"Why don't you just cut them off?" he suggested.

"Well, Clark Gable has big ears, too," she said, and sighed in resignation.

"He also has a mustache. You think I should grow one?"

"No."

"Then maybe you'd better take off the ears."

"Maybe so. What good are big ears without a mustache, right?"

"Right."

"Well, here we go," she said.

"Listen . . ."

"Mmmm?"

"Don't leave holes."

"Where the ears were, you mean?"

"No, I mean where the *hair* was."

"Stop worrying," she said. "I think I have a flair for this sort of thing. Really. I think it'll be a beautiful haircut."

"Yeah, well . . ." he started dubiously, and then heard the click of the scissors behind his right ear. He closed his eyes. He heard only the metallic rhythm of the scissors and Grace's shallow breathing behind him, and somewhere beyond that the distant sound of the ocean, not the usual crashing of an angry surf but rather the cavernous murmur captured in a seashell. *Click,* the scissors went behind his ear, *click, click,* he could feel the sun hot on his bare head, *click, click, click,* gaining more authority now. "Oh, this is going to be very nice," she said. "Really, it'll be lovely." He grinned and felt an odd contentment spreading through him. The steady click of the scissors almost lulled him to sleep. He turned once to look up at her, "Yeah, I almost *did* get your ear that time, mister," and saw the intense concentrated look on her face, the sunglasses very low on her nose now, the way his grandmother used to wear her glasses when she was sewing by the front window of the tailorshop in the waning winter light. He closed his eyes again.

"I'm getting hair all down me," she said.

"What do you mean?"

"Oooh, it itches."

He turned to look at her. The slopes of her breasts in the scanty top were crosshatched with pen strokes of fallen hair. She brushed them away with the flat of her hand, and then reached into the bra top and made a writhing motion, her face pulling into a grimace.

"You have the most uncomfortable hair in the world," she said. "Urggh, it's sticking to the suntan oil."

"You want some help there?" he asked.

"I can manage, thank you," she said. "Ick, it's all over the place."

"Listen, do you think I can get a shave and a manicure, too? So it shouldn't be a total loss?"

"Shut up and sit still," she said. "Boy, am I ever sorry I started this."

The scissors began clicking again. Grinning, he said, "Watch out for the lice."

"I am."

"I don't want to disturb them."

"No, I know that."

"They've been with me so long, I've begun to—"

"Will you keep quiet, please? I'm trying to concentrate."

"How's the hair doing? Still going down there?"

"Where it goes is none of your concern," she said.

"My regular barber doesn't have that kind of trouble," he said.

"No, I should hope not. What's this sticking up here in the back?"

"In the back?"

"Don't get dirty, you evil-minded thing."

"If it's in the back, it must be a cowlick."

"I didn't know you had a cowlick."

"I have all kinds of secret things you don't know about."

"Yeah, well, I'll learn, I guess," she said. "Oh, hell."

"What is it?"

"I cut off a little too much right there."

"Oh, boy . . ."

"No, it's all right. Just a little too much, that's all."

"How long is this haircut going to take?"

"Why?"

"I think it's beginning to cloud up."

"It was cloudy when we got here," she said.

"No, really, Grace. I think it's going to rain."

They had left the hansom cab and were walking down Fifth Avenue when the first drop struck him in the eye like a hurled egg.

"It's starting to rain," he said, and suddenly the sky broke apart like a huge water-filled sack splitting along its weakest seam, dropping its contents in a surprisingly swift deluge for which there had been no real warning. They began to run. They ran blindly because the falling water was everywhere around them and its suddenness had produced a sort of numbed shock that robbed them of everything but instinct. He clutched her elbow and tried to steer her in one direction but she shrieked and turned in the opposite direction, giggling in panic, and then he grabbed her hand and tugged her toward him, and they both almost slipped on the suddenly slick pavement, and threw their arms around each other to maintain their balance, and then ran with their heads ducked, she holding her bag over her head like an umbrella, he tugging at her hand and searching for an awning or a doorway or anything to protect them from this storm that had materialized in vicious fury and was threatening to drown them.

"This way!" he shouted. "Here!" And she shouted, "Where?" And he yelled, "Here, here!" And they ran up the low slippery long flat steps of a gray and solemn church, her heel catching on one of the steps and sending her falling headlong, the fall broken by his supporting hand and arm. The rain lashed about them as he tried to help her up. One of her stockings had ripped from the heel of her shoe clear to the ribbed top. He put his arm around her waist and pulled her to her feet and then, still supporting her this way, half walked, half dragged her to the open arched door of the church and into the dimly lighted narthex, where the first thing he saw was the font of holy water.

"Wow," she said, "what a rain! Where'd *that* come from?"

"Are you all right?"

"My leg hurts," she said. "It'll probably be black-and-blue in the morning." She pulled back her skirt and said, "Oh, hell, will you look at that? A good pair of nylons." Then, seeming to remember that she was standing in a church vestibule, she immediately covered her mouth with her hand, as though her mild swearing had been overheard. She pulled her head into her shoulders and stood with her hand covering her mouth, waiting for a holy repercussion. When none came, she shrugged and said, "Could we go inside? I'm *freezing* in this doorway."

As they walked out of the narthex and into the church itself, she whispered, "Ick, I'm soaked to the skin," and he whispered, "I am, too," and then their whispers trailed because they heard the music coming from above them, and the music, like the sudden storm, seemed to erupt from nowhere as though a wise and knowing, all-powerful, all-seeing deity were handling the world in an avant-God incoherent though orderly-to-Himself way. The music came from somewhere above in the organ loft, and Buddwing recognized it as one of the Bach fugues, just as Grace whispered, "Bach," and he nodded. There were two men above them in the organ loft, both unseen, one playing the organ in majestic frenzy, the other playing the violin in a burnished rich and somehow pagan response. The music swelled and echoed throughout the church, repetitive and seemingly endless, the mathematical symmetry of Bach resounding from the heavy stone walls of the nave, and rising to the vaulted domes, falling like the pelting rain outside to the altar dimly glowing with the light of votive candles. They backed away down the aisle, striving for a glimpse of the musicians. The unseen men played with a fervor bordering on fury. The organ exposition was vibrant and resounding, the violin answering the theme, transposing it a fifth upward, the rich blend flooding out over the center aisle and the crossing, flowing into the north and south transepts, the organ's countersubject booming intricately, the violin entering again an octave below, the music reaching out beyond the altar and into the apse and flooding each stone corner of the church. Tongues of fire lashed at wooden stakes, licked the robes of fettered martyrs. Thieves and prophets hung alike in crucifixion, the music soared in wildly ordered abandon, heathens danced by firelight, bodies glowed with sweat and paint.

They had backed down the nave toward the crossing and then past that almost to the altar, but they still could not see the hidden musicians. At the western end of the church, through the narthex and the open arched door, a streak of lightning illuminated the gray wet street beyond, and an old man ran by with a newspaper tented over his head. The votive candles danced in red and green glass cups, thunder boomed its echo above the vaulted canopy, the organ answered in its richly resonant voice, the violin descended in a strident spiral, the final chords of the fugue hung suspended in the air like softly falling dust, echoing, and then the huge stone church was silent.

The silence was as surprising as the earlier rain and music had been. The music still seemed to vibrate within them, their skin still tingled with its resonance; but like a star that had died centuries ago, its light still visible on earth, the source of the sound was gone, and the only true reverberation now was the empty boom of silence. Into the silence, the musicians whispered something to each other, still invisible, their voices carrying across the length of the church.

Buddwing and the girl stood with their backs to the altar, speechless in the whispering vault.

His hand sought hers.

Their fingers locked and were wedded.

This, then, is a consummation, he thought.

This, now, is a consummation on a narrow nuptial bed, the first consummtaion and the last, a fugue in itself, the overlapping subject and answer, and the endless quest, the parts introduced in succession and following each other in chase, in flight, in Latin *fuga.* She did not, as she had maintained, have a beauty spot near her left shoulder, but this was an unimportant incidental, he knew, for here on this bed and on the succession of beds to come, the parts introduced, he would learn who this woman was.

The apartment smelled of fresh paint—had he painted it himself only a month ago while she conferred with hovering seamstresses about her bridal gown? The furniture was new and clean, it smelled of the factory, its varnish was unmarred, its fabric unspotted. They had taken it from the packing crates not a week ago. The wood had splintered beneath the clawed end of his hammer as he pulled out the nails in squealing protest. The woman beside him on the sofa bed was new and clean, too, her gown diaphanous by custom, her hair neatly brushed, her eyes studying him in virginal anticipation. They had touched before, they had kissed more often, but they did not know each other yet, and now they would learn. They thought they would learn. Here, in preparation for the coupling that would follow, they brought two separately revolving universes and hoped for collision and knowledge. Viewpoints. The concurrent conversations he and Jesse had discussed, the deaf listener, the egocentric orator.

He smelled a subtle perfume in her hair, a scent of veiled mystery and erotic intrigue; she smelled the faint aroma of his male perspiration; it reminded her of her father's arms when he used to carry her to the rumble-seated Chevrolet. He felt her feathery blond hair and the paper-thin skull beneath, which he could crush in his hands; she felt the emerging bristle on his jaw, and wondered what it was like to shave, and his hands in her hair were gentle.

Viewpoints.

An apple is an orange.

She knew his kiss, he knew her kiss. His mouth was gentle upon hers, he thought, cushioned by her shy and soft and tenderly inquiring lips. She thought of her own mouth as voracious and thin; she wanted to bite his tongue, and his lips on hers were curiously harsh, his mouth was not at all tender. He touched her breasts and her nipples—he had touched them before—but there was nothing erotic to him about the practiced movement of his hands. He knew the nipples would pucker gently, and his hands worked in a repeated ritual, probing scouts in the employ of a bored and confident mercenary. My breasts inflame him, she thought, and this image of a rampaging, rapacious male animal, unable to control his hands, ripping off her blouse and her bra, violating her nipples, was erotic and stimulating and perhaps transmitted itself unconsciously to him because he found himself becoming erect, and he moved against her and put his mouth on her breast and flicked the nipple with his exploring tongue. She did not know the feel of an erection except as an outward experience, the uncoiling of soft flesh against her thigh; she did not know the inner surge and restless stirring, the mind-coupled anticipation, the flowing rush of passion to a single extending, unsheathed, sensitively expectant part of the body. She knew only the touch of his teeth on her nipples, alternately one and then the other, and whereas his tongue could feel the sudden stiffening, it was she who experienced her flesh distending and enlarging, she who felt that the tips of her breasts would burst through the expanding purple skin and fill his mouth, while only vaguely aware of the probing rigid arch against her thigh, which to him was all-consuming. She seized him more in conditioned response than in counterattack, but to him her grasp was wildly exciting; she became for him in that instant the fictional heroine foisted upon all American males from the moment of their birth, the passionate achingly aggressive female enflamed by the impending touch and sight of a man, the insatiable nymphomaniac. There was perhaps some of this in her, yes, the knowledge that her hand tentatively contained in curling warmth this live and growing member; yes, this knowledge was exciting and it spread in tingling electric tendrils to her groin where it became a vague and undefined urge. But more exciting to her was the certainty that for now she controlled this pulsing flesh, that it would grow immense at her command, that it was attainable through engorgement, that it could become an encircled, intimately possessed part of her solely because she urged it to. He knew only that her hand tightened on him, and he sought her womb in grasping reciprocation, the wished-for return. The natural ooze of lubrication became to him an imagined torrent of rushing female juices at the mouth of a dark and secret cave awaiting his exploration. Her breasts, her buttocks, her abdomen, the soft wet inner flesh of her thighs, all became targets for his questing hands, all thought of exciting her gone now in his own blind excitement which nonetheless excited her. It was he who at last invaded, and the feel to him was one of resisting wet lips and beyond that of a molten pool, a tunnel with live walls crumbling, a real invasion, yes, the thrust of undisputed force into a yielding and vulnerable interior—but this she did not feel. She felt instead an opening wide of herself, a stretching to receive. She felt on her quivering lips at first a hovering, tentative, round and rigid inquiry. She felt everything moving inward then, he and herself, a turning in; she felt a yearning need to accommodate and adjust to the width and the girth and the length of him, to enwrap, to gather and enfold. This was not to her an invasion. They stood at opposite ends of the same tunnel, seeing entirely different things.

But in his invasion, in the proud masculine power of his attack, there was also the fear of being surrounded, and so he pounded at yielding walls that had already succumbed, and nonetheless felt himself slowly engulfed by their very mucoid unresistance; he would lose himself inside her, he would become an irredeemable part of her oozing interior, he would explode within her and join her by osmosis. Powerless to command, powerless to retreat, he bludgeoned blindly and relentlessly, knowing that in his moment of supreme power, he would be inexplicably weakest. And in her receiving, in her vast and obliging female acceptance, there was the fear of losing control completely, the unspoken and frightening desire to allow this throbbing and engorging force to impale her unmercifully, to use her and abuse her, to pillage after abject surrender, to destroy and overwhelm and absorb, to mock in superiority, to degrade and debase, to turn her cheering street parade into a disorganized undignified rout.

Somehow out of these separately converging, touching, converging viewpoints; somehow out of this vague and mutually ignorant confusion of love and hate; somewhere out of an overwhelming need to satisfy, to give unselfishly; somewhere out of a contradictory urge to control and enslave, somehow, somewhere there arose a true moment of compassion where indeed the universes did collide, where indeed Buddwing and the girl were briefly joined together and wedded as they had promised to be. In this single ecstatic moment of exchange, they became one body, mindless; one driving force, genderless. They shared together a sense of mutual pity and contempt, of guilt and exaltation, of charity and supplication, of abundance and of need. In that moment, they clung to each other in total isolation and heard the echo of a billion sighs lost in the corridors of the night, and felt for the briefest tick of time that they really knew each other, when actually they had learned only that they were human.

# 14

He sat up in bed and grinned and said, "Let's make some coffee, okay? Would you like to make some coffee?"

"Sure," she said agreeably. "I've got some on the stove. All I have to do is heat it."

He was feeling very cheerful and cozy, and he liked being here with this girl, protected from the rain that oozed along the windowpanes and rattled in the street outside. The girl moved off the bed with a graceful swiveling motion, got to her feet, and walked to where her half-slip was draped over the chair. She put it on quickly, and then went to the stove in the kitchen. He watched her as she lighted a match. She bent to study the flame as it leaped from the jet. There was something about her pose, her attitude, that brought him great pleasure; the bent head, the concentration on her face, the curved back illuminated with a sheen of light from the windows facing Third Avenue, all were somehow familiar and reassuring to him. The apartment was very still, and the girl suddenly began humming as she stood with her hands on her hips and watched the pot of coffee. Outside, he could hear the clinging swish of automobile tires against the asphalt. The rain, the bookshelves bracketing the sofa bed, the girl's humming and the hiss of the tires, the panes dissolving in reflected neon from the street outside, all seemed of a piece, harmonious and serene. He grinned and lay back with his hands behind his head and tried to read the titles of the books upside down.

"Have you read all of these?" he asked her.

"Most of them," she said from the kitchen. "How do you feel?"

"Great."

"Yeah, me too," she said, and she grinned at him, and then turned to look at the pot again. He rolled over onto his stomach and looked up at the books.

*The Sane Society.*

*Interviewing: Its Principles and Techniques.*

*Our Inner Conflicts.*

*The Neurotic Personality of Our Time.*

*The Compulsion to Confess.*

*Essentials in Interviewing.*

*The Psychoanalytic Approach to Juvenile Delinquency.*

"Where's your basic black?" he said.

"What?" She turned from the stove with a small inquiring smile, her hands on her hips.

"Freud."

"Oh. I've got him down in the office."

"It's too bad I'm not Edward Voegler," he said cheerfully. "You could have had a ball with me."

"Why? Who's Edward Voegler?"

"An escaped lunatic."

"Oh, that's nice."

"Didn't you read the paper?"

"No. Where'd he escape from?"

"Central Islip." He paused. "For a while today, I thought I might be him."

"What made you decide you weren't?"

"I met a *real* lunatic."

"That's always a good gauge. Do you like your coffee very hot?"

"No."

"Neither do I. This is ready, then, if you want some."

"Yes," he said expansively, "yes, I want some. There is nothing I would rather have in the world right now than a good cup of coffee."

"Do you always get like this?" she asked.

"When?"

"After . . ." She shrugged. "After you make love?"

"How am I?"

"I don't know. Gentle, I guess. Your face looks very soft. You seem . . ." She shrugged again and sat at the table. "Just . . . soft." Naked, he got off the bed and went into the kitchen. He stood behind her chair and bent over her and cupped her breasts and kissed the side of her throat. "Hey," he whispered.

"What?"

"I love you."

"Okay."

"You're supposed to say you love me, too."

"I do."

"You do what?"

"I do love you, too."

"So say it."

"I love you, I love you, I love you." She paused. "Too."

"If you love me so much, why don't you pour my coffee?"

"I'm waiting for you to sit down."

"Do I need a tie in this place?" he asked, and she began laughing. "Because if I do, I'm sure I can borrow one from the head-waiter."

Still laughing, she went to the stove for the pot. She poured his coffee and then gently touched the top of his head and bent to kiss him on the forehead.

"Will you excuse me a minute?" she asked.

"Sure," he said.

He watched as she crossed the room. The bathroom door closed behind her. He heard her turn on the water tap.

Before their marriage, they had considered taking an apartment with a bathroom down the hall, but L.J. had said it was important for a new bride to have her own bathroom. L.J. had been married to the girl from Boston for more than a year by then, so Buddwing and Grace automatically assumed he knew what he was talking about. They had taken the more expensive Third Avenue apartment with its own bathroom, but for many months after they moved in, they had wondered aloud just what the hell L.J. had meant. Why did a new bride need her own bathroom? It was Grace who, with her curious combination of innocence and candor, came out of the bathroom one morning, woke Buddwing as usual, and said, "It's for putting in the diaphragm."

"Huh?" he said. "What?"

"Our own john. It would be very embarrassing down the hall."

"What would?" Buddwing asked sleepily.

"Putting in a diaphragm down the hall."

"Oh, yeah," he said, and rubbed his eyes.

Their bridal couch was the sofa bed they had bought on 34th Street, and upon which they were still making installment payments. The folding spring mechanism was bolted to the heavy upholstered frame of the couch, and one night while they were making love in a particularly energetic fashion, the head and part of the bolt snapped off, leaving a portion of the threaded body in the frame of the couch, and dropping the spring a good six inches from where it should have rested. In the morning, Buddwing Scotch-taped the broken head onto the frame and into the metal hole, where in some miraculous fashion it continued to support the spring, though in a rather lopsided manner. Grace went to the 34th Street store to complain about the broken bed, but she did so in such high good humor that they never came to fix it. In her eyes, he was sure, the bed had taken on a personality and an identity, which was all a part of being married, something like making coffee on one's own stove. He told her this one morning while she was washing in the bathroom. From behind the closed door, she said, "Oh, so who cares? We'll tell all our friends that our marriage is held together by a Scotch-taped screw."

Buddwing burst out laughing, but he heard no sound from behind the door. He went to the kitchen table, sat, poured himself a cup of coffee, and then said, "Hey, did you know that was funny?"

"Of course," she answered. "Why do you think I said it?"

"I never can tell with you."

"Ha, I'm a woman of mystery."

"Yeah."

"Yeah," she said, and opened the door.

She came to the table and watched him as he put cream and sugar into his cup. He lifted the cup to his lips very delicately, with his pinky outstretched, wearing the look of a bored, supremely confident, magnificently poised English peer taking his tea in the vicar's garden, totally unaware of his nudity. "Ahhh," he said, smacking his lips, "magnificent! This is mag*ni*ficent coffee!"

"Thank you."

"Aren't you going to have any?"

"I was just watching you."

"And?"

"Nothing. I love you, that's all." She gave a curious little wiggle, as though it were an involuntary shudder of joy.

"Do that again," he said.

"What did I do?"

"I don't know, that sort of writhing motion." He tried to imitate it.

"This?" she asked, and she did it again, and then laughed.

"I like it when you laugh."

"I don't laugh enough," she said. "I'm usually very solemn. I guess it's my Russian background. My parents are both Russian Jews, you know."

"I didn't know you were Jewish."

"Oh, sure."

"Really?"

246

"Well, *sure* really. What would I be doing otherwise? Trying to *pass* for Jewish if I wasn't?"

"You don't look Jewish," he said.

"Oh, boy," she answered. "The Chinese rabbi. You know that one, don't you?"

"Yes," he said, and smiled. "I meant, you look Italian."

"Who? Me? No. Italian? With this blond hair?"

"Northern Italians have blond hair."

"Yes, but still. Look at my face. It's a very respectable sort of Jewgirl face that you can find on the New Lots Avenue Express every day of the week including Sundays. It usually has blue eyes, though. That's the only difference."

"I still think you look Italian."

"*No, non sono italiana,*" she said. "As a matter of fact, I'm usually taken for Irish. I'm what is known as a Yiddishe shiksa." She turned suddenly on her chair and fell into his arms in a mock swoon of despair, the back of her hand pressed to her forehead. "Don't tell me," she said. "It's all over between us, right?" He laughed and was about to answer her when she said, "The truth, now! You were a Nazi storm trooper during the war, right? Worse yet, you were a baker." Still laughing, still trying to answer her, he jostled his coffee cup with his elbow and spilled half of it over the table. "Ah-ha!" she said. "See! It's true!" She turned suddenly in his arms, precariously balanced, and kissed him on the mouth.

On Thursday of each week, they both had classes that broke at five o'clock. They would have coffee in the Chock Full O'Nuts near the school, and then walk uptown to Klein's, where Buddwing would impatiently hang around while Grace shopped for bargains. She rarely bought very much, and never anything expensive, but she told him she was used to an extravagant way of life, and did not want to get out of the habit now that she was married to a starving young student. From Klein's, they would take the subway up to the theater district, have a meal in the Automat, and then see a Broadway show. Their tickets were always mail-order balcony seats, ordered months in advance,

$2.40 the pair. The actors they saw on the stage sometimes resembled performing fleas, but they enjoyed their Thursdays immensely, and considered them an essential luxury to which they were undeniably entitled. Actually, they allowed themselves very few luxuries. Occasionally, they would take a break from their studies each night and walk up to Addie Vallins' on 86th Street, where they would indulge themselves in banana splits brimming with ripe Burgundy cherries and toasted almonds at sixty cents apiece. Once they bought a hand-tooled edition of Shakespeare's plays for thirty-eight dollars, and on another occasion they had a wooden radiator cover designed and built by a carpenter in the Village for twenty-two dollars, simply because they could no longer bear looking at the huge cast-iron monstrosity in their living room. But for the most part, they lived frugally on Buddwing's G.I. allotment, asking neither his parents nor hers for help. At the time, if they had been asked what they thought of being married as opposed to being single, they both would have answered, "It's the same thing, except we live together. It's lots of fun."

Laughing, he tried to sop up the spilled coffee, but it ran toward the edge of the table and then dripped onto her slip.

"Ick, you're a slob," she said, and pulled the wet slip up over her thighs. "I tell him I'm Jewish, so he spills half a gallon of coffee all over me!"

"Are you really Jewish?" he asked.

"Sure, I'm really Jewish. What do you think? Yeah, really, really. I mean, I don't go to synagogue or anything like that. I'm not even going to my mother's Seder this year. But I'm Jewish, all right, the same way you're Jewish. In fact, the same way Adlai Stevenson is Jewish."

"Well, I don't know about me," Buddwing said, "but Adlai Stevenson *ain't* Jewish."

"Sure he is."

"No, I think he's Protestant. Maybe Episcopalian."

"What's that got to do with it? Only a very small percentage of the Jewish people in this world are Jews. As a matter of fact, there are many Jews who aren't Jewish at all. Being Jewish has nothing whatever to do with religion or culture or background. Harry Truman, for example, is Jewish."

"Oh, I see," Buddwing said. "Ah, yes."

"But *she* isn't."

"Who?"

"Bess."

"No, of course not," Buddwing said. "Come to think of it, we've had very few Jewish Presidents."

"I know, I know," she answered. "And that's odd when you realize some of the signers of the Declaration of Independence were Jewish."

"Like who?"

"Benjamin Franklin, for one."

"Right, and John Hancock."

"Sure. But did we have any Jewish Presidents in the beginning? Was George Washington Jewish?"

"Absolutely not."

"Or either of the Adamses? Or Jefferson? Do you know who the first Jewish President in this country was?"

"Who?"

"Abraham Lincoln."

"That's right," Buddwing said.

"Eisenhower certainly wasn't Jewish."

"Neither was Mamie."

"Or Nixon."

"Which is why they couldn't get along with the Russians," Grace said.

"Why?"

"Because Khrushchev *is* Jewish."

"Of course he is," Buddwing said. "He's an old Jewish grandpa."

"Right, and Castro is a rabbinical student. That's why they get along so well."

Buddwing snapped his fingers. "Hey! You know who else is Jewish?"

"Who?"

"De Gaulle."

"Right. And Senator Dirksen."

"Right, right, and Mayor Wagner!"

"*Very* Jewish. You know who isn't?"

"Who?"

"Nelson Rockefeller and Barry Goldwater."

"Abdel Nasser *is* Jewish," Buddwing said.

"Sam Levene and Molly Berg are *not* Jewish," Grace said.

"No, they're Jewish impersonators. Sophia Loren, on the other hand, *is* Jewish."

"Oh, of course! So is Vittorio De Sica and Marcello Mastroianni, For that matter, Italy is a Jewish nation entirely."

"No, not entirely. Gina Lollobrigida is not Jewish."

"How about Federico Fellini?"

"I think he's only half Jewish on his mother's side," Buddwing said, and they both burst out laughing.

"Philip Roth is not Jewish," Grace said.

"Neither is J. D. Salinger."

"But you know who *is* Jewish?"

"Who?"

"James Jones."

"Naturally."

"Norman Mailer isn't."

"Neither is Sammy Davis, Jr., or James Baldwin."

"No, nor Elizabeth Taylor."

"Marilyn Monroe was Jewish," Grace said.

"Yes, but Arthur Miller isn't."

"Neither is Frank Sinatra."

"But Pablo Picasso is very definitely Jewish," Buddwing said.

"So's Pat O'Brien."

"Right. And Spencer Tracy!"

"Certainly. And Jack Paar."

"But Johnny Carson isn't."

"Neither is Hugh Downs."

"Or Helen Hayes."

"Never! Listen," Grace said, "for that matter . . ." and then she stopped with a shocked expression, and buried her face in his shoulder and began giggling.

"What?" he said, smiling.

"Oh, no!" she said, giggling.

"Who? Tell me."

"I think . . ."

"Who?"

"I think Adolph Hitler was Jewish!"

"Oh, my God, you're right!" Buddwing said, and he erupted into laughter. He held her in his arms, rocking with glee, while she giggled into his shoulder.

"Oh, *please*," she said, giggling.

"I'm not *doing* anything!" he said, his stomach aching, tears running down his face.

"Please, I'll *wet* myself," she squealed, and they both burst out laughing again.

"Hey, watch it!" he shouted, laughing, losing his balance on the chair.

"Oh, my God!"

"Hey!" he said, and they fell noisily to the floor.

"Oh, I broke my arm," she said, giggling.

"Here, let me kiss it," he said, laughing, bringing her arm to his mouth and running his lips over the length of it with small noisy kisses.

"That tickles!" she screamed, and began tickling him in return, under the arms, on the soles of his feet, across his belly, until finally they both rolled onto their backs and roared hilariously to the ceiling. The rain was gentle against the windowpanes. There was the smell of coffee in the small kitchen. Their laughter trailed. She sighed gently, and closed her eyes, and he put his hand on her breast and felt the beat of her heart.

In his eyes, she was an enchanted being who had magically come into his life and filled it with a radiant glow. Never very imaginative himself, he entered into each new preposterous game she invented and played it with delight. He was even willing to listen to her astrological prognostications because somehow there seemed to be a distorted kernel of truth in each of her predictions. When she consulted her charts and then dolefully wagged her head because a Philosophy examination happened to fall on a day when Venus or Saturn were in conjunction with whatever the hell—he could never keep her signs and symbols straight—he felt a small pang of terror in spite of himself. He began to believe he had married some sort of woodland witch who stirred frogs and bats and eyes of newt into a huge caldron and muttered incantations to the stars to keep herself forever youthful, forever desirable, forever innocent.

He never knew what to expect from her next. She performed each of her magic tricks with the immunity of a child, never seeming either ridiculous or theatrical, no matter which preposterous pose or fantastic situation she was conjuring. She could feel perfectly confident in saying to a drunk lying in the gutter, "Shame on you," and then could suggest one Saturday night that they buy two bottles of Scotch (a luxury) and try to consume them both before they went to bed. She could cheat on an examination without batting an eyelash, and then launch a tirade against Russian diplomats who broke their word. She could turn her back to him one night with a frosty "Is that all you *ever* think of?" and then wake him at two in the morning with the sheet pulled over her head like a tent while she whispered seductively from its depths. She was totally mercurial, and it was her very unpredictability that made that first year together so completely alive.

If either of the two had any plans for the future, they were the plans of the very young, amorphous, fleeting. They had met when they were both freshmen and now, in their junior year, they were married. They talked continually of graduation as though it were some sort of mysterious rite that would pass them through an invisible barrier separating them from the real world of productive people. Once through that barrier, they would assume their rightful places in the order of things. But they had no notion as to where their rightful places were, or how they would go about occupying them. Their plans were spontaneous and ephemeral, providing excitement each time a new one was outlined. One week, they decided they would go to Paris as soon as they were graduated, and just bum around, drinking absinthe in the sidewalk cafés, and making love in garret rooms overlooking chimney pots. The next week, it was decided they would both go West for their master's degrees, either to the University of Colorado in Denver, or U.C.L.A. in Los Angeles. But the week after that, Grace suggested that they go to the Scandinavian countries for the summer, taking jobs as English-speaking guides on the bus tours, which would enable them to save some money for their future education. Buddwing bettered her idea by suggesting that they live in Puerto Rico for a while, where the sand was white, the sun was hot, and the income was tax-free. No corner of the globe was safe from their imaginary visits, no occupation too bizarre, no dream too fantastic. A new batch of travel folders flooded into the apartment daily, and they picked over the world like explorers impatient to set sail. Their dreams all hinged upon "graduation," that fabulous passport to the world of real adults. Once out of school, once free of the cloistered atmosphere of academics, they would come to grips with the world through discovering it—and would incidentally find themselves as well. They seemed unaware that at least some of their plans centered about a continuance of studies, an extension of the cloistered atmosphere that nourished them as surely as an incubator. "Graduation" would solve everything. "Graduation" would enable them to lay their further plans and choose their destinies. There was really no rush because they would have the whole summer to decide. In the meantime, they could live as they had done from the very beginning, in a curious world of make-believe that neither of them recognized as such.

"What are you thinking?" he asked.

"I'm trying to remember if we have enough liquor."

"Enough liquor for what?"

"Some of the kids are coming over later."

"Oh," he said. "Yeah?"

"Yes, about eleven o'clock." She paused. "What's the matter?"

"Nothing. I thought we'd be alone."

"Well, it's only nine-thirty."

"Yeah, okay."

"I'm sorry, but I invited them yesterday."

"Okay."

"I didn't *know* I was going to meet you, you know."

"I know that."

"I really hadn't planned on doing anything the early part of the night. In fact, I wanted to wash my hair and do some laundry, is all."

"Well, I'm sorry if I spoiled your plans," he said.

She rolled over beside him and propped her chin on one hand, her elbow bent, and looked directly down into his face and said, "Hey."

"What?"

"Cut it out."

"Okay."

"Because you know you haven't spoiled any of my plans."

"Okay."

"And we don't need this kind of crap between us."

"Okay."

"Because it's too good the way it is."

"All right."

"And anyway, I won't have to wash my hair now because the rain took care of that."

"But you *do* have to do your laundry."

"Yes, but the machine is right in the basement. I don't have to go out or anything."

"Good. I want to go down to the basement with you and help you do your laundry."

"What we could do, you know . . ."

"Yeah, what?"

"Well," she said thoughtfully, "it only takes a minute to carry it downstairs and put it in the machine, you know."

"Mmmm?"

"Yes, and we *do* have until eleven o'clock, or maybe a little after. One of the kids is in a show, you see, and they're picking him up and then coming over. So let's say eleven-fifteen, maybe eleven-thirty."

"Yeah, so?"

"So we could bring the laundry down, and then come up here while it's in the machine. It takes, oh, forty minutes, I guess. How does that sound to you?"

"I kind of wanted to watch your dirty clothes spinning around behind the glass."

"Well, okay, if that's what you want. But I thought since we've got until eleven-thirty, well, that gives us plenty of time."

"For what?"

"Well, for whatever you want to do with it."

"With *it?*"

"Yes, the time." She paused. She pushed her hand through his hair roughly and said. "What are you, a wise guy?"

"Yes," he said, grinning, "I'm a wise guy."

"You want it all spelled out, don't you?"

"Yes."

"All right, I'll spell it out for you."

"When?"

"Later. Come on, let's get dressed."

They were graduated on the fifteenth of June, 1950.

The commencement exercises were held on Ohio Field at the University Heights campus in the Bronx. Sitting beside Grace in his cap and gown, Buddwing heard the university registrar telling the gathered students and guests that this 118th graduating class was the largest in the history of the school, and he looked up at the glowering clouds on the horizon and wondered if it would rain. The university officials were used to soggy graduation exercises, since it had rained during four commencements in the past five years, but the promise of rain seemed like an ill omen to Buddwing.

9,158 degrees would be conferred today, the registrar was saying as Buddwing watched the clouds apprehensively. Fifty-five per cent of these degrees would go to veterans of World War II. How long had he waited for this promised day—through how many goddamn cacophonous nights in the middle of the Pacific Ocean with Japanese guns pounding, through how many dreary lectures in stuffy springtime classrooms, through how many eternities of crap courses and ten-minute quizzes and final examinations and papers due on Friday the twelfth? He hoped it would not rain. 5,866 bachelor's would be conferred, 2,885 master's, 196 doctor's, and 209 certificates in specialized fields, he had visualized this ceremony as taking place in brilliant sunshine, Get these troops out of the hot sun, Colonel, his face and Grace's touched by the glancing rays, the promise of the future. Now, with rain clouds threatening the sky, he listened while he was told that Alfred Lunt and Lynn Fontanne would receive jointly an honorary Doctor of Humane Letters degree. He was suddenly glad that he and Grace were receiving separate degrees, and he waited impatiently for the actual ceremony to start, frightened lest it begin raining before this culminating act was consummated.

He received his document and he shook hands with Dr. Chase, the school chancellor, and he went back to his seat, following Grace who was walking back off the platform, just a few paces ahead of him. When they were seated again, he covered her hand with his own and squeezed it gently.

It began raining before Dr. Chase could deliver his commencement speech. It rained lightly at first, and he and Grace sat with the other students and guests, hopeful that the clouds would blow over. But the drops began falling more heavily and more steadily, and one by one the gathered crowd began to run for cover. He and Grace stayed until they were certain Dr. Chase would not make his speech. They fled with the rest then, and learned in the Alumni Bulletin the following week that some five hundred foolhardy souls had remained seated throughout the entire downpour, college graduates who had not learned enough to come in out of the rain.

Their families were present at the exercises, of course, and Buddwing found this togetherness almost unbearable. He had never liked Dan and never would, and his presence at something that was terribly important to Buddwing and Grace seemed almost

an affront. Grace's father chattered on about his new Arabian
steed, and Grace's mother asked Buddwing's mother if she played
bridge, and would she like to join her weekly Mount Kisco game?
Grace pulled Buddwing aside and whispered, "I wonder who got
top billing?"

"Huh?"

"On their joint degree. Alfred or Lynn?"

"How do you feel?" he asked.

"What do you mean?"

"Well, just . . . how do you feel?"

"Stupid," Grace answered. "How do you feel?"

"Stupid."

"Fine way for college graduates to feel."

"Well, I guess we're stepping out into the world," he said. "I
guess that's why."

"Yes," she answered with a solemnity that startled him.

In the summer of 1950, Sam Buddwing, or whoever the hell he
was, stepped out into the world that was New York City and
began looking for a job. He had been advised during the commencement exercises that fifty-five per cent of N.Y.U.'s graduating class was composed of World War II veterans, and that the
class was the largest in the school's history. He had only to extend
these spectacular figures to Harvard and Princeton and Rutgers
and Yale and C.C.N.Y. and Fordham and Dartmouth and Cornell
and Syracuse and any and every college or university, big or
small, in the United States of America in order to determine
exactly how many eager young graduates were storming the
largest city in the world that summer, looking for work. These
were the young men who had invaded the fortress of Europe,
who had hedgehopped their way from island to island across the
Pacific, who had watched their comrades in arms die in muddy
ditches and steaming jungles, and they came now like a new invasion force, bristling with knowledge, the greatest peacetime
armada ever assembled, to storm the bunkers lining Madison
Avenue. They all carried parchments stating that they had completed the required course of study for a baccalaureate degree,

and they all came equipped with transcripts of their school records, and bright cheery smiles, and perfect speech learned in elocution courses. None of them knew what a buyer's market was. None of them realized that jobs which had once been going to high school graduates could, in this embarrassment of educational riches, now be bestowed upon men who had completed a four-year college course of study.

Buddwing did not know quite what he wanted, but he knew he had not gone to college to become a bank clerk trainee. He began seriously entertaining the notion of leaving for Paris with Grace, where they would indeed become bums, drinking absinthe and rotting their brains away with wormwood. They had their first serious argument the day she suggested that perhaps she could find a job to carry them through the summer, after which they could make further plans and either go on with their studies or go to Europe, or whatever.

"If I can't find a job, how the hell do you expect to find one?" he asked.

"I'm only offering it as a compromise suggestion," Grace said. "I mean, you *can't* find a job, can you?"

"I could, if you wanted me to go out digging ditches," he answered.

"Well, I don't want you to do that. But I wouldn't mind taking a job as a salesgirl someplace or—"

"The hell with that," he said. "You're a college graduate!"

"I don't think we can eat our diplomas, do you?" she asked.

"No. That's why I think we should go to Paris."

"We haven't got the fare."

"I could take some kind of job to earn the fare, and *then* we could go."

"All right, if that's what you want to do. I simply thought that, since my sign is Gemini—"

"Oh, come on, Grace, not that again. You don't really think—"

"Yes, I do."

"That's all nonsense and you know it."

"What was it that put me in bed for a month then, would you mind telling me?"

"You had the flu," he said.

"No, I had a touch of bronchitis."

"Dr. Manero said it was the flu."

"Dr. Manero doesn't know anything about it," Grace said. "When you're born under the sign of Gemini, the weakest part of your anatomy is your lungs. I've always had trouble with my lungs. I'm always catching cold very easily—you know that, honey, so admit it."

"I catch cold easily, too, and I'm Capricorn, so what the hell does that prove?"

"You don't catch colds, you get slight touches of rheumatism. If you're Capricorn, the weakest parts of your body are the knees, bones, and joints."

"I've never had trouble with my knees, bones or joints," Buddwing said.

"Except when you get a slight touch of rheumatism."

"I don't get slight touches of rheumatism, I get common colds."

"Well, you can call them what you like, but I happen to know," Grace said.

"Yeah, Omar the Mystic."

"Don't make fun of it," she warned.

"Queen of the Zodiac," he said.

"Because I don't happen to think it's very funny."

"No, that's because you have no sense of humor."

"That isn't my fault. I was born under Gemini. I'm not supposed to be some sort of flibbertigibbet scatterbrain."

"No, you're supposed to be intelligent, logical, and meticulous."

"That's right."

"Which is why you flunked Greek Mythology the first semester I knew you."

"I flunked Greek Mythology because Geminians always dissipate their energies. I'm a very changeable person, you know that. I start out to do something and then I lose track of it and start something else. That's very common if you're born under Gemini."

"Sure," he said.

"But that doesn't mean I'm not ambitious."

"No, I know that."

"Or sensitive."

"You're very sensitive," he said.

"Yes, and I say what I think, which is another characteristic of Geminians, and which happens to be burning you up right now. Huh? Isn't it?"

"No. You can always say what you think. Nobody's telling you not to say what you think."

"Well, then, it seems to me that an intelligent woman who's a college graduate should be allowed to go out and take a job if her husband can't find one to support them."

"Nobody's forbidding you to work. What do you think this is, the Middle Ages? If you want to work, work. I'll stay home and mop the kitchen floor and have the babies you're supposed to have."

"What do you mean by that?"

"By what?"

"By the 'babies' crack."

"Nothing. I simply thought that having babies was a woman's function, and that a man was supposed to go out and—"

"I'm not about ready to have a baby, so let's get off *that*, if you don't mind. You can't even keep the two of us fed, and you're talking about a baby."

"What am I, all of a sudden? A mental incompetent? I don't want to take a job that doesn't lead anywhere, is that so unreasonable?"

"Not at all. But is it unreasonable for me to suggest that perhaps I can help out? I thought this marriage was a partnership. If you *really* want to go to Paris, as you say, then why shouldn't I—"

"I don't *know* if I want to go to Paris."

"Well, what is it you'd *like* to do, exactly? Would you please tell me?"

"I don't know yet."

"When *will* you know? When we're both on home relief?"

"Look, Grace, I refuse to take some kind of jerky job. I am not a jerk, goddamnit!"

"All right, I grant you that. I have granted it to you a hundred times tonight. I will continue to grant it to you. All I'm suggesting is that—"

"Oh, go on!" he said angrily. "Go get a job. If you think you can get one, go ahead."

"Thanks. That's very goddamn encouraging."

"What do you want me to do? You've just cut off my balls, would you like me to garnish them with a little parsley?"

"Cut off your *what?*"

"Balls. B-A-double-L—"

"Now that *is* the Middle Ages. That is posi*tive*ly the Middle Ages. The concept of a man in armor, and a woman as a . . . child-bearing sow who mops the kitchen floor and—"

"Boy, you've got a real thing about babies, haven't you? What are you so afraid of?"

"I don't want a baby." Grace said. "I should think—"

"Oh, I know that. Oh, brother, do I know that. I mean, all the creams and jellies and tubes and insertions, and God forbid you're ten minutes late, wow, the fingernails get bitten down to the elbow, and the hair gets pulled—"

"I do not want a baby now," she said with dignity.

"Yes, I know."

"I do not want one."

"I heard you. Why not? How about answering that one?"

"Which reason do you want? I have about a hundred and ten."

"Give me all of them."

"All right," Grace said, holding out her hand and beginning to tick off the points on her fingers. "Number one, we have exactly forty-eight dollars in our joint savings account, forty-eight dollars, and the rent is due next week. Number two, you seem incapable of finding any sort of employment—"

"Listen, Grace, if you imply once more that I'm a Mongolian idiot who can't—"

"*You* said it, not me. Number three, I thought you wanted to go to Paris, and I don't intend to go there with extra baggage in my belly. And number four, I don't even know who the hell *I* am yet, and you want me to have a baby. What would I tell a baby? Your mother doesn't know who she is?"

"Oh, come on, Grace, you know who you are. Go look at your charts; they'll tell you. Look it up under Saturn in the tenth house of Taurus in conjunction with Venus in the third phase of the moon."

"Haha."

"I thought that was pretty funny."

"Yes, you would. You Capricorns are all alike."

"Well, your brother warned you, didn't he?"

"Keep him out of this. At least he's supporting his wife."

"Yeah, well, if *my* father owned half the goddamn horses in the world, maybe I could go out and set up my own office, too."

"My father has *one* horse. *One.*"

"And *one* precious daughter, *one*, who's starving in a Third Avenue tenement."

"Oh, the hell with this," she said suddenly. "This is stupid as hell. There's no sense even talking to you."

"All right, then, *don't*. But I'm not going to take the first crumby job that's offered to me. I've got a right to know who I am and what I am. You just remember that."

"I'm sorry if I confuse your identity image."

"And don't give me any of that college-girl crap-talk."

"I wasn't aware—"

"Well, now you're aware."

"Is it all right to talk in my own damn house without being interrupted?" she asked furiously.

"I'm sorry."

"Don't be so goddamn sorry after the fact. That's only Capricorn talking. The poor, lonely, misunderstood, hypersensitive, self-pitying little boy."

"I said I was sorry."

"Oh, *I'm* sorry, too," she said, and began crying. He stood beside her helplessly, leaning against the wall, while the tears streamed down her face. She wiped her nose on the sleeve of her robe and then turned her head away from him and wept softly. Snuffling back her tears, she said, "There's a draft in here. Would you please close the window?"

"It's ninety-sev—" he started to say, and then closed his mouth and went to the window.

"Thank you," she said. She sniffed. "Have you got a handkerchief?"

"Yes. Here."

"Thank you."

She blew her nose. She would not look at him.

"Honey?" he said.

"What?"

"I'm sorry if—"

"I'm all right now. Forget it."

"But you—"

"I was just feeling bitchy, that's all."

"I'll get a job, but . . . it has to be what I want. Don't you see that?"

She sniffed again, and nodded. "What is it you want?" she asked gently.

"Ahhh, what do I want?" He leaned his head back against the wall and a curious smile touched his face. "I want happiness growing on trees in a garden, Grace, to pick like big golden apples, to bite into, to feel the juices running down over our chins. I want the sun to be shining all the time, and I want your hair to stay long and golden, and your eyes to stay bright with wonder, and your mouth to taste of clover. I want a long white beach with an ocean like a murmur in a conch shell, and I want to kiss your fingertips and your navel, and make love under the sun and laugh when it rains, if it ever rains, but it'll never rain. And, oh, our babies'll be fat and healthy with your blond hair and my blue eyes, and God will smile down on us, Grace, oh Jesus, He will nod his big white shaggy head and smile on us, and shower us with happiness and joy. We'll live forever, honey, we'll roam the world like young Vikings, we'll go to England and Spain . . ."

"Yes, Majorca . . ." she said.

"La Costa Brava . . ."

"France . . ."

"France, yes, and Italy . . ."

"Rome and Venice . . ."

"Florence and Milan . . ."

"Yes, Milan . . ."

"Everywhere, darling, wherever we want to go, because we'll be so goddamn happy, and together, and in love, if only . . . if only . . ."

"What, darling?"

"If only you'll stay with me," he said.

She looked up at him in surprise. "Why, of course I'll stay with you."

"Always," he said.

"Always," she repeated.

"Grace?"

"Yes?"

"Don't . . . don't ever wonder who you are again."

"But—"

"Please. Because if you do . . . I won't know who I am, either. And then we'll both be lost."

# 15

THEY sat on the floor in the basement of the building with their backs to the cinder-block wall. They had made out a list of things they would need from the liquor store and the grocery, and now they sat with their hands clasped, and waited for the laundry to be done.

She was wearing her red cotton robe, tightly belted at the waist. Her left hand was clasped in his right, her head resting on his shoulder. He had put on his trousers and an old sweater. They were both barefoot.

The sounds of the building vibrated everywhere around them. The washing machine hummed and clicked and clattered steadily as it passed through cycle after cycle. Overhead, the water pipes clanged intermittently and dripped a small puddle of water against the opposite wall. There was the sound of an occasional toilet being flushed, the sound of footsteps and unintelligible voices above. A small window was at the far end of the basement. The rain had stopped, but a strong wind had come up, and the window rattled against the sash with each fresh gust. The myriad sounds encouraged whispering.

"What we could do," she said, "is get rid of it."

"How? That takes money."

"Aren't there pills or something?"

"I don't think so. Not for . . . well, not for getting rid of it."

"My father would give us money. I think he would."

"I'd hate to ask him. I mean, for something like this. Anyway, they'd tell you to go ahead and have it, Grace."

"Boy, this is what I really needed, all right. I really needed this."

"Well, we *are* married, you know. I don't see—"

"I'm scared to death."

"Why?"

"I don't know. My grandmother died in childbirth."

"That was in the old days, Grace. Nobody dies in childbirth any more."

"I'll bet it hurts like hell."

"No, they give you anesthesia. You never even—"

"Not until its head is showing or something. Ick, it's disgusting, all of it."

"It's a very natural thing, Grace. Women go through it every day of the—"

"Oh, shut up."

"I'm only trying to—"

"I know, I know, I'm sorry." She was silent for a long time. Then she said, "This throws Paris right out the window, doesn't it?"

"It needn't. We could—"

"Sure, we could carry a baby halfway across the world. We don't even know if the water's fit to drink there."

"I'm sure the water in Paris—"

"And inoculations. How can you take a newborn baby to Europe?"

"He won't be born for nine months, you know."

"Eight."

"Well, eight."

"Or actually seven months and about ten days." She shook her head. "I'm twenty-two years old, and I'm going to have a baby in seven months and ten days. Boy, that's something, isn't it?"

"Some women have them even younger that that."

"Sure, some women are stupid asses, too. I don't know how this happened. I swear to God, I do *not* know how this happened. Can we sue Margaret Sanger?"

"I don't think so," he said, and laughed.

"I mean, if they put a damn product on the market, you'd think it would work, wouldn't you?"

"It's not supposed to be a hundred per cent effective, honey."

"No, so we get stuck. Do you know what she said to me?"

"Who, Grace?"

"The woman at the clinic. When I went to take the rabbit test. They make you put it in, you know, to see if you've been doing it properly, all that. Ick, it's disgusting. Well, when she saw that I *was* doing it properly, she said, 'Are you sure you didn't leave it in the closet, honey?'"

"What did you tell her?"

"I told her, 'Sure, I left it in the closet. That's where we make love, in the closet.'" Buddwing began laughing. "Don't laugh," she said, "it isn't funny."

"Grace," he said, "the thing is, I wouldn't mind having a baby." She did not answer him.

"We're young," he said, "what the hell."

She still said nothing.

"We'd have a lot to offer a child."

"Like what?"

"Brains, beauty . . ." He shrugged, and then smiled.

"Would you please do me a favor?"

"Sure, honey, what?"

"Don't try to be comical."

"I'm sorry."

"You know when it must have happened?" she said.

"When?"

"That night we came back from L.J.'s house."

"You think so?"

"Mmm, yeah. When was that? August sometime? Just after you got the job—when was that?"

"That was August."

"Well, that's when it must have happened."

"Maybe."

"Well, at least it was good. That night, I mean."

"Yes."

"Boy, I'm really scared. I mean it."

"Honey, please don't be."

"You're not even supposed to *keep* this job. It's supposed to be a stopgap. I don't want to tie you down to something that—"

"Don't worry about me."

"Oh, I *have* to worry about you. I *am* you, don't you know that?"

"No," he said softly. "I didn't know that, Grace."

"Oh, don't be such a jerk all the time. I spend my whole damn day figuring out what to say to you, and what to wear to please you, and how to make you laugh, and how to feed you and—oh, the hell with it."

"I didn't know that," he said again, softly.

"I just don't want to get you hung up like this."

"I told you, honey, I *want* the baby."

"I don't want us to turn into . . . I don't know . . . shlubs. I don't want us to be like all the shlubs in the world, walking around with their fat bellies full of kids and their shabby flowered housedresses—boy, that scares me, honey. I don't want you going to a stupid job each day of the week and hating it and hating me and hating the baby and turning into a stoop-shouldered old man with threadbare pants."

"How's a baby going to change anything, Grace?"

"I feel changed already. I feel *fat*. Ick, I could vomit."

"You don't look fat."

"In fact, I *do* vomit," she said, and smiled.

"Now who's making the jokes?"

"Yeah, some joke. The radiant bride with the fat belly, puking all over the bathroom floor. What a charming picture to wake up to each morning."

"I love you, Grace," he said.

"I was wondering when you'd get around to that."

"Do I have to say it?"

"Yes, you damn well do. *Often.*"

"I love you."

"I suppose we'll have to tell them, won't we? Sooner or later. The folks, I mean."

"Yes."

"My brother'll flip. His baby sister, The Weeper." She grinned and said, "Well, he warned me."

"He certainly did."

"So I guess I've got no one to blame but myself."

"And me."

"And Margaret Sanger." She paused, and then sighed, and then said, "I'm scared."

He did not tell her that he was terrified.

If only, he thought.

Well.

If only

What we need is a break, that's all. You can't start this way, with nothing at all, and hope to survive. You can't start young and fresh and unscarred and step into this world. No, you can't. It's a devouring beast, and if you won't allow it to feed on you, it turns you against each other and you start feeding on yourselves. Because look at her, for God's sake. What is she? Twenty-two? And thinking it's all rolling out of bed with a laugh to make coffee in the morning, thinking it's all rainy Saturday afternoons hiding under the dining room table the way I used to hide with my cousin Mandy. Children. You don't take them and throw them into the street naked where the tigers are prowling, how can you? They need a break. All we need is any kind of a break. Ah, sure, self-pity. She said it, she was right, I'm a self-pitying son of a bitch, but I know that if we could only

Her brother could have done something for us; he could have

offered us something. What was his big expensive gift to us? A lousy toaster. Doesn't he know we need *money?*

I used to think, if only my grandfather were alive.

I used to think, if only Beethoven were alive, why, then I wouldn't be so alone. Why, then, together, all of us banded in a tight circle with our arms around each other, Jesse too with his hard muscular arms, all of us with our backs turned against those walls that are moving in, why, then we could hold, then we could push the walls back, could keep them from squashing us flat, if only I weren't alone. Because she can't help, you see, not the way she is now. She's too sweet and frail and confused, and she can't help to hold back whatever it is that's determined to flatten us, to drain all our young blood and leave us one-dimensional with only an angry helpless snarl on our flattened lips. We're too young.

We're too young to be flattened this way. But how can I stop it from happening if I don't even know who I am, if there's a hunger inside me to . . . to *be,* to grow, to live, to

"You *never* knew who the hell you were, and you've *always* been hungry."

Ah, sure, talk about it, the wisdom of the very old. Hungry where? At your fat and overflowing breast, was I hungry there? Lost where? In the dark jealousy of a love I could never consummate, hating him and loving him, knowing you were *ours,* yes, but really only his and never truly mine? Lost and hungry, yes, but why didn't you ever tell me? Why didn't you say, Sam, there are tigers out there, they are going to try to rip you limb from limb. Why didn't you tell me that, Mother darling? Why did you leave me to discover it for myself with a girl who had never been told, either, a girl who thinks I know all the secrets when I know none of them at all? Why didn't you tell me that I would have to go into the street naked and strangle tigers with nothing but love to protect me?

Tigers feast on love, didn't you know that? The smell of love is fat and rich to their nostrils, and oh, they want to sink their claws and teeth into it; there is too much love in this world for the tigers. Throw love in their faces, hold up love as a shield, swing love as a sword, stand naked with only love as a cloak, and they will pick your bones clean, and you'll never know who the hell you are or were.

The girl turned off the water tap.

The apartment was very still.

He sat alone and wondered who he was, and wondered why nobody had reported him missing to the Bureau of Missing Persons. He knew there was a Bureau of Missing Persons someplace in the city, and he knew that the first thing anyone did when her husband was late for dinner was to report him to that bureau and they would then send around two detectives who asked for dental charts. He had read the newspaper this morning, and the only person missing was Edward Voegler, from a mental hospital. He knew positively he was not Edward Voegler, so how come nobody had reported him missing? And if nobody had bothered to report him, was he indeed *missing*, or was it simply a case of nobody giving enough of a damn to *miss* him?

"Have you got a radio?" he called to the bathroom.

From behind the closed door, the girl said, "Yes, on the bookshelf. The left-hand side of the bed."

He found the radio, and turned it on. A group of little girls were singing a song that seemed to say, "I *love* him, I *love* him, I *love* him, and where he goes, I'll *foll*ow, I'll *foll*ow, I'll *foll*ow . . ."

Then why *didn't* you follow? he thought. Here I am, why didn't you follow?

"I like that song," the girl said from the bathroom.

"I wanted to get the news."

"It's too early for the news."

"It ought to come on at eleven," he answered.

"Come in here," she said. "I want to kiss you before I put on my lipstick."

He did not want to go to her because he suddenly felt the entire thing was her fault; she should have been more careful. It was not fair of her to grow as huge as a mountain with life clamoring inside her, a trembling volcano waiting to erupt; it was not fair. He wanted to get out of this apartment that restricted him, wanted to get away from this strange woman who was not Grace at all, not the Grace he had known, but rather some oddly deformed creature who moved ponderously and constantly complained of backaches. The little girls on the radio were shouting, "I *love* him, I *love* him, I *love* him," in eternal cacophony, but if she really loved him, loved him, loved him, why had she allowed this to happen? He could remember those nights in his father's car, their secret laughter about her brother Dan-Duke, could remember all of it with a painful nostalgia that made him wish she did truly love him, did indeed give enough of a damn about him to have called the Bureau of Missing Persons. He suddenly knew this was impossible. The voices of the chanting little girls gave way to the sound of what was supposed to be a beeping transmitter signal, and an announcer said that it was news time. He moved closer to the radio.

There was trouble of every kind in New York City and the world, and he listened to the woes of humanity while waiting to learn something about the specific woes of a very special human being who happened to be himself. But the radio told him nothing at all, and when the announcer was finished, a commercial came on in which a bratty kid kept yelling to his mother to bring some more Parks Sausages. He went to the radio and turned it off. The room was silent except for the sigh of the wind against the windowpanes.

He listened to the wind and decided to leave her.

Yes, he thought.

Yes.

Leave now. Go before it is too late.

Go kill all the tigers.

He stood by the window, looking down into the street.

Yes, he thought. You leave Grace now, and one day she is going to leave you.

The thought came into his mind unbidden, and he almost dismissed it at once because it was so utterly illogical. How could

she possibly leave him one day if he left her now? He simply
would not be there; you can't leave someone who isn't there. And
yet the very absence of logic in the thought seemed to make it
undeniably logical. Yes, it is true, he told himself. If I leave her
now fat and misshapen with a baby in her belly, why, she'll leave
me someday; that's all there is to it. He shrugged. There did not
seem to be much sense in pursuing the thought, since he had already decided to leave her, anyway. But he found himself negat-
ing the thought, and then discovered there was at least some hope
in negation.

If I do *not* leave Grace now, then one day she is *not* going to
leave me.

Something was still wrong with the thought, but he could not
imagine what. He had the oddest feeling that whatever was wrong
had to do with Grace herself, and that he could do nothing to pre-
vent her from leaving him forever whenever she wanted to. But
at least the thought provided hope.

Hope for what? he wondered.

Well, hope that everything would turn out all right.

That's the way it's supposed to work, didn't you know that?
You're supposed to go through the worst possible trials and
tribulations each day before the soap commercial, and then at the
end of the week everything is supposed to work out all right.
The cavalry is supposed to arrive. That's what the whole goddamn thing is about, don't you know? That's what keeps us
going, the certainty that everything is going to work out all right,
the mortgage will be paid, the villain will be vanquished, everybody will be rich and happy, and it will end in a clinch at sunset.

He suddenly found himself grinning. You think I'm afraid of
tigers? he thought. Ha! The cavalry's going to arrive. Who the
hell's afraid of tigers!

He went to the bathroom door and pounded on it furiously.
The door opened. She was wearing her red cotton robe, belted
at the waist. She looked out at him with a curious smile.

"Ah, *now* he comes," she said. "When I've already put on my
lipstick."

"Listen, Grace," he said.

Over her shoulder, he could see his own reflection in the mirror over the sink. His eyes were brightly glowing; there was a high, intense look on his face.

"What is it?" she said.

"What is *this?*" he asked. "A big goddamn city?"

"Yes, it's—"

"What is it? A big goddamn world?"

She was studying him curiously now, the smile no longer on her face, a look of serious concern in her eyes.

"Are you afraid of tigers?" he asked.

"Yes," she answered. "I'm scared to death of—"

"Neither am I," he said. "What the hell are tigers? We're both young, aren't we? We're both strong!"

"If twenty-eight is young, then I suppose—"

"We're going to lick this goddamn thing, Grace. We're going to make it turn out *our* way, the way *we* want it, do you hear me? You're twenty-two years old. Why the hell should you have to cry in bed at night?"

"What is it?" she said gently. "What's the matter? Is something—"

"It's not all making coffee and rolling out of bed on a Saturday morning, Grace. What the hell do they have out there? Tigers? Who's afraid of tigers? A little colored kid in the jungle made *pancakes* out of them, for Christ's sake!"

"What did you hear on the radio? Did something upset you?"

"They took his pants and his shirt and his shoes and his umbrella just like they've taken ours, Grace, but the cavalry arrived, didn't it? *They* wound up on the breakfast table, so who's afraid of them?"

"You're frightening me," she said.

"There's nothing to be frightened of. They made the rules, didn't they? All right, we'll *learn* the rules. We'll play the game their way, why not? We're together, aren't we?"

"Yes, darling," she said. "We're together."

"All I need is your help."

"I'll help you."

"I'm going to know who I am, do you hear that?"

"Yes, darling, I know you are."

"I need your help, Grace."

"I'll help you. I'll help you all I can."

"Do you know what I was about to do? I was about to leave
you, do you realize that? I was about to go out there alone,
Grace! What would you do then? What would you do alone,
with your big belly, in this empty apartment? What would you
do? You'd cry alone, the way I heard you crying night after
night, your back turned to me, while I lay there with every
muscle quivering, and the apartment closed around us like a
tomb, alone, Grace. How could I have even *thought* of it?"

She watched him silently, and then glanced across the room
toward the telephone. She seemed about to move toward it.

"We don't need anyone," he said. "Never mind that."

"What?"

"The telephone. Never mind any of them, the hell with them
all. We can do it alone."

"I thought . . ."

"What did you think? That I could actually leave you? Just
walk out of your life? Ah, no, Grace, that's *your* game, not mine.
What would you do then, huh? If I left? Weep alone for the
boy and girl who met in a park and tried to grow up together,
unaware that tigers can stunt your growth? They can, Grace, oh
they can, but not to us! What would you do, wipe away your
tears and consult your charts and notice that Gemini is under the
rulership of the planet Mercury, and that you were born in the
second decanate, eleven to twenty degrees, with the sun in as-
cendance? And then forget? Wipe away your tears and forget?
How could I leave you, Grace? How could I ever forget you?"

She did not answer him. She was biting her lip now and watching him worriedly.

"I want to be one of the tigers," he said. "I want to drink raw
blood."

He saw she was fighting to hold back her tears. She was twisting

275

her hands now, and biting her lip, and the tears were behind her eyes, ready to overflow.

"No," he said. "Don't cry."

"You frighten me. I'm worried about you."

"Don't worry about *me*," he said. "Worry about *them*! They're the ones who have to worry!" He walked swiftly to the window and threw it open. "Listen to me!" he shouted to the lighted windows across the street. "Listen to me, you bastards!"

"Darling, please . . ."

"Open your window eyes and look at me up here! Do you see me? This is *me* standing here! I am going to get all the things I need and want, and I am going to get them with these bare hands. Now, what do you think of that? Go ahead, turn out your bathroom light up there—what the hell do I care? You can't stop us, do you hear me?" He turned from the window. Very softly, he said, "They can't stop us, Grace." He walked to her and dropped to his knees before her. He opened the red robe and put his head against her belly. "I love you, Grace," he said. "I love what's inside you." He paused. "We're going to learn. We're going to beat the bastards."

She sighed deeply and gently stroked his face. He stayed on his knees before her, his cheek pressed to her belly, for what seemed like a long long time. Then he rose and stood before her with his head erect and his shoulders back. "I'll go down for the whiskey now," he said. "We're going to have our party. We're going to celebrate."

"Maybe *I* ought to go. Maybe—"

"No, you still have to dress." He smiled. "Don't worry about me, Grace. There's nothing out there that can harm me."

"I don't want anything to happen to you," she said.

"Nothing will happen to me."

"Or to us. I don't want anything to happen to us." She paused. She studied him for a long time, and then cautiously, she said, "Look, would you . . ." She bit her lip. "We can get help, you know. If you'd let me . . ."

"We don't need help," he said.

"It's just . . . I don't want to lose you."

He smiled and went to her and took her in his arms. "No, huh?" he said teasingly. "How come?"

"I love you," she said.

"You do, huh? Then how about giving me the money for the booze?"

She hesitated, watching his face. "You'll come right back, won't you?"

"I'll fly," he said.

She moved away from him and opened her handbag. "It's two blocks up. The liquor store. You'll have to look for a grocery. I don't know if any'll be open at this time of—"

"I'll find one."

She handed him a twenty-dollar bill. "Please hurry," she said. "I'll be worrying."

"Go put on your dress," he said. He kissed her lightly on the forehead, and went out of the apartment.

The streets outside had been washed clean by the rain, and everything glistened with the sparkle of fresh wetness. He breathed deeply of the air and walked two blocks up the avenue to the liquor store. He spent $6.94 for a fifth of Old Grand-Dad and $6.80 for a fifth of Black and White. In one of the side streets, he found an open grocery store where he bought two quart bottles of club soda for fifty-nine cents, six splits of gingerale for the same amount, a bag of potato chips for thirty-nine cents, a bag of cheese tidbits for twenty-nine cents, and a can of salted peanuts for thirty-nine cents. He had spent a total of fifteen dollars and ninety-nine cents. In addition to the thirty cents he still had from Gloria's five-dollar dole, he now had four one-dollar bills and one penny, for a grand total of four dollars and thirty-one cents. He was rich again.

He stopped on the street corner, the brown paper bag with the whiskey bottles in one arm, the brown paper bag with the groceries in the other. The buildings of New York rose around him like a wall of slitted eyes. Beyond that wall, there lay the world for his taking. With Grace beside him, he would destroy every tiger in these narrow canyons. He would drain a bottle of booze, and then shout a war cry in the streets. He would flush out all the yellow and black cats, seize them by the tails, twirl them over his head in exultant triumph, and then call Gloria Osborne at MO 6-2367 to tell her he was a giant, and perhaps go to eat a victory feast with her at Izzy's Cafeteria.

MO 6-2367.

Gloria.

No, not Gloria, but

"It's not your fault," Dan says.

These are the first kind words Dan has ever said to him in his life.

"I know it isn't," he answers.

"In case you thought it was."

"It just started wrong," he says.

"You'll have to call tomorrow morning," Dan says. "They need all that information. About how many people there'll be, all that."

"I'll be going there, anyway."

"I know, but . . . maybe you ought to sleep late, get some rest. You'll be there all day, you know."

"I thought I'd go early."

"There's no need for that. Molly and I will be there."

"All right, I'll call them."

"Unless you want me to handle it."

"No, I can do it."

"You'd know better than I, anyway. And it's your decision to make."

"Yes, I know."

They are silent for a long time. He walks beside Dan and tries to hate him, tries to hate somebody, but all emotion seems to have drained out of him.

"How will you be going?"

"What?"

"Tomorrow morning."

"I'll drive," he says.

"Do you think you should?" Dan asks.

"Why not?"

"I'd feel a lot happier if you took the train."

"I can drive."

"Still, you might be there late tomorrow night, and you'll be tired. Take the train. I'll drive you home tomorrow."

"All right," he says.

"Maybe we ought to get a schedule."

"All right."

They walk toward Grand Central. At the information booth, they ask for a Harlem Division timetable. He puts it into the inside pocket of his jacket without looking at it.

"You have the number now, don't you?" Dan asks.

"Yes," he says.

"You wrote it in the book, right?"

"Yes."

"You still have the book?"

He feels his pocket. "Yes, I have it."

"You won't forget to call, will you?"

"No, I won't forget."

"You won't forget, now, will you?"

"No, I won't forget."

MO 6-2367.

Again, as it had earlier this morning, the need to call that number seemed terribly urgent. As he walked, he began looking for a bar or a cigar store, the need rising, his pace quickening. He had promised to call, had he not? He had specifically written down the number so he would not forget to call. Besides, now that he was brimming with plans for the future, he felt he owed her a call, just a ring—Hello there, how are you, this is me again—to let her know she was forgiven. What the hell, he should not have expected her to know all the answers. He would tell her that he was strong and swift and ready to do battle. I am going to make you proud of me, he would say. He could almost visualize her

279

listening to him as he spoke. She would be standing in her bedroom with the phone tucked under her ear, and she would smile and nod encouragingly and benevolently, Yes, son, go kill all the tigers.

He went into a United Cigar Store and walked directly to the phone booth. He deposited his dime and dialed her number, MO 6-2367. His hand on the receiver was trembling. He listened to the phone ringing on the other end, and then Gloria's voice came onto the line, and his heart lurched.

"Hello?" she said.

"Hello there, how are you?"

"Who is this?"

"This is me again," he said.

"Who the hell is me again?"

"You remember. I was there this morning."

"What do you want? Another handout?"

"No, Gloria, I thought—"

"My husband is here with me," she said curtly, and hung up.

For a moment, he could not believe he was holding a dead phone in his hand. He stared at the instrument as though it had betrayed him, and then put it back on the hook and sat motionless in the booth, watching the grinning white face of the dial. He clenched his fist suddenly and banged it against the coin box, and then he picked up his bundles and walked out into the street again.

I only wanted to tell you what I was planning, that's all, he thought. I mean, I thought maybe, just maybe, you might be interested in knowing what the hell your son was planning. So what was all that business about a handout? Who needs anything from you? I'm a big boy now, sweetie; I can make it alone. I knew I'd have to make it alone from that day in Yokohama. I left you a long long time ago, sweetie, so what gives you the right to talk to me this way now, to tell me your *husband* is there with you? Your husband has always been there with you—is that supposed to be news? Who the hell needs you *or* him? I've got Grace with me, she's going to learn to growl and spit, we're going to run so far and so fast that neither of you will know where the hell we are, or even if we ever existed!

He nodded his head defiantly, and began walking back toward the apartment.

The blond woman in the black cocktail dress was waiting in a taxi at the next corner.

# 16

At first, he was not sure the woman was addressing him. As he approached the taxi parked alongside the curb, she lowered the window, leaned partially out of it, and called, "Hey, you! Do you want to be a trophy?"

Clutching his parcels, he glanced over his shoulder and saw that he was the only person on the corner. As though answering the question he was phrasing in his mind, the woman in the taxi said, "Yes, *you*. I'm talking to you."

He moved closer to the cab and bent down to look into it. The woman was in her middle thirties, wearing a very low-cut black cocktail dress and sitting forward rather carelessly on the seat, the dress riding high up over her knees. For a moment, her face seemed familiar, but then he realized the resemblance was only an illusion, the neon reflection from the bar on the corner softening her features in the dimness of the cab interior. Her blond hair was clipped close to her head, a coiffed tendril curling onto one cheek, a disorderly tangle falling haphazardly onto the other. There was a hard line to the woman's jaw and nose. Her mouth, smiling at him now, combined with her heavily made-up eyes to deliver an immediate impression of knowledgeability that even the neon glow could not conceal. Whatever she had once looked like—at eighteen, at twenty, at twenty-two, at twenty-eight—had been obscured by a shellacked veneer of smartness and chic, and something more than that: a cynical wisdom that seemed to shine through her eyes from within.

"What did you say?" he asked.

The woman was still smiling. "I asked if you would like to be a trophy," she said. She slurred the words, and it was then that he caught the whiff of alcohol and realized she was at least partially drunk. "I'm on a scavenger hunt. I'm supposed to bring back a tall man in a blue suit. What do you say?"

"Bring him back where?" he asked.

"Oyster Bay."

"That's an out-of-town call, lady," the driver said over his shoulder. "You know that, don't you?"

"You just tend to the driving."

"All I'm doing is telling you it's an out-of-town call."

"Do you want me to take your number?"

"Lady," the cabbie answered, "you can take my number if you like, all I'm doing is advising you that Oyster Bay is an out-of-town call, if that is where we're going now."

"That's not where we're going now," she answered. "We still have other things to get." She turned again to Buddwing. "What do you say?"

"Is this a gag?" he asked.

"Does it look like a gag? You're the first man I've seen in a blue suit. Is blue going out of style or something?"

"I didn't think it was."

"Neither did I. Come on, what do you say? If I have to drag a man back to that party, he might as well be good-looking."

"Well, that's very flattering, but . . ."

"What have you got in the bags there? Your lunch?"

Buddwing smiled. "Whiskey," he said.

"Ahhh, good, I picked a winner." She threw open the cab door. "In. Not another word. In."

Still smiling, Buddwing shook his head. "No," he said. "I'm sorry. I'm on my way somewhere."

"I'll help you get there," the blonde said.

"By way of Oyster Bay?"

"Why not? Oyster Bay is very nice."

"Come on, lady, where to?" the cabbie asked impatiently.

"Hold your horses, I have to look at this list. Now, what the hell did I do with it? Oh yeah," she said, and reached into the front of her dress and pulled a crumpled sheet of paper from between her breasts. "Can you give me a light back here?" she asked. The cabbie sighed and turned on the overhead light. The woman squinted at the list and then said, "I'm as blind as a bat without my glasses." She handed the list to Buddwing. "Can you make this out? Don't mind the Chanel, it's there by osmosis."

Buddwing took the sheet of paper, reeking of perfume, and studied the items typewritten on it, one beneath the other.

"You really *were* supposed to find a tall man in a blue suit," he said.

"What did you *think* this was? A clumsy pickup?"

"No, but—"

"Then why so surprised? Have you got a cigarette?"

"I'm sorry, I'm all out."

"Driver, have you got a cigarette?"

"Lady, have you decided yet where you would like to go?"

"No, I have not decided yet, and I asked you if you had a cigarette."

"Lady, I am a cab driver, not a butler."

"What's his number?" she said, turning to Buddwing. "I can't read it from here."

"It's 704163," the cabbie said, "and my name is Frederick Calabresi, and this is a Yellow Cab. Does that answer all your questions?"

"I don't want to ride with you," the woman said. She opened the door immediately and came out of the cab, legs flashing. She staggered on the sidewalk for a moment, clutched Buddwing's arm for support, and then said, "Pay him."

"Me?" Buddwing asked.

"Yes, you. All I've got is a hundred-dollar bill, and I don't want to break it. Pay him, for God's sake."

The cabbie threw his flag, leaned out the window and said, "That's two dollars and twenty-five cents."

Buddwing sighed and reached into his pocket.

"If you tip him a penny, I'll brain you," the woman said.

He paid the fare and tipped the driver fifty cents. When he turned to the woman again, she said, "Did you tip him?"

"No," Buddwing said.

"She's drunk as hell, mister," the cabbie said. "You better watch yourself," and he pulled away from the curb.

"What did he say his number was?"

"I don't remember," Buddwing said.

"Neither do I. Have you still got that list?"

"Yes."

"Will you help me find those other trophies?"

"I don't think so."

"You might as well stick around," the blonde said. "You've already got an investment in me." She smiled. "You *did* tip that louse, didn't you?"

"Yes."

"He didn't deserve it."

"You were kind of rough with him." Buddwing said.

"He never had a ride like that in his life," she answered. "*He* should have tipped *me*." She paused and looked at Buddwing unsteadily. "What's your name?"

"The hell with that," he said.

"Are you wanted or something?"

"No."

"So don't be shy."

"I'm the man in the blue suit, okay?"

"Sure, but what do I call you? Rover? Prince?"

"Call me anything you like, I don't care."

"What kind of whiskey have you got there?"

"Scotch and bourbon."

"Open the Scotch and we'll have some."

Buddwing hesitated.

"Come on," she said, "you're not going to deny a lady a drink, are you?"

"This is for a party," he answered.

"That's right," she said. "Sit down, we'll have a party."

"Look, really, I don't think—"

"A lousy drink? One lousy drink?"

"Well, all right, but—"

"Good, sit down. Here. Right here."

They moved toward the front step of one of the buildings, the blonde weaving uncertainly, Buddwing helping her. She sat beside him, and then opened her legs and pushed the black folds of the dress down between them. Buddwing opened the bottle and handed it to her. "Cheers," she said, and drank from the lip. "Ahhh, good." She passed the bottle back to him. "Read me the other things on that list, will you?"

"Why'd you come all the way here from Oyster Bay?" he asked.

"I didn't come from Oyster Bay."

"Didn't you tell the cabbie—"

"Yes, that's where we're going as soon as we round up this junk, but that's not where we started. Not where *I* started."

"Where did you start?"

"890 Park Avenue."

"Is that where you live?"

"No. That's where Sibbie lives. Sibbie Randolph. She's a friend of mine." She paused. "Do you know her?"

"No."

"She's a swinger," the blonde said. "Anyway, we were there for dinner, and somebody suggested that we have a scavenger hunt and meet out at Jerry's house in Oyster Bay at two o'clock. What time is it now?"

"I haven't got a watch," Buddwing said.

"*Every*body has a watch."

"Not me. Nor you, either, for that matter."

"Well, what time is it *about?* You must know that."

"It's about eleven-thirty."

"That gives us an hour and a half to round up this junk, if we're going to be out on the Island by two. I'm not supposed to be doing this alone, you know. There were four other people on my team."

"What happened to them?"

"Well, Sibbie and Ralph, I have a pretty good idea what happened to them. The other two, I don't know. I'm stuck with the list, that's all I know."

"This is quite a list," he said.

"Yes, but I've got *you* already, so that's a start, isn't it?"

"Don't count on me," Buddwing said. "I'm supposed to be someplace else right now."

"Oh, never mind that, give me the bottle." He handed it to her. She lifted it to her mouth, winked at him, said, "Cheers," and drank. "Ahhh, good," she said. "Here. Have some."

"I don't want to get drunk."

"Why not?"

"I told you. I'm supposed to be someplace."

"Where?"

"Well," he said, and shrugged.

"Oh, look how shy and cute. What is it, a girl? What are you embarrassed about? I don't own you."

"I know that."

The blonde grinned. "What was it? Did Mummy send you down to the store for some goodies, huh?"

"Cut it out," he said harshly.

"Ah, the beast emerges. I love bestial men. Give me that bottle." She took it from him again and held it to her mouth, taking a long swallow.

"You'd better go easy," he said.

"Why? I go hard or easy, however I want to. Any complaints?"

He shrugged.

"Good. No complaints, no backtalk, you're with *me* right now, and *she* can wait. Anyway, I can't read that list without your help. What's the first thing on it? Not the man in the blue suit, I know that. That was down near the bottom someplace."

"Well, the first thing on it is 'Five Hundred Thousand Dollars in Cash.' "

"Easy," the blonde said. "What's next?"

"Easy? Five hundred thousand dollars in cash?"

"Sure."

"I guess they mean play money."

"No, I guess they mean real money. If you consider five hundred thousand dollars real money."

"I do," Buddwing said.

The blonde shook her head. "Five hundred *million* dollars is real money," she said, "and even that isn't so much. It's all relative. Do you have any relatives?"

"A few," he said, smiling.

"I have all sorts of relatives," the blonde said. "I have enough relatives to go around the world and back again, twice, laid end to end." She sighed and said, "If you don't start drinking with me soon, I'm going to get angry. I don't like to drink alone."

"I think you've had enough, anyway," Buddwing said.

"Don't ever say that to me. Not if you want to be my friend."

"Okay."

"Okay, what's your name?"

"I don't have a name."

"Ah-ha, a mystery man, Secret Agent X-9." She paused and said, "That gives away my age, doesn't it? How old do you think I am?"

"Thirty-five."

"Yes, but I look thirty, don't I?"

"No, you look thirty-five."

"Flattery will get you nowhere," she said. "What's the second thing on that list?"

" 'A Black Cadillac Sedan.' "

"Easy," she said. "We'll call Carey."

"I have exactly one dollar and forty-six cents in my pocket," Buddwing said.

"It only costs a dime to make a call."

"Who'll pay for the car?"

"We'll charge it to my husband's business. What else is on that list?"

"We still haven't got the five hundred thousand."

"Stick with me, honey," she said, and winked. "Everything's easy. Just swing with it, and don't let the bastards get you down. Come on, come on, the list."

" 'Your Name in the Newspaper,' " he said.

"Simple. The penny arcade on Broadway and Fifty-second. We can get it there. What else?"

" 'Three Good Men and True to Testify to Your Character.' "

"That was undoubtedly Sibbie's idea. There are only five extra men at the party now, you know, so she naturally feels the need for a few more. Three good men and true, brother!"

"To testify to your character," Buddwing reminded her.

"That's all we need is three men to testify to *my* character. We'd better make it yours."

"But I'm not going along with you," he said.

"Why not? Look at what that list offers. Fame, fortune, adventure, romance, what more do you want?"

"Where's the adventure and romance?" Buddwing said.

"Me. I'm on that list someplace."

"No, you're not."

"I'm *better* than on that list. I'm *here*. I'm sitting right here next to you. Give me your hand." She took his hand. "You feel that? That's me. Now, come on, let's go get this stuff."

He looked at her steadily, appraising her.

"What's the matter?" she asked.

"I'm not sure it's what I want," he said.

"No? What *do* you want?"

"I don't know."

"Shake hands with everybody in the world."

"How are any of these things going to help me?" he asked.

"Help you *what*, for Christ's sake?"

"Help me to know who I am."

"Don't talk metaphysics," she answered. "Say what you mean."

"I mean, lady, I've been lost since six o'clock this morning."

"And no wonder. You keep asking stupid questions, you'll be lost the rest of your life."

"What did I ask that was so stupid?"

"You asked about identity. If you don't know what identity is, then you don't know anything."

"Tell me."

"Identity is five hundred thousand dollars, and a black Cadillac, and your name in the newspaper, and a beautiful blonde on your arm, and at least three lackeys to tell you how great you are. *That's* identity."

"Whose?"

"Yours, mine, everybody's. If you want it, there it is, right on that list." She smiled. "See? Didn't I say I'd help you?"

"How have you helped me?" he asked. "All I've got so far is a meaningless scrap of paper."

The smile turned into an impish grin. "You've also got a woman," she said.

"So?"

"So I'm doing what a good woman is supposed to do. I've listened to what you want, and now I'll help you get it, even if it scares hell out of me."

"Why should it scare you?"

"Because I don't understand you *or* the things you want. All I can do is feel your need, and try to help. I listened while you read your list to me, and now I'll—"

"This list is *yours*," he said. "Not mine."

"Is it? Forgive me. I thought you wanted to know who you are."

"I do."

"Yes, that's what you told me, remember? And I listened. And now I'm going along with you, to help you get—"

"You're twisting it," he said. "It's *you* who needs these things, and you're asking *me* to go along."

"Is there really any difference, darling?" she asked.

"Maybe not."

"There isn't, believe me. Come on, have a drink."

He hesitated, thinking over what she had just said.

"Come on, honey," she coaxed. "The night is young, and we've got a whole damn *city* to plunder."

He looked at her and nodded, and then took the cap off the bottle of Scotch. He put the bottle to his lips, drank, and handed it to her. She smiled over the rim of the bottle as she drank, and then pulled it away from her mouth and wiped a dribble of whiskey from her chin.

"Ick," she said, "I *hate* the taste of whiskey."

The chauffeur-driven Carey Cadillac picked them up on the southeast corner of 81st Street and Third Avenue. They got into the back seat, and the blonde crossed her legs and made herself comfortable, and then looped her hand through Buddwing's arm and said, "Now, the first thing we've got to do is get your name in the newspaper. Have you ever been to the penny arcade on Broadway and Fifty-second Street?"

"Yes," he said.

"Are you from New York?"

"I was born here."

"Have you ever been to Grant's Tomb?"

"No."

"Neither have I. How about the Cloisters?"

"No. But I've always wanted to go there."

"What on earth for?"

"So I could kiss Marjorie Morningstar under the lilacs."

"Excuse me, sir," the chauffeur said.

"Yes?"

"I'm double-parked, you know, and—"

"Take us to the penny arcade on Broadway and Fifty-second," the blonde said, and the driver set the car in motion.

"Have you ever been to the Queensboro Bridge?" Buddwing asked.

"I *live* right on Sutton Place," the blonde said. "The Queensboro Bridge is practically in my bedroom. As a matter of fact, I almost *jumped* off the Queensboro Bridge once."

"Why'd you do that?"

She shrugged. "I was feeling blue."

"You don't look like the kind of girl who ever gets blue."

"How do you know what kind of girl I am?"

"Well, I don't."

"Then don't tell me what I look like."

"I was only trying to—"

"Because nobody ever knows what goes on behind the four walls. This skin, these bones, they're the four walls. Inside, there's a secret person no one ever sees, no one. You probably know more about me right now than anyone else in the world."

"How come?"

"I never told anyone else about the Queensboro Bridge."

"You haven't really told me yet."

"There's nothing to tell. I got out of bed one rainy day, and simply decided I'd had it."

"Why?"

"How do I know why? I don't like rain, all right? That was a good enough reason. Motivation is only for the movies. Real people are motivated by whatever the hell comes into their heads at any given moment."

"And you were motivated by the rain?"

"No. I wasn't motivated by the rain."

"Then what?"

"What difference does it make? I was a kid, barely twenty-three. That was centuries ago."

"I'm interested."

The blonde sighed. She turned her head away from him as the car sped crosstown. She seemed almost to be talking to the reflecting glass of the window beside her, rather than to Buddwing.

"I lost a baby," she said. "I know that's not very great shakes

—what the hell, women lose babies every day of the week. But this was different, you see, because I hadn't wanted the baby in the first place; in fact we had even discussed getting rid of it. But then—you know how these things are—we decided to go through with it; he convinced me that everything would be all right. Well, you know, you're married, aren't you?"

"Yes," he said.

"Then you know."

"I *used* to be married," he said quickly.

"Do you have any children?" she asked, turning to look at him. "No."

"Well, then . . ." She shrugged and turned back to the window again. "He really wanted the baby, I think. Or maybe not, I don't know, maybe he was as scared as I was. But he convinced me, you see, he really convinced me that everything would be all right, and after a while I didn't mind the idea so much and then, I don't know what the hell happened, maybe the maternal juices began to flow, all at once I began looking forward to having the baby, and that was when I lost it. I lost it in the sixth month. It was very messy, ick, I don't want to remember it."

She was silent for a very long time. He thought she had finished her story, and then suddenly she said, "The night before the bridge bit, we talked about it. At long last, we talked about it, after walking around it for months, after pretending nothing so very terrible had happened. We finally talked about it, screaming at each other in that terrible cheap crumby little apartment we had, blaming each other for what? For my failure and for his failure, for the world's failure, for death, for life? Who the hell even knew what life or death were at that time? Who knew anything but the grind of waking each morning and facing each other with an unspoken accusation in our eyes, until that night when all the accusations flooded out?"

The blonde drew a quick sudden breath.

"It was raining the next morning," she said. "I got out of bed, and all I put on was my white raincoat, nothing under it, and an old pair of rubber boots I'd had since I was eighteen years old and going to N.Y.U. I walked onto the Queensboro Bridge, and I thought if this was what life meant, if this was what it was about, I didn't want any part of it. I wasn't going to wait around until they pulled me apart piece by piece and left me bleeding on the sidewalk. I'd do it myself, my own way. I'd break *myself* into a million pieces before they did it for me. So I stood on the bridge near Welfare Island, and I wondered if I should go back and leave a note, and then I decided no, the hell with a note, let him figure it out for himself. I looked down—I don't know why; the mind plays funny tricks. I was going to throw myself off, but I wanted to see where I was going to land."

She paused, and again drew a quick breath.

"There was a nurse down there, wheeling an old man around in the rain. She was holding an umbrella over his head. It was pouring bullets, and the two of them were marching around in the rain, it was crazy. And then suddenly the old man looked up and saw me standing on the bridge, way up there. And he smiled and waved at me." She paused. "So I didn't do it."

"Why not?"

"I don't know. I guess maybe I decided if an old man being pushed around in a wheelchair on a miserable day like that could find something to wave and smile about, what the hell." She turned toward him suddenly. "Or maybe I just decided that if I couldn't lick them, I had better join them damn fast. I had better go home and listen to that man of mine, and get him out of that goddamn dead-end trap before the jaws came clamping down —maybe that's what I decided. Whatever it was, when I got home, I wasn't so sure any more. I sat in our kitchen at the table— I still hadn't taken off the raincoat or the boots—and I just wasn't sure any more. I just had the feeling I'd only postponed something that was inevitable, why the hell bother? Just because a sick old man smiled up at me and waved? He was probably smiling and waving because he was looking up under my raincoat." The blonde shrugged. "Anyway, he saved my life. For all that's worth."

"You saved it yourself," Buddwing said.

"I'm getting sober," the blonde said. "You're a terrible influence. How'd I ever get involved with a person like you?"

"I don't know. Just lucky, I guess."

"Yeah, lucky," the blonde said. "Where's the bottle?"

"I like you better sober."

"Nobody cares whether you like me or not. Give me the bottle."

"No."

"Oh my, a difficult man," she said, and sighed. "When were you born?"

"January tenth."

"Capricorn, it figures. Not that I believe in *that* junk any more," she said, and shrugged. "I don't believe in anything any more, if you want to know. Not the stars, not God, not love, not marriage, nothing but the five hundred thousand dollars we're going to get tonight, and this Cadillac wrapped around us. That's all."

"How do you know we'll get the five hundred thousand dollars?"

"Because we need it."

"For what?"

"To win."

"To win what?"

"The game."

"Ahhh, the game. And when we win it?"

She shrugged. "We win it, that's all."

"What do we win?"

"The right to keep playing it," she answered. "The right to get two hundred dollars every time we pass Go. The right to stay *in* the game, that's all. Until we're bankrupt."

"Then what?"

"Then out. We pack our hotels and our houses, and we trade Boardwalk and Park Place for the Queensboro Bridge. When you're bankrupt, there's no place else to go."

"But you're never bankrupt if you win," Buddwing said.

"Aren't you?" the blonde answered. "You're married, go ask your wife. Go home and say . . . what's her name?"

"Grace."

"Go home and say, 'Grace, can you win and be bankrupt at the same time?' See what she tells you."

"I can't do that," Buddwing said.

"Sure, because you know what the answer'll be." She glanced through the window and said, "There's the penny arcade. Let's get your name printed in the goddamn newspaper. Just pull right up there, driver."

"Ma'am, there's a No Parking sign there," the driver said.

"We'll take that back to the party, too," the blonde said. "Rip it off the post, will you?"

"Me?" the driver asked.

"Yes, you. Do you want to be a lousy chauffeur all your life? Live a little."

"Well . . ."

"Come on," she said to Buddwing, and they got out of the car.

It was midnight in New York on Saturday night, and the Broadway sidewalk was packed with pleasure-seekers, all of them hiding their broken hearts from all the lights up there commemorating the fissures. The lights seemed determined to overwhelm by sheer size and candlepower, each blinking barrage showering onto the night a dazzle of swirling, skittering, racing, exploding illumination. A thousand times life size, a million times brighter than life, they blasted their wares to the street until the mind reeled dizzily. The people below, as though running to escape the falling debris of wattage, jostled against each other blindly, seeking the more human scale of the stores and restaurants lining the avenue. The shows had broken, the movies had let out, and now the Saturday night throng moved in a narrow canyon rimmed with shrieking illumination, like a herd of cattle ponderously and painfully avoiding an electrified fence.

There was very little equality in this crowd that moved along the sidewalk and overflowed into the street, constantly imprisoned by light. Whereas they were all here for pleasure, none of them had any intention of sharing it. This was not a unified crowd that had just come from the same football game, emptying an arena. This was, instead, a crowd pouring *into* an arena, and the only thing they shared was the uneasy knowledge that within this brightly lighted oval they themselves might have to provide the only entertainment. So they looked at each other suspiciously. Was that blind man leading his dog really blind? Were those teen-agers looking for fun or trouble? Was that real mink or imitation?

The Fourteenth Street shopgirl had spent all afternoon in a beauty parlor having her hair washed and tinted and teased and set and sprayed and lacquered into place so that a woman from Washington Mews could walk by and whisper to her escort, "My *God*, did you see that fright wig?" This was Saturday night, and a group of Puerto Rican teen-agers from Bruckner Boulevard could feel momentarily free to venture into the city as though they really did own a part of it. ("This place is getting overrun by spics," a second-generation Italian from Fordham Road would mutter to his wife.) This was Saturday night, and going too fast, moving into the past too quickly—how many Saturday nights would there be before the whole thing ended? This was a time for enjoyment, a narrow respite between Friday evening and Sunday morning. If there were drinks to be consumed, this was the time to do it; jokes to be told, tell them now; women to be laid, lay them quick before they turned on the lights and called the law; jigs to be danced, chanteys to be sung, rumbles to be started, riots to be led, dance them, sing them, start them, lead them—this was Saturday night and such a short time in which to cram all that pleasure, such a short time in which to realize the week-long dream. If you didn't make it now, you'd have to wait clear the hell to next Saturday, and who knew whether you'd be here or not by then?

They came out of the illegally parked limousine and pushed their way against the current of the crowd, walking past the front windows of the arcade, the monster masks, the practical jokes, the souvenir ashtrays and metal Empire State Buildings. The arcade

was crowded with teen-agers and older people who still remembered Luna Park. Slot machines bonged and blinked, rifles
popped, pellets pinged, a young girl in a bouffant hairdo shrieked
joyously to her boyfriend when she shot down a hundred and
forty Messerschmitts with an electronic machine gun. At one end
of the arcade, alongside a man who was painting nude girls on
silk ties, stood an elementary printing press and an ink-stained
man. A small crowd of people was watching the artist as he
dotted the nipples of a painted voluptuous redhead. A lone Negro
was watching the printer pull a wet newspaper from the press,
the headline stating A BOY FOR THE COHENS! Buddwing and the
woman walked directly to the counter.

"My friend wants his name in the paper," she said.

The printer looked up. "What do you want it to say?" he asked.
"Write it down here. No more than twenty-five letters, and
spaces count as letters."

"How long will it take?" she asked.

"Half hour. You can wait or come back, either way suits you."

"Think we can make five hundred grand in a half hour?" she
asked, and winked at Buddwing.

"Only way you can do that," the printer said, "is if I was to
run it off on this press for you."

"No, we need *real* money."

"That's a lot of loot, lady," the Negro standing at the counter
said.

"Not if you're lucky," she answered, smiling.

"You're lucky, huh, lady?"

"I'm lucky. This tall man in the blue suit here is my lucky
charm."

The Negro looked at Buddwing appraisingly, nodded, and then
said, "I believe you."

"We're thinking of robbing a bank," the blonde said. "Do you
know any banks that need robbing?"

"I know a couple in Birmingham that need robbing," the Negro
said, "but that's a long ways off."

"We were thinking of something closer."

"Five hundred grand is a lot of loot, lady," he said again. "Most banks don't keep that kind of loot over the weekend."

"You want a newspaper or not?" the printer asked. "I got work to do."

"We want it," the blonde said.

"Then write down what it should say, willya?"

"What shall we say?" she asked Buddwing.

The Negro grinned and said, "Couple Caught Robbing Bank."

"That's more than twenty-five letters."

"Blonde Breaks Bank?" he suggested, and then shrugged. "How many letters is that?"

"Why don't we just say I've been a big success at something?" Buddwing suggested.

"Yeah, just say he made it," the Negro put in. "So-and-So Makes It." He paused. "What's your name?" he asked. "We'll need it for the headline."

"I don't have a name."

"Every man has a name," the Negro said.

"I'm not Everyman," Buddwing said.

"How do you know?" the blonde said. She took the pencil from the counter, and on the slip of paper she wrote:

EVERYMAN MAKES IT!

"There. How's that?"

"A bit pretentious, don't you think?" Buddwing said.

"Well, that depends," the Negro said. "How many letters is it?"

The blonde began figuring. "Eighteen," she said. "Counting spaces."

"That's less than twenty-five, all right," the Negro said. "It ain't pretentious at all."

"I'm not Everyman," Buddwing said. "I'm me."

"And who are you?"

He shrugged. "Nobody."

"Maybe that's more to the point," the blonde said. She scratched out what she had written, and beneath it she wrote:

NOBODY MAKES IT!

"That's poetic, but untrue," Buddwing said. "We *are* going to make it."

"I believe you," the Negro said.

The blonde shrugged and handed the slip of paper to the printer. "Print it," she said. "We'll be back in a half hour."

"What kind of a headline is that?" the printer asked.

"What are you, a printer or an editor?"

"I'm only saying."

"Print it," she said. She turned to Buddwing. "Come on, let's go make our five hundred grand."

"Nobody makes it," the printer muttered behind them.

The Negro followed them out to the sidewalk. As they approached the limousine, he asked, "You serious about that loot?"

"Why? Have you remembered a bank someplace?"

"Banks are for putting *in*, lady."

"What's for taking *out?*"

"Crap games."

"Life's the biggest crap game going," the blonde said.

"Me," the Negro answered, "I don't dig symbolism. If you're looking for a *real* crap game with some real money in it, I know where. You interested?"

"I've got a dollar and thirty-six cents," Buddwing said, and shrugged.

"That won't get you in *this* crap game, man."

"Will a hundred?" the blonde asked.

"You hope to parlay a hundred bucks into five hundred grand?" the Negro asked, and shook his head.

"Why not? Will there be that much money in the game?"

"It's there, if you can take it home."

"We can take it home."

"I don't know," Buddwing said dubiously. "What's your stake in this?"

"Ten per cent," the Negro said.

"Of what?"

"Your winnings."

"We'd have to win a hell of a lot more than five hundred grand in order to afford your percentage."

"Tell you what," the Negro said. "Win five and a quarter, and I'll settle for twenty-five grand."

"Suppose we only win five? Or less than that?"

"Then my services are thrown in free. How about it?"

"You really *do* think we're going to make it, don't you?" Buddwing asked.

"Yep. I think you're gonna bust that game wide open."

"How come?"

"Man, when you're born black, you never know the smell of luck until it comes sailing down Broadway sweet and cool in your nostrils. When you and your wife walked into that penny arcade, I got such a whiff of it, it nearly overpowered me. I'd like a piece of it, man. Twenty-five grand is all I ask."

"You're on," the blonde said.

"Where is this game?" Buddwing asked.

"Up in Harlem. You ain't a segregationist or anything, are you?"

"Yeah, sure I am," Buddwing said, and grinned.

"So am I," the Negro answered, returning the grin. "I want to segregate all that money in the crap game from its rightful owners."

"Come on, let's go do it," the blonde said.

She was moving toward the limousine when the Negro said, "My name's Hank. I know your husband's name 'cause I seen it in the paper." He grinned broadly. "But I don't believe *we've* had the pleasure, lady."

The blonde hesitated. Then she opened the car door, winked at Buddwing and said, "Just call me Grace."

Spanish Harlem was in full swing by the time they arrived, overrun by sailors from a squadron of destroyers moored in the Hudson River, all of whom had come uptown in search of exotica and erotica. The only natives concerned with the sailors were the prostitutes and the muggers; each would have a chance at rolling them before the sun came up. The rest of the citizens ignored the fleet and went about their pursuit of gaiety as relentlessly as did the Broadway crowd. The bars lining Madison and Park were full of drinkers, the apartments in the side-street tenements rang with the sound of guitars and Spanish songs, teen-agers sat on front stoops and discreetly nuzzled each other and their bottles of Thunderbird. This was not San Juan or Mayagüez, but it was Saturday night and for a while the ghetto could ring with the same humor and joy that sounded in the town plazas back home. There would be some fights, yes, and perhaps some youthful gang members would test their muscles against each other, it being spring and the summer rumble season not being too far off, but for the most part the cops roaming in pairs would have nothing more to worry about than a few drunken slashings and some sailors with bumps on their heads.

The Housing Authority cop had no such worries since he was not in the streets but was instead up on the third floor of the City Housing Development on 114th Street, in an apartment overlooking Fifth Avenue. The Housing Authority cop was not alone in the apartment. He was, in fact, part of a group that numbered about a dozen people, all of whom were crowded around a blanket that had been spread against the living room wall. As Buddwing, Hank, and Grace moved closer to the group, the Housing Authority cop reached for the dice on the blanket, shook them in his fist, yelled, "Eight, right back!" and then hurled them mightily against the wall. Hank, Buddwing, and Grace, standing on the edge of the crowd around the blanket, watched the white cubes strike the wall, bounce off onto the blanket, roll halfway down its middle, and then stop dead, a five-spot showing on one die, a two-spot showing on the other. In deference to the ladies present (there were three including Grace) the Housing Authority cop muttered his swear word under his breath, and then looked sourly at his neighbor as though the man had hexed him. His neighbor, clutching a fistful of ten-dollar bills, ignored the glance, adjusted his rimless spectacles on his nose, and reached for the dice. Buddwing and Grace elbowed their way into the circle and watched while the man with the spectacles rolled a seven and then a six, and then failed to make his point. The dice passed around the circle to a young mulatto woman named Iris, who picked them up and chided them gently as though they were a pair of skittish lovers, and then rolled them easily against the wall, her palm opening, the dice striking the wall and rolling back with a three-spot showing on one, and a one-spot showing on the other.

"Two to one, no four," a tall beefy man in a dark gray tropical suit said, and Buddwing was surprised to see Grace hold out her hundred-dollar bill, and say, "It's a bet." The man in the gray tropical took her bill and tucked it together with his two bills between the forefinger and middle finger of his right hand while he continued to agitate for further bets, "Two to one, no four," and the mulatto girl picked up the dice and blew her breath upon them as softly as a lover's kiss, and again eased them out of her white palm and against the wall. They rolled back showing a pair of deuces, Little Joe, four the hard way. Grace collected her money—their stake had grown on a single roll of the dice to three hundred dollars—and Iris, the mulatto girl, put fifty dollars on the line and picked up the dice again, smiling a secret smile at them and again brushing her breath against them like a kiss.

"I'm with her," Grace said. "Three hundred dollars she's right."

"It's a bet," the man in the tropical suit said, and he handed Grace three one-hundred-dollar bills.

Iris whispered, "Come on, you mothers," and immediately rolled an eleven.

"How we doing?" Hank asked at Buddwing's elbow.

"So far, so good."

Hank was looking around the circle of bettors and trying to determine where the big money was. To take five hundred and twenty-five grand out of this game, it was first necessary to know who were the real gamblers and who were the Sunday drivers. There was no bookie in the game, and all bets were being made between the individual players, which meant that the odds were true odds, without a house percentage working against the players. It was entirely possible for his companions to win very big money here, provided they bet against the people who had it, and provided luck was with them. Hank nodded in approval when he saw that Grace was betting against the man in the gray tropical suit, since he was very big wood, a pusher who worked a lot of high schools in the Bronx. In addition to him, there were two other big gamblers in the game, both of whom were clutching fist-spiked handfuls of bristling bills, and one of whom had bound bills lying in front of him on the blanket in ten- and twenty-thousand-dollar packets. Hank nudged Buddwing gently and, with successive nods of his head, pointed out the heavy spenders in the game. Iris, meanwhile, had rolled a seven and another eleven, and Grace's bankroll had mushroomed to twenty-four hundred dollars, which was still several hundred thousand short of their goal. On the next roll, Grace switched to betting the girl wrong, wagering the full twenty-four hundred dollars. The girl rolled a five, a six, and a seven in rapid succession, and Grace picked up her forty-eight hundred dollars, and grinned up at Buddwing.

The dice passed to a thickset man with an Irish-looking face. He put a five-dollar bill on the blanket, and Grace bet him wrong for two hundred dollars. He sevened out almost immediately, and she picked up the four hundred and now had an even five thousand dollars as the dice were passed to her.

"You roll," she said to Buddwing and handed him the dice. "Five grand he's right," she said, and extended the five thousand dollars.

One of the big guns in the game looked at Grace appraisingly, shifted his eyes to Buddwing, moved his cigar from one corner of his mouth to the other, and then softly said, "Bet," and held out his five thousand dollars.

Buddwing picked up the dice.

"How do you feel, man?" Hank whispered into his ear.

"Lucky," Buddwing said.

"Roll 'em," the man in the tropical suit said.

"We want a seven," Grace said.

"Here's your seven, honey," Buddwing said, and hurled the dice against the wall. They bounced back onto the blanket. One of them stopped dead almost immediately with a six-spot showing on its face. The other die rolled and then went into a long spin and finally fell flat on the blanket, showing a one-spot.

"Seven!" Hank said, and Buddwing picked up the dice again.

"Bet the ten thousand," Grace said.

"It's a bet," the man with the cigar answered.

"You don't leave no room for error, honey," Iris said to Grace.

"We can't lose," Grace answered, and watched as Buddwing shook the dice in his fist.

"*Sev*en now!" he shouted, and threw them against the wall.

One die hit the wall and bounced straight up into the air like a rocket going into orbit. The players watched it reach its apogee and then fall swiftly to the blanket, where it struck the other die, changing the number on its face. Both dice rolled an instant longer and came to a stop.

"It's a seven!" Grace yelled.

"We've got a hot shooter in the game at last," the Irishman said.

"Roll the mothers," Iris said.

"What do you want me to bet?" Grace asked him.

"All of it," Buddwing said.

"Put part of it on eleven," Hank said.

"Why?"

"I got a feeling."

"Grace?"

"Okay with me," Grace said.

She put five thousand dollars on the blanket and was immediately faded by the man with the cigar. She held up the rest of the money and said, "I've got fifteen thousand says he elevens."

"I'll give you fifteen to one on that," the man in the tropical suit said.

"The right odds are *sev*enteen to one," Hank said gently. "You know that."

"Oh, boy, we got an accountant in the house," the man answered. "Okay, seventeen to one. Is it a bet?"

"It's a bet," Grace said.

They were laying bets all around the blanket as Buddwing picked up the dice again. In his mind he was trying to multiply fifteen thousand dollars by seventeen, which was what the payoff would be if he rolled an eleven. He clenched his fist around the dice and began shaking them.

"That eleven's a one-shot bet, you know that, don't you, lady?" the man in the tropical suit asked.

"She knows it," Hank said.

"Fifty dollars, he elevens," the Irishman said.

"Bet," someone across the blanket answered.

The tall thin man wearing rimless spectacles held out a thousand-dollar bill and said, "Would anyone else care to give me seventeen to one on that?"

"You're covered," the man with the cigar said.

"Come on, these dice are cooling off," Buddwing said.

"Oh, don't let 'em cool, honey," Iris said.

"Any more of that eleven action open?" a young man needing a shave asked.

"Right or wrong?"

"Right."

"How much?"

"Ten bucks."

"Come on, sonny, Mickey Mouse is across the street."

"Who'll give me seventeen to one?" the unshaven young man persisted.

"All right, all right, it's a bet," a redheaded woman said.

"Can I roll these damn things now?" Buddwing said.

"Go ahead, roll."

Buddwing shook the dice again.

"Talk to 'em first, baby," Grace said.

"We want an eleven," Buddwing said.

"Come on, you mothers," Iris said, "give the man his eleven."

He raised his fist over his head, shook the dice once more and, as he threw them against the wall, shouted, "Ee-*lev*-en!" The same shout went up from half the players around the blanket at the same moment, so that the word "Ee-*lev*-en!" struck the air at the same moment the dice struck the wall. They hit savagely and rolled back savagely and savagely came to an abrupt stop. There were only two ways of making an eleven as against thirty-four ways of making any other possible number, and there was a whole hell of a lot of money riding on those two cubes as they stopped dead on the blanket like a pair of fists connecting. For a moment, the players were startled by the sudden halt of the dice. A six-spot and a five-spot stared up from the blanket, but nothing seemed to register on the players' faces. It was as though a rain dance had provided rain immediately and unexpectedly, drenching everyone before he'd had a chance to work up even a fairly good jig.

"He made it," someone whispered, and the right bettors began laughing and slapping each other on the back and picking up their winnings while the wrong bettors stared sourly at the dice still lying on the blanket.

"How much have we got now?" Buddwing asked.

Grace, counting bills feverishly, looked up and said, "Just a second."

"Come on, let's roll them dice, honey," Iris said.

"We've got two hundred and sixty-five thousand," Grace said, a shocked tone in her voice.

"Yeah, and it's all my money," the man in the tropical suit said.

"Bet it all on the next roll," Buddwing said.

"Hey, go slow, man," Hank warned. "We lose it, and we're out of the game."

"If we win it, we're out of the game, too. Even money on that would give us five hundred and thirty thousand."

"Still . . ."

"Put it on the line, Grace," Buddwing said.

She hesitated a moment, and then looked at Hank. Hank shrugged.

"Yes or no?" Grace asked him.

"Go," Hank said, and Grace put two hundred and sixty-five thousand dollars on the blanket.

"Who'll fade it?" she asked.

"That's a lot of action, lady," the man in the tropical suit said.

"We thought this was a real game," Hank answered.

"Yeah, it's a real game, all right. You come in with a single bill, and you're busting up the joint."

"That's gambling," Hank said. "If you want to play jacks, maybe we can go to the Y and round up some little girls."

The man in the tropical suit closed his eyes gently and pulled a grimace, and then opened his eyes slowly and stared directly at Hank and said, "I know guys on the bottom of the river."

"So do I," Hank said. "You fading or not?"

"I'll take a hundred grand of it," he answered.

Across the blanket, the man with the cigar said, "I'll take another hundred."

"There's sixty-five open," Hank said.

A small blond man who had been betting quietly up to now, but whom Hank had recognized as one of the bigger gamblers, took three twenty-thousand dollar packets of bills from the inside pocket of his jacket, and threw them on the blanket. He pulled a roll from his side pocket, removed the rubber band from it, and peeled off five one-thousand-dollar bills, which he put onto the blanket with the rest of the money.

"I think that covers it," he said softly. "You want to roll now?"

"If you don't mind," the man in the tropical suit said, "I'd like to see those dice before you roll."

"What is this, a Warner Brothers movie?" Hank asked.

"I don't know what kind of a movie it is," the man in the tropical suit said. "I only know you won more than two-and-a-half grand from me on the last roll, and I've got another hundred thousand riding on this one. Now, maybe that kind of loot don't give me the right to examine those dice where you come from, but where I come from, three hundred and fifty-five grand buys a lot of seats at the RKO Palace."

"Show him the dice," Hank said.

Buddwing handed the dice over. "Don't cool 'em off," he said.

"I just want to make sure they ain't *too* hot," the man answered.

He held the dice close to his face, one in each hand, and tried to wobble one against the other, and then studied them for cut edges or shaved sides, and then turned each die to each of its sides, matching the number against the same number on the other die. The dice were flush-spotted, which meant they would have been extremely difficult to load, and very easy to detect if they had been loaded, but he examined them minutely nonetheless. Still unsatisfied, the man in the tropical suit passed the dice to the man with the cigar and said, "What do you think?"

"Now, let's not handle those dice too much, huh?" Hank said.

"If you don't mind, Mac," the man with the cigar said, "*I* got a stake in this, too."

He took the dice and, with his hands in full view of all of the players, went through the same scrutinizing examination the man in the tropical suit had just conducted.

"What do you think, Harry?" he asked.

"I think five hundred and thirty grand on that blanket calls for a fresh pair of dice," the man in the tropical suit said.

"Why? There something wrong with those?" Hank asked.

"He made three passes in a row," the man with the cigar answered.

"If these dice are straight," Hank said, "there's no rule I know of that says he can't make a hundred passes in a row."

"It's the *shooter's* option to change the dice, isn't it?" Grace asked.

"Not if they're crooked," the man with the cigar answered.

"The dice were in the game when we got here," Hank said. "If they're crooked, they were crooked for everybody."

The Irishman standing next to Iris said, "Give him the dice, and let him shoot."

The young man who needed a shave, and who had bet ten dollars on Buddwing's eleven on the last roll, and who now had a hundred and eighty dollars, looked directly at the man with the cigar and said, "Give him the dice."

The thin man with the rimless spectacles looked at the wall and said to no one in particular, "The dice are straight. Let him shoot."

"There're your three good men and true," Grace said, and she smiled at Buddwing.

"Well, how about it?" Buddwing asked. "Are we shooting craps here or what?"

"What do *you* think, Harry?" the man with the cigar asked.

The man in the tropical suit answered, "I don't know, Alfie. What do *you* think?"

The quiet blond man, who had sixty-five thousand dollars riding against Buddwing, very calmly said, "Give him the goddamn dice. This ain't no nursery school."

"The *same* dice, please," Hank said, and watched as Alfie handed them back to Buddwing.

"Is it okay to roll?" Buddwing asked.

"Roll," the blond man said.

"Roll," Harry said.

"Roll," Alfie said.

"Make it a good one, honey," Iris said.

"Now, easy, man," Hank said.

"Go, baby," Grace said, and Buddwing shook the dice in his fist and bounced them off the wall. They rolled back and came to a stop.

"Ten," Harry said.

"Your point is ten, mister," Alfie said.

"Easy," Grace said.

Buddwing picked up the dice. All around the blanket, the bettors were laying right bets, wrong bets, proposition bets, flat bets, come bets, point bets, one-roll-action bets, hard-way bets, none of which concerned Buddwing. All of his money was on the blanket already, two hundred and sixty-five thousand dollars. All he had to do to double it was roll a ten before he rolled a seven. He shook the dice and threw them.

"Eight," Harry said. "Your point is still ten. Two to one, no ten," he said and held out a fistful of bills.

"I'll take fifty of that," Iris said, and handed him her money. "Now, *go*, man," she said to Buddwing. "Make them mothers behave."

"Come on, baby, we want a *ten!*" Buddwing said, and threw the dice.

"Four, the easy way!" Alfie said. "You're off this hard-way bet, mister," he said to the Irishman.

"I know it. Ten dollars on the five."

"Three to two, here's fifteen," Alfie said. "Roll 'em, mister."

Buddwing threw the dice again.

"Nine," the blond man said. "Who'll take the odds on the six and eight, six grand on each, six to five?"

"It's a bet," the redhead across the blanket said.

"Ten grand, Red."

"Here you go."

"Roll."

"*Talk* to them, baby. *Talk* to them," Grace said.

"Come on, Mac, do it."

"Now-come-on-TEN!" Buddwing shouted, and rolled.

"Eleven," Harry said.

"You're close, baby," Grace said.

"Three to two, no five."

"Bet."

"A hundred on any craps."

"Eight to one, you're covered."

"Here we go, *ten*, baby," Buddwing said, and rolled.

"Six," Grace said. "Where's that ten, baby?"

"Coming up, sweetheart, just for you."

"Roll it, baby, *give* it to me."

He did not know how many times he threw the dice in the next five minutes without rolling either a ten or a seven. He only knew that the action around the blanket was frantic now, and that thousands upon thousands of dollars were being wagered on each successive throw. The big gamblers had been betting Buddwing wrong from the moment he had rolled the ten, giving the odds, and had lost thousands more in addition to their initial investment, the fate of which was still undecided. Moreover, the balance of power seemed to have shifted somewhat. Iris and the young man who needed a shave and the thin man with the rimless spectacles and the Irishman were all holding fistfuls of crumpled thousand-dollar bills and trying to drum up some action. Reluctantly, the quiet blond man gave Iris eight-to-one odds on the hard ten, and she handed him her thousand-dollar bill and then turned to Buddwing and said, "Now *really* do it, man. Two fives for me."

Grace looked at the blond man and asked, "May I talk to those dice a minute?"

"Go ahead, talk to them."

She was reaching onto the blanket for the dice when Alfie shifted his cigar in his mouth and said, "Are you rolling or is he?"

"Why, *he* is," Grace said.

"Then leave the dice alone."

"Your friend said I could talk to them."

"Let her talk to them," the blond man said.

"How do I know she won't switch them?"

"With that dress she's wearing, would you mind telling me where she could hide another pair of dice?"

"You tell him," Grace said, smiling, and picked up the dice. She held them between her thumb and forefinger and rubbed them lightly over her crotch. Then, with a wide grin, she said, "There. I just talked to them, baby. Now, shoot." She threw the dice across the blanket to Buddwing, and they rolled to a stop near his knees, one die showing a five-spot and the other showing a two-spot.

"You just took the *seven* off the goddamn dice!" Alfie said angrily.

"That's just what I did, mister," she answered, grinning. She turned to Buddwing. "Now give me my ten, baby."

"I told you we shouldn'ta let her touch the dice."

"They're the same dice," the blond man said.

"She took off the seven."

"So go say a novena. What the hell are you, a gambler or a witch doctor?"

"You want to inspect them again maybe?" Hank asked.

"Oh, roll the goddamn dice and get it over with," Harry said.

"Damn guy's been rolling since last Tuesday," the blond man said.

"Okay, here we go," Buddwing said, picking up the dice. "I'm making that ten, and then I'm going home."

He glanced at Alfie, and then Harry, and then the blond man, hoping for some sort of indicative reaction to his statement, testing them. If he did roll his ten, he would pick up five hundred and thirty thousand dollars from the blanket, and obviously that would be the time to say good night. But would the three gamblers allow him to bust open the game and then simply leave?

"Come on," he said, "I want to go home," and he began shaking the dice in his fist, watching for a reaction.

"Make your ten first, mister," Alfie said, "and then we'll see about going home."

"Make it the hard way," Iris said. "Come on, honey, two sweet fives."

Buddwing shook the dice again. He was sweating heavily, and he was very thirsty, and it occurred to him suddenly that this was hard work and that even if he won he might wind up with a hole in his head.

"Don't wear out the spots."

"Roll 'em."

"Ten, baby," Grace said.

"Here we go," Buddwing said, "ten now, give me a ten now, give me a TEN!" and he hurled the dice against the wall. They struck soundly and bounced back spinning.

"We want a ten," Iris intoned as the dice continued spinning, "two fives, two fives, two fives."

The dice continued spinning.

"The damn things are trained," Alfie said.

"Come on, lay down," Harry said to the dice, and one of the dice fell at his command, showing a five-spot. The other die was still spinning, but no one was talking now. They watched its whirling motion breathlessly, their fists clenched, their bodies tense. The die was slowing now, wobbling, it seemed ready to fall, it gave a short death rattle and then rolled over onto its side. It was showing another five-spot.

"You *did* it!" Grace shouted, and threw herself into Buddwing's arms and kissed him full on the mouth. At the same moment, Hank reached onto the blanket and picked up their winnings. He turned to them quickly, pulled them apart, and steered them away from the blanket. The three gamblers were busily paying off bets around the blanket, but the blond man looked up as Buddwing approached the door, and then very quietly said, "You going someplace, mister?"

Buddwing turned. "Yes," he answered. "We're leaving."

"You're taking an awful lot of money out of this game," the blond man said softly.

"That's right."

"Ain't you gonna give us a chance to win it back?"

"Would you give me the same chance?" Buddwing asked.

"Well, now, a *gentleman* would."

"There ain't no gentlemen in crap games," Hank said.

"I'm just con*cerned* about you, that's all," the blond man said softly. "That's a lot of money to be carrying around with you at this time of night."

"We'll be all right, don't worry," Buddwing said.

"I think he'll be fine," the young man who needed a shave said, and he walked away from the blanket and took up a position beside Buddwing.

"So do I," the Irishman said, and went to join them.

"I'll help see you home," the thin man with the rimless spectacles said, and walked to where the others were standing in a small defiant knot.

"What the hell is this?" Alfie asked. "Are all the winners quitting?"

The blond man kept staring at the group near the door. It seemed to Buddwing that he was trying to decide whether to shoot them on the spot, or let it go until a later time, or perhaps postpone it indefinitely. Harry and Alfie were flanking the blond man now, their feet wide-spread, their hands hovering about the openings of their suit jackets. Buddwing was certain they were carrying pistols. He hoped they were good shots because he preferred not to crawl out of there a cripple. At the same time, he hoped the blond man—who had seemed fairly reasonable throughout the course of the game—would be just as reasonable now. And while he was waiting to be shot or pardoned, it suddenly occurred to him that he and Grace now owned five hundred and thirty thousand dollars. He wiped the sweat beads from his lip.

"I know guys on the bottom of the river," Harry said menacingly.

"Argh, shut up with your guys on the bottom of the river," the blond man said. He looked at Buddwing again. "Double or nothing on the five hundred thousand," he said. "Highest roller."

"No," Buddwing said.

"You're just gonna walk out like that, huh?" the blond man said. "Without so much as a fare-thee-well?"

"Fare-thee-well," Buddwing said, and opened the door.

"Hey, smart guy," the blond man called after him.

"Yeah?"

"Don't come back. Not you, and not your friends, neither."

They went out into the hallway. Behind them, the blond man said, "All right, let's shoot craps here."

# 17

As the limousine headed downtown once more, Buddwing discovered a few things about the three good men and true who had come to his assistance in the third-floor apartment.

The thickset Irishman, as it turned out, was an Off-Broadway character actor named Sean Murphy. He confessed immediately that he had been scared to death of the three hoods in the apartment, but that his acting experience had seen him through his fear, since he had once played the part of Alan Squier in a summer stock production of *The Petrified Forest*, and therefore knew all about handling people like Duke Mantee.

"Summer stock is not life," the thin man with the rimless spectacles informed him. "I happen to be a lawyer. That's why *I* was certain none of the men in that game were ready to commit homicide."

"How could you tell?" Murphy asked.

"Homicide would have endangered their livelihood, which is gambling. Homicide is a felony. Gambling is only a misdemeanor."

"What's a misdemeanor . . . uh . . . I'm sorry, I didn't get your name."

"Harris, Roger Harris. A misdemeanor is something like spitting on the sidewalk."

"Were we guilty of a misdemeanor?" Buddwing asked. "By being in the game?"

"Certainly," Harris said. "That's the trouble with the world today. The laws are so unrealistic."

"The trouble with the world today," Murphy said, "is that not enough quality shows are being done on Broadway. The actor must look to Off-Broadway if he wants to do anything serious. And then, in order to supplement his meager income, he's forced to break the law by entering illegal crap games, which are misdemeanors, as you just said. He has to go all the way up to Harlem to find a game which, if he's caught in it, will—"

"Think of all the poor colored kids up in Harlem," Grace said, "who never even get to *see* a Broadway show."

Hank smiled benignly and said, "That's right. The trouble with the world today is that not enough colored kids get to see Broadway shows."

"Who'd *want* to see a Broadway show?" the unshaven young man asked. "All you pay for there is the privilege of watching another man's neurosis, usually homosexual in nature, and usually badly expressed."

"You sound like a writer," Murphy said.

"I am," the young man answered.

"What's your name?"

"Mike. My point is that even if—"

"Listen," the driver of the car said suddenly, "the *Off*-Broadway shows aren't too good, either."

"Why don't you tend to your driving?" Murphy said, somewhat testily.

"I'm trying to, but look at this traffic, will you? If you want to know the *real* trouble with the world today, the *real* trouble is the condition of our streets and highways. Our speed has outgrown our technology. Man is embarked on a supersonic voyage to nowhere."

317

"You can say that again," Grace said. "How can anyone possibly have any sort of image prolongation when he's constantly threatened with nuclear annihilation?"

"Well, that isn't exactly what I meant, ma'am," the driver said.

"Look at our milk supply," Grace said, ignoring him. "Do you know how much strontium 90 is in our milk supply right this minute?"

"*Whose* milk supply?" Hank asked. "The world's, or yours personally?"

"That's right, switch it to tits," Grace said. "What do you care about the thousands of unborn freaks?"

"Honey, I was born a freak," Hank said.

"The trouble with the world today," Harris said, "is the long delay in getting civil rights cases to trial. I've had a case on the docket for close to five years now. Involves the rape of a white girl by a Negro, present company excluded, of course. He certainly had every provocation."

"She asked him in to chop up the chifferobe, correct?" Mike asked.

"No, she came to his apartment naked with a bottle of bourbon in one hand and a daisy in the other."

"She was only trying to find her own *chemin*," Mike said.

"In addition," the driver said, "all this traffic is polluting the air with poisonous gases."

"That's no worse than polluting the Broadway air with the stench of garbage," Murphy said.

"Or making Le Pavillon too expensive for poor colored kids," Grace said.

"The thing I'd like to know," Hank said, "is why there are no colored mannequins in the store windows of America."

"I marched in protest," Grace said. "All the way from Sutton Place to City Hall."

"When was this?" Murphy asked.

"Oh, twelve years ago, I guess."

"Why did you march?"

"I was pregnant at the time. My doctor said walking was very good for me. A hell of a lot he knew."

"I wrote a letter to Commissioner Barnes," the driver said over his shoulder. "I told him that unless we solve our traffic problems, this city will become hopelessly obsolete. Our technology has outgrown our speed, that's the trouble with the world today."

"I attended a meeting of Actor's Equity," Murphy said. "I told them that the struggle in the world today is to enlarge our Off-Broadway theaters beyond that arbitrary two-hundred-and-ninety-nine-seat limit. That's the trouble."

"Would anyone like to play Who's Jewish?" Grace asked.

"The Black Muslims are a threat," Hank said. "The trouble with the world today is lunatic-fringe groups. I went to a rally in Harlem. I told them there is no difference between white men and black men except the color of our skins."

"We all drink the same contaminated milk, don't we?" Grace asked. "Wouldn't anyone like to play Who's Jewish?"

". . . Pinter and Ionesco as compared to Williams and Inge . . ."

". . . General Sessions, Part II. Well, how is anyone expected to . . ."

". . . changed it to a one-way street overnight. When I got to the corner . . ."

"I wanted to be a respected and successful writer," Mike said to Buddwing. "That's why I spent all that time studying the respected and successful writers. After all, there must be something that causes the critics to go wild over a book, don't you think? A book has to hit *some* kind of nerve, isn't that right? I mean, after all, there must have been something that prompted Gilbert Millstein to call *On the Road* 'an authentic work of art,' don't you think?"

"Gilbert *who?*" Buddwing asked.

"Or *The New Yorker* to say *By Love Possessed* was a masterpiece, don't you think?"

"I should hope so," Buddwing said.

"Reviewers," Mike said, and shook his head. "That's what's

wrong with the world today. Reviewers. They all deny the writer the one luxury to which he is automatically entitled."

"And what's that?"

"The right to fail. Take that away from him, and you also rob him of the courage to dare. In this country, if a man writes a bad book, the reviewers behave as though they've caught him exposing his genitals on a crowded subway car."

"That's only a misdemeanor," Harris said.

"Well, I happen to believe that even writing a *bad* book is important."

"Certainly," Harris agreed. "I was merely pointing out that it isn't necessarily a felony."

"Book reviewers are all frustrated Negroes, anyway," Hank said.

"Writers are all frustrated actors," Murphy said.

"Lawyers are all frustrated chauffeurs," the driver said.

"The entire *world* is frustrated," Grace said. "Nobody'll get off anybody else's back."

"I'll tell you," Hank said. "I don't *want* you to get off my back. All I want to do is marry your daughter."

"If you mean that," Mike said, "you could marry my daughter tomorrow. If I had one."

"Of course I mean it," Hank said. "You want to know what equal rights means to me? Equal rights means I'm a man, just like you. And if I'm a man, then I don't want no other man telling me who I can or can't marry. Any Negro goes around shouting for equal rights and then claims he don't want to marry *your* daughter, or *his* daughter, or *anybody's* daughter, why, he's just somebody who's asking for manhood and saying he don't want it at the same time."

"I agree with you," Harris said. "This is all a matter of sex."

"Sex, my ass," Hank said. "This is all a matter of identity."

"I think Harry Belafonte is very sexy," Grace said.

"Fifty years ago, you wouldn't have."

"I think Floyd Patterson is very sexy, too."

"You're talking about two nice, safe, gentle Negroes who are acceptable because they're clean and handsome and fit into what the white man *thinks* a Negro should be, which is a *white* man. The day you think Sonny Liston is sexy, *that's* the day the Negro in America has finally made it. I'll tell you something very funny about this whole civil rights megillah—"

"Would anyone like to play Who's Jewish?" Grace asked.

"Robert Mitchum is Jewish," Murphy said.

"The funny thing about this entire knotty problem," Hank went on, "is that most white men can picture themselves in bed with a colored girl very easy, but they just can't seem to reverse it and picture a blonde in bed with a black man. And that's where identity comes into the picture, and that's why I *do* want to marry your daughter. Why do you think I want to go to school with you? Why do you think I want to vote? Because I want the same power that you have. I'm not asking to be a citizen— hell, I'm a citizen already, second-class or not. I'm asking to be a *powerful* citizen, I'm asking for the right to make five hundred thousand dollars, and have a black Caddy, and a blonde on my arm if I want one, and my name in the goddamn newspaper, and a minimum of three flunkeys to tell me how great I am every day of the week. I want the right to be whoever I *want* to be, that's all."

"Come on," Grace said, "let's play Who's Jewish."

"Anne Bancroft is Jewish," Murphy said.

"Judge Learned Hand is Jewish," Harris said.

"John Updike isn't," Mike said.

"What the hell am *I?*" Buddwing asked suddenly, and they all turned toward him.

"What?" the driver said.

"Nothing," Buddwing answered. "Never mind."

He crouched in the corner of the limousine, suddenly very confused. There was laughter everywhere around him now as name after name was suggested—he's Jewish, she isn't—and then Hank began telling the joke about the man who went to Heaven and looked at God—"Well, to begin with, she's colored"—and they all laughed again, and then the driver told them a racy story about a celebrity he had driven only last week, and they all listened knowledgeably, and then Mike gave his own capsule review of *Last Year at Marienbad*. "Are you listening?" he asked. "Here's the review: Last last year year at Marien, bad bad bad," and they all laughed again. It seemed to him that Grace's legs were crossed too dangerously, and her skirt pulled too high. It seemed to him that the talk was too fast and too glib, that no one was really saying a damn thing about what was really wrong with the world, but was concerned instead only with what was wrong with his particular corner of the world.

It seemed to him he had heard all the jokes and opinions before, had shared the gossip. It seemed to him he had played every game ever invented. It seemed to him he had seen the crossed legs and exposed knees of a million women, had peered into the low-cut tops of all the gowns in the universe. He had been driven in this same expensive automobile listening to the same talk from the same articulate people for the better part of his life, and none of it made a damn bit of difference. He *still* didn't know who he was.

"Have you got that money?" he asked Grace suddenly.

"Yes, I've got it."

"It doesn't help a damn bit," he said under his breath. "None of it does," and was glad that no one heard him. The car was racing down a comparatively empty stretch of Lexington Avenue, preparatory to turning west and heading for the penny arcade where the newspaper headline would be waiting. He knew the headline would not help, either. Edward Voegler had been headlined earlier today, but how had that helped the poor frightened lunatic hiding somewhere in the bushes of the world? He listened to Grace's brittle laughter, and he remembered the time so long ago when they had tumbled out of bed to drink their coffee and to start a spontaneous game that they had played automatically and apathetically a thousand times since. He stole a sideward glance at her and wondered how this chic and highly lacquered, slightly drunk and provocative blonde sitting beside him in a Cadillac sedan had ever possibly evolved from the simple girl who had tried to study Greek Mythology in the park outside N.Y.U. He looked at Hank and wondered if Hank knew what that headline back at the penny arcade would say when they picked it up. NOBODY MAKES IT!, that's what it would say, don't you know that, Hank? Fight your battle for civil rights, become the man you want to be, get your five hundred grand and your black Cadillac and your blonde, if that's what you want, and then add them all up, and Hank, my friend, you'll find that you're only starting, that somewhere along the line while you were fighting so goddamn hard for all the things you thought you needed, you lost the very thing that mattered most to you.

He was suddenly seized with an urgent desire to get out of this car and away from these chattering people. It can't all be gone, he thought, it can't be too late, I've got to get back.

"Driver," he said, "stop the car. I'm getting out."

"What do you mean, you're getting out?" Grace said.

"We're all going to Oyster Bay, man," Hank said.

"I'm going back," Buddwing said.

"Back where?" Grace asked.

"Back," he answered. "Stop the goddamn car!"

The driver pulled the car to the curb. Buddwing got out quickly and was walking away from it when he heard Grace's voice behind him.

"Hey, you," she said.

He turned. "What do you want?"

"You *can't* go back," she said.

Someone in the car laughed, and Buddwing turned away and began running. Behind him, he heard Mike shouting, "Didn't you ever read Thomas Wolfe?" and then they all burst into laughter again, and the car gunned away from the curb, while he continued running down Lexington Avenue, turning left on the corner and heading for Third. The secret, he thought, was to find those two people who had spilled coffee on the table and rolled onto the floor laughing. The secret, he thought, was to find the person he had been this afternoon, the person clean and new who had met a virgin girl in an autumn park. He quickened his step. Third Avenue was deserted, save for a few late strollers; he supposed it was close to one o'clock in the morning. He felt again the way he had felt on Central Park South just after he had come out of the Plaza, when the world was empty and the birds trilled their high and heady music to his ears. He began running down the sidewalk. He saw the apartment building in the middle of the next block, and he grinned and ran faster. He was about to enter the building when he stopped on the front step and looked up at the numerals over the door, and realized all at once that he did not know Grace's address.

Wait a minute, he thought. It was

Wait a minute, it began with a nine, I think.

Just hold it a minute.

Well, look, the numbers here all begin with a thirteen, so it couldn't have been a goddamn nine, did you even look *up* at the numbers when you went into the building?

Well, wait, it was near a liquor store, wasn't it? Wasn't there a liquor store a few blocks away? Jesus, how many liquor stores are there on Third Avenue, or was it a liquor store at all? Yes, of course it was, but wasn't there a bakery downstairs? Or a stationery store? Wait, it could have been a petshop or a saloon, it could have been a pizzeria, it could have been

Look, Grace don't do

The numbers here all begin with a thirteen—was it thirteen nine something? No, it

Just hold on a minute, will you, because the address is on the tip of my tongue, who are you kidding, you never knew the address! Grace, the world is on the tip of my tongue, we can beat this whole damn system, I'll remember in a minute, please don't do anything stupid. He was suddenly overcome with a wave of panic so great that he leaned against the side of the building and closed his eyes and stood there limply with his heart pounding and his knees trembling, and it was then that his head began to throb and he knew that he was in for another migraine.

At first, he did not want to open his eyes. He did not want to open them and find that his vision had blurred again, not now when he was so close to making a new start, not now when he knew that everything would work out all right if only he could get back to Grace. But instead, he opened his eyes at once. There was no time to waste. The thing to do was to find her building immediately before his vision began to blur. It had to be some-where along here, didn't it? He was *in* the damn apartment not three hours ago, it couldn't have simply vanished!

He walked rapidly up the avenue, his head throbbing, waiting for his vision to blur at any moment. He knew he was on the right side of the avenue, but he saw nothing that looked even vaguely familiar to him. He was certain he had come too far uptown, and then certain he had not come far enough uptown, and then certain he was walking in the wrong direction. He began wondering if she lived on Third Avenue at all, and not possibly Lexington or Madison. Then, as he walked, he felt a slowly dawn-ing hope when he realized that all he had to do was look her up in the phone book—Grace MacCauley, that was her name; all he had to do was look her up and find her address that way. He almost walked into an open candy store and then he remembered that she was Jewish. How could a Jewish girl be named Grace MacCauley? How could Harry Truman be Jewish? Hadn't they said he was Jewish? How could Floyd Patterson be colored and white at the same time? Why wasn't Beethoven a deaf com-poser instead of a kid who wanted to go to Pratt Institute and who died on Tarawa? How can he be a face on the roof of Il Duomo? How can God be a crazy old man who followed me from N.Y.U.? Isn't anyone what he seems to be? Doesn't any-one have an identity? How can *I* know who *I* am if I don't know who anyone else is?

Grace, for crying out loud, this is a hell of a time to cop out on me. Where *are* you? Listen, I'll start yelling in a minute, Grace, I swear to God! I'll yell Grace MacCauley at the top of my lungs and wake up the whole damn neighborhood. She's not Grace MacCauley, he thought, she hasn't been Grace MacCauley for a long long time. You stupid jackass, she isn't Grace at *all*, don't you know that? Not Grace MacCauley and not Grace *anything*. She is a Jewish social worker you picked up on Broadway. She sent you down for booze because some of her friends are coming over. What time is it now? Are they still there? Come on, Grace, cut this out! Now, where's that damn apartment of yours?

In desperation, he began looking up at the lighted windows in the faces of the buildings. He saw a thousand window slits peering back at him intently, he saw a girl in one of the windows turning down a bed, he saw a man in another stroking a dog's head—Dan, he thought. Dan MacCauley, of course. Why, *that's* his name, of course. He's her brother, isn't he, so his name must be Dan MacCauley, so all I have to do is call him up and ask him where Grace

No. No, we don't want to do that, do we? No, he wouldn't cooperate. He wouldn't give me the address even if he knew it. No, I don't want to call him. Besides, *he* isn't what he seems to be, either. Nobody is. He's not a man, he's not someone who'll help you when you need it, he's a dog-man trained to leap at your throat, he's no different from any of the tigers, how'd a louse like him ever get a sweet kid like Grace for a sister? Hey, Grace, yoo-hoo, where are you? Yoo-hoo, Arthur, here I am, he thought, and suddenly he looked up at the windows lining Third Avenue and felt the same painful isolation he had known on the dock watching the disembarking passengers. It seemed to him that life pulsed in each of those warm amber rectangles, the woman who sat up there leaning on her windowsill with curlers in her hair, the man sitting by the window reading his newspaper, the girl taking off her blouse and then belatedly coming to the shade to pull it down. No! he thought, don't pull down the shade, don't cut me off! I want to come back! I want to be among the living!

His vision blurred then.

What had earlier been a thousand amber slits now became two thousand, all denying him entrance, all refusing to recognize him. He ran down the avenue searching each window, shaking his head. It seemed to him that shade after shade went down, life after life was suddenly snuffed out until the avenue was a wall of glowing blind rectangles. He darted into the doorway near the bakery only because it seemed to be a haven from this suddenly hostile wall of glowing blinded eyes. There were garbage cans stacked for the night on the ground floor behind the staircase. He sat on one of them, breathing harshly, not knowing where he would go next, his head pounding. The hallway, the staircase, the feeble naked light bulb all blurred out of focus in the excruciating pain of his headache. He reached into his watch pocket and took out the remaining gelatin capsule, and then put it on his tongue, and tried to force it down without any water. He choked on the capsule, and spat it out, and then sat helplessly on the garbage can while he continued to cough, certain he would retch. The coughing spell passed. The pain in his head, aggravated by the coughing, was unbearable. He tried to focus on the ejected gelatin capsule, which lay on the floor not three feet from the garbage can, but he saw only a blurred amoebalike smear on the asphalt tile of the vestibule. He closed his eyes. The yellow light flickered in the darkness of his skull.

He did not know how long he sat on the garbage can with his eyes closed. When he opened them again, his vision was still blurred, but the panic was gone and he was able to appraise the hallway calmly between the rising and falling waves of pain that attacked his temple. The hallway seemed familiar. The mailboxes outside, the naked hanging light bulb—wasn't this the hallway he had

He rose slowly to his feet. Through his blurred vision, he tried to overlay this hallway onto the hallway he remembered, the one Grace had led him into earlier tonight. Wasn't that the same wallpaper? Hadn't there been a stain just there? And that tear in the carpet on the stair tread, wasn't that there before? Cautiously, he put his hand on the banister and began climbing. He could not remember which floor she lived on, but he knew it was high up in the building, certainly the third floor, or perhaps even higher. He could hear the sounds of life again. They came from behind closed doors, muffled, but definitely the sounds of life. He stopped in the third-floor corridor and looked at the closed doorways all around him. There were four apartments on the floor. He could hear a television set going in one of them. In another, there was the sound of someone coughing. He knocked on the nearest door.

A woman's voice said, "Who is it?"

Don't ask me that, he thought. For Christ's sake, above all, do not ask me *that*. "Grace?" he asked. "Is that you, Grace?"

"There ain't no Grace here, mister," the voice said.

He knocked on the door adjacent to it. He waited while he heard footsteps approaching the door, and then the door opened, and an old woman in a nightgown peered into the hallway. He mumbled his apologies and knocked on the next door, and the next, and both doors opened almost simultaneously, and two strange faces looked out at him, and he turned away apologetically and gripped the banister and ran up to the fourth floor. He knocked on all the doors in rapid succession, running from one to the other without waiting for a response, and then standing in the middle of the hallway while the doors opened everywhere around him. Let me in, he thought, let me back in, and he looked at the strange faces in the hallway, and then seized the banister and climbed the steps two at a time to the fifth floor. If I reach the roof without finding her, he thought, I will jump off into the street. A door opened on a little boy in a bathrobe, another on a tall man in his undershirt, a third on a woman with cold cream on her face. He knocked on the last door in the hallway and leaned against the jamb. When the door opened, he did not look up at first. And then he raised his eyes, and she was standing there.

She was wearing flannel pajamas and her hair was loose around her face, and there were tear stains on her cheeks, and her age showed in the lines around her eyes and her mouth, in the sag of her breasts and the slight protrusion of her belly beneath the pajama bottoms. But his vision was blurred, and he saw two Graces standing side by side in the open doorway, and one of them had long blond hair and bright youthful eyes, and he smiled at her and said, "Grace, I almost lost you. Oh God, I almost lost you."

"You did," she answered.

"Wh—"

"The party's over," she said, and slammed the door in his face.

# 18

A COOL wind was blowing in off the East River.

He came down into the street, and deliberately headed into the wind, walking toward the river. His head was throbbing and the long, deserted street ahead of him was double-exposed, the streetlamps swirling into shifting patterns of light, stretches of darkness, and then blurred light again, the wind cool on his cheeks and on his mouth. He needed time to think. He could not think with his head pounding like this. The river wind would cool his face, and the headache would recede, and he would go back to the apartment and talk to her gently through the wooden door, until she turned the bolt, and eased open the door, and let him back into her life. He did not for a moment believe it was all over. They had argued violently a hundred times before, she had slammed a thousand doors in his face, but it could not be over, it could never be over.

It was cold by the river.

The breeze he had sought was a harsh sharp wind that whistled angrily over the water, slapping waves against the shore pilings. He pulled up the collar of his jacket, and thrust his hands into his pockets, and began walking uptown. In the distance, he could see the lights of the Triboro Bridge, hung mistily against the sky. Through his blurred vision, everything had taken on a quality of softness, the bridge lights nuzzling a curiously fuzzy sky, the clouds blending into blackness, Randall's Island and North Brother losing the perspective of distance, a dredge out on the water pounding in time with the beating pulse at his temple, but silhouetted curiously against nearer blurred lights, Hell Gate hanging on the horizon, shrouded. He walked close to the iron railing bordering the river, shivering from the cold, watching the lights in the distance. There was no fog, but he felt as though he were walking through layers upon layers of mist, each foot coming down gently and easily upon a soft bank of cloud into which he sank knee-deep without effort.

He was alone by the river.

The noises of the city were distant and impersonal. Because his feet sank into deep layers of mist, he did not even hear his own footfalls. Because the pounding at his temple coincided with the steady beat of the dredge, he heard neither, and walked steadily and easily, wafted gently on a mild current of air that carried him without conscious direction to a half-understood goal.

He was going to his grandfather's tailorshop.

He looked up at the street sign across the East River Drive and saw that he had come as far uptown as 101st Street. He did not quicken his pace. He continued drifting easily and dreamily, the sound of the dredge behind him now, passing Benjamin Franklin High School, and then 116th Street, and knowing the tailorshop was on First Avenue just off 117th Street, but continuing on past 117th and then going as far as 120th Street. He crossed the Drive and walked past Pleasant Avenue and saw P.S. 80 ahead in the middle of the block, and crossed to the side of the street where the school sat hunched in darkness.

He stopped on the sidewalk.

He looked up at the school, and tried to remember himself as a boy there—what had they called him then, what was his name? He could remember Miss Taxton, and the time she took him and another boy in 2A to her house in Larchmont for lunch on a Saturday afternoon; they had bounced a golf ball on the large flagstone terrace behind her house; he had thought it was the biggest house in the world. He could remember Mrs. Flynn, who was tall and string-bean-thin and with whom he had got into a heated argument at the Boys' Club on 111th Street where the school used to take them to swim every Friday afternoon. He could remember Mrs. Davidstein and the project on Mexico for which he had drawn a picture of a peasant in white sitting against a pale yellow wall taking a noonday siesta, and he could remember learning the words in Spanish to "*Cielito Lindo.*" Mrs. Harnig had been his favorite, a very tall woman very much like his mother, who would say "Oh hell" whenever anything went wrong, and who took his side in the argument with Mrs. Flynn that day at the Boys' Club. He could remember all of this, but he could not remember his name. He could remember who he had been—but he could not remember who he was.

He walked past the school and up to First Avenue. He crossed the street and stopped on the corner, looking up toward Second Avenue where the elevated structure used to be. He could barely recognize the street. He turned left on First Avenue (the *pasticceria* was still there on the corner) and began walking downtown, following the route he used to take from the school each afternoon (the coal station across the street was gone), crossing 119th Street and continuing on down First Avenue until he was almost to 117th Street, and then stopping and looking for the tailorshop. He did not expect to find it there still, but he at least hoped the façade of the shop would be the same, that whether the inside now housed a delicatessen or a butchershop, the outside would still be the same. There would still be the wide front plate-glass window with the hanging light bulb, and the door with the handle he used to reach up to grab.

But he recognized none of the stores in the row; everything seemed to have changed. He stood on the sidewalk staring at the darkened stores. His headache was receding, but his vision was still blurred and for a moment it seemed that one of the shops glowed with a gentle warmth; it seemed for a moment that snow-flakes danced on the air, and he could hear the tinkle of the bell over the shop door, and a familiar welcoming voice saying, "Come in, you must be frozen. Annie, make him some nice hot chocolate." He blinked his eyes. The stores were dark, eyeless in the night.

He began walking again.

When he heard the music, he thought his mind was playing a grotesque trick. His vision was beginning to clear somewhat, but now that the blurred distortion was vanishing, it seemed as though an auditory distortion were taking its place. As he came closer to 116th Street, he realized he was indeed hearing music, and he followed the sound, turning the corner and heading toward the bar in the middle of the block. There was a lighted doorway alongside the bar, with a steep flight of steps leading downstairs, and the music came from somewhere at the bottom of the steps, as though emanating in a burst of light from the center of the earth. A boy of about seventeen, wearing a tuxedo, was standing on the steps with a teen-age girl in a pink gown. Buddwing peered down the steps curiously, and the boy smiled and asked, "You looking for the wedding?" Buddwing smiled and said nothing. "You'd better hurry," the boy said. "The beer and sandwiches are almost gone."

He realized all at once that he was ferociously hungry, and he nodded at the boy, and then started down the steps, the girl in the pink gown smiling at him as he went by. The light grew stronger, the music louder; the narrow sharp flight of steps opened suddenly onto a wider mirrored alcove. The man he saw in the mirror did not startle him. He did not know who the man was, but at least the face, the body, were familiar to him; these had not changed since he had first seen himself early this morning at the

Or was that yesterday morning?

Was it tomorrow already?

333

He turned back toward the steps. "Do you know what time it is?" he asked the boy in the tuxedo.

"Almost two o'clock," the boy said.

"Thank you," he answered, and turned again toward the mirror. He had been awake since six o'clock yesterday morning, and it was now two o'clock *this* morning, and the man in the mirror looked very tired, older perhaps, but certainly not at all wiser. He smiled at himself sadly. Inside the hall, the band had begun a spirited tarantella. He straightened his tie and walked into the brightly lighted room. He searched for the food first because he had the feeling someone would detect him as a crasher and throw him out, and he wanted to make sure he got something to eat before that happened. The reception was still going full tilt, with distant cousins from Red Bank whooping it up in the middle of the floor with relatives from 114th Street and Second Avenue.

"Hey, Dominick," someone shouted to a bald-headed man dancing vigorously with a young brunette, *"Piano, piano! Ti viene una strocca!"*

*"Una sincope, stupido!"* the bald-headed man answered, laughing, and wiped his sweating brow as Buddwing spied the bar across the room and headed quickly toward it. The man behind the bar was obviously a relative or a close friend, because he was wearing a dress shirt with his black bow tie loosened and dangling down his starched front, and with his sleeves rolled up and his arms wet from dipping into the icebox for sodas. His tuxedo jacket was hanging on a peg behind the bar, and he looked up at Buddwing as he approached and then grinned amiably and said, "What'll it be, friend?"

"What've you got?"

"Ham or ham and cheese. Beer or soda."

"I'll have a beer and two hams," Buddwing said.

"You the bride or the groom?" the man asked, and turned toward the keg of beer behind the bar.

"A little of each," Buddwing said.

"Oh, you know them both, huh?" the man asked, drawing a glass of beer.

"Mmm," Buddwing said.

"Rosie is my cousin," the man said.

"She's a nice girl," Buddwing answered.

"You telling me? I know her from when she was running around with her pants wet. Now look at her, getting spliced." The man laughed. "Two hams, right?" he asked, and put the glass of beer on the bar top. "You from this neighborhood?"

"No," Buddwing said.

"I didn't think so. I ain't from around here, either. Well, technically, anyway. I'm from Brooklyn. But my wife lived here, you know. So when we got married, we wound up here."

"I see," Buddwing said.

"We were married right in the church on a hun' fifteenth, matter of fact. Oh, it made my mother sick, believe me. She had to come all the way from Brooklyn, oh, it made her sick."

"I know what you mean," Buddwing said, smiling. "My wife's parents live in Mount Kisco, so any important family function takes place up there."

"Sure, naturally," the man said. He reached into the large cardboard box behind the counter, and put two sandwiches in waxed paper bags before Buddwing. "It's nice up that way, though, ain't it?"

"Oh, sure," Buddwing said. He took a swallow of beer. "That's good beer."

"It ain't getting warm, is it?"

"No, it's just right."

"The keg's almost gone. This'll probably be breaking up soon. Look at them two nuts. They ain't even left yet."

Buddwing looked across the hall to where the bride and groom were circulating among the guests, accepting congratulations and good wishes, passing out small white boxes of candied almonds. Like the wedding in Milan, he thought, and then pushed Milan out of his mind.

"Is something wrong?" the man behind the bar asked.

"No, no. Nothing."

"You keep blinking your eyes."

"I have a bad headache, that's all."

"Why don't you eat something? Maybe you're hungry."

"Yes, I am."

"Go on. Sit down over there someplace and eat your sandwiches."

"Thank you," Buddwing said.

"You sure you feel all right?"

"Yes, thank you."

"Because if you don't, you see that guy sitting there in the blue suit? That's Dr. Solomon, he brought Rosie into the world. I mean, if you don't feel so good."

"No, I feel fine, thanks."

"Well, go sit down anyway, why don't you? You look a little green around the gills."

"All right, thank you," Buddwing said, and he nodded and walked away from the bar and to a table at the far side of the hall. The band was playing *Vicino il Mare*, a mandolin picking out the tune to the accompaniment of piano, drums, and trumpet. Someone cracked a dirty joke to the groom, and he burst out laughing while the bride stood by in becoming blushing innocence. The sound of Italian floated on the air around him, pierced by the pizzicato mandolin, the brittle tinkle of laughter, the pleasant hum of celebrating people. The man behind the bar had said he looked a little green around the gills, and he did feel very weak now as he pulled a chair out from the empty table, felt his knees would fold beneath him at any moment, they had stumbled into the Milanese wedding last summer in the midafternoon, searching for a bar after the suffocating heat on the roof of Il Duomo. On the roof, he had pointed to one of the cherub faces carved into the stone icing and said, "He looks like someone I used to know." Grace, with her back to the sun, the sun glowing in her hair, brass against brass, had answered, "*You* look like someone I used to know."

He took one of the sandwiches from its waxed paper bag and bit into it. The sandwich was dry, no butter, no lettuce, two slices of lean ham on a starchy roll. He washed it down with a swallow of beer. The band was playing a medley of Italian favorites now, *Torna a Sorrento* and *Tra Veglia e Sonno*, and *Maria, Mari*, and finally *Luna mezz' 'o Mare*. The laughter around him rose as an old man with a walrus mustache began singing the lyrics at the top of his voice. He was joined by two portly men at another table, and suddenly the hall was ringing with the words, echoing from the walls to assail Buddwing where he sat alone at his table, with a dust-dry sandwich and a glass of flat beer.

> *E la luna mezz' 'o mare:*
> *mamma mia me maritari*
> *Figghia mia a cu te ddari?*
> *Mamma mia penzaci tu.*
> *Si ti rugnu 'o pisciaolu,*
> *iddu va, iddu veni,*
> *sempe 'u pisci ne mani teni . . .*
> *Si ci pigghia 'a fantasia*
> *ti pisciulia figghiuzza mia.**

She had given him the gold ring with the black stone the day before they left for Europe last summer. He had looked at the inside of the ring and said, "From G.V. Is that all?"

"Those are my initials," she said, "aren't they?"

"Yes, but shouldn't it read 'From G.V. With Love'?"

She shrugged and said, "The love is understood."

In Paris, there were a great many business people to meet and talk to, and therefore a great many parties—cocktail, dinner, midnight buffet. They had practiced their French assiduously before the trip, speaking nothing else for days before their flight, and in Paris they had ample opportunity for putting the language to use. It became a little more difficult on the road, where the pure French became somewhat bastardized, making it harder to understand and be understood. From the Esso booklet, he memorized the sentence, *Faites le plein, s'il vous plaît, et vérifiez l'huile et l'eau*, impressing no one but himself, and at a total loss

---

* Used by permission of the copyright owner.

when it came to answering automotive questions put to him by garage attendants.

She was wearing a light plaid topcoat the day they discovered the Roman arena in the small French roadside town. It had been raining all morning, and then the rain stopped abruptly, leaving behind it a cold and gloomy day, more like October than August.

"October always makes me sad," she said.

"This is August," he said.

"Still," she answered.

The arena was not marked in any of the guidebooks, nor had they even remotely suspected that the Romans had ever advanced this far into France. The town, in fact, was a combination of incongruous elements. It seemed to be a typical French country town, but there was undeniably a Roman arena in its center; and beyond the arena, its sign clearly visible from the upper rim of the stadium, was an English tearoom. The sign, moreover, was lettered in English, the black letters centered on a field of white, TEA ROOM, so that for a moment he felt oddly displaced and wondered exactly where the hell he was, France, Italy, or England.

To further confuse the conglomerate geography, as Buddwing stepped down over the tiers of seats and onto the arena's turf still wet with the morning's rain, he had the feeling that he was walking into an American football stadium. He looked back and up at Grace, who was standing on one of the stone tiers, her hands in the pockets of the plaid coat. He grinned and chanted, "Give 'em the ax, give 'em the ax, give 'em the ax . . ."

"Where?" she said automatically, but her mind seemed to be elsewhere; her eyes were preoccupied.

They drove into Milan on a Saturday, and checked into their hotel at noon. The streets were mercilessly hot, and the lobby of the hotel seemed shaded and almost cool by comparison. The desk clerk took their passports and then looked at Grace in surprise and said, "*Credevo che fosse italiana.*"

"*No,*" she replied with a strange pleased mysterious smile, "*non sono italiana.*"

338

"*Tutti in Italia la prendono per italiana*," Buddwing said.

"*Certo, che sembra una settentrionale*," the desk clerk answered, and rang for the bellhop. The room was sleek and modern, with a huge double bed, and a mirrored wall, and a marble bathroom with a dozen mysterious knobs and hoses. But the air conditioner was out of order, and the moment they stepped into the room, they were assailed with a contained heat more formidable than that in the streets outside. Buddwing went to the phone immediately and asked for the desk.

"*Questa stanza è impossibile*," he said. "*L'aria condizionata non funziona.*"

"*Si, signore*," the desk clerk answered, "*ma non è soltanto la sua stanza, signore, è la stessa cosa in ogni stanza nell'albergo. Qualche cosa è successo al sistema centrale.*"

"*Mi vuol dire che non c'è neanche una stanza fresca in tutto l'albergo?*"

"*No, signore. Tutte le stanze sono ad aria condizionata. È soltanto che per il momento il sistema centrale non funziona, e così ci sarà un piccolo ritardo per giungere alla temperatura giusta.*"

"What do you mean by a short delay?" he asked in English, and then said, "*Ma, quanto ci volere . . . ci vorrà per accomodarlo?*"

"*Ci stanno lavorando adesso, signore.*"

"*Quanto tempo ci vuole?*"

"*Non dovrebbe essere troppo, signore.*"

Buddwing covered the mouthpiece with the palm of his hand and turned to Grace. "What do you think?" he asked. "There's something wrong with the central cooling system. They're working on it now."

"I'm exhausted," Grace said. "We might as well stay."

"*Va bene, grazie*," Buddwing said into the phone, and hung up. He turned to the waiting bellhop. "*Va bene, puo lasciare le valige*," he said, and then tipped him. They stripped to their underwear as soon as the bellhop was gone, and began unpacking their bags. He was carrying a small portable typewriter in a metal case, and he put it on a table near the single large sealed window

in the room. Grace went into the bathroom to bathe, and he lay
on the bed in his undershorts, sweating profusely, and fished
into his wallet for the telephone numbers of his business con-
tacts in the city.

There was no answer at the first number he called, and when
he dialed the second number, he got a scatterbrained secretary
who could not understand his Italian.

"*Vorrei parlare con il signor D'Amore,*" he said slowly and
patiently.

"*Ah, si, si, il signor D'Amore. Ma non è qui proprio adesso.*"

"*Bene. Dove l'aspettiamo?*"

"*Scusi?*"

"*Quando arriveremo?*"

"*Scusi?*"

"Look, for . . ." He paused, regained his patience, and then
calmly said, "*Dove si trova il signor D'Amore?*"

"*Ah, ah! È a Como.*"

"*Quando ritorna?*"

"*In una quindicina di giorni,*" the secretary said.

"*Grazie,*" Buddwing said, and hung up.

"What is it?" Grace called from the bathroom.

"D'Amore's at Lake Como. He won't be back for two weeks."

"Oh, that's great," Grace said.

"I couldn't reach Danaro, either." He looked at the list in his
hand. "I guess I'll try this last one."

"What?"

"I said I'll try this last one."

"All right." She paused. "This water is brown," she said.
"Ick, it smells like sewer water."

He dialed the last number on his list and got an answering
service that told him Signor Casoscorso had gone with his family
to Positano for their yearly summer holiday, could she take a
message? He said, "No, thanks, no message," and hung up. "Well,
what the hell do we do now?" he called to the bathroom.

"What do you mean?"

"None of them are here. Why'd we bother coming to Milan?"

"There must be things to see here," Grace said.

"This leg of the trip was supposed to be business. We didn't have to come to Milan if we wanted to sightsee."

"Didn't you write ahead?"

"Of course I wrote ahead. Damnit, they knew we were coming."

"The Paris leg was business, too," Grace said.

"What?"

"Nothing."

"Well, what are we supposed to do now?"

"I don't know," Grace answered, and then very softly said, "I guess we're stuck with each other."

They ate lunch in the hotel dining room and then napped away the afternoon. The air-conditioning system was repaired before they went out for dinner, but not before the sun glaring through the hotel window had partially melted the rubber roller on his typewriter. That evening, they ate green noodles and chicken *cacciatore* in a restaurant near the Galleria. The city seemed deserted. They had very little to say to each other during the meal.

In the middle of the night, Grace woke up screaming.

"What is it?" he shouted, alarmed.

"The man," she mumbled, "the man."

He put his arms around her and held her close. "What man?" he asked gently.

"In the wheelchair," she said. "He's looking under my raincoat."

"All right, honey," he said, "try to get back to sleep."

"Why didn't he let me?" she said, and then rolled away from him, and buried her face in the pillow.

On Sunday they went to see the cathedral.

The roof of Il Duomo was a tangle of intricate arches and buttresses, a sculptured maze that challenged the eye with its interwoven complexity. The sun was dangerously hot, baking the roof of the cathedral, each carving arc of stone fringework casting a narrow unprotective shadow. They walked the roof heavily as though caught in the sticky strands of a giant spider-web. When Grace peered over the edge of the roof to the piazza below, she suddenly swayed back dizzily against him, and it was then that they decided to find a cool bar someplace.

The streets of Milan that Sunday last summer were virtually empty. Every now and then, a lone automobile would cruise past, but for the most part they seemed alone in a city that had been rendered mute and inanimate by the heat. They wandered into the wedding reception by accident, hearing music at the back of a *trattoria* and entering only to discover that a private party was in progress. Then, because they were Americans and because the heat had generated a desperate sort of camaraderie among those who were foolhardy enough to challenge it, they were invited to sit and have a drink. The bride's father was an immense sweating man in a black morning coat and striped trousers. He told them he had a brother in Los Angeles, and that he considered their sudden arrival at the wedding an omen of the highest possible good fortune. *"Un ottimo augurio,"* he said. He introduced them to his daughter, a radiant dark-haired beauty in a satin bridal gown with wet circles of sweat under the sleeves. She was clutching the arm of her groom, a pale smiling youth who continually wiped beads of perspiration from his brow.

They were so young. They were so very young, and chattering in high excited Italian, passing candied almonds among the guests, drinking toasts, listening to the coarse Italian honeymoon jokes, laughing, brimming with plans for the future, shining with youthful dreams. Buddwing and Grace sat at the small table in the outdoor garden of the *trattoria*, surrounded by festivity. They watched the newlyweds, and an unsettling gloom began to spread over them, a gloom they could not understand until later, when they were back at the hotel.

The air conditioner was working, it hummed serenely, it filled the room with purified, cooled air, it immunized the room against the world outside, providing a sterile cubicle in which they could face each other at last, and see each other.

They had taken off their clothes and Grace was standing in

front of the mirrored wall when he padded up beside her. They looked at each other in the mirror, and he said, "You're really very small," and she did not answer for a moment because she was staring at this man who had always thought of her as being tall, staring at this man in the mirror and not recognizing him, either. And then, because they both felt simultaneously that the mirror images were lying, that these two people who peered back at them were not really *themselves* but some falsely distorted representations, they turned from the mirror and faced each other, and looked.

It ended in that moment, he supposed.

Whatever had existed between them until now, whatever thin thread of hope held them to each other, whatever memories of a small park or a crowded French restaurant or a cloistered automobile or a deserted sunny beach or a wedding ceremony in a huge stone church vibrating with the sound of organ and violin, whatever crushed dreams, whatever lost goals, whatever forgotten youth, all vanished in that moment.

They were staring at strangers.

They stared in shock and surprise because they were naked to each other at last, and embarrassed by their nakedness, and filled with the terrible mutual knowledge that these two people, who looked out of unbelieving eyes at strangers, were strangers to themselves as well.

"Oh, Jesus," Grace said.

"Grace," he said in sudden panic, "do you remember—"

"Oh, Jesus," she said.

"Grace, the times we—"

"We met a million years ago," she said flatly. "We're dinosaurs. We're extinct. We're dead." Her voice lowered. "We're dead."

"No," he said.

"We're dead," she repeated.

"No," he said, refusing to accept the words. Who the hell were these pale and naked strangers staring at them from the mirror, crowding into their lives? No, he thought, we've come too far for this, we know each other too well, we've fought too hard for whatever tiny shred of life we've managed to grab, no! This isn't happening to us, he thought. Grace, there is still something for us.

His eyes met hers in the mirror.

I know you, he thought.

Please. I know you.

Please, we have been through so much together.

Let me see your eyes.

The eyes were pale, drained of color, drained of emotion, drained of hope. He had seen these eyes on a night long ago when they had hoarsely shouted accusations to each other, had seen these same pale and frightened eyes the next day as she sat at the kitchen table in her white raincoat, Grace, what are you doing with your raincoat on?

I tried to kill myself, she said.

Don't be ridiculous.

Yes, I tried to kill myself.

Honey, honey, and he took her in his arms, and gently she wept against his shoulder. Is this what life means? she asked. Is this what life is about? He did not know, and so he could not tell her. He comforted her, kissing her tear-stained face and holding her close, and putting his cheek against her hand, and like conspirators they whispered the afternoon away and made love afterward and found a strength somewhere. Her eyes came slowly back to life. The color returned, and with it a determination and then something more than that, a resignation, a burning intensity.

Eleven years ago, the boy and girl who had met in a sundrenched secret autumn park when the world was concerned only with Greek mythology and the touch of a hand, eleven years ago the boy and girl who had learned each other's ways in a city as glittering as the universe, eleven years ago the boy and girl who had solemnly vowed to love, honor and cherish in a huge stone church trembling with the sound of music, eleven years ago the boy and girl who had begun living together with faces clean and bright, eyes hopefully gleaming, who had come through a pregnancy and a miscarriage and all the bitter recriminations that followed, eleven years ago this boy and this girl had fervently whispered their vows anew, reaffirmed their bond, and declared to themselves and to the world that they were one, that they would not be defeated, they would survive, they would endure, they would triumph.

Eleven years ago.

Now in a hotel room in an Italian city, they saw each other after all those years, after all the clever golden people and pretty conversations, after all the cocktails delicately held and whiskey bottles drained, after all the lifted skirts and covetous hands and sly and secret insinuations, after all the deals and propositions, after all the countless necessary homicides, the lies, the petty thefts, the alibis, the threats—after all of this, after all the jazz of everyday living, the jazz that pounded and vibrated and moved away in a dazzling modulation to another distant chord, changing so imperceptibly from chord to chord, from note to note, that the change was not at all visible until now, until this moment when all the autumn leaves of a park outside a school seemed to fall in a simultaneous ear-shattering crackling rush that drowned out even the distorted jazz-throb and left them standing before a mirror in Milan, two sophisticated, intelligent, educated, experienced, successful Americans who suddenly realized they had passed Go once too often—the goddamn game was over and they were bankrupt.

"We're dead," Grace said, and this time he did not contradict her.

In Portobello last summer, the street band marched through playing "Midnight in Moscow," and he bought the clock against her wishes because nothing mattered after Milan. There was a giant smudge on the bass drum where the padded stick repeatedly struck the same spot. The name of the band was lettered in a semicircle on the drum, THE LIMEHOUSE REGULARS. The band marched with a ragged beat, and the music echoed in the crowded street as he bought the clock that would later hang on the living room wall throwing minutes into eternity while he walked with rising dread over the green carpet.

The band was playing "Melancholy Baby." The bride and groom were saying their farewells discreetly, trying to sneak out of the hall and up to their waiting car. The ham sandwich had stuck in his throat, and he washed it down with the warm beer, and then rose suddenly and walked toward the steps, past the mirrored wall, without looking back at himself.

"They leaving yet?" the teen-age boy in the tuxedo asked. His face was smeared with lipstick.

Buddwing nodded and climbed the steps.

MO 6-2367

Mount Kisco, he thought. Not Monument.

Mount Kisco 6-2367

It was too late to call now.

It was too late to do anything now.

"There's nothing we can do now," Dan had said, and that was when they had gone to the movie together.

He began walking.

He did not know who he was, nor did he any longer care. They had both been dead since that Sunday in Milan, and perhaps for years before that, and he didn't give a damn, he simply didn't give a damn. He had said that to Dan on the telephone, "I don't give a damn." You don't mean that, Dan had answered. "It was over years ago," he said. You shouldn't say that. "It was over years ago," he repeated.

The house had filled with strangers, and Dan had suggested that they get out of there, take in a movie, there was nothing more they could do now, the arrangements had all been made, Mount Kisco 6-2367, there was nothing more they could do. He had gone back to the silent Sutton Place apartment after he had left Dan. He knew he should sleep, it was very late. He had gone into the bedroom overlooking the Queensboro Bridge, and taken his wallet and change and keys and placed them on the dresser top. He had removed his watch—he never slept with his watch on; she had once said to him, "Take off your watch, for God's sake! I want you to be naked"—and then put his handkerchief on the dresser beside his other stuff and then turned and stared at

346

the bed, and simply walked out of the apartment with no intention of ever returning to it.

He was very tired.

It was close to three o'clock in the morning, and New York
City was asleep. He walked clear across Italian Harlem and into
Spanish Harlem, I once broke the bank in Spanish Harlem, did I
ever tell you that story? and then into Central Park. He was not
afraid of muggers. The worst they could do was kill him when
they discovered he was carrying only a dollar and thirty-six
cents. As he entered the park, he reached into his pocket for the
money and then suddenly threw it in the air over his head. "Here,"
he shouted to the night, "take it! You've taken everything else!"
The bill fluttered silently down to the path. The coins jingled
behind him and then were still.

There was life hidden in the bushes of the park.

There were lips to be kissed, and breasts to be fondled, worlds
to be explored. There were assassins lying in wait. He did not
care. He was already dead.

He walked the entire length of the park from 110th Street, and
then found a bench near the Fifty-ninth Street lake. He was bone
weary. He stretched out immediately, and closed his eyes.

He thought at first he was dreaming.

The memory came so swiftly, the pictures flashed into his mind
with such clarity, that he thought at first he had fallen asleep at
once and begun dreaming instantly, this apartment is too still.

He unlocks the door with his key; this is unusual because he
has rung the bell and she usually comes to the door to greet him.
He stops in the hallway; there is no sound in the apartment save
for a gentle swishing sound somewhere in its secret depths, that
and the ticking of the clock on the wall, the one he bought in
Portobello. He does not move. He stares at the carpet. And then
he places one foot before the other and begins walking in the
direction of the swishing sound. He stops outside the bathroom
door and again hesitates, and then reaches out for the knob.

He turns the knob.

Something is glittering on the tile near the sink.

347

He sees the glittering object, but his eyes move up and away from it swiftly, and then he notices that the water tap is turned on, and he realizes without surprise that this is the swishing sound, and he sees her toothbrush lying on the rim of the sink, the open tube of toothpaste beside it, why does she never replace the cap on the toothpaste? He sees the sleeve of her red robe then, the same red cotton robe she has worn since they were married, sees the red sleeve in the open crack of the bathroom door.

He opens the door wider.

For a moment, he cannot move, he cannot think, he cannot scream.

She is wearing her white raincoat.

She has fallen behind the bathroom door, and in an instant of recognition, he realizes she is wearing the raincoat and not her robe. The red sleeve he saw is a sleeve drenched with her own blood. She is lying in a pool of her own blood. There is a trail of blood from the sink, she has opened her wrist at the sink with the glittering razor blade and held it under the water and then weakened and staggered back from the sink and dropped the razor and fallen to the floor behind the door. Her blood spreads over the tiles, her eyes are open wide and staring, her mouth is open, there is blood in her hair and on her naked breasts, he knows he will vomit. He stumbles back against the tiled wall. He shakes his head. His senses return. For a soaring gleeful instant, he thinks, I'm glad! and then suddenly whirls and smashes his bunched fist against the tiled bathroom wall, cracking the stone on his ring. Why did you do this? I love you, why did you do this?

MO 6-2367 was the number of the Mount Kisco funeral home, he was to have called them yesterday morning to tell them how many cars they would need to follow the hearse when they put his dead wife in the ground, when they covered his Grace with earth, when they

"No!" he screamed.

He sat upright on the bench and stared into the darkness. His heart was pounding, his hands were trembling.

"No," he whispered softly.

In a little while, he fell asleep.

He awoke.

He could not have been asleep for more than a few hours, and yet he felt curiously refreshed, coming instantly awake without passing through that fuzzy borderland he usually associated with rising. He knew exactly where he was. He seemed only mildly surprised to discover he was wearing his street clothes, but then he supposed one did not sleep in pajamas on a wooden bench in Central Park. He sat up and rubbed a hand over his face, not to wash away any weariness—more, he suspected, as a gesture of habit. Then he glanced across the path and beyond the iron railing to where the ground sloped to a small lake. The lake ended in a narrow finger capped by a huge outcropping of primeval rock, the man-made concrete of Fifth Avenue beyond and in the distance, and behind that a pale blue sky.

Who am I? he wondered.